His for the Taking

Thinking to find answers, Damron stared into her eyes. Beautiful. Those eyes so dark a brown and fringed with lush, thick lashes that would surely feather his cheeks when they kissed.

Ah. Kissed.

Gazing at her mouth, he swallowed. Full and luscious. Ripe. She must have sensed his growing desire to taste her there, for the tip of her tongue peeked out to dampen her lips. At that moment, she looked delicate and sweet, the perfect maiden . . .

Always Mine

Sophia Johnson

ZEBRA BOOKS
Kensington Publishing Corp.
www.kensingtonbooks.com

ZEBRA BOOKS are published by

Kensington Publishing Corp.
850 Third Avenue
New York, NY 10022

All Kensington titles, imprints, and distributed lines are avail-
able at special quantity discounts for bulk purchases for sales
promotion, premiums, fund-raising, educational, or institu-
tional use.

Special book excerpts or customized printings can also be created to fit specific needs. For details, write or phone the office
of the Kensington Special Sales Manager: Attn. Special Sales
Department, Kensington Publishing Corp., 850 Third Avenue,
New York, NY 10022. Phone: 1-800-221-2647.

Zebra and the Z logo Reg. U.S. Pat. & TM Off.

First Printing: August 2006
10 9 8 7 6 5 4 3 2 1

Printed in the United States of America

For my loving husband, Gil,
who every evening continues to pry me away
from the keyboard when dinner is ready.

To my daughter, Lorrie, and her husband, Carlo,
who gave me my first computer and challenged me
to stop reading and start writing!

To my daughter, Valeri, and her husband, Tony,
whose support and encouragement means so much.

And with many thanks to Delle Jacobs,
my wonderful critique partner,
for her everlasting patience.

Prologue

North Wales, 1072

Curious gazes and speculative whispers followed the man's lithesome progress. His cloak billowed like wings, so swift was he in ascending the steep path. All would later swear his feet never touched stone.

No one dared intrude on his solitude, though should anyone need him, he was always there. 'Twas the fact he had aided their grandfathers, e'en their great-grandfathers, that stopped them.

He ne'er aged.

The mystic stood atop the highest point of the cliffs overlooking the turbulent sea and waited for Cloud Dancer to descend. His gaze followed the great eagle's flight. Tilting his head, he listened to the shrill calls from the sky telling him what he had waited centuries to hear.

Brianna is coming.

He gloried in the approaching storm and laughed as the howling wind whipped the hair back from his face and lifted the brilliant-hued feathers on his cape. The mantle cracked and rose about his body. His arms reached heavenward, and he felt as though he were about to glide with the wind to the eagle above.

His eyes lit and his lips lifted in a smile of joy and anticipation. With but a whisper of sound, Cloud Dancer landed on his wrist. It was a testament to the man's strength that his arm did not drop from the eagle's weight. They needed no words, each understanding the other, as they looked to the northeast toward Scotland. The storm would reach there shortly. He had much to do before he could start his journey. Raising his arm, he sent the great eagle back to soar and dip amidst the roiling clouds.

"Damron's beloved will return at last," he whispered to the wind. "Ah, *mo fear beog,* my little one. Your soul is much wiser now, and his love will not frighten you. I won't be there to greet you, but he will. 'Tis time you meet again and accept your fates."

His hands rose to enfold the talisman that hung low on his chest. He lifted his face to the heavens and closed his eyes. One word left his lips. Caught by the wind, it roared as loudly as the crashing thunder.

"Come!"

Chapter 1

Lydia Hunter was drawn to the man in the ink drawing the first time she saw him. She had cried out to him then, calling him *her* "Lord Demon," and sobbing like her heart would break.

She was five years old.

Every summer she left New York to return to the Highlands and Blackthorn Castle. She *had* to come. His soul called to hers. Each passing year, the pull toward him strengthened. And now, after a mind-wrenching divorce, the need to be close to him had turned to heart-pounding urgency.

She stood in front of the faded likeness of Damron Alasdair Morgan, an eleventh-century laird of Clan Morgan, which hung on the freshly painted wall of Blackthorn's museum.

Needing to imprint his features firmly in her heart after the year's absence, she blinked to clear her contacts and drew closer to study the drawing. Damron's dark, wind-blown hair reached just above his shoulders. A wisp of a lock had strayed over his forehead, and in her heart's memory, she could see him reach an impatient hand to shove it away. Strong brows arched over cynical eyes. An arrogant nose rose above firm, sensual lips and a chiseled jaw. Nothing softened his unyielding expression.

Her sight blurred. She blinked again. Compelling eyes stared back at her. Accusing her.

She couldn't look away. It was as if he demanded something from her. She yearned to touch and caress the face in the drawing. Her chest hurt with the urge to wail the way she had as a child.

"Why couldn't you love me?"

Puzzling flashes came more frequently today. Surely they couldn't be memories. The images were of the man who could be a demon when he was angry. She felt anguish, too, that he kept hidden just out of reach. Now, more than ever, she knew he begged something from her. What could it be?

"Mommy, why is the lady crying?"

The child's voice broke the hold Lord Damron's likeness held on Lydia. She sniffed and ducked her head to swipe the tears away. Would he forever have this strange power over her? Even when she became ninety years old?

Her ragged sigh answered her. She forced herself to leave him and go into the museum to browse through the timeworn antique shop. She stood aside while chattering schoolchildren lined up at the exit with their teachers and headed out to their waiting bus.

The shop manager's gaze lit with recognition when she spied Lydia against the wall. She hurried over, and without a word, handed her an antique brooch. Lydia stared at it. Sharp pains of distress jolted through her. They took her breath away.

Her gaze darted to the woman's face. "Where did you find this?" Her voice sounded hoarse, distressed.

"Behind an old safe we were replacin' last eve." Nodding at the brooch, the woman's forehead creased. "No one remembers seein' it before. It's like it hid until the perfect moment to be discovered." Her brows near met. "I ken it waited for you."

The brooch tingled in Lydia's hand. She turned it around and around. It was familiar. She studied the circle of Celtic knots with the head of a falcon on either side. Though little remained of the Latin words etched around it, she knew what it read.

"With a Strong Hand," she whispered. She rubbed her thumb over the area. "The Morgans' motto." She clutched it to her heart and nodded.

The woman ducked her head, agreeing. "Seein' how much you love Blackthorn, I wanted to offer it to you first."

"Thank you." Lydia's voice quavered. She felt a sharp prick, and looked down. The pin that secured the brooch was shaped like a fist holding a dagger. A thin stream of hot blood streaked her palm. She ignored it.

Lydia wanted the brooch. She didn't care how much it cost. She had to have it. Reaching inside her tapestry vest, she shoved her passport aside, grasped her credit card and handed it to the woman.

The manager smiled and wove her way through the customers to the nearest register.

Lydia fought her trembling fingers as she tried to pin the brooch to her pullover sweater.

She rubbed her eyes, then sucked in her breath and stood transfixed when a thick haze drifted through the portrait room doorway and surrounded her.

The deep gray mist shifted. A man's strong fingers reached to cover hers and fastened the brooch over her heart. His skin was warm. He opened her hand, groaned on seeing the blood there, and lowered his mouth. His tongue lapped the blood away, then soft lips kissed the spot. He lifted his head and studied her face. His breath feathered against her cheek. All the while, his intense green gaze held her prisoner. Her heart lurched as she inhaled the scents of sandalwood and spices. And man.

He moved closer. His presence brushed against her. She gasped, feeling his hard body, his muscles, his heat. God help her. Had she lost her mind? Did she imagine it? But then, did she also imagine the sounds? His voice, like a summer breeze, spread heat over her.

"I would have yer vow, Brianna. Promise me! Promise me ye will ne'er . . ." The urgent words spiraled around her, fading.

Tears streaked down her cheeks. Her heart ached at the anguished plea. Without hesitating, she whispered the reply she knew he sought. "I promise. I'll never leave you. Not even through eternity."

No sooner had she spoken than Lord Damron's image sighed and faded away. The mist followed.

Seeing the manager heading toward her, Lydia fought for composure.

"Thank you so much for holding the brooch for me," she stammered. Forcing a smile, she signed the receipt. After giving the woman's shoulders a quick hug, she hurried outside. She needed fresh air. Surely it would clear her mind and settle her racing pulse.

Her shoes echoed on the stone stairway leading to the top of the tower. The most intact portion of the castle was here. The ruins of the lord's rooms always soothed her, and as she wandered through them, she cupped a hand over her brooch.

Deep in her soul she knew this place. She patted the stone walls that seemed to welcome her. In these old chambers, comfort enveloped her like strong arms, no matter the season. It was very tangible today. Her imagination continued to run more rampant than usual, for she felt an irresistible need to leave the rooms and stroll along the curtain wall leading to the barbican.

Others might hide from the weather's passion, but Lydia delighted in the wind that whipped vigorously enough to nearly pull the clothes off her body and mist so thick she could taste the wetness.

She looked out over the cliff side at the pounding surf. A sigh of appreciation for the dark, strange beauty of the day passed her lips. Her sadness disappeared. Happiness bubbled through her like newly poured champagne, and she grinned with pleasure.

A large bird, flying high above, circled and drifted lower and lower. The sharp voice of a raptor called to her.

The wind blew harder, tugging her coat open to crack in the air behind her. Laughter rolled from deep within her, bursting past her lips. Her scarf flew off, freeing her hair. Smiling, she threw her head back and thrust her arms to the sky as if entreating the heavens to carry her to the eagle calling from above.

The wind strengthened into a gale, carrying a voice as deep as thunder that commanded:

"'Tis time you meet again and accept your fates. *Come!*"

The mist became a downpour. Thunder roared. Lightning flashed in the sky. Another gust of wind, stronger than before, lifted her in invisible arms. Could she fly as she had in her dreams?

She felt no fear. She heard the call of the raptor, the sound of his wings. So close now. Suddenly, the wind released her.

Her arms flew out, searching for balance. The back of her hand scraped against cold, rough stone. Her feet scrabbled to find firm ground but landed in a puddle, only to slip from beneath her again.

Falling backward, she screamed and grasped the brooch over her heart. Her head hit cold, unforgiving stone.

Chapter 2

Northumbria, England, 1072

"Why are King William's men bringing a Scotsman to Saint Anne's Abbey, and why cannot I go to Ridley?" Brianna Sinclair's chin began to quiver and her eyes filled with frightened tears. She rubbed a palm over the tip of her nose, disliking the acrid smoke of the tallow candles placed about the dim room.

The abbess shrugged. "'Tis not the king's way to tell a woman what he plans. We will learn of them shortly." She gripped the cross hanging from the thick black cord around her neck, and her lips moved in silent prayer.

"Why has not Uncle Ridley come for me? Everyone knows I am soon to wed Sir Galan at Ridley. Now King William forbids me to leave the abbey until this Scotsman comes! Why, Alana?" She twisted her hands together and looked at her sister for comfort. "Something terrible is going to happen. I feel it! You do also."

"Shh, calm yourself, little one." The abbess' voice was a soothing blanket of love falling around her sister's shoulders. "I know not why. You are the king's ward. The messenger says only that you must tarry until Lord Morgan arrives. Mayhap you will not have to wait long."

"What if the king has changed his mind and does not want me to wed Galan?" Brianna gasped and pulled back from Alana. "This Damron of Blackthorn is a Scot. They lay waste to all we hold dear here on the borders. I will not wed a barbarian. A Scotsman killed Father! If not for them, I would long since have married Galan and had little ones." Her arms wrapped around her lower waist as if protecting those not-yet-conceived babes.

"Aye, a Scotsman killed our father. But do not Saxons also raid into Scotland and kill fathers of families there? 'Tis the manner of fighting men on both sides of the border," Alana said.

"I am told they fight even as they dine. 'Tis common knowledge they rape their brides and beat them each sennight for sport. And baths? They never bathe! I could not abide the stench." Brianna frowned and tilted her nose as if she sniffed the air.

Alana hugged her young sister close to her chest. "Come now, think on it. Fortunately, we have old Roman baths on our lands. If we had not, we might not have become accustomed to bathing. Our men fight often. They sometimes beat their wives. As for rape—'tis part of a warrior's reward. They fight the harder for it."

"I *will not* have him. I want Galan. We will marry afore this beast arrives."

Brianna dutifully attended the noon prayers for sext. She purposefully arrived late so she would be at the rear of the chapel. Kneeling on the cold marble floor with her head bowed, she peeked up to study the women. About ten paces in front of her, twelve pious ladies knelt in six rows. Deeply engrossed, they recited their prayers.

She winced, for she had never been able to attain the inner peace that seemed to radiate from the praying women. Was God impatient with her for her rebellious spirit? The priest had told her for she must bow to God and the king's will in all things.

She eased off her shoes and slipped them under the braided rope at her waist. Breathing a silent prayer for God to forgive her for disobeying the king, she added a much more fervent one that Alana would understand and not be angry with her.

As she backed out of the chapel, her gaze darted around. No one was about. She would ride to Ridley and wed Galan. Slipping quietly along the walls, she made her way to the stables where Sweetpea greeted her with a happy whinny.

"Shh, love, lest they hear us. You do not want to live with Scotsmen. Why, they might even find you a rare delicacy." Her whispered words quieted the fawn-colored mare. She took in a deep breath, savoring the familiar smell of hay, and listened to the soft huffs of the horses.

The shudder coursing through her body found a twin in her mare. Sweetpea shook herself and tossed her head as if dislodging a horrid thought. Sitting on a small mound of hay, Brianna put on her shoes. The special saddle her Nathaniel had made her to celebrate the day of her birth hung close by on the wall.

Nathaniel had always been there for her whenever she was in trouble. He was a man full grown before she was even born, though he never seemed to grow older. If he were here now, he would tell her what to do, she thought mournfully.

Soon, she had the mare ready to ride. Walking on tiptoe, she led the horse to the stable entrance. Above all, she did not want the men her Uncle Ridley had assigned to protect her to hear her leave. Just as she mounted and settled her foot in the stirrup, her groom came running toward her. She urged Sweetpea forward.

"Milady, halt! Brigands be in the woods. Ye must await yer guards," the groom shouted, waving his arms.

Brianna didn't heed him. She spied a farmer, stooped with age, pulling a creaky cart laden with vegetables through the entrance. Delighted to find the heavy wooden gate open, she streaked across the small courtyard.

She rode hard for several leagues, before she burst out of the dense forest into an open field. She laughed with triumph, for Ridley Castle was but a short distance ahead. Galan would know how to keep her safe.

That noise? Thunder? Nay, 'twas the sound of many hooves beating the earth, the creaking of saddles, and the heaving snorts of horses being ridden hard. Her laughter died in her throat.

On the opposite side of the clearing, a troop of warriors thundered toward her. None had the long blond hair or beards of Saxons. They wore the strange helmets and shields of the king's Norman soldiers.

They came so rapidly! Did they mean to ride her to ground like a wild animal? She was too late leaving the abbey. Happiness turned to terror. She jerked the reins to turn her mount and flee back to the safety of the woods.

"Please God, please God. Help me!"

No sooner had she breathed the prayer than her faithful Sweetpea stumbled. Tossed over the mare's head, she felt a scream catch in her throat. The ground rushed up to meet her.

"Do ye ken King William's thinkin', Connor? Have I no' told him I dinna want to wed again, to take this whey-faced Saxon as bride? Over and again?"

Damron shouted above the drumming of the horses' hooves. It was no strain for him, as he forever bellowed when riled. His Scottish brogue thickened.

Connor's deep laugh lightened Damron's scowl and cooled his temper. His cousin and first-in-command was always able to soften his mood.

Ahead, a beautiful fawn-colored horse burst from the woods. The rider's hood fell back and, as he watched, long tresses broke free from their ribbons to fly like a brown silk banner behind the woman's dainty head. Even from this distance, the sound of her laughter reached them. What had caused that glee? That jubilant mood? The moment she spied them, she foolishly tried to force her horse around to gallop away.

"Lucifer's nails! Does she not have wits to see she can injure her horse on this ground? Why is she alone?" Damron shouted.

The horse stumbled, pitching the girl headfirst to the rocky ground before it also fell. Damron clenched his teeth and urged his mount to greater speed. On reaching them, he hauled back on the reins. Great clods of earth flew in the air from their horses' hooves.

He threw himself off the saddle and hurried over to inspect the horse. It struggled to its feet, blowing and stamping, throwing dirt in all directions. Connor knelt to tend the girl.

After Damron seized the mare's reins and brought the horse under control, he stroked over the animal's quivering legs while he crooned endearments.

"By God's grace, she did not cripple the mare."

Connor looked at him with raised brows. Damron turned his attention to the girl, whose skirts had flown above her knees.

"A few sharp smacks on her nether parts would teach this little fool not to be so careless. Her mare looks to be of un-usual stock. She should be a fine breeder." Damron scowled at the girl's small form. "Not so this slip of a lass."

A knight could easily replace a woman, but a well-bred and trained warhorse was his most valuable possession. Damron treated his own mount, Angel, better than most men treated their wives.

Nudging Connor aside, he crouched beside the girl. Her head rested against a rock streaked with blood. He moved gentle hands over her head and body much as he had tended the mare. He turned her onto her back and stared at the rock.

"Christ's wounds, Connor, 'tis shaped like a fist." He put the odd stone in his cousin's hand. "Does it not bring to mind our motto: 'With a Strong Hand'?" He huffed, his face hardened. "This maid is beyond foolish. I have a mind to tell her master he must needs use a strong hand to rein her in."

After Damron tore off strips of the girl's shift and wiped the blood from her face, he bound a clean strip around her head. He continued to check the front of her in the same manner as he had her back, feeling over the curves of her hips and waist as his hands moved up to her ribs.

Encountering soft mounds beneath the tunic, he unthinkingly tightened his grip.

'Twas no maiden but a woman grown.

The eagle's call screeched in Lydia's ear. The world lurched and whirled in a mad rush of air that went on forever. She felt less tangible than a gnat's wing. At last, the sensations changed, eased and fell away. She felt herself slide like a baseball player onto home plate on muddy ground, then into something solid.

Her head throbbed. Her ears roared. Her lids wouldn't obey her mind no matter how hard she tried. They stayed clamped shut and refused to open. Nothing on her body responded. As she focused on each breath, she willed herself not to panic.

With each heartbeat, mind and body merged. Her skin tingled. She felt the ground beneath her. She heard men's voices and the gentle huff of a horse. One eyelid struggled open enough for her to see a face that had to be pure imagination.

"Ohmygod. Ohmygod."

A man leaned close to study her lips. Surprise lit his face.

"Devil take it. Ye willna curse. Are all Saxon lasses so ill bred?"

In her blurred vision, she saw two identical images of a face from hell. Her eyes widened at the sight. As fierce as that double image looked, it was two too many for comfort. Finally, the faces merged to one. A shiny conical helm with a gold-plated nose guard covered the man's head. It hid all but his eyes and jaw. He looked like a giant hawk, with icy green eyes that stared into hers.

She studied those eyes. A spark of recognition caused momentary panic. Why? What had she to fear from him? The man scowled. Trying to return the favor, she winced from the effort. She touched her throbbing forehead, finding cloth bound around it. It was warm and wet. Blood? Had this man tended her? Fingers tightened on her breasts. Startled, she realized the strange face belonged to hands that now squeezed her tender flesh.

"You damned toad! Take your hands off my breasts."

Though she meant to sound assertive, her words were little more than a squeak. Appalled at her display of weakness, she squared her jaw and jutted her chin.

A bark of laughter drew her glance to the left. A second man knelt there. He had removed his helmet. Coarse brown hair flowed around a face with amused brown eyes. He grinned at her with lips that looked as if they often smiled.

"Hm. I ken 'tis the first time a lass has likened you to a lowly creature, cousin."

"Lucifer's horns, woman. Ye *willna* curse."

Damron's brow furrowed into a ferocious scowl. His hard gaze locked on hers as he eased his hands from her breasts.

She knew he did so at his leisure, letting her know it was his decision, not hers.

He clasped her arms instead and ignored her efforts to pull away. "Lucifer's teeth. What do ye think ye are doin'?"

"Lucifer's teeth have nothing to do with it. Aren't you listening? Or have you yelled so much you've made yourself deaf? I told you to remove your hands. I've a good mind to report you for molesting me." She glanced at the sky and muttered, "When did the rain stop?"

"It hasna rained today, rude lass."

"Why are you in costume? Where's the regular guard?" Had she missed reading about a Highland Festival today?

"In costume?" The man leaned closer. "Regular guard?"

She started to glower at him, but decided against it. Her previous efforts hurt too much. Instead, she squinted her lids and tried to look mean.

"You'd better leave before I get *really* angry." She gritted her teeth against the thudding pain raging through her head and tried to pry his fingers from her arms.

The man with the pleasant face burst into laughter.

"Connor. Leave off." The harsh words sounded threatening.

"Quiet! Both of you. I have a splitting headache." She made her own demand as loud as she could. The results impressed her.

She studied what she could see of the tyrant's face. It wasn't much. Why didn't he take off his helmet? Conflicting smells came from this body so close to hers. A whiff of sandalwood merged with sweaty maleness, leather, and the pungent odor of armor and horse.

"Oh, hell and damn. Why won't you go away?" She caught her breath as tremors of foreboding flowed over her like waves.

Damron ignored her. No one, much less a wee lass, had ever had the nerve to order him, the future Laird of Blackthorn, about.

He turned his glare on Connor, warning him he was on touchy ground. His cousin muffled his amusement. His warriors and the king's escort were listening and watching. He straightened and eyed them, noting their grins quickly fled and their gazes looked heavenward.

Damron waited as ten Saxon warriors bearing the Sinclair crest on their shields galloped toward them. They did not approach with swords drawn, for the king's escorts were readily visible.

A man, who appeared to be a groom, vaulted off his horse. He hopped from one foot to the other, craning his head to peer around Damron.

"Who is this ill-mannered lass? Why was she unescorted?" Damron scowled, his hands fisted on his hips.

"My lord, 'tis Lady Brianna Sinclair. She lives with her sister at Saint Anne's. My gentle lady started afore her escorts were prepared."

The woman on the ground threw out her arm and knocked Damron on the ankle. "I'm not Brianna, I'm . . ."

The groom, wringing his hands, broke in. "We could not catch up to her. She is long used to evading her escorts."

Damron's face tightened, his lips thinned. He had sent the herald ahead to inform the abbess of Saint Anne's to expect him. *This* rude girl was Lady Brianna? Why had she left the abbey, and why was she riding west toward Ridley?

This wisp of a lass, who bristled with defiance, was his docile, obedient bride? As if he could somehow burn her to cinders and she would disappear, he glowered at the Saxon woman he was forced to marry. Not caring if he sizzled the lady's ears, he shouted, "Lucifer's pocked arse."

No doubt she heard him, for her eyes rolled up and she looked to have slipped her mind again.

He vaulted onto Angel's back. Heaving a disgruntled sigh, he spread a heavy plaid across his lap. His brows furrowed, he motioned for Connor to hand her up to him. Fortunately, Connor kept his amusement tightly contained while Damron settled her to his satisfaction.

He snapped an order to her groom to ride ahead to Ridley and tell them of the injured lady. Looking around at her Saxon men, Damron spoke in disgust.

"Gowks, all of ye." Jabbing a thumb over his shoulder, he ordered, "Ride to the rear." Once they were under his control, the fools would soon learn not to disgrace themselves.

Angel's gait started too roughly, and Brianna moaned. He signaled the big stallion to a gentle walk as he studied the woman in his arms. Her hair, a deep chestnut color, flowed long and thick with curls that clung to his fingers. Brown brows were shapely arches above long-lashed eyelids. A small, aristocratic nose, generous full lips tilted up at the sides. Her lower lip looked plump and inviting, begging to be teased. Her small body felt delicate and helpless. His rage began to ebb. His arm tightened to draw her closer. She smelled of roses and sunshine.

Not for long. The girl whimpered. Before he knew the reason for her distress, she spewed her stomach's contents on his tunic. Though he cursed, his hands were gentle as he wiped her face and held her head high so she would not choke.

They traveled the forest road and came out at a large, grassy area to the front of Ridley Castle. Expecting them, the gatekeeper had raised the portcullis. Armed men lined the wall walks and the inner courtyard.

They crossed the drawbridge and passed through the barbican. Damron's eyes roved over every inch of the ground and walls. He noted anger in the glares directed at him and saw the men's hands tighten on their sword hilts. Though he kept his eyes straight ahead, he did not miss a single detail.

Damron was suspicious of the lass the king would burden him with. Lady Brianna appeared far from the meek, biddable girl William had portrayed. Also, the king had casually mentioned a petition from Sir Galan of Ridley seeking permission to marry. Had he sought Lady Brianna? Mayhap William had not told him all?

Once he and Baron Simon of Ridley entered the baron's solar, Damron waited patiently while the baron read the king's missive informing him that Damron had complete authority over the Sinclair and Ridley honors. Ridley eyed him warily, no doubt wondering at the king's actions.

"I would know more of the Lady Brianna." Damron leaned forward in his seat. "Is the lass often fashious and disobedient?"

"I have never known Brianna to be anything but mild of manner and obedient. She never disobeyed her father, God rest his soul. She has been an angel with me." Baron Ridley's face flushed with indignation.

"If not disobedient, is she mayhap prone to reckless urges? To be willful and not seek manly guidance afore she acts? Mayhap to refuse it?"

The baron's eyes opened wider. His face turned redder as Damron's harsh voice demanded answers. "Nay! She has always known her place."

"Why then did she flee the abbey when she knew I was to arrive?" Damron's eyes narrowed to slits as he studied Ridley.

"I know not why. Mayhap she sought only to take exercise and became frightened on seeing your warriors."

"Exercise?" Damron snorted with disbelief. "Alone? With her escorts far behind her?" He shook his head and posed the one question that most begged an answer.

"Is the lady oft alone with a knight in your service? A Sir Galan?"

The baron fairly hopped with agitation. "Nay. Never are they alone. Our Brianna would not dream of such base behavior."

Damron nodded. He would learn more on his own than what this man would tell him. To his way of thinking, at the very least the young woman was headstrong. She could have easily worked her wiles on such an easygoing man as the baron and met Galan in secret.

In their chambers the following evening, Damron paced from the door to the window opening and back, time and again. "What think ye of all we have learned, Connor?"

"At Saint Anne's this morn, Abbess Alana vouched for Brianna's honor." Connor sat on a stool close beside the window. He turned a small cup of ale around and around on the table, admiring the painted design on it. "She believes her sister bolted from fear of the unknown. What possessed William to even hint to Sir Galan that there could be a marriage between the two? Her honors are too vast to bestow upon a mere knight." Connor rolled his shoulders, then stretched his arms out with a sigh of pleasure.

"In his cups, of course." Damron had no need to hide his irritation, for Connor well knew his dislike of their old friend's overindulgence in food and drink. "'Tis a cruel thing that he does."

"Dinna fight so hard against this edict of King Malcolm and King William's, Damron. They must needs foster peace on the borders. William could have demanded you as hostage at Abernethy. Instead, he proposed a union between a powerful Scottish family and his own Saxon ward. 'Twas a clever move. Only you would think a lovely young bride with such wealthy holdings a punishment.

"'Tis natural he demanded you. He thinks to do you further honor." Connor raised a hand, questioningly. "'Tis his way. Do you not remember the first year we fostered with William's family and he gifted you with your destrier, Angel? You disarmed the knave intent on stabbing him in the back. A future Scottish laird and the future king of England—what an unholy pair you made."

Connor chuckled. "You always with a scowl on your face and William forever in a temper."

Damron returned to his arguments and refused to talk of those early years after his father's death, when he divided his time between Scotland and Normandy. He strolled over to the bed, picked up a plump pillow and kneaded it as he walked a few paces. Whirling, he threw it back on the bed.

"This 'lovely young bride' is a Saxon." He spit the words out like they somehow tasted foul. She was older than most brides because of the Conquest. William had said she had seen twenty summers. "She is scrawny and weak. How will she survive Highland livin' in the best of summers, much less in months cold enough to break the tarse off a man?"

He glared at the braziers of hot coals placed about the room. He threw off his tunic and padded barefoot to the wooden shutters. He opened them wide and stood motionless, welcoming the cold air flowing over him.

"Why must they need fires when 'tis warm?" he muttered.

He stared at the glittering stars. They looked like clusters of fireflies in the evening sky. He didn't want another wife; he had loved before upon first sight. Her face and form had been of rare beauty, his Genevieve, but her character was steeped in darkest deceit. He shuddered.

He longed to punch William's arrogant nose. Eight years earlier, he and William had been together in the Norman court. Damron had been wed to Genevieve but a short time then. He had visited his mother's kin in Rouen and returned to the court a sennight earlier than expected. He had ridden hard to surprise his love with a locket, studded with precious sapphires, securely resting in his pocket. 'Twas Genevieve's name day.

Instead, it was Genevieve who had surprised him.

Damron had no wish to marry again. He could not trust a woman. A jagged scar near his groin was a constant reminder why. Now King William and King Malcolm forced Brianna on him. A wife was naught but trouble and heartache. His leman, Asceline, tended his needs and well knew her place. He had no need of a wife.

He blinked away the images that haunted his mind, realizing Connor had called his name several times.

Connor's gaze searched Damron's face. "What is your intent?"

"I must needs watch Brianna for a sennight. Her behavior is by far too strange for the biddable, sweet-tempered lass William described. What has he not told me of her?"

"Aye, she did not appear to be easily led by a man." Connor strode over to a corner table and poured water in a basin. He washed his face and hands, then splashed cold water over them.

"One saving grace is that, since I am their new overlord, I can draw much-needed men from the Sinclair and Ridley garrisons." Damron felt some small satisfaction. "We could well use the extra warriors to supplement Blackthorn's army, with the Gunns always nipping at our borders. They are becoming e'er more bold of late. I want no more of our families grievin' because we did not have enough warriors to protect them."

Images of his slain father and brothers, along with Connor's parents, filled Damron's mind with pain. He thought about their loss when he and his cousin had been eleven summers old.

He snagged the green tunic he had thrown on the bed and tugged it over his head. "I will judge for myself what manner of person she is. *Honor!*" He snapped the words in disbelief.

"Aye," Connor said, drying his face. "Abbess Alana believes a woman can have honor the same as a man. A strange belief."

"'Tis not possible." Damron secured his sword about his waist. Its weight soothed him as he strolled to the door and glanced back. "Wait for me in the great hall. After I look in on Brianna, I will join you."

* * *

Lydia awoke in a darkened room. Somehow, she must have lost her contacts. She squinted, trying to make out the vague shapes around her. She was in a bed unlike any other on which she had slept. The sight of the wooden frame, complete with a white canopy and heavy green bed curtains tied at each post, made her blink in disbelief.

Across from the foot of the bed was a door with leather hinges and a strange latch instead of a doorknob. Beside it stood a heavily carved wood trunk. A brace of candles illuminated it.

Her headache reminded her she had been visiting the ruins of Blackthorn Castle when the winds of the freak storm had tossed her down on the stone walkway. At least she thought that was what happened. Other images kept intruding.

Like a camera snapping pictures, visions flashed before her eyes—strange horsemen galloping toward her, the ground flying up to meet her after a horse stumbled, her fear as she braced for the fall. Odd. She'd never ridden a horse in Scotland.

How could she have these visions? And men shouting. Who were they? And why had she called out to God to help her? Now where in blazes had that memory come from? Was it a dream? She winced as an angry jab of pain rocketed through her head.

She'd better solve her problems in order. There seemed to be many of them. Where was she? She didn't recognize the room. Why had they brought her here after the storm instead of to the Bed and Breakfast where the museum staff knew she always lodged?

Hearing a soft rustle of clothing, Lydia turned her head to see a young woman sitting in a chair close by. She had black hair and sky blue eyes. Her face looked familiar, and she appeared close to Lydia's age. The woman sensed her gaze, for she shot up from the chair and hurried over.

"Oh, Brianna, you truly did it this time. He says you ran away. I thought you were going to die when I saw all that blood. That horrible man ordered everyone about like he was the king, and Papa let him." She stopped rambling long enough to draw a breath before she continued. "Mother said that after they left the solar, Father's face and neck were red, his hair stuck up, and he looked like a cock." She jammed her fists on her waist and frowned indignantly. "Mayhap she has trouble with her sight? He has never looked like a chicken to me."

Brianna? Does the woman mistake me for someone else? Of a sudden, fear clogged Lydia's throat. *My God! She speaks Old English, and I understand her. And that obnoxious man earlier. He spoke Norman French, and I answered him in the same tongue.*

Though she had a master's degree in historical linguistics, along with one in genetics, she had never thought she'd one day use any of the earlier languages. She'd had a flare for them. She sent a thank you heavenward to her parents, for they had been renowned historians and taught her a love for all things ancient. After listening carefully to the rapid fire of words, she spoke.

"My name is not Brianna. It is Lydia Hunter. Who are you?"

"'Tis I, your cousin Elise. Can you not see me? Of course you are Brianna." She nodded so vigorously her chin hit her chest. "You are a Sinclair, and Sinclairs are not hunters. Are you playing a game? When you fell on the rock, did it hurt your eyes, too? You have been asleep for two days. Mother said your brain might not work too well, but she never said anything about eyes."

Her worried gaze studied Lydia. "You keep blinking. Are you going to be sick again? You spewed on the giant, and he grumbled something fierce. Do wait until I get Mother." She raced to the door, barely opening it wide enough to slide her slim body through.

Lydia gingerly pushed herself up and edged back against the hard wood of the headboard. The dizziness had gone, and the pain in her head had diminished to dull pounding. On seeing her arms and hands, she frowned, stretched her fingers wide and held her arms close to her eyes. Why did they seem different? Puzzled, she rubbed her eyes, then gripped the edge of the covers and peered beneath them. Never had she seen such a nightgown, other than in drawings of medieval women's clothing.

Was she dreaming? Or had she stumbled on a medieval festival in full swing? Glad to have thought of a reason for the strangeness of her surroundings and memories, she began to relax.

A wooden screen painted with colorful Celtic designs closed off one corner of the room. She slid off the bed, and when her bare feet touched the cold stones, her toes curled. Shivering with each step, she made her way to the screen and peeked behind it. Atop a stand was a pitcher of water and a large bowl with several white cloths beside it. Tucked beneath was something that looked like a chamberpot.

She shuddered and decided to wait for Elise to direct her to the bathroom. A hint of sound caught her attention. She glanced over her shoulder to see a young man ease the door shut, and then stride toward her.

"Get out! This room is occupied." She stabbed her finger toward the door, anger giving her voice the tone of authority she needed. Even so, it sounded different. It lacked its usual depth.

"Do not be afeared, Brianna. 'Tis I, Galan." In several long strides, he reached her and grasped her shoulders.

Before she knew his intent, his warm lips caressed her cheek. She gasped and flattened her hands on his chest and shoved, but she may as well have tried to move an ancient oak. He did not budge.

The door burst open, striking the wall with an earsplitting crash. She cried out as her gaze flew to the doorway to see who had stormed into the room.

Chapter 3

A very large man filled the doorway, blocking out the soft glow of rushlights on the landing. Although the room was too dim to see his face, Lydia read anger in his taut body and widespread legs. It had to be the obnoxious man from the clearing who stood there.

He was still in costume.

Everything here was much more authentic than at any Medieval Festival she'd ever attended. She'd better abandon that idea in favor of her dream theory. Surely she'd absorbed more of her mother's books on medieval life than she'd realized. The actors' clothing and the room's furnishings were much as she had seen portrayed in the tomes. Even more puzzling was the ease with which everyone spoke Old English and Norman French.

"If ye dinna wish to mourn their loss, remove yer hands from her," the man ordered Galan. His words were thick with menace as he placed his powerful legs firmly in a battle stance.

Lydia felt the full force of his possessive gaze sweeping over her.

"Ye shame yerself, Brianna! Get ye back in bed."

Lydia's skin flushed that the men had seen her in such a

thin garment. She dashed over to yank the sheet off the bed and hold it up under her chin. Humiliation escalated to anger.

"My name is not Brianna. You have no right to barge into my room, and certainly no right to tell me what to do. This person may be in your command, but I am not." She thrust out her chin and narrowed her eyes. She used the same tone that had never failed to quell her ex-husband, Gordon, when he sought to usurp her control over the Genetics Research Laboratory. But today she sounded different. She must be more frazzled than she thought.

A feral growl rumbled from the man's chest. Exuding pure menace, he stalked toward her. He was playing the part of the arrogant medieval lord of the castle far too seriously. She had the feeling he never ignored a challenge.

Especially from a woman.

Prickles of unease scampered up her back, much like mice scurrying to their hiding places on hearing a hungry cat's meow.

Elise hurtled into the room. "Brianna, I found—eeps!" She squeaked and skidded to a stop, then made a wide detour around him.

An elegant woman followed Elise, carrying a candle and shielding its flame. Whatever he was about to say he kept to himself.

"Come!" Grasping Galan's shoulder, the man left the room with him.

"I brought Mother." Elise pointed over her shoulder at the woman. "'Tis your Aunt Maud, in case you forgot her name, too."

"Dear, do not shout so. I am sure the fall did no damage to Brianna's ears." Lady Maud's eyes twinkled with amusement. She handed the candle to Elise and brushed back the hair from Lydia's forehead. Gentle fingers examined the cut and swollen area there. "You will have a colorful brow for several days, but 'tis easily hid if your hair is done in the proper way, Brianna."

"My name isn't Brianna. It's Lydia." She began to wonder if these people didn't understand her, for they stubbornly continued to call her Brianna. And they acted familiarly. As if they really believed they were related to her.

"Does your head hurt less this day?" Lady Maud motioned Elise to move the candle closer while she studied Lydia's eyes.

Fireworks flashed through Lydia's head again. She couldn't remember ever having a headache in a dream. Another urgent problem made itself known, and she squirmed. "I have to use a bathroom. Would you please tell me where it is?"

"Bathroom?" Lady Maud's brow lifted, but when Lydia shifted from one foot to the other, her eyes lit with understanding. "Of course, dear." After patting Lydia on the shoulder, she motioned toward the screen and quietly left the room.

"A chamber pot? I can't believe it." Lydia shook her head, mindful not to cause the pounding to increase. This room was too fine to be in a cheap hotel. "Surely you have a modern bathroom somewhere close by?" When Elise still looked puzzled, Lydia added, "Garderobe?" Seeing her blank expression, she added, "A place to pass water?"

"Oh, that? 'Tis but a tiny alcove with an open seat overhanging the wall. Blessed heaven! You should be glad not to use it this day."

Elise's words rose as Lydia ducked behind the screen. "'Tis wet and windy. You always say you hate the cold air swirling up on your behind."

"Why don't you open the door and announce it to the world? Some of the hotel guests might not have heard you." Great, now she was grumpy. Why couldn't she have modern conveniences in her dream? "Humpf, I don't understand. I bet I'll wake up to find this dream's a nightmare and I've wet the damned bed."

"Oh, nay! Do not tell me you wet the bed," Elise wailed.

Lydia peeked around the screen and saw her scramble and

search over the bed for wet spots. When she found none, she plunked down at the foot and waited.

Hearing someone scratch at the door, Lydia ducked back behind the screen. She wasn't about to parade around in front of anyone else.

Two men carried in a wooden tub, followed by servants with buckets of water. After filling the tub, they placed the rest of the water beside a brazier of hot coals. When they left, she went over to stare at the tub.

Well, hell and damn. They really don't have a bathroom.

"What is the matter? Come. Soak away that foul salve so I can wash your hair. Mother had broth made for you. She says hot broths make a person sleep. You need lots of sleep so you will re-member you are Brianna." Eyeing Lydia, she frowned. "Lots and lots of sleep," she repeated and nodded for emphasis.

"I'm not going back to bed. What is that sweet smell?" She stilled, realizing she had never dreamed a smell before.

"Truly, Brianna, your memory worsens. 'Tis your favorite rose-scented soap, of course."

When Lydia got into the tub, the soothing hot water came up to cover her breasts. She reached for the cloth and pot of soap and carefully washed her face. Elise insisted on sham-pooing her hair.

"I have washed away the blood and dirt. Tilt your head back so I may rinse it."

When the soap was gone, Lydia pushed the hair from her face, feeling her tresses' unfamiliar length. Her eyes widened.

"Please. Open the shutters." Seeing Elise's blank look, Lydia pointed to the window opening. Elise scampered over and unlatched the shutter, letting in the soft afternoon light.

Flowing over Lydia's shoulders was a mass of dark chest-nut hair with deep hints of auburn. Her hands shot up, splashing water over the sides of the tub. Elise jumped at the soaking she received.

"Oh . . . my . . . God." For the first time, Lydia realized how changed she herself was. Disbelief filled her as she stared at her arms and studied her hands. She lifted her legs abruptly, again sloshing water over the sides of the tub. She gasped. Her legs were shorter, more slender. Why, they even looked delicate, as if she had never run a marathon or rollerbladed.

"Merciful saints! Why are you flopping around?" Elise cupped her hands beside her mouth and stage whispered, "Are you having a brain fit? I must get Mother. Please, do not drown while I am gone."

"Don't you dare leave. Sit still while I figure this out." Her heart pounding, Lydia forced herself to breathe slowly and calmly. She stared at her legs and shook her head. It can't be. Grabbing the sides of the tub, she stood and looked down.

Her breasts were small but perfect with tips the color of pink roses. A flat, firm stomach followed. She looked lower still to see her woman's mound tufted with soft brown hair. When she spied firm thighs without a hint of cellulite, her knees folded and she dropped down into the tub.

"Oh, Brianna, you will surely drown if you do not stop." Elise darted around the tub like a frightened squirrel.

"Let me think." Lydia's mind was in turmoil. She felt her face. Although the slender nose felt familiar, the rest seemed more delicate. Never had she dreamed that she had a different body. Yet it had to be a dream.

Still, it felt real—her painful headache, being hungry, feeling everything she touched and even smelling the rose soap. Most important was the relief she felt when she used the chamber pot. That, too, had never happened in her dreams.

Stepping from the bath, she wrapped herself in a drying cloth and went to sit beside the large brazier to dry her heavy length of hair. Trying to arrange it with the wide-toothed comb Elise handed her, she soon discovered her long, curly tresses came with a problem. Patiently, she untangled the snarls as Elise rummaged through the carved trunk.

"The scullery maid said that giant Scotsman went to Saint Anne's after matins this morn and returned in a rage." Elise briskly shook several garments in the air. "He challenged every one of your Saxon guards to meet him in the training field." Eyes wide with fright, she lowered the garments and whispered, "Do you think he has skewered them with his sword?"

Lydia knew she was talking about the macho man who thought it was his God-given right to command her.

"Not damned likely. Uh, where are my things? I must get dressed. Does the hotel serve the evening meal at sunset?"

Elise flapped the handful of clothes close to Lydia's eyes.

"Blessed saints. You cannot go below." Elise waved her arms around adding an extra denial. "You do not see your clothes and you forget your name. I do not understand half of what you say, for your speech is most strange. Mayhap 'tis that rock's fault?" She sounded hopeful.

After Elise slipped a delicate silk smock over Lydia's head and followed it with a light green tunic, Lydia sat on the edge of the bed and pulled on the old-fashioned hose. Hmmm. How did she secure them around her thighs?

Noting her hesitation, Elise shook her head and clucked her tongue. She came over to tie green ribbons above Lydia's knees. Not trusting her to do it right, Elise slipped soft leather shoes on Lydia's feet and cross-gartered them about her ankles. Satisfied that she didn't need further help, Elise hurried over to lift the door latch.

"I will have Cook prepare a tray with broth and mayhap some bread and cheese." She tugged at the heavy door.

"Hold on there. What about my underwear? You don't expect me to go naked under here, do you?"

"You are not naked." Elise giggled and let go of the door to come back and lift the hem of Lydia's tunic. She pointed beneath it. "Look. Did you forget having your smock? Why do you dress? We may not go below. That Scotsman ordered that you not leave the room until he says you may." Another thought struck her, and she moved her hands to guard her bottom. "Oh, nay, you are not going to get us a beating, are you?"

Lydia snorted and headed for the door.

The young woman scurried to stand against it, her arms and legs spread wide to make a barrier. "You cannot," she whispered. Her face blanched. "We must be careful. Father Jacob will read the banns this coming Sunday."

"Bans on what? No. Don't tell me. I'll bet he means to banish women from the dining hall." Huffing in disgust, Lydia tugged Elise away from the door.

Elise's frightened gaze searched the room as if looking for support there. She grabbed hold of Lydia's clothing and dug in her heels.

It didn't work.

Lydia found the landing was as strange as the bedchamber had been. It was like many castle interiors she had seen, though she had never visited this one in her travels. Everything was in perfect condition. They had placed rushlights at close intervals so a person could see well enough not to stumble. Their smoke gave off an unfamiliar smell. A bubble of excitement welled up.

How would her imagination fill in the details? She hoped she didn't awake before she could explore a little. Elise still clung to her clothing like a stubborn limpet.

Determined to go below, Lydia towed her behind her as she went down the stairs.

Men and women filled the large hall, and everyone was speaking at once. Fascinated with the bright clothing and the room's arrangement, she stared around her.

A fireplace, tall enough to walk into, filled much of the wall to the right. Surely a Norman influence? Picturesque tapestries covered the rest of the stone walls, along with weapons of all kinds. Bright banners hung from the rafters, their vivid colors muted by a light haze of smoke. Trestle tables with benches stood in orderly rows about the room.

Scant seconds later, a large body blocked her sight. Two big booted feet went toe to toe with hers. Behind her, Elise squeaked like a mouse. She let loose of Lydia's clothing, then bolted away.

"Brianna, turn and get ye back above. Ye will stay abed until ye return to yer senses."

His curt commands left no doubt who was speaking. Staring at his shirt, she gave herself a mental kick, for her knees had started to shake. She tried to glare up at him, but he stood so close her gaze could not stray above his chest. She wasn't about to back up. He'd think he had intimidated her.

"Huh. I have my senses. And do stop calling me Brianna. My name is Lydia." The heat coming from his body seeped through her own clothing. With each breath, she inhaled his scent of sandalwood and spices. Intoxicating. What a shame he didn't have a pleasing personality to enhance his sexuality.

"Ye are mindsick, woman. Anyone who canna remember their name is in need of rest. Go to yer bed, else I will take ye myself."

"My mind is not sick." As if instructing a child, she spoke slowly, distinctly. "My memory is fine." Macho man was ruining her interesting dream. In the early days of her marriage, Gordon had thought to control her every movement. She had soon disabused him of that. She wasn't about to put up with this stranger's overbearing ways. She scooted around him before he knew what she was about.

He looked ready to object further, but he didn't. The man named Connor, whom she remembered kneeling beside her in the clearing, said something to him she didn't catch.

"Allow me the pleasure, Brianna." Galan appeared at her side and held out his arm to escort her.

She put the tips of her fingers on his forearm and marveled

at the hardness there. He must work out daily. Their footsteps stirred the rushes under their feet, releasing the soft scents of rose petals, thyme and rosemary, adding a pleasant touch to the medieval atmosphere in the room.

Galan seated her beside him at the high table, and after glancing around, she saw several people separated her from where the aggravating man sat. If she could not see him, he also could not see her.

Young attendants silently brought basins and poured water for them to wash their hands. Another handed them drying cloths. A servant placed a large, flat piece of stale dark bread on a platter between her and Galan. Ahh, a trencher? Her imagination seemed quite accurate. They each had a silver goblet for wine, but no eating utensils were on the table.

Servitors placed platters of salmon, steaming venison and roasted boar stuffed with mushrooms nearby. As the smells drifted to her, her mouth began to water.

Galan removed an eating knife from a sheath at his side and lifted a sizeable portion of salmon onto the trencher.

She had no idea how she was supposed to eat it. Why couldn't she dream of a time when they at least had wooden forks? Galan whispered to her and held a portion to her lips. Carefully, she took it without her lips touching him. It tasted divine.

Leaning forward, she stole a quick glance at the head of the table. Disgruntled, she rubbed her eyes. She couldn't see any of the faces there clearly. She huffed in disgust. Why couldn't she have decent eyesight in her dream? Lord, what she wouldn't give to have her contacts. She squinted and finally saw Lady Maud's husband help her with the salmon in the same fashion.

Feeling the hard gaze of the warrior upon her, she jerked back and took a gulp of wine. It was a big mistake. Never had she tasted such dry red wine. She slapped a hand over her mouth to keep from spluttering it over the table. She preferred a dry red, but this was so dry it near withered the insides of her cheeks. The platters of food no longer enticed her. Blast! It was the Scotsman's fault. He'd ruined her appetite. She'd probably be so hungry when she awoke that she'd eat two of the large, famous English breakfasts.

Listening to the conversations around her, she became more familiar with Old English. She had no need to speak, though, for when someone asked her a question, Elise supplied the answer. The young woman chattered on and on, reminding Lydia of an excited teenager.

Each time Galan leaned close, she felt ripples of disapproval radiate from Mr. Macho at the head of the table. He acted like a jealous boyfriend.

"Brianna, I have a surprise for you. I have worked long and hard to please you with it," Galan whispered in her ear.

"Oh, God. Do you think you can go slower on the surprises?" Since she had entered Blackthorn's museum, she'd had one shocking surprise after the other.

"Are you talking to God, Brianna? Father Jacob will be back for matins at dawn. After mass, you can talk to him and he will tell you what God thinks." Elise nodded encouragingly.

Smiling at Brianna, Galan took a lap mandolin from a page and bowed to her. He sat on a stool in front of the table and began to play. The music had a beautiful melody.

As his voice filled the room, its quality held Lydia spellbound. Hearing the words, she realized he was singing a love song. From the many knowing smiles of everyone seated near her, it wasn't an unusual event.

Galan called forth something lurking in the back of her memory. Flashes of a stolen moment in a draped window enclosure. The feel of his body as he clasped her to him. She blinked and shook her head. No way could that be a memory. How could she remember anything about Galan? This was a dream, for heaven's sake. He ended his song with a flourish and returned to sit beside her.

She leaned her head close to his and put her hand on his arm. "Galan, I don't believe I've ever heard a more beautiful song. I hated for it to . . ."

Suddenly, her bench wobbled dangerously, almost spilling her onto the stone floor. She jumped up like a startled rabbit, lost her balance and landed on Galan's firm thighs. As she scrambled off him, her nose bumped against a hard-as-marble chest.

That impossible man again! She knew, for she had stared at that same chest earlier and recognized his clothing. And his enticing scent. Leaning back against the table while rubbing her nose, she tilted her head to look up at his face.

Surely her eyes played tricks on her?

"Ye will return to yer room. Now." The words sounded forced between grim lips. He scooped her up in his arms and stalked toward the stone stairwell.

Lydia struggled and pushed at his shoulders. His grasp tightened.

"Keep ye still, or I will put ye o'er my shoulder." He glowered down at her as an added warning.

Lydia felt the blood drain from her face. Because of the Norman helm he had worn in the clearing, and because of the dark bedchamber above, she had not seen him clearly before. He couldn't possibly be the man whom she thought she was seeing. Not even in a dream. No foggy mist that enveloped them in the antique shop separated them here. She could feel his heat, his flesh. She smelled his scent that caused her blood to race through her body.

"Tell me your name, Demon. Tell me your name." He couldn't be the man in the ink drawing. It wasn't possible!

"Damron, woman, not Demon. My name is Damron, and well ye know it." His words grated with impatience.

"No. Not just Damron. Tell me all of it." Her words quivered with apprehension. She had to be sure.

"Damron Alasdair, of the Morgans at Blackthorn Castle. What difference does my full name make?"

"You can't be. You're dead!" Lydia gripped the neatly braided hair at his temples. She drew his face closer. Shock rippled through her.

Her shout echoed off the stone walls. "How can you be here? You've been dead for centuries!"

Chapter 4

Damron surged up the stairway two steps at a time, wanting to get Brianna to her bedchamber and out of his arms as quickly as possible—before he shook some sense into her. From his first sight of her riding toward him days before, she had acted nothing like the biddable young woman he was promised. She had enticed Galan, leaning toward him when she spoke. Even touching him familiarly. Damron's stomach churned, remembering Brianna's rapt expression when the young man sang.

Why, she did not act like a meek lass who had lived in an abbey, but like a headstrong lad who thought to ignore his authority. She would have found herself soundly thrashed as soon as she had disobeyed his orders and appeared below—were she a lad.

Damron kicked the heavy door to her chamber. It crashed back against the stone walls for the second time in her recent memory. Quick strides took him across the room, where he dropped her on the bed.

"Ack!" She spread her arms and clutched at the covers.

Elise ran through the doorway and skittered around him as he whirled and stalked from the room.

"Oh, Brianna, whatever will you do?" Elise twisted her hands together and looked about to cry. "Everyone heard you yell that Lord Damron has been dead for hundreds of years. Why, he would be dust by now. He was furious. I am afeared they will lock you in a tower like they did Great-grandmother Elyn."

"Lock me away?" Lydia's arms flailed as she fought the feather bed mattress and sat upright to stare at Elise.

"Yes, like Great-grandmother. They said she fed her husband wormy meat and yelled he was a vulture and should eat carrion." Elise's eyes widened as she recalled the story about her relative.

"They thought her possessed and tried to drive Lucifer from her. The priest shaved a cross on the top of her head. It did not help." She gasped and stared at the crown of Brianna's head. "Mayhap they will think you are like her. Oh, 'twould be a sin to shave such beautiful hair."

"If he was as obnoxious as Lord Damron, he probably *was* a vulture." Her palms began to sweat, her heart to race. She took quick gasps of air. This was no interactive dream about a medieval castle. It's the real thing. *God, help me!*

Knowing she was hyperventilating, she fought for control. *There's no paper bag here to breathe into, so calm yourself. Pass out now, and they'll march in here and shave your head before you know what's up!*

Lady Maud came into the room making soft, soothing sounds. "Mayhap you left your bed too soon, sweetling. Surely 'tis the reason for your strange ravings." She handed Lydia a pewter cup. "Drink this, and by the sun's next rise, you will be to rights." She smiled kindly at Lydia before putting her arm around Elise's shoulders to coax her to the door. "Come, love. If we keep Brianna awake with our useless talking, she will not get the healing rest she needs."

Left alone, Lydia sniffed the hot liquid but decided to pour the brew out the window. She had no idea if the herbal concoction was safe. Perhaps Damron had persuaded Lady Maud to add a sleeping potion to it. Now was not the time to sleep. She needed to think, to sort out this strange dilemma before Elise returned for the evening.

She undressed and examined the clothing, noting the texture of the material, the simple design and the stitches that held it together. Her anxiety grew while she folded each article. Finally, she climbed into bed, prepared to pretend a deep slumber if they checked on her.

No sooner had she done so than the latch lifted and someone quietly entered to stand over her. Her eyes were lightly closed, and she tried to keep her breathing deep and rhythmic. She did not need to see her visitor. His scent reached her nostrils.

He studied her so closely that his warm breath stroked her cheek, bringing to the surface another puzzling memory. The scene flashed behind her closed lids, and she almost gasped aloud. It was much clearer than any of the strange memories she'd ever had.

Damron, his weight on his arms, covered her. His dark brows arched questioningly above green eyes that stared hotly down into hers. His full, sensual lips hovered close to hers. "This?" His teeth nipped gently at her skin as he trailed kisses to the tip of her breast. Slowly, hotly, he licked the nipple there, then gazed into her eyes. "'Tis this ye like?" His voice husky with passion flowed over her. She moaned softly. "Do ye love me, henny?"

She refused to answer. He clenched his teeth, causing a jagged scar, which ran from the left corner of his lips down across his jaw, to whiten. His thick black hair was longer. The thin braids at his temples fell on each side of his face to lightly brush her sensitive flesh.

He was naked.

* * *

The erotic vision caused a wild swirl of heat to race through her body and puddle in the pit of her stomach. Her mind cleared when the flesh-and-blood Damron began to speak.

"Ye are not as they said," he whispered, his tone bitter. "Either all was a lie, or the rock has done more harm than the bruises that show."

Though anger and frustration radiated from him, his touch was gentle as he smoothed the hair back from her forehead. His fingers combed through her thick curls, then strayed to trace her lips.

The bewitching scent from his hands caused an involuntary catch in her breathing. He stilled, then lifted his fingers. Was he afraid he was waking her? Several moments passed before he moved away.

She did not dare twitch a muscle. After hearing the door close, she peeked through thick lashes. She was alone.

Over the years, she had learned much about the Sinclair and Morgan families. Brianna's mother died after birthing her, and her sister, Alana, took over the duties as mother. When Brianna was eight years old, the baron founded Saint Anne's Abbey with Alana as its abbess.

Damron Morgan was noted for his temper and strong will. After his marriage to Brianna, she gave him two sons, but their history said she later leapt from the parapet of Blackthorn Castle.

"Not bloody likely," Lydia muttered aloud. She had never believed it, for Brianna had lived at the abbey with Alana. She damned well would never put her immortal soul in danger.

How in blazes did she get here in Brianna's body?

Had all those misty flashes of strange memories over the years belonged to a previous life? Even at five years old, when she had seen Damron's likeness, she claimed he *belonged* to her. Her father told her she misread Damron for Demon, though she now believed it was more than a child's mistake. She remembered the feeling of fierce possession that filled her as she bought the brooch, the face and voice that begged her to vow she would never leave him. It was Damron's as surely as it had been tonight.

When she'd walked high above on the castle parapets, the wind had blown as furiously as a hurricane gust and lifted her into the air for scant seconds before dropping her back against hard stone. Her head struck something. Then, darkness. She'd heard the raptor's voice, felt the flutter of its wing feathers.

She had moved through black nothingness until the echo of a frightened voice cried out, "Please God, please God, help me!" The sensation of moving ended then with a sense much like slipping on a muddy river bank and sliding into the water.

She'd felt another blow to the head. More darkness. When she again became aware, she had struggled to make her body respond to her mind. Had her soul returned to a former life then?

She had often thought about the journey of souls, but always in the sense that souls went forward into another time. What if her matured soul was called back to relive a previous life? Maybe this explained why she had felt such a tie to the drawing. If she had once been Brianna, it would account for those strange images that did not belong to Lydia.

Was there a way back? One thing she knew for certain. If she indeed was in a former lifetime, she had no intention of leaving the way the early Brianna had.

Hours later, Lydia woke with tears streaming down her face. The same nightmare often plagued her. An unseen man accused her of betraying him. A flash of light hit shiny metal, a sword raised to strike. Her mouth opened in a soundless scream.

Someone stirred beside her. She was not at home in her bed. Before she could stifle it, a distressed cry escaped her lips.

Elise turned over, and Lydia forced herself to lie still. She broke into a cold sweat. No longer could she hope the past days were a dream.

"Oh, Brianna, you look frightful." Elise raised up on an elbow. "Have you been crying? Did you not sleep? Does your head hurt? Your forehead does not stick out like an egg this morn. Do you want to stay in bed today?" She bounced up with the exuberance of a colt.

"No, I haven't been crying, yes, I did sleep, no, my head doesn't hurt, and I don't want to stay in bed." Lydia forced herself to smile at the sweet young woman and watched her as she rose and went about her morning ritual.

While they slept, someone had built up the fire. Other objects, not there the night before, were on the washstand. She watched Elise wash her face and hands, then rub a small branch with green foliage over her teeth. After she worked a soft-looking woolen cloth over each tooth, she rinsed and nibbled sprigs of parsley that were beside the first greenery.

Once Elise was finished, Lydia went over and discovered the cleaners were sprigs of hazel. They cleaned her teeth much better than she expected. The parsley freshened her mouth even more, but she wished she had a toothbrush and toothpaste.

She finished and dressed, the clothing no longer feeling strange. Though it was more comfortable than modern garments, she felt unnerved without underwear. Determined to make the best of her life, she beckoned to Elise.

"Come, let's do some exploring."

Elise scampered after her. They collected warm hunks of bread and thick slices of dark yellow cheese as they threaded through the early diners in the great room. Elise grabbed two apples, stuffed them in her pockets, and stuck another under her chin. Lydia didn't catch up with her until she reached the stables. As she passed the stall housing Damron's white destrier, the horse reached out his huge head and snorted.

"Ha! What misguided soul named you Angel? Lucifer better suits your personality," Lydia muttered as the huge warhorse stomped and shook his head at her. Was he reprimanding her as harshly as would his master?

Several empty stalls separated him from Sweetpea. The beautiful mare tossed her head and nickered, begging attention. When Lydia drew close and the horse bumped her shoulder in an unmistakable sign of affection, she felt a surge of joy. She stroked the warm, soft hair between the mare's eyes and whispered, "Hello, love." On hearing her voice, Sweetpea shook her head.

"So. You think I talk strangely, too. Don't worry, sweets, I have your treat." She reached into her pocket for an apple that wasn't there. "What happened to your apple?" When she realized she had expected one to be there, she caught her breath.

"Do not fret. You keep forgetting your name, so I knew you would forget her apple. I brought it for you." Elise grinned and handed one to her. "You do talk strange, but 'tis lovely. Like when you sing with Galan."

As Lydia offered the apple to Sweetpea, she raised an eyebrow and would have questioned Elise about this business of lovely singing. Why, after her friends had told her she shouldn't even hum in the shower she was so off key, she only mouthed the words of the hymns during church service.

A sense of heat and a tingling awareness on her nape warned her of Damron's presence. Sweetpea tossed her head and stamped her hooves. When a strong, tanned hand brushed across Lydia's shoulder to pull the mare's ear, the traitorous horse seemed delighted. Damron stood so close, he pressed against Lydia's back. She could hear his deep voice rumble in his chest as he spoke to the mare.

"Ah, my treasure. How lovely ye are with yer dainty neck and beautiful face." Damron's breath ruffled her hair as he caressed the mare's ears and ran his strong hand sensuously down the mare's neck. "Soft as velvet. So warm and soothin' to the hand. What a magnificent body." As his hand continued its caress, Sweetpea quivered and tried to move closer to him. "So eager to please me. What noble offspring ye will bear."

"Huh. I'll bet he doesn't talk that sweetly to a woman," Lydia muttered to herself.

She tried to deny the heat that went through her at his words. Pressing close to the rails to keep from brushing against him as she edged away, she stole a look at him and was again struck with his appeal.

His face wasn't what she would call beautiful for a man. Each feature lent strength. His broad forehead and prominent brows accented demanding emerald eyes. She had always wondered about their color. A straight, arrogant nose added character, while sensuous lips graced a strong jaw that refused to yield to any softness. She forced her gaze from his lips. Why did she have this insane urge to taste them?

His energy flowed over every inch of her, feeling like lightning strikes. Pivoting on her heel, she sprinted for the door. She felt his heated gaze explore her back.

Damron had not missed the tension that rippled through Brianna when he pressed close to her at the stall. Nor did he miss seeing her nostrils flare, catching his scent, as he studied her profile.

Had she known he was speaking of her while stroking the mare, she would have run from him as swiftly as a hare from a hunting dog. 'Twas her dainty neck and beautiful face he admired. Her skin that he found soft as velvet when his hands had roamed over her checking for injuries after her fall.

He had not missed the heat that built and radiated from her, nor the quiver that ran through her when she scoffed that he would not talk that sweetly to a woman. Her pupils had dilated, ever so slightly, when she studied his face.

On eyeing his lips, the tip of her tongue had moistened her own. He had no doubt that along with her fiery nature would come an equally heated passion. And, with God's help, 'twas she who would bear him noble offspring, did she but know it.

For several hours, Brianna and Elise roamed the floors of the castle, climbed the winding stairways and opened doors to look in each room.

"Elise, why are there no rushes on the other floors?" From all she knew of the period, it was the custom to cover the floor space with them. They collected debris pitched from careless hands, and the leavings of the hounds and falcons. "And how is it that everyone seems to bathe frequently?" From what she had read of the eleventh century, they were afraid of bathing.

"Why, because of your Nathaniel, of course." Elise stared at her with worried eyes.

"My Nathaniel?"

"Do not tell me you forgot Nathaniel?" Elise gasped, sounding both scandalized and horrified simultaneously.

"Indulge me. My mind is a little foggy today." She took hold of Elise's arm, for she looked ready to take off at a run to fetch Lady Maud.

"Ever since I can remember, you have always called Lord Bleddyn your 'Nathaniel.' You allowed no other to call him such. If we did, you wrestled us onto the ground for the doing." She eyed Lydia warily. "Do you remember now?"

When Lydia shook her head, Elise sighed. "He believes dirty rushes cause diseases. Mother has the rushes in the great hall changed often. And Bleddyn claims bathing will not open the body to ill humors but will aid in healing wounds."

Lord Bleddyn? That hadn't told Lydia anything, because she still didn't know who he was by either name Elise called him. She knew better than to question her further, for the girl was already peeking warily at her from the corner of her eye.

When they reached the top floor, they stepped out on the walkway that bordered the inner bailey and connected the main building to the tower housing the buttery and pantry. The wind pulled their hair and whipped their clothes about their legs. Lydia felt a jolt of panic, remembering another time of standing high above a castle and feeling the wind take control of her body. She grabbed the wooden railing.

She sensed someone's gaze and glanced at the opposite walkway. Damron watched her. She turned her back on him, squared her shoulders, then followed Elise to the outer bailey. Before going below, she stopped to study the view.

At the far corner of the outer bailey was a small orchard. As she admired the denseness of the trees, she was startled by a vision of herself laughing as Galan chased her among them. When he caught her, his warm lips kissed her forehead. Shock jolted through her. What was between Brianna and Galan?

The vision left as quickly as it came. She took a deep breath and held to the wall, calming herself with the view. The land was beautiful. Green fields stretched to the edges of the forests, and verdant mountains loomed in the distance.

How wonderful not to see houses jammed together. No planes flew overhead. No cars streaked down crowded highways, polluting the air and harassing the ears.

Elise ran down the stairway at the next corner and shouted back to her.

"Hurry, Brianna. Mother told me last eve that Galan is to

take us for a special outing. She says it might help your memory to come back the sooner."

When Lydia followed, she found they were again at the stables. She grinned as Elise, with help from a groom, scrambled awkwardly onto a mare.

Galan came to put his hands around her waist and seated her on a strange, boxlike saddle. He gave her a soft squeeze before releasing her, then turned and gained his own saddle.

Closing her eyes, she hoped she would adjust to the saddle. Lydia was an accomplished rider, and her training took over when she held the reins in her hands.

The next half hour was most pleasant. The trees had begun to wear their summer colors. Yellow and violet wildflowers carpeted the ground. They stopped at a lake where wispy trees overhung the water. After a servant spread a blanket for their comfort, their escorts moved to a discreet distance.

Galan retrieved food from a bag tied to his saddle, and placed a loaf of flat, heavy oat bread, a wedge of cheese and a roasted chicken on the cloth. A flagon of ale and three goblets joined the food.

As they ate their meal, Lydia felt that someone besides Elise and Galan watched her. Each time she looked up, she could not see who it was. Surely it must be her imagination.

"This next sennight will be as years, my little love," Galan whispered in her ear. His lovely blue eyes gazed into hers as he pressed ever closer to her side.

Strange, but she didn't feel awkward with him. His nearness felt natural. The early Brianna must have been very fond of this man. Oh, my. How fond? Had she allowed his caresses? Perhaps more?

"If only time would fly as swift as eagles," Galan murmured. He began to nuzzle the sensitive skin below her ear with hungry, nibbling kisses.

Good heavens. Just how intimate had the two been? She

jerked, and his nibble, a little too eager, decided it. She yelped and shot to her feet.

"What is it? Did a bee sting you? Oh, my goodness, do run before it gets you again," Elise advised as she jumped up and started doing a little dance of worry, hopping from one foot to the other as her gaze searched for the flying assailant.

Galan turned a bright shade of red. Elise shouted, "Blessed St. Bridgit! It has stung Galan also. He is turning purple. Quick, we must get him home." She started twirling in circles searching for their mounts and escorts.

Connor emerged from the sheltering line of trees, surprising Lydia. Had he been the one spying on them?

Her eyes opened wide. His sparkled with amusement.

"It's my fault," she blurted. "I thought a lizard climbed onto my shoulder. I jumped like a ninny."

Connor grinned and arched his brows at her. She scowled back. Without a doubt, he had seen the reason she had bolted up. She motioned to Elise and Galan.

"Come, let's cool our feet in the lake before going back to the keep. Galan, I promise I won't jump and cause a foolish commotion if a fish swims close."

Galan shot her a look of gratitude as he joined them at the water's edge. Lydia removed her shoes and lifted her hem to her ankles to enjoy wading. She wriggled her toes through the muddy silt, and then stood still, waiting for the water to clear again. Were there minnows darting out from their hiding places and inspecting her toes? No one spoke. She filled her lungs with fresh air and soaked up the surrounding beauty. After several minutes, everything was back to normal.

The return ride wasn't as comfortable as it had been when they set out. Connor purposefully rode beside her, forcing Galan to drop back beside Elise.

"Did you enjoy your outing, before the amorous lizard nibbled your neck, my lady?" Connor did not bother to suppress a chuckle.

"It's a good thing I didn't swat it. It could have bitten me, don't you think?" she asked softly.

"Happily it did not. I would have had to skewer the bold invader for being on territory that doesna belong to him."

His reply sounded like a quiet threat; his gaze had turned serious. What right did he have to question her?

She frowned. "The territory doesn't belong to anyone, Sir Connor. Was there a reason for your presence in the woods?"

"I had reason, Lady. And this territory does have a master."

Before she could reply, they came out into the clearing before the keep. Connor called to a knight named David to take his place, nodded to her and spurred his horse forward. She watched until he disappeared through the gatehouse into the outer bailey.

As they approached the outer walls, she again felt that prickle on her skin that warned someone studied her. Looking up, she discovered the source. Damron stood atop the barbican.

His hard green gaze raked over her, his look declaring he had the right to explore her at his will. His intensity felt like hands searching over her body. Goose bumps spread over her flesh, for she *remembered* those strong, callused hands from another time, undressing her, caressing each inch of her flesh as he uncovered it.

And her own instant reaction to his touch! Eagerness.

Damron had been supervising the training of Brianna's Saxon escorts, intent on molding them into disciplined warriors. Never again would they be so foolish as to allow his wife to stray from their protection.

In the bailey below, warriors scaled walls and sprang over

ditches, while others practiced vaulting onto saddles fixed atop wooden horses. Seeing Connor approach, he went down the stairway to meet him.

"What mischief have you to report?" His cousin was as wise as he in the ways of women. If Brianna's behavior was less than ladylike with Sir Galan, Damron would see they regretted it.

"I think you needna worry the lady will let him sniff too close." Connor's eyes gleamed with amusement as he related the incident to Damron. "The young man's face did not lose its fiery glow until we came from the forest."

"I will see it turn blue if he oversteps again. I like it not he thinks he has the right. If Brianna isna the innocent they told me, they will find hell a welcome respite!"

He would see she spent the rest of her days guarded and locked away at Saint Anne's Abbey.

The muscles in his jaws twitched as he went to meet her. He put his hands around a waist so small his fingers touched in the back. After lifting her to the ground, he moved her hair aside to study her neck. She tried to jerk away.

"Dammit! Take your hands from me." Her voice quivered with indignation as she pushed at him.

She reminded him of one of the prickly cats belonging to his half brother, Mereck. Her nose wrinkled disdainfully, no doubt from the pungent odor of his body heat and the chain mail that covered him. Did the lass expect a warrior to smell like flowers?

His anger simmered. "My name is Damron, not Dammit. You will cease your strange words."

"Damron, Demon, Dammit are all the same to me," Lydia muttered after she stepped back out of his reach. She stifled the urge to kick his shins. She had long ago learned to control her fiery temper, but this man, whose drawing had so fascinated her, seemed to provoke her worst behavior. His eyes narrowed dangerously.

She decided she'd better leave and give his temper a chance to cool. Whirling around, she hurried over to the stairway that led into the keep.

"Oh, saints help us, Brianna. I thought he would throttle you. He told Father yester eve that someone must needs take you in hand. Let us stay from his sight. If your head had not been bleeding the day you fell, he would have thrashed you. He said someone should have years ago."

"What? A thrashing? He must be out of his mind."

Elise nodded. "Father was so aggrieved he spluttered when he talked and turned red. Mother was so afeared he would swoon she threw a cup of ale in his face." Elise heaved a gusty sigh as she rushed up the stairs.

No one had laid a hand on Lydia since she was four years old. She had slipped away from her parents and tried to crawl inside a suit of armor at Blackthorn's museum to find the man hidden there. Everyone had come running when they heard the crash of collapsing armor. Her father had swatted her bottom once, not because of the armor, but to impress on her never to wander off on her own again.

When she passed through the heavy door of the solar, she took a deep breath and tried to calm herself.

Elise sat on a cushioned bench and began to pluck the strings of a harp, and when Elise started to sing, Lydia realized she knew the words. She began to sing along with her.

Elise's earlier comment about her singing with Galan had surprised her. Her attempts to sing had been a joke between her and her parents. Her words cracked like an adolescent boy. From the time she was a child, whenever she heard beautiful voices, she felt that a giant hand had squeezed her heart. But today, the notes came out strong and sure, without a waver or a squawk.

Happiness surged through her, as if someone had returned a rare and valuable gift lost for many centuries. When Elise began another melody, Lydia again was familiar with the song, but felt she hadn't heard it for a very long time. As her confidence grew, her clear soprano increased in volume.

They lingered in the solar for the remainder of the day. When they returned to their room, handmaids were there filling the tub. The two buxom young women giggled and talked about the knights they had helped to bathe earlier.

"I was ta help the dark lord. He would but let me soap his back," one said wistfully. "He scrubbed like he would wash the skin from his body. He grumbled about Saxons and their prissy noses. When he stood for me to rinse him, he turned so I could not see his male member." She giggled and wriggled her eyebrows.

"Ha. Ye'd best stay clear of that one. The other man seems eager enough ta share his lovin'," her companion said.

"Aye. I made sure soap got in the dark lord's eyes so I could take a look. He has a fearsome scar from the hair of his maleness down a hand width inside his thigh! Someone must have been jealous of sech a huge tarse and ballocks and tried ta rid him of them."

"Lucky you were out of his reach when he wiped his eyes. He was right angered," her companion replied.

Picturing Damron naked, complete with scars and soapy water trailing down his body, made Lydia catch her breath. "Don't you dare get attracted to him," she mumbled to herself.

"Oh, cousin! I would never be so brave," Elise whispered behind her.

"Brianna still acts strangely." Damron paced his sleeping chamber like a caged beast. "David reported she searched every floor, opened doors and looked under furniture to study it. After their ride, the women secluded themselves in the solar. He believes her voice is unusual. I will have her sing for me. Mayhap she has redeemin' qualities I havena yet seen."

Connor quickly defended her. "She has many good qualities. She is kindness itself to everyone, has loving patience with Elise, and always smells sweetly of roses and heather."

"Were I ye, I wouldna let myself be so close as to catch her scent. Ye could end with blood on yer pretty face."

Connor shrugged and grinned. "One of her best qualities is her spirit. She is no timid creature who cringes when you scowl. If you push her too far, you are the one likely to have a bloody face," he teased as he cuffed Damron on the shoulder.

Damron scoffed at the idea. Once she learned he was her lord and master, she would not dare lay a hand on him. If his plans for the next several days went aright, he would soon know more of this unusual lass.

Before dawn broke the next morning, Lydia forced herself to stillness so Elise would not wake. She needed to think. Several times the previous day she had sensed that something was familiar that should not have been. Earlier, she had hoped it was because she had read so much about medieval times. Now, she knew it was because she had lived it before.

Moaning softly, she curled into a tight ball. Her brain screamed what her mouth could not. "Why! How could this happen? How am I going to stop it? Will I ever go back?" She prayed to her mother and father, both gone two years before in a plane crash. If only she could talk this over with them.

The sound of horses tramping in the bailey drew her to the window. Clutching the neck of her sleeping garment together, she looked out. Rushlights on the outer walls of the keep lit the area below. Riders milled about in helmets and mail. A flash of white to the left caught her eye. Angel. When the destrier's rider looked up at her window, his gold-plated nose guard caught the light, making it gleam like the sun. She felt his hard stare.

Damron had sensed she was there, though he could not see her. Quickly, she stepped back from the window. She heard the clop of many hooves, the creaking of saddles and words softly spoken. Were he and his men continuing their journey to Scotland? She took a deep breath. Hopefully, she would find her way back to her own time and body before they met again.

From this moment on, she must think of herself as Brianna, or everyone would believe her crazed. What year and month were Lord Damron and Lady Brianna wed? She broke out in a cold sweat. Though she had never felt such a strong sexual attraction to any man as she had for him, she couldn't marry him. How could she commit her heart, her soul to a relationship when she didn't know whether she would be here for the rest of her life, or be whisked back to the future at any moment?

In times of stress, she often rode before dawn. As the sun crept over the horizon in the early morning hours, it brought peace to her troubled mind. Dressing in deep green, she combed her hair and tied it back with a ribbon. Fastening a heavy black mantle about her shoulders, she made her way down to the stable. The stable master came to tend her.

"Please ready Sweetpea. I want to ride before the day begins. I wish to do so astride." She prepared herself for his protest.

The man did not seem surprised. He called for an escort and placed a boy's saddle on Sweetpea. After checking each fitting, he helped her mount. He turned his head when she threw her right leg over the saddle. As she rode through the gateway with four men in front and four behind, she sighed with relief.

Brianna reveled in Sweetpea's power as she rode through the woods. The wind slipped her hair loose from the ribbon, and her tresses flew around her head as free as the tall grass blowing around them. Husky laughter rose from deep in her throat. She urged Sweetpea on until the men trailed behind. They let her take the lead. It was evident they were used to the way she rode.

The beauty of the morning enthralled her. The sun began to rise over the eastern mountains, and its fiery light turned the tips of the wet leaves and grass to jewels.

A mischievous gust of wind whipped her mantle up from her legs, leaving them bare below her knees. As she drew in a deep breath of pine-scented air, she took pleasure in the feel of the horse and the early dawn. Finally, she realized the sounds of her escorts had diminished. She panicked.

"Oh, damnation. Don't tell me I've lost them again!" she shouted. Again? Her eyes widened at the memory. The sound of hoofbeats thundering ever closer caught her attention. She glanced over her shoulder.

A horse length behind, Damron rode on Angel. With the intense glare of his slitted green eyes and lips set in a grim line, he did indeed look the demon she had named him.

Chapter 5

Damron had quelled Angel's restless stomping in the front bailey, before even a hint of dawn lit the sky. The air around him sparked with sexual awareness he felt only when Brianna was nearby. He sensed her gaze studying him and glanced from the corners of his eyes. She was not here, even hidden in the shadows the rushlights did not reach.

He tilted his head back to peer at the window opening above, but he did not see her lurking there. He did not need to. His body sensed her. Blood throbbed through his veins, and his nostrils flared as if he caught her female scent. He stared at the darkened window until his instincts told him she had jumped aside from it.

Lifting his hand high and making a small circle, he signaled the men to fall behind him as they left the castle grounds.

"Marcus, take them deep into the woods. See they work hard. The Saxon men from the Sinclair estate are now mine as their overlord. They must learn to fight amongst fallen trees and the dangers of rough terrain." Damron waved them forward, then moved into the deep forest shadows to wait.

Brianna was up to some mischief.

Soon after, she rode from the castle, her guards close

around her. As he watched, she urged her mare forward until she rode a horse length ahead of them. Their larger steeds were no match for the fleet mare. Had she not learned a lesson when the mare threw her afore? The reckless lass was again putting herself and her mount in danger.

He pressed Angel forward, his body humming with tension. Why had she left the castle? Did she plan a tryst with Galan? The thought that they might be lovers made him want to strike out. Genevieve's treachery ate at his soul, feeding his mistrust of Brianna. He would not tolerate another unfaithful wife.

He pictured a black mantle stretched atop dew-wet grass with Brianna sprawled on it, her glorious brown hair spread around her naked body. His mind's eye saw Galan approach her.

Cover her. Claim her.

Damron's jaws clamped tight to stifle a groan of agonizing pain that tore from his chest.

He would kill any man who dared make love to his bride.

Brianna's exultant laugh floated back to him. The sound tightened his loins. As he drew abreast of each of her guards, he jerked his head toward the keep. After he had sent the last man on his way, he urged Angel to close the distance between him and Brianna.

Brianna glanced over her shoulder, her eyes startled.

She was wise to be wary. Galloping alongside her, he folded his hand over hers on the reins and slowed their horses.

"For heaven's sake, Demon! What are you doing here?"

Not answering, he brought them to a stop. Her eyes widened at the speed with which he dismounted. Silent still, he hauled her from the saddle to stand before him.

He stared at her. She met his gaze, flinched and looked aside. Clearing her throat, she tried to pull back from him. He tightened his grip on her shoulders.

"All right. I know. There's no need to remind me. Your name isn't Demon. It's Damron. Still, that's no reason to get your tail in a wringer." She wriggled her shoulders, but the more she moved, the tighter he gripped. "Let go. You're crushing me."

"What do ye think ye are doing, lady?" He forced his voice through a tightly held jaw. Her nearness was causing his body to respond against his will. Then, remembering her strange words, he hesitated a moment. "Tail in a ringer? What is this?"

"Oh, blast. It's an expression." Brianna thrust her nose in the air, looking like a stubborn wood sprite.

His gaze roamed over her and noted her hair was loose and flowing about her shoulders. Why had she not covered it? His eyes narrowed as he stared. Her clothing clung to her body. She had not worn a smock under her green tunic. The thought stirred his blood.

"Were ye so anxious to meet yer lover ye did not take time to don proper attire?"

"Why, you nasty-minded Scot." She threw the words at him like darts, and with each one, she poked his chest with a finger. "Of course I was meeting a lover. I planned to meet a legion of lovers. Couldn't you tell? Didn't you see all those men with me? They were to keep me from getting lost . . ."

"Dinna be knotty-pated, lady. Ye well know what I mean. Whom did ye race to meet? Do ye have a tryst with Galan?" His lips curled in a snarl, and he gave her a light shake.

"What the he——, uh, devil's a knotty pate? Whatever it is, I'll soon be one if you don't stop rattling my brains." She shoved at his chest. He didn't budge. She shoved all the harder. When he released her, she tottered.

He grabbed for her arm, missed and grasped her breast instead. Before he could react, Brianna struck at his wrist and yelped in pain. He flushed and drew back, dropping his hands at his sides.

"That's twice you've grabbed me there." Her voice wavered. "I won't have it."

"'Tis sorry I am, Brianna. I did not mean ye harm. If ye

would act as ye should, we wouldna so oft be at odds." His voice softened as he tilted her face up to study it.

"Now it's *my* fault you grabbed me? Act as I *should*? How is that, pray tell? Bow and grovel and beg for you to squash parts of my body? You're a bleeding tyrant, that's what you are."

"Ne'er have I hurt ye apurpose. Had I done so, ye wouldna long be standin', ye fashious henny."

"Don't yell at me, you medieval chauvinist pig!" Brianna's nostrils flared. Clutching his arm, she rose to the tip of her toes and made a vigorous swing at his face. Before her fist could reach his jaw, he caught her wrist.

"Enough!"

Frighted by the thunder of his voice, birds squawked and flew out of the surrounding trees.

His patience was at an end. Pulling both her hands behind her back, he hauled her close. He didn't understand her witless chatter. Or her willful manner.

Where was the demure, obedient bride William had described? If he did not know better, he would think she was an imposter and not Brianna of Sinclair, the king's ward.

Studying her flushed face, he admitted she was far more beautiful than he had expected. He felt the softness of her back and, when his hands started to roam, he resisted the overpowering urge to cup her bottom in his palms.

Had another man already done so? Thinking to find answers there, he stared into her eyes. Beautiful. Those eyes so dark a brown and fringed with lush, thick lashes that would surely feather his cheeks when they kissed.

Ah. Kissed.

Gazing at her mouth, he swallowed. Full and luscious. Ripe. She must have sensed his growing desire to taste her there, for the tip of her tongue peeked out to dampen her lips. At that moment, she looked delicate and sweet, the perfect maiden William had described. His sex stirred and hardened against her stomach.

Until now, he had seen only the strange-talking lass who did not know her place, who mistakenly thought herself his equal. That lass who aggravated him, yet quickened his heartbeat. As he dipped his head preparing to satisfy his craving, he caught himself.

He would wait until he learned what was between her and young Galan. He would not take another man's leavings.

Disgusted with himself for wanting her, he grasped her waist and deposited her astride Sweetpea.

Brianna's clothing clumped around her hips as she landed with a thud. More than ever, she was acutely aware of her bare bottom. Well, hell, even her racy red thong would be decent right now. Flushing, she snatched the bottom of her tunic and jerked it down over her legs.

When Damron placed her feet in the stirrups, she saw his gleam of satisfaction. She grabbed the reins, only to have him yank them from her, turn and mount Angel.

Surely this flesh-and-blood Damron couldn't be the man in the drawing. The man who had stolen his way into her heart.

"Why did ye not use a woman's saddle, Lady?"

She clamped her lips together and refused to answer.

"Why were ye so mindless as to gallop yer mare as if ye were a warrior? When Sweetpea threw ye afore, were ye not injured enough?" He waited a moment.

Closing her eyes, she listened to her dual memories. He was right. When the early Brianna left the abbey and galloped over the rough ground, she had been reckless. Her face heated.

"Answer me."

"Had I been astride at the time, I wouldn't have lost my balance." She ignored his impatient snort.

"Have you no feelings for yer beautiful mare?"

"Of course I do. I would never harm Sweetpea." How could he think such a thing of her?

"And yer men? What of yer foolish disregard for those whose duty it is to protect ye?"

"What do you mean? They were already up and about. They seemed pleased for the early ride."

"They will not be as pleased when I mete out their punishment for allowin' ye to again come in harm's way, or for aiding ye in a lover's meeting."

"What? For heaven's sake, why would you punish them? They did nothing wrong. I told you before, I was not seeking a tryst, and I wasn't in harm's way." He couldn't really mean to hurt them, could he?

"Ye did not know what lay ahead. A wild boar or masterless men could have awaited ye."

She swallowed and met his gaze. These were cruel times. She was sure a reprimand or slap on the wrist wasn't what medieval lords called punishment. Did he mean to whip the men or discipline them in some other horrible way? She couldn't let that happen.

"Please, Damron, don't harm them. They did nothing wrong. I've always liked riding free. If it's going to cause anyone harm, I'll not do it again."

He nodded his head, looking satisfied. She let out the breath she'd been holding. He had accepted her promise.

"'Tis plain yer father neglected teachin' ye yer place."

Her place! She gritted her teeth and clamped her lips together. For everyone's sake, she would have to curb her words and be more diplomatic with him. They entered the castle's grounds and approached the stable. When Damron brought Sweetpea to a stop, she dismounted before he could reach her. Biting her tongue, she made a dash for the keep. Dealing with

Damron was stressful enough without provoking his disgusting "lord and master" attitude.

.

Hearing laughter behind him, Damron whirled. Mirth filled Connor's eyes. "What amuses ye?" Damron stalked over to stand toe to toe with him.

"You do, of course. You have the look of a frustrated knight, and the lady appears angry enough to slay a dragon. What ruffled her feathers so badly she took off like a frazzled bolt of lightning?"

"Huh! She canna keep her temper for the space of a dozen heartbeats. Dinna mention feathers to the lass. When I dubbed her a fashious henny, she tried to flatten my nose."

Connor laughed again. A stone flew through the air and clattered between them. Looking up, Damron saw Brianna glaring at them. He turned, slammed a fist in his open hand and took a step forward. She sprinted up the stairway. He nodded, satisfied.

"I told you she would try to bloody your face. Did she find a boulder to aid her height?" Curiosity glinted in Connor's eyes.

Damron rubbed his chin and chuckled. "Nay. She raised up on her toes and steadied herself on mine own arm. When she tried to bring her fist to my nose, her effort had my undivided attention."

"For a wee lassie, she has the temper of Mereck. Your half brother's rage erupts like a crack of thunder. I like this bold Brianna." Connor's eyes twinkled.

"Dinna think on it, Connor," Damron warned. "Do ye know what else she said? That I grab her breast apurpose and am a 'shovingist pig.'"

"Ne'er have I seen a woman so heedless of consequences. She tweaks my anger to the point I yearn to thrash her bottom. Hmmm, I have noted her face betrays her every emotion. She canna hide anythin' from me." The thought pleased him.

* * *

Later that afternoon, a small army of warriors arrived. The outer bailey filled with Highland Scots wearing shirts and plaids. Damron looked over the Blackthorn men he had left with Mereck at Sinclair Castle, Brianna's ancestral home that was now his. Once his half brother selected a steward and was sure he would manage the castle properly, he sent the men to rejoin Damron.

Added to his own Scots were twenty men-at-arms Mereck had carefully picked from Sinclair, and the five Norman knights that left William's service to follow Damron. He and Connor were already training Brianna's Saxon guards. Although Damron resented being forced to take another wife, he was most gratified for the extra men to defend Blackthorn.

The back of his neck tingled. Knowing what he would find, he turned and glowered upward. Brianna stared out the solar window. Eyeing his men. In a silent demand that she withdraw, he scowled and jerked his head. When she ignored him, Connor snickered. Damron cursed and ordered the men to follow him into the great hall. Among the Saxons in the room, his Norman knights stood out with their darker hair and eyes, his Highlanders because of their greater size.

Brianna descended the stairs, looking beautiful in a yellow tunic, her chestnut curls held back from her face with a light yellow silk veil and a gold circlet. Damron saw her gaze dart around the room. She looked far too interested by his way of thinking. As he approached her, she folded her arms across her breasts, protecting them. Connor chuckled beside him.

Spying Galan from the corner of his eye, Damron moved to block his path. Brianna tried to detour around them both, but Damron grasped her elbow and led her to the raised dais.

"Act with dignity afore my men, Lady," he whispered with a tinge of menace. Though he did not yet want her to know she belonged to him, he wanted her by his side. It would be his trencher that she shared, his fingers from which she accepted choice bits of meat.

"You don't need to tell me how to act, Damron."

Her voice was so low he bent closer to her. His gaze met hers; she hooded her eyes. Her soft skin, smelling of a mixture of heather and roses, stirred his blood. After he seated her on his left at the high table, Connor effectively hemmed her in on the other side.

Cook's servitors soon brought forth steaming platters heaped with roasted duck, venison and mutton, smoked haddock, boiled goose, salmon and bowls stuffed with food that Brianna didn't recognize. She tried to identify the different spices used when the aroma of the platters reached her. Surely she detected sage, rosemary, bay leaves and ginger? Damron filled their trencher with succulent helpings from each serving.

Silver chalices, etched with scenes of wild birds, sat between each couple. Jeremy, Damron's squire, filled theirs with wine. Damron offered the cup to her.

Brianna took a small sip. Not the too dry red wine she'd had before, this was dark and sweet. Oh, how she wished she had a margarita, or a rum and Coke. She had a notion that getting through this dinner would require more bracing than the wine offered. Before they came below, she had told Elise she had lost her eating knife. Thankfully, Elise didn't question her, but gave her another. She took it from the holder on her girdle and reached for a portion of duck.

Damron's hand covered hers and slipped the knife from her fingers.

"Nay, my lady. Ye will have no blade between us." His eyes flashed a challenge. "Let me serve you as your young swain so enjoyed doing."

When she opened her mouth to object, he slipped a juicy sliver of duck between her lips. She had no choice but to eat it and, when she swallowed, a bit of salmon swiftly followed. She raised her hand in protest.

"Eat what I feed ye without protest," he commanded softly.

"I can feed myself, sir." She started to reach for another portion of duck, but found her wrist grasped and held to the table.

"Smile and act with decorum, like a proper maiden." He placed her hand in her lap while still holding her wrist.

The heat of his fingers scorched through the material of her clothing to her thighs, sending shivers up her spine.

"Release me, sir, or you'll get a scene they'll talk about for the next century."

"Will ye give yer word to act with dignity?"

"If you stop mistreating me, I will." When she nodded, he released her.

"Lady Maud said you planned to leave when your men arrived." She glanced pointedly around at the extra men in the hall. "I will welcome the dawn."

"Why, my lady, you wound us." Connor claimed her attention. "I thought our leavetaking would sadden you. Blackthorn is far distant from Ridley." Looking sorrowful, he wagged his head at her.

Of course their Highland home was far from Ridley. What did he mean? Before she could ask, Damron placed a slice of apple so close she automatically took it between her teeth. When he handed her the chalice of wine to cleanse her palate, she downed half its contents. She grinned at the surprise on his face.

He regained the chalice and turned it to the spot where her mouth had touched. The tip of his tongue slid sensuously over the cup's rim as if he caressed her lips. His heated gaze held her prisoner.

A bead of red wine remained on his lower lip. She couldn't wrench her gaze from it. How would it feel to take his soft flesh between her teeth and tug? To slide her tongue over it?

Though his domineering ways raised her hackles, she couldn't deny the powerful sexual attraction she felt for him. Shifting on her seat, she swallowed and turned to Connor.

"Tell me, Connor, what is knotty-pated?"

"Why 'tis tresses blown into knots, lass."

Suspiciously, the corners of his mouth twitched.

"Knotted hair? Why did you think that?" Elise leaned forward to look at Brianna. Impatiently, she slapped Connor's hand as he waggled a chicken wing beneath her nose. "'Tis someone foolish, Brianna." She grinned as she evaded him. "Do you not remember when Galan was yet a squire and called you a babe on your tenth name day? You called him a knotty-pate then. He wrestled you to the ground. Mud covered you both. Your father dunked you with water before you could go into the keep. You told him you heard the stable boy call the old groom a 'knotty-pated old ram.'"

Brianna's eyes widened. When she reached for the wine, Damron snatched the cup from her reach.

"Dinna even *think* on it." He shifted to face her. "With the strange way ye have been actin', ye deserved the title."

"I'll give you that one. But what is a fascist hen? And don't tell me it's a chicken race. I won't believe it." Brianna's eyes narrowed at him.

"Ah. A fashious henny, Brianna?" Connor's eyes sparkled with mischief. "In Scotland, when a lassie is troublesome and in need of discipline, we call her a troublesome little hen. Her master will swiftly put her in her place."

"I thought you both of Scottish birth, Sir Connor." Elise's whisper halted conversation, and those closest craned forward, listening. "How is it you have Norman and Scottish knights? You both speak French, except when the gia—, er, uh, Lord Damron is angered. Then I cannot understand him."

"Damron's mother is from Rouen, Normandy," Connor replied. "We fostered there with her relatives, who are also part of King William's family. As for Damron, when riled, his brogue leaps to his tongue."

Damron glared up at the heavy wooden beams, looking as if he contemplated something unpleasant.

Lady Maud turned the conversation by suggesting they would enjoy a musical evening. She motioned for a squire to bring a harp to set in the open space before the high table. Elise caught Brianna's hand and led her around the table to stand near the harp, and Lady Maud's sister, Cecelia, took out a flute from her tunic pocket.

After the first strains of music began, Brianna sang a solo. She avoided looking at Damron and pretended the room was as empty as the solar had been. When she finished, she started to sing a duet, expecting Elise to blend in.

At the sound of Galan's beautiful tenor, surprise jolted through her. Why did she remember another voice, a baritone as rich as sweet chocolate, singing this duet with her? She kept her gaze on Galan while he approached her, yet deep in her soul's memory another man strode toward her, his voice the one she expected. The closer his vision came in her mind, the more her heart surged. His face was a blur, but there was no mistaking his large frame. It was Damron's voice she recalled.

Brianna became lost in the music. As the passion of the song increased, so did her own. Her heart began to pound. Her eyes clouded. She was thankful when the song ended.

Several animated duets later, Galan began an unfamiliar melody.

> *My love is made of grace and beauty,*
> *Skin so soft as feathers light.*
> *Breasts to fill my hands with wonder,*
> *Hair that clings and holds me tight.*

His hands molded her form in the air, then the backs of his fingers caressed her cheeks. When he sang of her hair, his fingers fanned through it and brought a curling handful over her right shoulder.

When his words tapered to a whisper, the notes fading, Galan placed a gentle kiss on her forehead. She did not pull away.

Damron clenched his hands and glared at the knights openly lusting over Brianna. Seeing his fierce scowl, the men shifted their interest to Elise.

"Ne'er have I heard such a perfect blending of voices," Connor murmured.

"I have heard far better." Damron ground out the words between clenched teeth.

"Could it be green fingers of jealousy I sense travelin' your mind, cousin?"

Damron turned, stomped Connor's foot and then exploded from his seat.

Startled, Brianna swung around. She blinked and focused her mind back on the room.

"I wish you Godspeed on the morrow, my lord," she said. "Surely it will be many months before we meet again?"

Damron's smile looked decidedly wicked. She made a quick curtsey and fled the room. His triumphant bark of laughter trailed her, spreading a cloak of fear around her shoulders.

Chapter 6

"I thought you would be first to rise this morn, Brianna."
Elise's voice rang with excitement. When Brianna pulled the
covers over her head, Elise tried to tug them down.

"Don't tell me it's morning. Didn't we just go to bed?" Brianna groaned and clung to the blanket. She cracked open sleepy
eyelids to squint at the window opening. This was more than an
early rise. Barely the faintest hint of dawn showed in the starlit
sky. She had never been a morning person. She needed two cups
of strong coffee to appreciate the breaking day. Well, rats. She
wasn't going to get caffeine here. She blinked and tried to get her
wits about her.

Already fully dressed, Elise flitted between the trunk and
the bed, spreading Brianna's clothing across the bed.

"Hurry. Father Jacob will read the banns this day." Elise
tugged Brianna to the washstand and waited, her back turned.
No sooner had Brianna dried her face and hands than Elise
whipped off Brianna's sleeping garment. Before Brianna
could lower her arms, a deep rose smock floated over her
head, followed by a light rose tunic.

Smoothing the tunic over her smock, Brianna admired the
design of oak leaves done with silver threads the seamstress

had embroidered at the neckline and tip of the tunic's long, flaring sleeves. She tied a braided rope girdle interwoven with silver cloth low on her hips, the way Elise wore hers.

Fully awake now, she stifled a yawn and daydreamed about the steaming mug of sweet, creamy mocha chocolate cappuccino she always bought at her favorite coffee shop near her work.

"Come," Elise urged. "'Twould be a pity for Father Jacob to scold us for being late on such a special day." She grabbed Brianna's hand and rushed her through the castle and out into the bailey.

"What's so special about today?"

Elise skidded to a stop and rolled her eyes. "The banns." She waved her hands in front of Brianna's eyes as if to wake her. "Do not tell me you forgot the banns? Blessed saints, 'tis worse than forgetting your name." She linked her arm with Brianna's and urged her into a sprint toward the chapel.

The cool morning mist dampened Brianna's cheeks. She shivered, but not from cold. Prickles of warning scampered down her back as something just out of reach teased her memory.

The chapel stood atop a small knoll in the rear bailey. The Ridley family awaited them inside the entrance to the balcony and their private pews.

Galan's face glowed with satisfaction. He offered Brianna his wrist and escorted her to sit between himself and Elise on a padded bench covered in bright red linen. Brianna glanced around, admiring the elaborate carved railings and the exquisite statues in niches along each wall. Brianna spotted several Morgan knights seated below, but neither Damron nor Connor was among them.

The mass was lengthy, and she fought to keep the priest's droning voice from lulling her to sleep. As the service drew to an end, Father Jacob smiled up at her and raised his arms high.

"I have a most pleasant duty to perform—the avowal of an intent to wed."

Brianna smiled back. She didn't smile for long.
Father Jacob began with a prayer.

*Lord God our Father, You have called Your children
to paths not yet taken, through hardships
not yet discovered.
Give us faith to go with good courage,
knowing that You are guiding us,
and Your love supports us; through Jesus Christ our Lord.
Amen.*

"Brianna Sinclair and Galan Ridley desire that prayers be made for them that they may enter a union in the name of the Lord."

The priest studied the room. "Should anyone wish to challenge this, speak now or forever hold your peace."

"What?" Brianna shot to her feet. All sleepiness had fled.

Everyone below the balcony gawked up at her like hungry nestlings waiting for worms.

Behind her on the balcony, a resonant voice rolled like approaching thunder through the chapel.

"I have most serious objections, Father Jacob."

Damron! Brianna's scalp tingled. She whirled around to stare at him.

"Lady Brianna canna wed Galan Ridley."

She nodded her head and almost shouted she couldn't marry anyone. Instead, she gulped and decided she'd better hear him out.

Dressed in full Highland regalia, Damron stood inside the doorway. He wore his hair brushed back from his face, a long, thin braid at each temple. Leather thongs tied the neck opening of a wide-sleeved white shirt.

Around his waist, a heavy leather belt secured a woolen tartan in muted colors of green, blue and black. The end of the material rested over his left shoulder, where a brooch pinned the tartan to his shirt. Her heart lurched, for it was the brooch from the drawing, larger than the one she'd bought at the antique shop.

One hand rested on the sword hilt at his side, drawing her attention to a leather pouch riding low on his hips. Her gaze continued down past his handsome knees, where white gartered stockings covered his calves and ended at his leather shoes.

The man in the drawing had sprung to life.

Brianna's heart raced, and blood thrummed through her veins. Damron was the most handsome man she had ever seen. Had they been in the twenty-first century, she would have found him impossible to resist. Ha! Until she learned of his domineering ways.

"What mean you, Lord Damron?" Simon Ridley's voice quivered with alarm. "Baron Sinclair had no contracts signed before his demise. Why, we received word from King William that he approved of Sir Galan."

"The king has changed his mind," Damron replied for only those involved to hear. "He bestowed the baron's honors on me. Lady Brianna is part of those honors."

Brianna's ears rang. Bright flashes of memory streaked through her brain. She heard a voice from far away say, "The king's man requests you ready yourself to travel when Lord Damron arrives."

Quick flashes jolted her—of stealing away from mass at the abbey and then of seeing the ground flying beneath her horse's hooves. They faded in time for her to hear Damron's absurd claim that she was part of his award.

"I'm no man's possession." Her lips pressed thin with suppressed fury. Why, he talked as if she were a piece of land. The chauvinistic jerk!

"Oh, but ye are, lass," Damron crooned with a wicked glint in his eyes. "Ye have been my *possession* for o'er a fortnight."

"No one can own me. I'm not property that can be sold." She stiffened in defiance.

"Ah, my sweet-tempered lassie. Ye are well and truly my *property*." He rolled the last word slowly, decisively from his lips. His countenance became stern and immobile. "We are wed."

"Wed? How could we be, if I have no memories of it?" Every muscle in her body tensed. "You are wrong, sir. If we're truly man and wife, you would have spoken of it when you came upon me in the clearing."

She had recalled other memories. Why not this most important one? Wouldn't she sense it?

Damron nodded to Connor, who cast her a chagrined look.

"You are in truth his wife, Lady Brianna," Connor said. "Lord Damron married you, with Queen Matilda standing in for you, in both King William and King Malcolm's presence. And by their insistence."

"A wedding by *proxy*?" Brianna near shouted the word.

"Proxy?" Connor tilted his head, a look of uneasy puzzlement on his face.

Brianna ignored the question and turned to Damron.

"When did this so-called wedding take place?" She stared at him, demanding an explanation. "From what I know of proxies, the bride must be notified."

"'Twas in a village church outside Abernethy a fortnight ago," Connor offered without meeting her gaze.

She stared at Damron in disbelief. "Do you mean to tell me you married a woman without her knowledge? That *can't* be legal."

Damron looked surprised by her anger.

She wasn't just angry. She wanted to scream. Her fists tightened until her nails bit into her palms. Taking a deep breath, she tried to calm her building temper.

The nerve of the man. He hadn't mentioned the marriage to

her so he could check her out. Like she was a prized brood mare! He wanted to be sure she was worthy of his great honor. Why, he was even more arrogant than Gordon had been.

"You neanderthal! You've been here for days and didn't take the time to tell me of it?" With each word, she stepped closer to him. The jerk looked surprised she wasn't overjoyed with his news.

She grabbed his shirt at the neck and tugged. "You blasted giraffe, lean down so I can talk to you. Explain how this monstrous thing occurred."

"Neanderthal? Giraffe? Cease yer crazy name-calling. Calm yerself." He gripped her waist and lifted her until they were eye to eye. "I sent two messengers. When I spoke with the abbess, she advised me the first man ne'er arrived. 'Tis likely brigands came upon him. The only word she received was to prepare ye for travel."

He started to set her on her feet. Before he could, she fisted her hands and boxed his ears.

His eyes widened in disbelief.

Taking advantage of his surprise, she kicked his shins.

Seconds later, she hung face down across his shoulder like a sack of dirty laundry. Air whooshed from her lungs, and when she caught her breath, she clamped her teeth together to keep from screaming curses at him while in the chapel.

Galan tried to reach her, looking intent on tearing her from Damron's arms. Connor stepped aside and two of Damron's warriors approached Galan. Though he struggled, they subdued him, locking his arms tight against his sides.

"Put me down, oaf!" Brianna pummeled Damron's back as hard as she could. When it had no effect, she pinched and tried to use her sharp elbows to get his attention.

On exiting the chapel door, all hellfire flew into her. "You obnoxious, overbearing bastard!" She pounded him with her fists and kicked her legs trying to dislodge his arm. He didn't miss a step. She bent her left arm and used her elbow to hit him on the back of the head. He didn't twitch. If he didn't release her, she'd snatch him bald. She twisted around, grabbed a handful of his thick black hair and yanked as hard as she could. His head jerked backward.

He ignored her. Disgusted, she filled her hands with his tartan, lifted it and tugged. By God, she'd strip him bare. Leave his beautiful naked ass for all to see. Cold air rushing over his nether parts got his attention.

"Lucifer's cursed horns!" He set her on her feet with a thud. "Cease this untoward behavior, Lady, or I will deal with you as a child." He adjusted his tartan, clasped her hand and pulled her toward the keep.

She had to run to keep up with him. He drew her into the baron's solar at the rear of the great hall and rested a heavy arm around her shoulders to keep her from bolting. Pressed against him, she caught his enticing male scent. For an instant, she forgot her mind-boggling predicament.

"Ye are William's ward, after all. Why are ye surprised he arranged yer marriage? Surely yer own father, God rest his soul, wouldna have sought yer approval in selectin' a man to husband ye." He softened his hold on her.

"It doesn't surprise me that William arranged it. It's the way it was done." She snapped the words at him with bitter resentment. "Without any regard for my wishes. My feelings."

From his blank look, she knew he didn't understand. In these times, women had no say in the matter. If William had wanted, he could have married her to an ancient with five hairs on his head, an even fewer number of teeth and warts on his nose.

"You say we were married. I want to see proof with my own eyes." She tried to shrug free from his restraining arm. He didn't let her.

In all her research on Damron, she had never seen mention

of a proxy marriage. She had believed the likeness of him had shown a man with a strong, admirable character. A man with integrity. No matter how much she was drawn to him, the more she thought of his colossal nerve to marry a woman and not make sure she knew of it before the fact, the more resentful she became.

"My word is proof enough, Lady. Ye belong to me as much as the sword at my side, my weapons, my clothing or my warhorse." He dropped his arm from around her shoulders.

His words were as hurtful as a slap on the face. "Your horse? You think of me, a woman, the way you think of an animal?"

Even her cheating husband in the twenty-first century had treated her as his equal. Her chest ached with disappointment. "I'll have the marriage annulled." She stepped back from him and folded her arms across her chest.

Damron lowered his face until his nose touched the tip of hers. Her eyes crossed.

He paused after each unyielding word. "There will be no annulment, Brianna."

"Like hell there won't." All of these past days at Ridley, he'd been spying on her. No wonder Connor was close when Galan took them on their outing. Other times, too, she had felt someone watched her.

"What if you had come to collect your bride and found she had one eye and few teeth? If I had displeased you, you would have gone to William and told him to stuff it." She wanted to stamp her foot. Her fingers itched to throw something.

"Do ye think ye *please* me with your damnable temper?" His voice hardened. "Yer speech that better suits the stable is supposed to be *pleasin'?* Yer deliberate attempts to fan my anger are *pleasin'?* Lady, ye fall far short of pleasin' me."

Why did his words cause such pain? She blinked back threatened moisture. If Baron Ridley and his family hadn't arrived then, she would have disgraced herself with tears.

Connor, the last to appear, carried several parchments.

Brianna cleared her throat, hoping to relieve the ache there. "May I see them, please?" She strode over to the table beside the window opening and held out her hand. He raised a brow at her as he unrolled the parchments and spread them flat. She held her temper, remembering medieval men didn't believe women intelligent enough to master reading. When Damron raised a brow, she stifled the urge to kick his shins again.

Afraid that she would be unable to understand the documents without time to study them, she took a deep, calming breath. Stepping aside, Damron waited with widespread legs. Her gaze followed the elaborate writing across the page and sighed with relief. She blessed her mother for having so often requested her help in deciphering ancient documents.

On the twelfth day of June in 1072, Queen Matilda stood as proxy for Brianna Sinclair. King William bestowed Damron with Stonecrest and Ridley castles, Rothbury and Bellingham manors and various other properties formerly held by Brianna's father, Cecil Sinclair.

Matilda and William's signatures were prominent, as was Damron's after his own pledge. Though it was unusual for the times, Damron had been generous with her in the marriage contract. In the event of his death, he settled a considerable amount of money on her, along with the deed to Rothbury Manor, not many leagues from Stonecrest. His firstborn son would inherit his title and lands in Scotland. A second son would receive Stonecrest Castle and half his English holdings.

She blinked, remembering the early Brianna had birthed him two sons.

Her legs turned to rubber. Damron slid a stool close. She settled onto it as gracefully as a one-legged duck.

"My lady, are ye satisfied our marriage is fact?"

"We can still have it annulled," she whispered. "We don't deal well together, and the union has not been consummated."

"There will be no annulment, wife."

For all that his voice was soft, the words were said with steely resolve.

"You made it clear I'm not pleasing to you. Why wouldn't you wish to find someone who is?"

He ignored her.

"We will leave as soon as ye gather yer clothin'. 'Tis a long journey to Blackthorn, and I have been gone far too long."

"I'll not flit off to the wilds of Scotland with someone I barely know." Her heart pounded against her ribs. "You've waited this long, so you shouldn't mind a short delay."

How could she begin a marriage with a man who was so very unlike the person she had believed him to be? A man who thought her no more important than his horse?

"I will wait until dawn." His voice was firm. "See yer possessions are ready, else ye will leave with what ye have on yer back."

He looked at Lady Maud, as if seeking her aid for Brianna.

Lady Maud, her eyes glistening with unshed tears, came over and put her arm around Brianna's shoulders.

"Come, love. We will help gather your clothing."

Brianna had hit a brick wall. She couldn't run away. What good would it do? She'd be alone in a strange land, a strange time. She would be a suicidal fool to wander around the countryside. It would be like walking in her underwear down the most crime-riddled streets of a crowded, modern city.

Here, if she was lucky, she'd be found by Damron or a Ridley search party before she was a mile away. If a stranger found her, she'd soon be struggling beneath him in the dirt. If she lived past the assault, she'd become some lout's slave.

Damron would never agree to an annulment. It was how

his first marriage ended. This proud man would never allow another woman to disgrace him.

While Maud went to the kitchens to see to what should have been a betrothal banquet, Elise and her aunt Cecelia spent the next hour showing the servants what to pack in the sturdy trunks. When Brianna looked around the now familiar room and knew she would be leaving it, she shivered with apprehension.

What if she left Ridley and this was where she had to be to find her way back to her own time? But then again, she was in Scotland when the storm struck and sent her here. To return, perhaps she needed to be high atop the battlements at Blackthorn Castle.

Elise, her face mottled from crying, handed her a heavy green tunic and hose for traveling. Cecelia took Elise by the hand and said they would search the storage room for young men's leggings. The garments resembled heavy pajama bottoms with feet, and would be suitable for riding. Brianna could still hear Elise's sobs and the older woman's murmurs of comfort as they went down the stairwell.

Brianna sat on the floor as she slit the green tunic and another brown one down the center so she could ride astride. Fortunately, the tunics had ample material.

"'Tis unfortunate ye learned of this in such a way," Damron told Galan. "All must follow as the king decrees. We canna turn from that." In the baron's solar, he let Galan talk freely as he watched him pacing back and forth.

"We planned to wed," Galan whispered, his heartbreak in his words.

"No matter the circumstance, ye canna intervene in what the king has ordered."

Little did the young man know Damron was as much displeased at being forced to marry as Galan was at losing his Brianna. But now that Damron had control of Brianna's honors, he would fight to the death to keep the security they represented for Blackthorn. They were a steady source of income, and more important, of fighting men.

"You had not the right to wed Brianna without her knowledge," Galan said. "You neither sent greetings nor informed her of her status."

"I had the right," Damron said quietly. "King William demanded it. I did send word, though the man ne'er arrived."

William insisted on the proxy marriage, knowing Damron would have held off the deed as long as possible. Mayhap until he was old and gray, Damron thought wryly. Once he was safely wed, even Malcolm of Scotland turned a deaf ear to his requests to delay fetching his bride.

"Do you not care how cruel you have been to her?" Galan stared at him, his eyes reflecting his ruined dreams.

"I need not answer to ye, Galan. Only to my king. As ye must also." He frowned, declining any more discussion on the matter. The deed was already done.

Damron realized the havoc he had created. He and Connor had been arguing over the matter when the mare pitched Brianna onto the ground. He knew he had been churlish to marry his bride and not come for her immediately, but duty had forced him to go to Mereck at Stonecrest to see to its garrison and repairs.

'Twas a shock to Brianna. She had planned to live her life close by Ridley. Now, she was uncertain of her future in a land many considered barbaric. He couldna fault her for fighting him earlier, though she had been unduly angry when he told her she was his property. Her independence was strange. A husband conquers, but she refused to be conquered. Like his family motto, *With a Strong Hand,* he would control her.

Damron turned to the baron. As Ridley's overlord, he outlined what he expected. Yearly, he had improved Blackthorn's defenses until they were as strong as any castle in Normandy. He would do the same with Stonecrest and Ridley.

They spent the rest of the morning riding over the land. Damron inspected and pointed out areas that needed attention. Within the castle walls, the baron assured him Galan was in charge of the defenses.

After they returned to the solar, Damron spoke directly to Galan as he explained his plans. He sketched what he wanted done. With these improvements, Ridley's fortifications would be impossible to breach. He had no doubt Galan would do a masterful job. He was used to sizing a man's honor.

When finished with his instructions, he went out into the bailey. Entering the dim stable, he sighed with relief. The familiar sounds of horses and the smell of freshly strewn hay all soothed him. Away from the gaping eyes of the castle inhabitants, he rolled and flexed his shoulders, relieving his tense muscles.

Horses were so much less complicated than people. He called softly to Angel, who ignored him. With his great head facing Sweetpea four stalls away, Angel whinnied, courting the mare with batting eyes, demanding her attention. His antics went unrewarded. Occasionally, Sweetpea snorted and shook her head, denying Angel's invitations.

Damron grinned. How alike they were to their human owners. The mare could deny the stallion if she wished, but when the time was right, she would have little say in the matter of a mate, much like her human sisters. Or her human brothers, for that matter.

He told Brianna's groom to ready Sweetpea to travel. While he watched the man prepare the mare, he thought about selecting a smaller mount for Brianna. When they reached Blackthorn, he wanted his bride in one piece.

As if his thoughts had drawn her, Brianna rushed headlong

into the stables with Elise following behind. Her eyes widened on seeing him, and she skidded to a stop. Elise crashed into her back, propelling them forward.

Brianna all but fell into his arms. He folded them securely around her and brought her close against his chest. He inhaled her fresh, appealing scent. Her warm flesh pressed tight against his length quickened his blood. Anticipating the night to come, his loins hardened.

Elise took one look at his face, squeaked and darted back out the door.

"Hmmm, wife, will ye have such enthusiasm about all yer endeavors?" he murmured in her ear.

His raspy voice and burgeoning sex told Brianna what endeavors had come to his mind. His embrace tightened.

She tossed her head with a disgruntled expression, much as Sweetpea had responded to Angel. He held back a laugh.

"If I'd known you were here, ogre, I would have run in the opposite direction." She pushed against his chest as she talked.

"Name me ogre if ye will, wife, and I will be as ye call me," he whispered. When his lips touched the sensitive flesh beneath her ear, a shiver coursed through her. He studied her face, but she could not meet his gaze for long. Did she plan to run from him a second time?

"To what purpose did ye race into the stable?"

"I came to make sure they groomed and pampered Sweetpea before we leave."

"'Tis good ye are here. I would have ye choose a gentler mount." He relaxed his hold on her. She sprang back from him.

"Sweetpea is as gentle a mount as can be found. If you're concerned because of my fall, don't be. Sweetpea is unused to me riding that boxlike saddle from the abbey and didn't like my skirts. They startled her."

"Dinna dream to ride as ye did in the woods with yer

clothin' raised to display yer flesh for all to see." His muscles stiffened and his eyebrows rose as he contemplated her.

"I have garments for riding astride, sir. Not a speck of skin will show."

"Explain this attire to me."

Annoyance crossed her face. Aye. She could not hide her feelings. Her lips tightened before she replied.

"It's a slitted tunic and a special pair of leggings found for me by Lady Cecelia. Not only is it safer to ride this way, but I'll keep Sweetpea to a faster gait."

He had already decided to allow her the saddle, but wanted to see how hard she would work to convince him. Mayhap he could even coax a kiss from her?

"I have no thoughts of allowin' ye to delay us. I willna cross Scotland at a snail's pace. We will be ridin' hard, and I dinna believe ye can keep up. If not, ye will ride behind one of my men."

She rose to the bait. Anger flashed in her eyes at this male insult.

"You want me to ride pillion?" she all but shouted. "I will not ride on a horse's butt behind some unwashed warrior all over Scotland, sir. By the time we got there I'd be nothing but a giant bruise."

"If I decree ye ride on a horse's 'butt,' as ye so elegantly deem it, or run behind holdin' its tail, ye will do as I decree." He narrowed his eyes and stared down at her. "I have the safety of my men to look to afore thinkin' of yer delicate arse and whether or not it will gather a few bruises."

"Are you telling me your men are more important than your wife?" She looked at him and sucked her teeth in disgust. "I'm not hugging some smelly man's back more than a hundred miles. If you think I will, you're in for a rude awakening."

"Wife, I decide how ye are to ride. Ye will do as I say. We depart afore the sun rises." His gaze bored into hers.

She stared back, her body taut with anger. He noted the instant she realized, by the force of his will, she had to bend to him. To prove his point, he gripped her face and kissed her with savage possession. Waves of lust hardened him near to bursting, as he rocked his hips against her warm stomach.

Eyes spitting barely controlled rage, she lurched back from him. He saw her struggle not to strike his face, for her open hand lifted, then jerked down to scrub over her mouth. Stiff and proud, she spun around and marched out of the stable.

His brow quirked, watching her. So much for his "coaxing" a kiss from her sweet lips. The sway of her hips and the memory of her soft mouth and body heated his blood with anticipation.

He would have no easy time of it when he claimed her as his wife this night. E'en so, by the next sun's rise, she would be well used to pleasuring him.

Chapter 7

Brianna eyed the bulging clothing trunk beside the door and sighed. Now that she had a few minutes before she had to appear at the feast, her stomach churned.

What in God's name did a woman in this century do when she found herself wed without having known of it? One thing for certain, she couldn't tell Damron of Blackthorn to take his marriage contract and stuff it up his nose, then storm out of the castle.

Hearing Connor call from outside the bedchamber door, she welcomed the distraction. After she bid him enter, he thrust an oblong wooden box, embossed with bold Celtic symbols gilded with gold leaf, into her arms. She'd seen such a treasure as this only locked behind a glass case in museums.

"My Lady, Lord Damron wishes to present you with a gift. He requests you honor him this night by wearing it at the feast."

The box's weight startled her. What lay inside it? She raised her brows, curious. "Stones?"

"Not of the kind you think." His eyes twinkled as he turned to leave.

"Blessed saints. Mayhap the giant is chivalrous after all." Elise peered over her shoulder. "Quick. Open it."

Brianna sat on the bed and examined the beautifully carved

box. She lifted the lid and gasped. Nestled in a bed of blue silk was a girdle made of round gold discs. Each disc was delicately etched with the Pictish symbol called the Double Disc, signifying the marriage of two families. Filigree gold loops chained each disc to the next. The clasp was a larger disc rimmed with rubies. At its center rose a huge, brilliant sapphire. She lifted the girdle by the chain and admired the clasp as it twirled, catching the light to splash rainbows of color over the whitewashed walls.

"Oh, my, Elise. Isn't it beautiful? Hmmm. I noticed you have a lovely black silk tunic. May I borrow it?"

"Saints, Brianna! Lord Damron expects to see you dressed as a bride, not a widow." Elise sucked in a loud breath. "Surely, a mourning outfit will prod his anger."

"Oh, but the tunic is elegant. Rather sexy, actually. It will make a splendid background for this exquisite girdle." The one thing she could control tonight was what she wore. "Besides, what can he do with so many people about?"

She knew him well enough now to know he despised scenes. Besides, even if he created one, nothing could be worse than what had happened to her *back* in the future. Back in the future? It was strange to think of it as back and not forward. She had walked in on her husband George and his, uh—*administrative assistant*. His secretary had said he couldn't be disturbed. He was involved in the final editing of his paper on stem cell research. Lydia knew it for a lie, for they had worked on the edit together.

She'd wrenched open the heavy mahogany doors. Gordon, mouth agape and pants puddled around his ankles, stopped in midthrust. His *assistant,* sprawled atop the desk and unable to see the door, urged him on, kicking her heels against his bare buttocks. After one heart-stopping look, Lydia had whirled on her spike heels, leaving both conference room doors thrown wide in her wake. It was a wonder the collective gasps from the department staff didn't create a vacuum strong enough to draw them closed.

She'd had no trouble getting a swift divorce.

Lydia shook off her ugly memories as she started to dress. Elise fidgeted while watching Brianna don a gold-colored silk smock and the black tunic. When Brianna moved her shoulders, the sheer smock peeked from the v-shaped neckline. A gold-colored veil, held in place by a twined black and gold circlet, flowed over her unruly brown curls. Elise helped her fasten Damron's gift low on her hips.

The time came to go to the great hall, and when they arrived at the landing she hesitated, to gather her dignity. The chatter and tumult of the crowded hall quieted.

"Ah, little lady. He has seen you," Connor murmured behind her.

All eyes focused on them. Over them all, she felt Damron's cold green stare as it traveled from her head to her toes.

A path opened before him. His gaze pinned her as he sauntered to stand at the foot of the stairs. His clothing was much as it had been that morning, but more formal. The shirt was of fine material. Ruffles streamed from the sleeves, and white silk ribbons tied the shirt at his strong bronze neck. Her heart fluttered.

He again wore the plaid drawn over his left shoulder and fastened with the brooch she remembered. A beautifully engraved leather belt and scabbard secured the material around his waist. His hand gripped the hilt of the ceremonial sword there.

Garters below his knees held fine white stockings, and his shoes were of soft dark leather.

His body taut, he studied every inch of her. Her flesh tingled and heated under his hot, intense scrutiny. She controlled the urge to twitch.

He exuded raw, masculine power. Alluring. Enticing. As she studied the strong angles of his face, she swallowed. Her gaze came to rest on his wide, generous lips. It was a mistake. The scar at the corner there gleamed white in his tanned face.

He was way beyond anger. He was furious.

Perhaps she should have thought longer before pricking his pride? How would a medieval man react to his bride wearing black? Well, hell. She was about to find out. One thing she did know: he wasn't enchanted.

She squared her shoulders and met his gaze. She raised her left brow. *What can you do?*

She started when she sensed his reply. *This night. Ye will see this night.* His lips had not moved.

Brianna's defiance did not surprise Damron. That she had shown it in such a challenging way, did. Deliberately, his gaze roved over her body, undressing her in his mind.

He studied her intently. His gaze started at the top of her veiled head to drift down to the tips of her shoes peeping beneath the black hem. His blood smoldered as he browsed back up to linger on her hips. He stopped for an instant to admire her slender waist and flat stomach. A minute nod of his head acknowledged his gift clinging there. Ah. 'Twas nestled against her body's hot core.

His heated perusal next halted on her softly rounded breasts. Picturing them. As every fiber of his being focused, he imagined how he would suckle the rosy tips hidden there. He wet his lips. They pursed, as if around her delicate nipple. He allowed his gaze to be more suggestive. To show his lust. A triumphant surge flowed through him as her nipples hardened and pressed against her clothing.

Aye. Brianna would respond quickly to his loving. Genevieve had never enjoyed love play, no matter how tender. Mayhap taking Brianna to wife would not be a hardship after all.

He continued to show his lust. Her skin flushed a soft rose.

When he met her eyes again, she squared her shoulders. He admired her bravado, for her eyebrow quirked at him.

Ah, she questioned him about her attire. He answered her with his eyes, his thoughts.

This night. Ye will see this night!

Her hands twitched. She understood. He smiled.

He leisurely walked up the remaining steps and took her hand, placing it on his own.

"I see ye are in mourning," he murmured.

Her fingers were icy. She was not as composed as she pretended. He watched her expressions.

"'Tis perchance for yer lost love?" He saw no response. "Nay? Hm. For yer soon to be lost innocence, then?"

Her startled gaze flew to his. Her hand jerked.

"Ayc!" His chuckle was soft. Wicked.

He turned to face the guests in their bright, colorful garb overflowing the great hall.

"Come."

Damron led her through the still open path to the dais in front of the lord's table and turned so they faced the room. Baron Ridley and his family stood behind them.

"My Lords. Ladies. I present to ye my wife, Lady Brianna." His voice held more than a note of possession. He gently pressed her shoulder. "Acknowledge the bond, Brianna."

"My lord, do you now place your foot on my neck?" She bowed gracefully, deeply.

"Nay, lady. I prefer yer bottom, where it rightly belongs." When she bowed even deeper, he took her elbow and forced her to rise.

His men cheered the announcement, pleased at the turn of events. Ridley's guests stood, their mouths agape. No doubt, they had expected to hear of Brianna and Galan's betrothal.

"In the presence of King William and King Malcolm, I wed the Lady Brianna by proxy in London. I came as quickly as possible to collect my lovely bride."

"Huh! Quickly? That's a crock of droppings," Brianna muttered, shifting away from him. His arm draped around her shoulders and hauled her tight against his side.

"That was ill-advised, wife," he warned softly. "Had anyone heard yer remark, I would have been forced to correct ye afore everyone."

Brianna had no doubt what he meant by "correct." Her anger simmered. She tried to pull from his side, but he did not let her move so much as an inch. Taking her elbow in a firm grip, he led her to sit beside him at the high table in the place of honor.

Baron Ridley lifted his goblet high in a toast. "In the sad absence of my good friend Baron Cecil Sinclair, I wish our dearly loved Brianna a long, happy life with Lord Damron of Blackthorn. May your union be fruitful and loving."

Brianna and Damron shared a gold wedding chalice. She took a hearty swallow. Catching a glimpse of Galan over the rim, his soul in his eyes, she swallowed the rest of the wine before Damron could move it from her. When Damron's squire refilled the vessel, Damron grasped her hand to wrap her fingers around it. His strong, hot hand covering hers, he brought the cup up to his lips. His eyes stared into hers, warning her, as he drank. While the round of toasts continued, he kept possession of the cup, allowing her only small sips.

Cook marched triumphantly into the hall carrying a roasted peacock resplendent with its decoration of feathers and colorful clusters of grapes framing it. Servitors struggled with platters laden with wild duck in wine sauce, quail, and then goose cooked with garlic came next. Fish, lamb and poultry followed.

She had no appetite, but Damron insisted on feeding her as he had before. She didn't care for the taste of peacock and turned her head aside after the first bite.

"Wife, ye will eat what I have placed at yer lips." His voice was hard and impatient.

She stubbornly clamped her teeth together.

"Ye will eat, or it will remain afore yer mouth until Hades freezes. Ye have had too much wine. I willna have ye unaware of our weddin' night."

She glared at him. When she took the meat into her mouth, she nipped the tips of his fingers as forcefully as she dared.

Not even the smallest muscle in his face twitched as his gaze held hers.

She released him, only to have him sensuously trace her lips with the tips of his fingers. He lowered his forehead to hers.

"Do so again, and ye will be leavin' the banquet as ye did the chapel," he murmured. His warm breath teased her chin.

Fortunately, the massive doors of the keep burst open, distracting him. A great gust of wind flirted with the rushlights and blew out the brace of candles near the entrance.

In the doorway stood a man of the same height and as broad of shoulder as Damron, but with a fearsome demeanor. His hair, black and long, was shaggy around his face. His eyes were as black as a stormy sky. A high, chiseled nose above firm and well-defined lips added distinction to his face.

He had painted the left side of his face blue, and on the right a ragged scar in vivid red ran from his hairline down across his eye. It ended at the corner of his mouth. He wore a brilliantly colored, feathered robe over a black tunic and leggings. He waited, as still as a windless midnight. Hands fisted on his hips, he stared at Brianna.

Damron sprang to his feet, his nostrils flared. Feeling the stranger's gaze draw her, Brianna also rose to stare at him as he crossed the room.

"Bleddyn. Welcome." Baron Ridley shouted his greeting. He, Galan and the Ridley knights stood with obvious respect for this unexpected guest. Elise clapped her hands with glee.

When Brianna could see him clearly, she studied his savage appearance. As his gaze bored into hers, comforting warmth flowed over her.

"Nathaniel." Her voice was a bare whisper.

She didn't understand her reaction to this man who stood before her. But she knew in her heart he was her loving friend, that she could trust him above all others.

"Mo fear beog, my little one. You arrived safely. Have you no welcome for your pet?" His voice husky and deep, Bleddyn tilted his head to the side, studying her. "I came when I knew of your marriage. It has taken a sennight to travel here."

Reaching across the table, he cupped her face and placed a soft kiss on her lips.

Damron growled. His hand shot out to grip Bleddyn's wrist in a vise. Their eyes met. With a slight flick of his arm, Bleddyn broke the hold as easily as he would have a child's.

"Do not be concerned, my lord. The lady is as a sister to me," he said softly.

While the Ridley family greeted him, and the castle's knights and ladies called to the savage-looking man, Brianna made room between herself and Connor. When Bleddyn walked behind Damron, he nodded to him. "May I seek audience with you and the baron? 'Tis most urgent." On Damron's nod, he looked satisfied, and sat.

Brianna smiled and turned to Damron's squire. "Spencer, please prepare a trencher large enough to feed an army." On hearing her request, Bleddyn grinned. "Well, sir, did you plan to scare our Norman guests out of their wits? You know they are not accustomed to Welsh ways."

Brianna's mind flashed memories of her Nathaniel picking her up and dusting her off when as a child she fell off her horse. He had immediately put her back on and encouraged her to ride again. He had held her while she cried after he told her of her father's death. Alana stood at his side. She knew it was Alana, for the woman wore a habit. Recognition jolted through her, remembering the woman's eyes. They were the same as Lydia's mother's in the twenty-first century.

Not a glimmer of doubt remained. She had returned to a former life.

"'Sir?' Why this formality, little one? Am I no longer your Nathaniel who followed you to pick you up each time you fell?"

"Is she in the habit of fallin' from her horse?" Damron's tone was silky as he stared hard at her.

"Nay, Lord Damron. She is a more accomplished rider than many men. I referred to her childhood when she learned to toddle. She was but ten months of age and determined to outwit her sister, Alana. She tried to walk at every opportunity." His expression turned tender. "After several steps, she lost her balance. I would follow to save her bruising. If I was not fast enough to catch her, I was there to kiss the tears away."

"Was it then you knew of your gift?" Elise stretched forward to see Bleddyn more clearly.

"Nay. It came over many years," he replied quietly. "You need not be afeared for Brianna, for I will keep her safe."

Baron Ridley took the opportunity to stand and signal for the entertainment to begin.

Damron leaned close to whisper in her ear, "Do eat, my love. I would have yer mind clear of wine this night."

His breath tickled her ear. Shivers rippled down her back as his teeth nipped gently on her earlobe, then licked the spot. She gasped. His smile turned more erotic as he drew back.

He left the table with Connor, Bleddyn and the baron.

Brianna broke out in goose bumps, only to become hot as fire in turn. Damron was far too arousing. If she didn't gain control of her senses, how would she resist him? A sharp stab of panic jolted her.

Baron Ridley offered each man a cup of wine as they took their seats around the sturdy table. Damron sat nearest the window opening, grateful for the refreshing breeze drifting through it.

"As soon as I knew of your intent to take Brianna to Scotland," Bleddyn said, "I came as speedily as I could."

"If it took ye a sennight to reach Ridley, how did ye learn of my presence here afore we arrived?" Damron interrupted. His gaze searched the Welshman's face.

"Do you place credence in witches or warlocks? Or mayhap believe Lucifer has visited someone with a dark gift?" Bleddyn's gaze studied Damron.

"I have no patience with foolish beliefs. God has blessed some men with the power to heal, or to know when trouble brews. My half brother, Mereck, oft hears peoples' thoughts. I have honed my own instincts to feel an enemy's approach. What has this to do with yer knowin' of me?"

"At Stonecrest, when you received King William's missive demanding you fetch your bride, I felt your wrath and displeasure. When Brianna attempted to run from you, and Sweetpea tossed her to the ground, I knew your anger." Bleddyn hesitated a moment. "You will take her to the Highlands. I sense danger to her along the way, and even more when she reaches Blackthorn."

"Ye dinna think my fighting skills honed enough to defend my wife? Or do ye suggest 'tis I who poses a threat to her?" Offended, Damron narrowed his eyes.

"Nay. Nor do I doubt Sir Connor will be a staunch defender. I, too, have a special gift. It warns me whene'er danger threatens our Brianna. Had I believed 'twas from you or one of your men, I would not have allowed you to leave Stonecrest."

Damron's jaw squared. This man was more than arrogant. "From whence comes this peril?"

"I know not. But I have *seen* her attacker. He is but a vague shadow. No visible surroundings hint as to his identity. Even so, I *know* it will happen. I will travel with you. When we reach your Blackthorn, we will find what threat awaits her there."

"Bleddyn speaks true, Lord Damron." Baron Ridley leaned

toward him as he spoke. "Often he is forewarned of danger to Brianna. She was but a youngling when he raced to pull her from deep water where she had slipped from the bank. He taught her to swim soon after. When she was a budding young woman, a misguided swain sought to pluck her from her home. He had not taken her more than three leagues before Bleddyn caught up with them."

"Along with my skill with weapons, I am knowledgeable in the healing arts," Bleddyn said. "'Tis fair I warn you that should you deny me, I will follow at a distance. I will protect her with or without your consent." His tone left no doubt of his resolve.

The Welshman's calm authority stiffened Damron's spine. He did not like the thought of this man hidden in the deep forests that lined their way north. Having Bleddyn, or "Nathaniel," where he could watch him would be best.

"Ye may join us under one condition. Only if ye agree will I allow it. Make no mistake, sir. *No one* may trail us without my consent. Ye must swear an oath to me."

"I swear to no man." Bleddyn bounded to his feet. "I am no knight beholden to *any* man. I come from an ancient family and rule my own lands in Wales. I am more than your equal."

His hand on his sword, Damron moved close in challenge.

Baron Ridley edged between them. "Bleddyn ap Tewdwr is descended from the ancient Druids of Cymru and of Cadwallon, King of Gwynedd. Some name him a mystic for his many skills. Perhaps a vow between peers will give you the assurance you require, Lord Damron."

Damron studied the Welshman's face. "Will ye pledge from this day forward, until the threat to Brianna passes, ye will hold yerself true to me? That ye will protect my lady wife until ye request that I release ye?" He watched Bleddyn's eyes for any hint of wrongful intent.

From inside his tunic, Bleddyn removed an ancient talisman held by a gold chain. The light in the room brightened.

Ancient Druids had etched symbols into the surface of the heavy, round pewter. Around the edges were linked hounds, each overlapping the other. The hound denoted the otherworld. At the center was a triangle. The left side of the triangle had a salmon for divine wisdom. An eagle flew on the right as king of the sky, and at the bottom snarled a wolf, proclaiming the wearer a powerful warrior.

At the triangle's center was a jagged bolt of lightning.

Holding the talisman, Bleddyn repeated the vow as Damron had uttered it, staring deeply into Damron's eyes.

Damron's body tingled as if a current passed between them until the Welshman returned the talisman to its resting place.

"I, Damron of Blackthorn, pledge from this day forward, until the threat to Brianna passes, that ye have my and my men's protection. I will hold true to ye until such time as ye request to leave." Damron studied Bleddyn's eyes, then nodded, satisfied at what he saw there. "Let us return to the feast. I have neglected my bride far too long."

On reentering the hall, he tensed. Brianna sat next to Galan laughing up at him, her face flushed with pleasure. Her head was near touching his shoulder. When she leaned forward to speak with Elise, her neckline moved slightly, baring the top of a perfect golden breast.

He stalked up behind her, his footfalls unheard in the noisy hall. His hand slipped beneath her hair to the nape of her neck. Steely fingers clamped around it as he urged her to her feet. She tried to dislodge him. He did not budge. He turned her, his arm following her around until she faced him. Pulling her tight against his chest, he bent his head close to hers. Anger roiled through him as he hissed the words between his teeth.

"If ye value yer life, dinna e'er again display yer charms to another."

Chapter 8

Damron's warning struck Brianna like a burning, palpable thing. His hand gripped her head, and to anyone else, he must have appeared like a husband anxious to be alone with his wife.

Anger and defiance simmered in her. This flesh-and-blood man had the strong character she had sensed in his likeness. But with it came a domineering and ruthless manner. She couldn't remember anyone or anything that affected her more with such conflicting emotions.

Damron's eyes glittered as he removed her circlet and veil, then bent slowly, his lips hovering so close to hers she felt their warmth. His thrilling scent enveloped her. He, that living man from the drawing, made her breasts tingle with anticipation, her pulse race with longing. Why did he wait? She began to quiver, then gasped. Her breath caught.

'Twas for that he waited.

Hot lips claimed hers, his tongue plunging into her mouth to conquer hers, asserting his possession.

Anger flashed, tamping physical desire, that he would kiss her so in front of everyone. She thrust at his chest. When she couldn't budge him, she stamped on his foot.

In reprisal, one hand shifted to the small of her back. Holding her motionless, he ground his hot, turgid sex against her stomach.

She understood his message. She stilled.

His kiss softened, changed.

The tip of his tongue explored the corner of her mouth, then moved to trace her lower lip, tugging it between his teeth. In no hurry, he nibbled softly.

His breath was sweet. He tasted of wine and mint.

The kiss deepened with eager passion, sending waves of moist heat to the joining of her thighs. Her knees quivered. His arms tightened, a pleased growl rumbling from his chest.

Connor's hearty laugh and men banging their pewter tankards on the tables finally reached his ears. He eased his face from hers and lifted his head.

Brianna drew a deep, steadying breath and clasped his shoulders. How could Damron so quickly spark passion in her? Never had she felt such a heated response, not even to Gordon's expert lovemaking. She must put distance between them.

"Take your hands from me."

"Are ye certain 'tis what ye wish?"

Studying her flushed face, his mouth spread in a slow, secret smile. She knew he had not missed the tremors that ran through her, the softening of her lips. Nor the quaking of her limbs. And they all had pleased him.

Brianna twisted toward the room. He removed his support, yet his arm hovered just inches away. Her knees buckled. His arm snaked around her waist to steady her while he gave a short bow to the room, thanking them for their applause.

His dark brows arched over sparkling green eyes filled with laughter. On releasing her, his hand brushed her breast. Seeing his gaze change from laughter to smoldering, sensual heat, spoke of the physical union he would expect in a very short time.

Her heart vaulted to her throat. How could she have ignored that vital intimacy he would demand from this marriage? Medieval men took their bride's maidenhead seriously. If she was lacking one, disaster awaited her in the wedding chamber.

"Blessed St. Elizabeth," she exclaimed, surprising herself. *When did I start blessing saints?*

"Nay, not St. Elizabeth, Brianna," Elise corrected. "'Tis the month of June. Julitta is your favorite saint for this month." Her head bobbed as she continued. "Is your memory still scrambled?"

"It has been many years since you have mixed your saints and their months," Bleddyn chuckled. Seeing the question on Damron's face, he explained. "When startled, Brianna calls on her favorite saint born in that month. She and Elise began this practice when they were children and surprised by a special happening."

"Huh. Brianna has called on other than saints lately." Damron's tone turned husky. "What upset ye, wife?" He leaned close and whispered in her ear. "Or mayhap 'tis naught but impatience for the marriage bed? Hm?"

The tip of his tongue traced the shell of her ear. She could not stifle a soft gasp or the flutter in the pit of her stomach. Her thoughts were of the bedding all right. But not with impatience.

Fear best described it. Why couldn't she sense if the early Brianna and Galan had engaged in more than petting?

She stilled as her Nathaniel leaned close and murmured, "Do not be afeared, Brianna. Damron is the mate God intended for you. Do not anger him unduly, and he will go gently with you."

"How did you know what I was thinking?" While looking into his eyes, she mouthed the words, for the tips of his fingers touched her lips in a signal for silence.

"I have ever read your thoughts." He smiled at her. "Do not be afeared. I will not intrude when you do not wish it."

The tumultuous arrival of tumblers amid the beating of tabors and the wail of a hirgorn, the Welsh trumpet, interrupted them. The clamor in the great hall rivaled any sports bar in New York City on a late Friday evening.

Damron's jaw tightened as he watched Galan. The man's gaze never strayed from Brianna. Damron had not wanted the burden of a wife. If he had not sorely needed extra men and the coins he could draw from her estates, he would have defied both kings.

Every day he remembered the horror of seeing the mutilated bodies of his father and brothers, and Connor's parents. The raiders had meant to take Damron's family hostage, but Blackthorn's men had fought too fiercely. He would not allow anyone under his protection to meet such a death.

Though he had no wish for a wife, now that the two kings had saddled him with one, he would not allow any man to intrude. He guarded his possessions jealously. Genevieve had taught him why he should. Brianna was *his*. He must needs remind Galan of that. While the acrobats cleared from the room, he leaned toward Brianna.

"Wife, I wish ye to sing for me as ye did last eve. Let us say it is a farewell to yer maidenhood. And to yer loving swain." His gaze narrowed on the handsome young man.

"Please, Damron, don't be cruel. This evening is difficult enough for Galan."

"I insist. This will be the last ye will sing with him." Damron edged his voice with steel and showed no hint of sympathy. "I have bid my wife sing for us," he said as he stood and faced the room. "'Tis a farewell to her past, and a salute to her future as my lady in Scotland. Sir Galan will accompany her."

Taking Brianna's cold hand in his, he helped her to rise and led her to the center of the room. When he again sat, he beckoned his and Connor's squires to him.

Cecelia and Elise played lively ballads for the singers until the guests demanded the love songs Brianna and Galan did so well. Their voices gathered strength as they became engrossed in the music.

Galan began the song that had caused Damron to bolt from his chair the night just past. He tensed his legs to rise, wanting no further display of emotions as had happened afore. Bleddyn's gravelly voice halted him.

"Patience, Lord Damron. You already have much to regret. If you wish love in your bed, go gently. Do not push her."

Damron settled back and did not answer him. When the melody ended, Galan began another arrangement he had not sung before. It took but a few words for Damron to realize it was Galan's goodbye to the woman he loved.

Too late now, Damron regretted his harsh demand. He watched a tear steal down Brianna's lovely cheek. When they reached the last verse, the two magnificent voices blended.

> *The time has come to bid farewell,*
> *The life we planned is not to be.*
> *Your love will ever live in my heart,*
> *Your precious memory to comfort me.*

As the words faded, Galan removed a gold chain and large pendant hanging close to his heart. Light glinted off the stones as he placed his gift around Brianna's neck to nestle between her breasts. His trembling hands freed her hair and spread the shining brown curls around her shoulders. The backs of his fingers caressed her face, and his thumbs wiped the tears from her cheeks. He ignored those pooling in his own eyes.

Damron tried to rise. His lower body refused to move. He glared at Connor, believing he had placed heavy hands on his thighs to hold him to his seat. No one touched him.

"Come, my friend," Bleddyn said close to Damron's ear.

"You have blundered badly. Let them say their good-byes without interfering. They are hurting for each other."

'Twas the mystic who controlled him!

Damron seethed as he listened to their quiet words.

"Be happy, love. Do not worry for me." Galan placed a soft kiss on her brow.

"Nor you, me. I will come to no harm. Don't sorrow but begin a new life." Her arms slipped around him in a fierce hug.

The room thundered with men stamping and yelling their appreciation, while their ladies daintily wiped moisture from their eyes. Brianna curtseyed and Galan bowed to the room, before they made their way back to their table.

Damron rose, free now, his body tense. He took her arm to help her to sit.

"I'll never sing for you again. I promise you," she murmured.

Brianna did not look his way, but he knew her vow was meant for him. Her words stabbed his conscience. His spiteful demand had cost him much. The beauty of her voice would have been his greatest treasure.

The guests, becoming more boisterous as they consumed large quantities of strong ale and wine, began shouting for the bedding to begin.

Damron studied Brianna, watching her reactions. Nay, she was not as William had said she would be. She was far more. True, no subservient lass but a challenge, one he could not easily dominate. Mayhap even a woman he would grow to respect as he did his mother.

She drew in a deep breath. He suspected she thought of those people who would come into the bridal chamber to view their naked bodies for flaws. Aye, she panicked at the thought. Noting Galan's taut face, Damron knew he also dreaded what was to come. It would be a knife in his heart seeing his love prepared to accept another in her bed.

Brianna's face grew ashen. Her eyes widened in alarm. It was the first time he had seen her truly frightened. He rubbed his chin, studying her. Mayhap she feared the bedding ritual as much as the marriage bed? Rising, he took her fingers and urged her to her feet.

"'Tis time for ye to go above, wife. I will join ye shortly." He escorted Brianna, along with the women of her family, to the foot of the stairs. Connor joined him there. Both faced the room, ensuring none of the rowdy celebrants followed.

The guests called ribald suggestions on how Damron could ensure his bride screamed with pleasure this night.

If he was man enough. What with him wearing skirts and all!

He took their ribald humor gracefully. With a meaningful look toward the lord's table, he urged the baron to signal for the next entertainers to enter.

A troupe of actors performed a bawdy play that depicted a blushing virgin avoiding her lustful mate. A man, with a huge wooden phallus making a tent of his tunic, chased a buxom woman. Her heaving breasts diverted the guests' attention. Their antics soon filled the room with laughter until the skit was over.

When it came time to escort Damron above, he bowed low and raised his hands for quiet.

"I must disappoint ye, good people, but I am well able to divest myself of my garments. With the help of my bride." A gleam lit his eye, and he licked his lips and wriggled his brows. The men responded with catcalls and hoots.

"Let us see proof yer tarse and ballocks be manly enough to satisfy a lusty Saxon woman," a bearded knight yelled.

"Aye. Mayhap they be as scrawny as a starved hound," hooted another.

Bleddyn and Connor joined him at the foot of the stairway.

Damron's hearty laughter filled the room as he waved and turned away. He was intent on waylaying his bride. His tartan swayed as he took the steps two at a time.

Standing close beside the stairway and looking upward, a portly woman shrieked with glee. "Blessed saints! Why, 'tis like a destrier's. He be more'n ample to please his bride. Aye, and many a longing wench, too."

Damron shook his head, chuckling, then sobered as he thought of what was ahead. Spencer and Jeremy would have carried out his instructions to the letter, he was sure of it. He smiled with satisfaction.

'Twas time to show his wife what he planned to do about her wedding attire.

Brianna's legs wobbled. She fought to control her trembling. Virginal thoughts didn't frighten her. She had found great pleasure in her sexual life with her husband, for that had been the only successful part of their marriage.

If Damron had been a man in her future time, she would be more than willing to be his wife in more than name. Eager even, for she'd had many fantasies about him over the years. However, that Damron was the man in the drawing.

What frightened her was this dominating man who so obviously looked forward to making her his wife. And the circumstances. She'd read enough about medieval ceremonies to know what to expect.

When he came to her, he would be naked beneath the robe around his shoulders. Family members and ranking noblemen would accompany him. They were there to see whether the couple had any hidden imperfections. No way would she be the main act in some medieval peep show! She'd not allow it, even if she had to fight him tooth and nail.

As they approached the room, Lady Maud chatted about how they had prepared it for the wedding night, no doubt believing Brianna had forgotten the rituals as she had that her name was Brianna.

"We sprinkled rose petals on the wedding bed and tied herbs with silk ribbons to the draperies. Silver bowls hold samples of the most fruitful seeds we plant to ensure your union is blessed with many children."

Brianna knew she would give birth to two sons. What would they say if she told them only two children would be forthcoming?

"Wedding chalices are on the table with a silver decanter of special mead," Lady Cecelia said. "Each night, for a full cycle of the moon, you both must drink from it. It assures the wedded couple of an heir within the year."

Elise opened the door, jolted to a halt, then threw up her arms. "Blessed Virgin! Someone stole Brianna's wedding night."

"A wedding night cannot be stolen." Lady Cecelia's chuckle ended with a gasp when she peered over Elise's shoulder.

They crowded around the door, gaping into the chamber.

The wedding preparations had disappeared. Nothing that belonged to Brianna was in evidence. They searched the room, but the only articles found were Elise's own.

The mystery so preoccupied them, they startled when Damron's resonant voice filled the bedchamber.

"I thank ye for escorting my wife, ladies. Ye need concern yerselves no longer. Brianna is in my hands now."

Elise shrieked. Spinning around, she sent the privacy screen crashing to the floor. Moments later she landed on it.

Damron's lips twitched as he helped her to rise and patted her head much as he would have a favored pet. His eyes blazed at Brianna, and with purposeful strides, he was soon at her side.

"My lord, this is improper," Maud protested. "Everything is missing, and we have not yet prepared your bride."

"Do not be troubled. I have changed the custom to better suit the circumstances. My wife believes I have been neglectful. Tonight I would change that. I am eager to serve as her handmaid. Ye need not fear I will be clumsy."

Before Brianna could protest, he scooped her into his arms.

"Blast it. Put me down. I'll not allow it." She tried to wriggle free. "Why do you always have to prove your manliness?"

"Nay. Allow or not, as ye wish. I say what I will permit. Ye will but agree," he warned. "Soon ye will judge my manliness for yerself. I dinna doubt I am more than passably endowed to pleasure ye."

At the door, he grinned at the women and bowed as easily as if he held an infant. "My wife and I bid ye good eve, ladies. We will see ye at dawn." His long strides carried them from the room.

"Put me down, Damron," Brianna demanded. Her panic welled again. If she couldn't control such a simple thing as this, how was she going to thwart his intentions?

"Nay, again, wife. Ye will go quietly, or I may change my mind." He stopped, as if debating. "Perhaps ye prefer a public bedding after all? In Normandy, they sometimes arrange for guests to bear witness to the deflowering. Hm. Is that yer wish? It often adds spice to the husband's *manliness* to prove to everyone his prowess."

She gasped in horror. Oh, my God. He wouldn't do such a disgusting thing. Would he?

"Do ye ken my meanin'?" He studied her face. "We are not so far from the stairwell that I couldna summon an audience."

Brianna, her heart in her mouth, tried to scramble from his arms.

"Ah. Be that yer choice, wife?" Damron's voice filled with soft menace.

Chapter 9

Damron would never permit anyone to witness their love-making. Knowing Brianna would constantly battle him over control, he did not regret using such shameful tactics. What was his would *always* be his. Picturing her naked and panting beneath him, his eager shaft engorged and pulsed.

She belonged to him. Unseen. Untouched by anyone.

He turned and lifted her higher in his arms. She stiffened and near screamed in panic.

"Please, Damron. Don't do that to me."

"Rest easy. We have but arrived at our chamber."

He bumped the toe of his boot against the door, and Spencer opened it, his smile beaming. Damron entered and released Brianna's legs, but kept her body pressed firmly to his. Sliding her down his length, his swollen tarse thrust against the apex of her thighs.

Suppressing a grin, he watched her face while she became increasingly aware of his bulging manhood. Her eyes were wide, astonished. Satisfied, he released her and looked around the room. All was as he ordered.

"I thank ye for so aptly following my directions," he said to Spencer and Jeremy. He opened his weapons chest and gave each squire a beautifully wrought Scottish dirk. "Ye may rejoin the festivities. I willna need ye until dawn, Spencer."

The young men thanked him, and with shy grins, bowed before leaving the room. Damron bolted the door behind them.

A cheerful fire burned in the fireplace, warming the chamber. A fur rug lay before it, and a comfortable chair with a matching table stood close. The decanter of mead and chalices were on a small table beside the bed, as were the cakes and a silver bowl filled with the seeds that promised fertility.

He noted her reactions as she took in each item. He almost allowed a smile when she ventured a look at the bed. A rosy blush spread over her soft skin. His gaze followed it till it reached the edge of her neckline. His amusement faded when Galan's pendant came into view.

Scowling, he removed his ceremonial sword and put it in his war chest. Her wary gaze followed his every movement. Slowly, he removed the clan brooch and let his tartan droop over the belt at his waist. His fingers loosened the silk ribbons of his shirt and removed it. She blinked and her fingers twitched as she eyed his bronze chest and the dark mat of hair that covered it.

He padded over to sit on the chair, conscious of her heated stare on his back. He removed his leather shoes, and the garters that held his stockings below his knees. As he moved, his clothing shifted and exposed his muscled thighs. She stared at them as he slid the stockings from his feet.

When he stood to unwrap the tartan, she gasped and turned her back to him.

"Ye will soon grow used to my body, Brianna. Would ye help remove my clothing?"

"I'd as soon unwrap a snake," she whispered.

"No, my sweet," he chuckled wickedly. "'Tis no snake, though it springs upright when it desires."

He could imagine the blush that suffused her face. She kept her back to him. Grinning, he knew she dared not turn for fear he was naked. Spencer had neatly folded his robe atop the clothing chest, and Damron slipped it on. Soon after, he moved close behind her.

"Ye may look now, wife. I willna offend yer virgin eyes. Come, I have poured wine. 'Twill calm ye and give ye warmth."

"It is quite warm in here. I'm not in the least cold."

His lips twitched. "Hm. Then 'tis for me ye tremble?"

"I'd like wine, after all."

Cautiously, Brianna turned to find Damron holding both goblets and wearing a black robe open to his waist. Dressed as he was, he looked less the medieval man. She blinked rapidly, took a deep breath and tried to appear calm.

When he handed her the wine, she took a healthy swallow. Glancing down, she saw his *manliness* was looking forward to bed sport, as it was called in medieval times.

How was she going to thwart physically becoming his wife? She couldn't be intimate with him. What if she got pregnant? She couldn't stand it if she had a child and her soul took flight again.

As Lydia, she had never become intimate with a man she didn't love. Her friends had teased her about being old-fashioned. Physical closeness meant relationships to her. *Lasting* relationships.

God help her. She was in love with this man before fate whisked her here. Although the living man wasn't as easy to love as the man of her fantasies, she couldn't dispute her sexual attraction to him. More than she had ever felt for any man. A low groan escaped her. She could not let Damron possess her body.

Heavens to Murgatroyd! What if, in the middle of making love, her soul decided to flit back to where it came from? That poor early Brianna would be in for the shock of her life. She giggled.

Damron took the goblet from her hand and attempted to draw her close.

She balked. Dug in her heels like the sturdiest mule.

"Stop. We must talk." She hoped she sounded commanding.

"Lucifer's moldy horns, woman, I dinna wish to speak. I would do far better things with my lips—all of which will pleasure ye."

"You've proven we're married, but I don't *feel* married." She backed up slowly. "*You* were there before the priest, not me."

"I will summon a priest, if it will clear yer mind." Step by step, he followed her, looking more masculine, dangerous and impatient by the moment.

"We weren't married with our families present. Until we are, I cannot give myself to you."

That was a good idea. Surely he could understand a woman's sensibilities. She turned her head to judge the distance to the wall. Thankfully, it was still a good five feet away. "I'll feel we are living in sin, and I won't do that."

She took a giant step back. He glowered at her.

"Lucifer's pointy ears! We are o'er a sennight from my land. I dinna intend to wait."

He took a quick step forward, grasping for her.

Swerving, she avoided his hands and hurriedly stepped aside. All men liked to eat. His wife's knowledge of his preferences would surely be important to him.

"We hardly know each other. I have no idea what you like to eat."

"Eat? Lucifer's stomach, woman." As she scooted back, he made a swift grab for her. And missed. "'Tis not food I crave but ye in that bed."

"Stop! My sister isn't here. I can't share your bed. She would deem it a mortal sin, she would." Brianna's head bobbed like her neck had given up trying to hold it aloft. Oh, God, even to her ears she sounded crazy.

"What?" he spluttered. "Ye want yer sister abed with us? Lucifer's . . ."

Her mouth gaped. Crude man! Had he been about to curse some part better left unsaid? She scowled at him.

"You know my sister's an abbess. How disgusting can you be to suggest such a revolting thing?"

"Enough! We will ha'e no more of this trumpery. Ye are but tryin' to deny me."

When she forgot to retreat, he grasped her shoulders and drew her close.

Do not anger him further, Brianna.

Nathaniel's voice echoed in her head. Oh, Lord. Could the Welshman see and hear what was going on? Not thinking, she spoke aloud.

"Leave. You said you'd not intrude when I didn't want you."

I cannot see you. If you tell me not to hear your thoughts, I will not. I leave now, came the soft reply.

Damron hoisted her in the air until her nose was inches from his and glowered at her.

"Leave ye? Nae intrude?" Damron spluttered. "I dinna say I would leave when ye wished it, and I winna leave this room. Ha'e ye gang wholly daft? Do ye ken what I say, lass?"

Huh? Hearing his thick brogue, she almost giggled and said no. He held her so close her eyes crossed. She leaned her head back to see more clearly, and wished she hadn't. His eyes were squinted in fury. The veins in his temples throbbed.

"I'm neither daft nor deaf. I was telling my thoughts to leave and not intrude." She patted his bare chest soothingly. "It's like praying aloud. We often did it at the abbey." My, he felt good! And smelled even better. She was relieved to see the veins in his temples didn't bulge as badly as before. She'd best get on with the rest of it.

"Will you please put me down? Could we have more wine?"

She smiled as sweetly as she could while he lowered her to the floor. She was thankful for one thing: that enormous bulge no longer tented his robe. *Lord, but he's impressive.*

He had been furious the day he waylaid her in the woods,

but not as livid as he was tonight. Although his brogue was heavy, at least he hadn't called her *henny*.

"Come. Let's relax a bit," she urged.

Pressing his goblet into his hand, she quickly sat on the fur rug beside the chair. Finally, he settled in the chair. After several minutes, she turned her head and found he regarded her much as he would some alien creature that had found its way into his presence. He sipped his wine, his hot gaze not leaving her.

She wished he would drink enough to make him mellow.

As they studied each other, his jaw jutted aggressively. His face finally lost its flush.

"My lord, you have won the battles in the chapel and in the study, and this encounter tonight. If you force me now, our life together will end as harshly as so many others have done."

Damron slammed his goblet onto the table.

"'End as harshly?' What know ye of my first marriage? Who has been fillin' yer ears with things that hasna to do with ye?"

"No one has mentioned a first marriage, but I didn't believe a man of your age has never been married."

She had forgotten Genevieve. She tried to look properly distressed.

"Blessed Saint Julia. I'm sorry for your loss. I shouldn't have reminded you of it."

"Julitta," he mumbled. "Bleddyn said 'tis Julitta for June, not Julia. And I havna lost anythin'. I had the marriage annulled."

"Then it couldn't have been a happy one." Her voice faltered when he bounded out of the chair.

He paced back and forth, visibly thinking. Finally, he looked like he'd come to a decision. Taking a deep breath, he stalked around her. She got to her feet, disliking his looming above her. They stood face to face. More aptly, face to chest.

"I know what ye are about. Ye think to confuse me until I forget why we came to this room. 'Tis not going to work."

His gaze bored into hers, and she feared he guessed her every emotion. Instead of railing at her, he turned her so her back was to him as he spoke.

"I dinna want open warfare in my bedchamber. I come to it for comfort and respite from troubles, not to fight another skirmish. I will wait to deflower ye until we have a proper ceremony afore Blackthorn's priest.

"No one must learn ye are intact. Give so much as a hint, and I will take ye wherever ye are. Make no mistake. If 'tis in the front bailey on the ground, or in the great hall during a meal, that is where ye will lose yer maidenhead. Do ye ken?"

Brianna listened intently to his deep baritone and felt his steel will behind it. His body heat warmed her back.

"Have ye an answer for me, wife?"

"You agree not to bed me until we reach your home and are married before a priest? You'll give us time to get to know each other?" She glanced at him over her shoulder.

"Ye ken the outcome if ye break the trust?"

"I understood every word."

I can manage him quite nicely. All it took was a little patience to find the right arguments. She was pleased with herself.

His soft grasp on her shoulders turned her to face him. She shivered and forced her voice not to quaver. "You needn't help. I can manage."

"Ah, little bride. Ye knew when ye wore black ye sent me a message." He spoke quietly, but firmly. "I also let ye know what I felt about yer selection, if not in words, then by looks. I promised I would disrobe ye this night, and I will. Ye should have thought before throwing such a challenge. Be still, so I may finish my task."

He unhooked the beautiful girdle he had given her, and his hand circled her hips to gather the chain.

She eyed him as he strolled to her travel chest. She blinked hard and stared. His muscles flowed with power. He moved with graceful confidence in every step. Oh, my, he had beautiful feet. Never before had she seen a man's feet and thought them anything but serviceable. As he bent to put the girdle in its wooden box, his robe tightened, accenting the muscular power beneath. Her hands itched to run them down his back and his taut, manly arse she'd glimpsed that morning.

I've never seen anyone move as sexily as he does. Maybe it's the wine that makes him look so appealing? Desire flamed through her. It had been a very long time since she had felt that. Not since the night before Gordon's last business trip. Before the phone call from her friend the next morning telling her the truth. The thought cooled her blood. Were medieval men as unfaithful as modern males? Probably more so, since they rarely married for love.

As Damron closed the box, she remembered she hadn't acknowledged his gift. "Thank you for the beautiful girdle. I've never seen anything like it. Was it crafted in London?"

"No, I had the trinket done in Glasgow. The chest has been in my family for many years. My Scottish grandmother loved turning wood into art. This was her finest effort. I sent for it at the same time."

When he returned to her, he looked with distaste at Galan's gift. On the pendant, three horses pranced around a circle. They held their arrogant heads high with nostrils flaring and hooves meeting in the center. Their eyes were deep amber, emeralds formed the flying reins, and tiny rubies shaped their hooves.

"Ye will not sleep in another man's gift." His emerald eyes stared into hers, and his lips compressed. He lifted the gold chain free of her hair and slipped it over her head. After he placed it on the table, he came back to complete his self-imposed chore.

She stood on the rug facing the fire. He gathered her hair and spread it over her left shoulder, then quickly untied the black tunic's lacing. She caught her breath, feeling the backs of his warm fingers on her sensitive skin.

He had considerable experience at the job. Was it from undressing his first wife? She scowled. Or his leman? A hot streak of jealousy shot through her. Had Damron kept his mistress close during his first marriage? Ha, in these ages it was the leman who undermined a couple. In modern times it became business *associates*.

Gathering the black silk in his big hands, he lifted the garment over her head. She stood in the gold smock, uncomfortable in her near nudity. When he led her to the chair and she sat, she folded her hands over the joining of her thighs.

Going down on one knee, he slid her shoes from her feet. He ignored her efforts to hide herself. When he reached beneath the smock to pull her hose down her legs, she saw his strong, tanned hands through the flimsy material. She jerked and blushed furiously.

"Be still. I ha'e no wish to tear yer hose."

"If I may get a sleeping garment, I'll put it on. Will you be sleeping on the rug, or would you prefer I slept there? It's all the same to me, so you decide."

"On the rug? Oh, nay, my lady. Neither of us will sleep anywhere but on that bed. I agreed I wouldna deflower ye. I did not promise to sleep alone. Ye must think me a great gowk if ye believe I would do so."

"Oh, for heaven's sake. A gowk?"

"A gowk, Lady, is Scots for a fool."

"I'd never think you a fool. A little strange in your thinking, but never a fool."

Damron strode to the bed and picked up the exquisite night garment resting there. He stared at Brianna standing before the fire. The flames highlighted every inch of her body with a fiery glow. He groaned. He wanted to explore all he saw, but he would stick to the plan he devised while they argued.

This woman was different. Connor's sister, Meghan, was the only other woman he knew who was close to Brianna's personality. Both had fiery tempers, stubborn streaks and determination. Abbess Alana had spoken of Brianna's honor. Meghan and his mother had honor, but he had seen none such in any of the women of the royal courts. Mayhap the excesses of the courts corrupted them?

'Tis true, he wanted peace in this marriage. He would wait to learn what manner of woman she was. For certs, she was a challenge. Her strong will dared him to dominate her. To have her come to his bed willingly, he must needs outsmart her.

Over the coming nights, he planned to entice her body unmercifully until she begged him to deflower her.

He looked at her and quirked his brow. She did not move. He crooked his finger. She shook her head.

"Mmm. Ye are beautiful standin' afore the fire, wife." He lowered his voice and let it throb with passion. "Yer clothing vanishes as if by magic."

Desire tightened his face. Looking embarrassed and shy, she came to him. As he removed the smock, her dainty breasts were bared for the first time. She covered them with her hands. He struggled to look unaffected while he held the sleeping garment over her head and waited.

She hesitated, then lifted her arms. Her eyes closed. Clenching his teeth, his hot gaze traveled over her as he lowered the gown. He quickly turned her so she would not see his lust.

His fingers spread through her chestnut hair. A rumble of pleasure sounded in his chest as the curls clung and spiraled around his fingers. He spread it across her back and over her shoulders and studied her firm bottom peeking through the material. His mouth went dry. He tapped her shoulder to let her know he was finished. She looked up at him, her brows raised. When he said nothing further and padded over to the other side of the bed, she sat on the edge of the mattress and waited.

He poured the special mead into the goblets and put them on the table. The honeyed brew was potent, but he no longer wanted to restrict her from becoming too mellow.

She jumped when he came to her, picked her up in his arms and strode toward the fire. He barely heard her mutter low, "Heavens, he has a penchant for carrying women." He sat in the big chair and settled her comfortably on his lap.

"You don't need to hold me. I can sit somewhere else."

"Lady wife, there are no other chairs, as ye well see."

"I prefer sitting on the rug. Ask anyone and they'll tell you I like to sit on rugs."

"If ye wish to sit on the rug, do so."

She started to climb off his lap. Holding her gown so it wouldn't ride up, she wriggled closer to his knees.

A groan caught in his throat as her little rear squirmed against his suffering tarse. He stilled her movements and slid from the chair with her in his arms. After stretching his legs out, he leaned back against the chair.

"You needn't give up your comfort, Damron. I can sit here by myself." She frowned up at him.

"Nay, my love. I wouldna dream of it." His voice was low and silky. He rolled his shoulders, causing the robe at his chest to open further.

She shifted to put her back more to him, hiding her body. He uttered an oath and handed her a chalice. If she did not sit still, he might spend himself while she remained virgin.

He studied her dark brown eyes and silky chestnut hair, and offered a toast. "May we have a brawny heir with eyes as dark brown and rich as the earth, hair the color of the leaves at All Hallow's Even, and the strength of his grandfathers." Touching his chalice to hers, he urged her to take a swallow.

She did, and added her own toast.

"May we have a healthy, strong daughter with hair as black as the night, eyes as green as new leaves in spring and the wisdom of all her grandmothers." They again sampled the mead. "We shouldn't be drinking this now," she added worriedly.

"If we dinna finish what they prepared for us this eve, we will insult the mead-maker."

After several more sips, she stopped trying to hide herself and rested against his chest.

"I would tell ye about the people ye will meet when we arrive at Blackthorn. Would that interest ye?"

He started with his grandfather Douglas, and she became so engrossed in listening that she relaxed and continued to drink her mead. She did not notice when he refilled her chalice. He ran his fingers through her hair and spread it over his chest like a silken scarf. She didn't protest.

He kept her thoughts occupied as he described everyone at his home. She nestled back against him, unwittingly giving him a heart-stopping view of her delicate breasts and the front of her gleaming body. As he gently explored her, his thumb teased a nipple. Her ivory breasts were small with beautiful rose tips. They were far lovelier than the heavy globes of his leman.

His heart pounded. She moved, causing his robe to open over his legs, but she was unaware of it. His blood coursed thickly through his veins. He gritted his teeth and called on his iron will for control to keep from ravishing his bride.

She did not notice when he slipped her gown from her left shoulder. He cleared his hoarse voice and continued talking, stopping occasionally to place soft kisses along her neck and shoulder. His tongue slowly outlined the rim of the sweet shell-like ears that had captivated him since the first time he saw them. Tugging the dainty lobe between his lips, he suckled it.

She started to pull away. He stopped his tender assault and continued the story as if nothing had happened.

After she again settled quietly, he ventured further. His hand stole around to stroke down over her neck and between her breasts, finally to rest on her midriff. He turned her so her back rested against his left arm. His right hand stayed where it was.

Diverting her attention by recounting his cousin Meghan's humorous escapades, he ever so slowly nudged her gown down to her waist. It was a whisper of feeling she did not notice. She took another swallow from the cup he kept filled to the brim.

He rained soft kisses across her forehead, down her nose, and across her cheeks. His fingers ran through her hair and moved to the nape of her neck to caress her there, soothing her further.

Brianna was more relaxed and comfortable than she'd been since she awakened on the ground with the groom jumping beside her. Listening to Damron's beautiful voice and sipping the mead, her limbs felt like creamy butter.

Hm. Mead was a most comforting drink. Not harsh like bourbon. It couldn't have much alcohol in it. Wouldn't she be unaware of her surroundings if it was? Her cup had barely gone down. She was pleased with herself for taking such ladylike sips.

Everything felt so right. So perfect.

"Tell me, wife, of yer own childhood," Damron whispered.

She kept her eyes closed and concentrated to recall events she could relate. If she changed some of her memories, they would fit with the current time. She told him of the time she first saw his likeness, though he did not know it was him.

"When I was barely five years old, my father took me to visit a formidable castle. While there, I wandered off and found myself alone in a long solar. Several ink drawings lined one wall. One in particular caught my eye. It was of a man wearing clothing much like you wore today. I could not see his face.

"A warrior in a strange suit of armor stood beside it. I was very polite and asked him if he would lift me so I could better see the drawing, but he ignored me. I thought perhaps because of the armor, he couldn't hear me, so I tried to climb up his legs to better talk to the man inside. I and the armor clattered to the floor in a dreadful bang. I screamed and cried, terrified that I had killed the invisible man inside.

"When my father found me, I kept saying, 'I wanted to see!' and pointing at the drawing. My father picked me up, and I saw the man in the drawing for the first time. I declared to Father, 'He belongs to me!' Then I began to cry and kept saying, 'Why didn't you love me?' I couldn't stop crying and begging the man to love me. It was not until the next morning when I finally quieted. Every year thereafter, I asked Father to take me to see the drawing, though I never again caused a scene."

Streaks of desire shot to the pit of her stomach, finally making her aware of his hands and lips moving over her. His kisses were gentle and coaxing, and his tongue ran along the closure of her lips to beg entrance.

Her mouth parted on a sigh. His tongue was hot and sweet as it explored her mouth, and she knew she had never had a kiss that felt so right. It wasn't too much to ask of her that she give him kisses. After all, they *were* married.

He was really being a gentlemanly knight, even with all she was denying him. How many modern men would agree to wait what surely would be weeks before bedding their wives?

When he coaxed her tongue into his mouth, she reveled in the silkiness of the insides of his lips. She was disappointed when his mouth left hers and his lips traveled from her chin, down the center of her neck, and over her chest to stop between her breasts. She jumped as his hand cupped a breast and kneaded slowly. He soothed her with the soft, rumbling sounds that so often came from him.

Her head tilted back. His lips caressed her neck again,

before roving down to her breasts. When he gently kissed and tugged a hard nipple, she pulled at his hair.

Oh, my God. She was resting against his naked body—well, almost naked body! How had her own garments fallen to her waist? She gasped. His hand cupped her sex. Her flesh was on fire.

She struggled to regain her composure and moaned. What he was doing felt so right. So very good. She hated to stop him. Aware that his hot and throbbing manhood pressed beneath her thighs, she panted and tugged on the braids at his temples.

Damron's hand cupped her damp mound and gave it a soothing squeeze as he took his mouth from her breast. He blew softly on her wet nipple, puckering the skin around it. Her sex throbbed on his palm, wanting more. Her face felt aflame as she tugged at his wrist and struggled with her gown.

"Little wife, I promised I wouldna take ye, but I did not promise not to touch ye. Ye must allow me this. Come. It grows late and dawn will soon be here." He carried her to the bed and placed her on the sheet. She pulled the bedding up to her chin. Smiling at her, he pinched out the candles.

The fire's embers were bright enough for Brianna to see him clearly. She couldn't drag her gaze away as he removed his robe and placed it across the chair's back. She swallowed, eyeing the soft black hair that matted his chest, then narrowed down over his taut stomach. The light reflecting from the fire turned his skin a beautiful bronze as he padded over to the bed. It also illuminated the many white scars scattered across his chest and arms.

Recalling the servants' comments, she let her gaze dart to his left thigh. She gasped on seeing the still-red scar from his knee up to his groin and studied it. Heaven help him! How had he survived such a wound?

He stepped forward, and her gaze riveted to that special place. She couldn't look away.

His hard, pulsing shaft rose from its bed of black curls in front of two large sacs. His size was startling. Nothing in her life had prepared her for this sight. She began to wonder if men had lost some measure of their *family jewels* as the centuries advanced? Hearing his wicked chuckle, she pulled the covers over her head, mortified he had caught her staring at his turgid sex. The bed swayed as he stretched upon it.

"Come, Brianna. Ye will be air starved. Dinna be shamed. 'Tis natural to be curious about a man's body." He tugged the covers from her face and placed a chaste kiss on her forehead, turned his back to her and settled down to sleep. Only when she heard his even breathing did she close her eyes and give in to her tired body.

Damron studied her face in the dim light. When he had palmed her moist mound earlier, her bemused expression told him he had made a good beginning on his plan. Now, the tumultuous day and the strong mead finally did their work. She slept soundly.

Damron's hands slid to her gown and lifted it over her hips to ease it from her. Satisfied, he drew his naked bride into his arms and against the contours of his body.

Chapter 10

Damron, his heart beating, near breaking his ribs with its thumping, stalked the woman's shadowy figure as she laughed and danced away from him. His feral growl should have halted her in her tracks, but she wantonly tormented and teased him till his raging loins demanded retribution.

"Yield, afore I take ye on the floor." His voice husky with passion, he grasped for her arm. Naught but thin air filled his hand as she twirled out of reach.

She laughed and shrugged her shoulders, letting the transparent silk undergarment slip over her pale skin to come to rest in the crook of her arms. Teased by the slithering fabric, the dark nipples on her ample breasts thrust outward, luring him as she danced backward, widening the gap between them.

Shielding her flesh from his gaze, yet allowing her straining nipples to peep between her spread fingers, she taunted him. He wet his lips, preparing them, then lunged forward to clasp her heated flesh to his.

He fell with her onto the bed, ready to mount the supple form molded against his. The move jolted Damron awake to a throbbing tarse straining for release. His mind cleared.

'Twas not his leman.

He took a deep breath and fought his body for control, before drawing away and slipping the covers off his wife. She stirred. Her hands moved over the bedding. Did she search for something? He edged closer, but only enough that she would feel the heat from his body. She scooted back until she pressed tight against him, then sighed with satisfaction.

The room was dimly lit, but enough that it outlined her ivory body. Soft as a breeze, his hand wandered over her, enjoying her silky skin. His fingers moved down over the dip in her waist, and after caressing her soft stomach, they feathered over the curve of her hip to cup her bottom.

Her body was artlessly open to him. He laid the palm of his hand on the crease of her buttocks, his fingers resting on the heat of her secret place. He groaned with pleasure.

She stirred, restless now. He removed his hand and drew his legs tight to her bottom. She mumbled, caught hold of his wrist and snuggled his hand between her breasts. Though not the way he had expected to spend his wedding night, it did have its merits.

Damron was pleased with her reaction. Each night, he would tempt her body with pleasure while her defenses were down. Undermining her resolve not to mate with him would be a challenge.

Pretending sleep, he forced a few gusty snores.

Brianna's eyes flew open. Having had an outrageous dream of a man whose face was in shadows, she was disappointed to have awakened too soon.

She gasped. Why was she hugging Damron's hand between her breasts? Her naked breasts? Huh? Where was her gown? He slept curled around her, his rigid member snuggled against the crease of her bottom. His breezy snores ruffled her hair. She inched her legs forward and shifted her hips away from his warm body. He twitched restlessly. His hand fumbled until it cupped her breast, and after a lusty grunt, he resumed snoring.

Brianna waited. Then waited longer. The blasted man didn't move. He seemed in a deep sleep. Where had the covers gone? She raised her arm and felt across his hot back. A light mist of sweat covered the splendid muscles there.

Slowly, careful not to wake him, she gripped the covers to slide them over them both, then again tried to pull away. She barely moved before he dragged the bedding off again. His hand sprang back to burrow between her breasts. The blasted man's body shook, so why did he pull the bedding off?

"Mmmff," he breathed into her hair. Whenever she attempted to move, it interrupted his snoring. She stayed put.

Maybe his hardness was that *man's thing* that happened while they slept. Even so, she didn't want him to awake and find her so conveniently placed. Sighing, she closed her eyes.

Brianna was sure she hadn't slept an hour more before a booming voice awakened her.

"Wife, if ye would break yer fast afore we leave, rise and don yer clothing. Do ye require my help?"

Damron, dressed for travel and looking rested, loomed over her. She remembered waking in the night and finding she had discarded her gown. Her face flushed hot as a backyard barbecue. Something tangled around her legs when she moved to sit up.

She peeked beneath the covers. She wore her gown.

Popping her head back out, she blinked and tried to mask her confusion with a smile.

"If you hadn't snored and kept me awake, I would be up and dressed by now." She gathered the covers around her body and stepped, as calm and graceful as a model, across the cold floor.

"Snore?" His eyes glinted with amusement. "I ne'er snore."

"Ha, you should hear yourself." Self-conscious now, she went behind the corner screen, longing for the privacy of her modern bathroom. She listened to him moving about the room, and heard the door open, then close. She sighed. She was alone. Hurrying, she tended her needs and dressed. Head lowered while she gathered her long hair and tied a ribbon around it, she came from behind the screen. If she hadn't spied his boots not more than a foot from her toes, her head would have butted against his chest. Her face flushed. He hadn't left.

"Come. I would see if what ye would wear is appropriate."

"Why? I've always suitably attired myself."

"Oh? 'Tis suitable to bare yer legs when ye ride, and for a bride to wear a black mourning gown, Lady?"

He sauntered around her, then lifted the back of her tunic to see how much freedom her leggings gave her. She frowned. When he grasped her bottom and squeezed, she whirled to swat at him. She stopped, her hand in midair. The sheets. Where were they?

"Blessed saints! They're gone." She worried her lower lip between her teeth. "They'll expect proof I'm a virgin."

"Aye. I have taken care of it." Smiling, he turned her to face him. "I would have ye wear my morning gift, wife." He draped a clan tartan under her arm and up over her shoulder, securing it over her breast with a silver brooch.

She stared at his big hands. Smelled his scent. And saw the brooch. Celtic knots formed a circle with the head of a falcon designed on each side. The pin was a fist holding a dagger upright.

Blinding flashes of light streaked through her head. She saw his foggy image in the ruins of Blackthorn, his warm hands pinning this same brooch to her sweater. She lurched, near losing her balance, and grasped for his arm.

Had that been an ancient memory from this day? Only a

great, enduring love could outlast the centuries to show itself in such a way. Her fingers dug into his arm. She fought the fear rising in her. What would happen to her, to him, if their love grew to such heights, and she suddenly returned to the twenty-first century? A whimper escaped at the thought.

"Lady, is aught wrong?"

"No. I'm just tired from too little sleep." She cupped her shaking hand over the brooch, and warmth spread from it. It was where it belonged.

"Thank you, Damron, it's very beautiful. I'll treasure it always."

Damron's eyes lit with pleasure, and his face softened on hearing her words.

When they entered the hall, all gazes turned to inspect her. The women's faces mirrored concern. Not the men's, though. Damron winked. They leered and thumped him on the shoulders like he'd scored the winning goal in the World Hockey Championship.

Disgusted, Brianna frowned.

"Careful, love. Dinna let yer temper lead ye to trouble."

He grinned at her, to all appearances a man very pleased with his wedding night. The scoundrel exaggerated his help in seating her.

She slapped at his hands, and her frown deepened to a scowl. Deliberately, she bounced down on the hard seat to disprove his insinuations.

"Easy, love. Ye will harm yer tender flesh further," he cautioned.

He filled her cup with ale, then ladled hot porridge into a bowl and spread butter over it before he placed it close to her hand. After slathering honey atop a hot scone, he set it beside her bowl. Only then did he serve himself. He was playing the gratified husband to the hilt.

"Brianna, are you able to travel so soon?" Lady Cecelia whispered after they finished eating and Damron moved to join Connor and Galan by the fireplace. "I prepared you a salve. You have but to apply it twice a day. Do not despair, dear. We all adjust. But you would do well not to anger your husband."

Brianna thanked her and put the small earthenware pot into the pocket of her leggings. Though Lady Cecelia had sealed it with wax, its smell was pleasant. Was it a beauty treatment? Perhaps Cecelia had heard of Damron's leman.

Soon Maud moved close to speak to her alone, gently hugged her and also handed her a small pot. "Men are selfish in their excitement, dear. Entreat him to go more gently," she advised, her face flaming.

Elise, her eyes bloodshot and swollen from crying, ran over to grasp Brianna around the neck. "Take care, Brianna. I will miss you terribly," she wailed. Brianna hugged her tight and soothed her with little shushing sounds and pats on the back.

Damron cleared his throat, signaling he wished Brianna to hurry. When they gathered outside, all the villagers were there.

"That good man who made such *encouraging* wedding mead, please come forward." Damron grinned, and everyone's gazes shifted to Brianna.

She pinched him.

"After sampling yer mead, I dinna doubt my bride will birth an heir within the year. I thank ye heartily."

The nerve of him. He drank most of the mead—didn't he?

"Swaggering braggart." She pinched him again, harder, for emphasis.

His arm whipped out and tugged her against his side. Gripping her chin, he kissed her soundly. When he lifted his head, her traitorous lips tried to follow his. He smiled.

"I see our benefactor has made himself known. I thank ye, my good man. As ye can see, we still feel its results. Do ye have sons of yer own?"

"Aye, my lord, I have. Four strapping boys and a fine daughter, all less than seven summers old." After Damron tossed him a bag heavy with coins, the man's chest puffed out and he strutted about like a pleased bantam rooster.

While they said their good-byes, Damron kept his arm around Brianna's shoulders. Finally, after a frown and nudge from Connor, he released her and allowed Galan to come say his farewells.

Galan took her hands in his and brought them to his lips to kiss her knuckles. "Take care, Brianna. If ever you have need of me, I will come."

From the earnest look in his eyes, she knew he would move heaven and earth for her.

"Don't worry about me, Galan. Nathaniel will see that I come to no harm." Before she could say more, Damron urged her down the remaining stairs to Angel.

She dug in her heels.

"Wait. You said I could ride Sweetpea."

"I said I would think on it." He gained his saddle and placed a folded blanket between his thighs. When Connor lifted her up to him, Damron settled her on the blanket. "Are ye comfortable, wife? I wouldna have ye suffer more tenderness."

Brianna rolled her eyes and poked him in the ribs with her elbow. As everyone called their farewells and waved, Damron urged Angel into a trot. He kept a firm grasp on her waist while she leaned far out and waved until they were all out of sight. In so short a time, she had grown fond of the people at Ridley.

Her stomach fluttered with nervous excitement. What would she find at Blackthorn? In the twenty-first century, she had felt such a strong empathy for the ruins. How would she react to the intact castle? And to the man she must resist, else she would lose her very heart and soul to him?

After a while, she squirmed and again stuck her elbows in

his ribs. He didn't seem to mind. Her elbows did, for his chain mail was unforgiving. Disgruntled, she continued to make a nuisance of herself in hopes he'd let her ride Sweetpea, who was being led behind a young squire.

"Settle yerself, lady. If ye think to gain my attention, ye have. Wrigglin' yer sweet arse against my manhood has aroused my interest." He waggled his brows at her. "Ah! I understand. Ye wish to stop so we may seek our privacy in the woods?"

"Ha, you wish!" He smelled too good for her peace of mind. She was increasingly aware of the juncture of his thighs and the bulge that grew by the minute. "Can I ride Sweetpea?"

"Nay." Damron let Angel prance and misbehave until she grabbed his arms to keep her balance.

Driving an old jalopy without springs for ten hours would be more comfortable than riding a horse for five. And quieter, too. Damron and Connor's shouts over the clamor of mounted men made her ears ring. It must be this habit that caused him to yell so often. After they continued for what seemed the better part of the day, she squirmed in earnest. Grabbing both sides of his jaw, she forced his head down to look at her.

"You insufferable demon. Stop this damn horse."

"Dinna shout. If ye need privacy, ye have but to ask. We meet Bleddyn just around the next bend."

He spoke true, for Bleddyn awaited them at the border into Scotland. He smiled when he saw the expression on Brianna's face.

Damron lifted her to the ground. She shoved his hands away, but had to grab hold of Angel's mane to keep from falling in the dirt. The huge horse looked down at her, jerked his head and all but sent her flying into the bushes. Damron steadied her.

"You nasty-tempered, evil bag of bones." Brianna fisted

her hand and whopped Angel below his left ear. She grabbed that same ear and tugged, shoving off Damron's restraining arm.

"If ever you dare do something like that again," she shouted into Angel's ear, "I'll take that part of you that you love the most and feed it to the wolves. Do we understand each other?" She gave his ear another yank, then let go.

Trudging into the woods to take care of her needs, she muttered about uppity men and their ornery horses. When she adjusted her clothing to return, the jars of salve in her pockets clacked together. She recalled the concern on the ladies' faces when they gave them to her, and Elise's frightened expression. Heat rushed from her head to her toes.

No longer wobbly, she charged out of the woods. Her arms swatted bushes as she flew past, yelling for Damron. Connor ran toward her, as though expecting to find a wild boar chased her. She flew past him and headed for the man she wanted to bash.

Damron placed his hands on his hips and waited. She tried to grab his chest, but couldn't get a handhold because of his hauberk. Frustrated, she grasped the braids at his temples. Seizing her wrist, he stared into furious eyes.

"Control yeself, Brianna." Damron hauled her to the side of the stream, out of his men's sight. "Ne'er, if ye value yer hide, come at me in such a way again. I willna tolerate it."

"Did you lop off a chicken's head on the bedsheets?"

"And dinna yell at me," he bellowed. "I nicked myself with my sword. It bled too freely afore I could stop it." He grinned. "Mayhap it looked like I tupped ye in haste."

Before her gaping mouth closed, he turned and left.

He entered the woods with his men, and she supposed they would take care of personal business. So she wouldn't see anyone wetting the forest floor, she kept her gaze downcast. Tearing a hunk out of the bread someone had placed on a blanket, she started nibbling on it. When she glanced up, she saw Bleddyn studied her face. He grinned.

"You're doing it again, sir. I'm glad you think it's funny, because I don't. Men are all alike." The humor of the situation finally got to her, and she giggled. No wonder the women had been so worried about her!

Before she could say more, the warriors returned. They had crossed into Scotland and now wore either tartans gathered at their waists or breeches. She didn't know which she liked best—the bare legs of the plaid wearers or the snug-fitting breeches that left nothing to her imagination.

Atop Angel, Damron scowled and beckoned her to him. She ignored him and hurried to Sweetpea. Before a dozen steps, she found herself lifted to the blanket on Angel's back, Damron's arm securely around her.

"Do you always snatch women off the ground when they're not looking? We're far from Ridley, so why can't I . . .?" Her voice trailed off as his arm tightened and air whooshed from her lungs. She jerked her head around to protest.

"Dinna vex me!"

One look at his face was enough to keep her silent. She huffed and turned to study the scenery. This mode of transportation might be slow, but you saw much more of the countryside atop a horse than you did in a speeding car. Scotland in the eleventh century was so very beautiful. What a world of difference between this early time and the future. The dense forests now covering much of the land were no longer there in the future. She took deep breaths of clean, fragrant air and mourned the beauty that would be lost.

She was anxious to speak to Nathaniel. Did he know about her? Would he think her a witch if he learned she had lived in both centuries? She gulped. If he did, he wouldn't treat her so kindly. Would he?

Nathaniel's voice answered in her mind. She was barely

able to restrain herself from twisting around to see him. Would she ever grow accustomed to his uncanny ability?

You need not fear me, little one. I came to ease your way in this life. You have known many things that interest me. I have seen your memory pictures of a time far ahead.

The Scots are great lovers of tales. Perhaps you would weave one to tell us? No one else will know 'tis truth. We Welsh have always believed Druids could travel between time, and the Scots have their own legends.

Brianna relaxed against Damron. Did Nathaniel know how her soul had transferred back to this former life? When they reached Blackthorn, would he tell her?

She felt and heard no answer from him. He had broken the connection between them.

For the better part of an hour, she tried to ignore Damron's hard body behind her. Finally, she pushed back against him, gathered her tunic between her legs and grabbed her right knee. She twisted around and threw her leg over Angel's neck so she sat astride.

"If I have to ride with you, I'm going to be comfortable," she grumbled. She squirmed and rearranged herself, ignoring Damron.

He soon drew her notice.

A sound rumbled from his chest that was felt more than heard. Glancing down, she spied bronzed, muscular thighs feathered with dark hair pressed against her legs.

She went as still as Lot's wife.

Modern Scotsmen wore briefs under their kilts. Did medieval men wear some cloth contraption? Surely they did. She stole a hand up his leg, looking for the edge of his tartan to pull it down. Instead, she encountered the hot, bare flesh of his inner thigh. Her hand jerked like he'd scalded her. When she tried to inch forward, his arm tightened around her.

That part of him, ever growing of late, pressed against her spine. Every hot, steely inch of him. Wasn't he ever flaccid?

She tried to look for his clothing without lowering her head. She saw the edge of the material but couldn't reach it.

It was a dilemma, one best dealt with by falling asleep.

When Brianna awoke, she was no longer astride Angel but again resting across Damron's thighs, her face snuggled to his throat. It was damp. "Aw, crud." She'd drooled all over the man's neck.

They pulled off into a clearing, and Damron lifted her from Angel. He held her upright, his arm supporting her waist. His somber eyes stared down, questioning her.

Assuming he wanted to know if she could stand, she put her weight on her legs and groaned when they protested. While grasping his arm, she lifted each leg in turn until sure they would hold her before she let go.

He nodded, released her and went about the business of ordering the camp for the night.

Jeremy led her to a stream where trees offered shelter from the men's sight. He'd stand guard at an appropriate distance. She looked around and grinned. She and her parents had camped frequently, so bathing in the stream wasn't a hardship.

The cold water was. Bathing quickly, she dried herself and pulled on her clothing. When she started to return to the camp, she didn't go far before she knew she'd gone in the wrong direction. Doubling back didn't help. She'd lost the stream.

Oh, bother, everything had disappeared. The only familiar thing was the sound of the birds as they welcomed the evening. Taking a great gasp of air, she shouted. "Jeremy? Where are you?"

Moments later, he came crashing through the bushes. When they reached the camp, Damron's eyebrows raised when told she was lost no more than fifty paces from where the squire had left her.

"Do ye have a poor sense of direction, wife?"

"I wasn't really lost. I was looking for wild berries."

One glance told her he didn't believe her, but he kept silent as he helped her sit. Jeremy and Spencer spread the evening meal on a large cloth. They would eat grandly tonight as Lady Maud had Cook provide them with roasted chicken, lamb and grouse, along with boiled carrots and baked bread.

After they had eaten most of their meal, Bleddyn spoke. "Brianna is a fine weaver of tales. She has agreed to spin one for us this eve."

She smiled, hearing the men's pleased shouts. Not knowing how they liked their stories to unfold, she decided to use the same opening parents have throughout the ages.

"Once upon a time, in a land far away, the people had many tribes, much like you have in Scotland," she began. "They called these people the Indian nations." Skillfully she spun her story, describing their skills at horsemanship, how they painted themselves and their trophy taking. Concentrating, she sent Nathaniel the sound of an Indian war cry.

"In earlier days," he spoke up, "my ancestors took the heads of brave enemies, for it gave the man's wisdom and strength to the captor. Sometimes they coated the skull with gold. 'Twas always given an honored place in the keep."

At that point, Damron suggested they end the story and seek their rest.

"After today's hard ride, you will sleep soundly, Brianna," Bleddyn soothed.

"Hah. No one will sleep, sir. Damron snores like rumbling thunder. He'll keep everyone awake."

"Me snore, wife? Ye are mistaken." Damron looked down his nose at her with the dignity of a king. "I ne'er snore. Ask anyone."

"I have known Damron all my life and he hasna e'er kept me awake. Mayhap you did hear thunder last eve," Connor added.

"No, it wasn't, Connor. Believe me. He snores."

When they entered the tent, Brianna saw a pallet with a

wool blanket covering half the tent floor. Damron excused himself and left. She undressed down to her shift and stretched out on the bedding, then covered herself with the blanket. This small tent was much more intimate than their room at Ridley had been.

She pretended she slept when he returned. Hearing clothing rustle, she peeked. His body was beautiful. Her mouth went dry. Seeing his sex, she squirmed.

Oh, yes, Damron had it right. He was more than ample.

He stretched out beside her, then pulled her close to study her flushed face.

"Brianna, ye are my wife. 'Tis yer right to view my body as 'tis mine that I see yers." He lowered his head, and his lips closed over hers. He kissed her like he would linger at it all night.

Her heart hammered against his chest. Did he feel it? When she didn't open to him, the light pressure of his thumb on her chin urged her to let him enter. He explored her mouth, running his tongue over hers in greeting. He thrust deep, then slowly withdrew to repeat the intimacy again and again.

The hair on his chest teased her nipples through the thin undergarment, hardening them. He cupped his hand over her breast, testing its weight. His palm rubbed gently across the pink bud, and when it hardened even more, he bent to suckle it.

Her hands tightened on his shoulders. Her breathing quickened when he became more aggressive. Finally, she panted and tried to push him away. His expression became stern.

"Nay, wife. Ye willna deny me this. I vowed not to take ye. I did not promise I wouldna kiss and find pleasure in yer body." Her face flushed. "I know how to make ye forget e'en yer worst aches, love. Would ye like me to show ye?" Devilment twinkled in his eyes.

"Thank you, no, I'm not the least sore." Her blush warmed her neck and chest. She had no doubt he was so skilled at love play that he could make a woman forget the color of her own hair. Or her name.

He chuckled and continued his gentle wooing. His wet lips trailed kisses to the hollow of her neck before he licked a path up her skin to her ear. His hand seared a path down her taut stomach to cup her dewy sex. He gently rotated the base of his thumb there, causing heat to pool between her legs.

Shivers of delight raced through her. She arched to him. When she moaned, he placed a chaste kiss on her forehead.

"Pleasant dreams, wife."

Wrapping his arms around her, he put her head under his chin and settled himself. His breathing slowed and deepened.

Brianna tried to put distance between them, but his arms tightened. She knew she'd still be awake at daybreak.

She wasn't going to get any sleep. No, sir. Not even for a minute.

She sighed. And slept.

Chapter 11

Darkness surrendered to soft hints of light. Awakening birds sounded their first chirps as they broke their fast several days later. Brianna avoided looking at Damron, and if words were necessary, she kept her gaze on his chest.

"Wife, did ye not sleep well? Mayhap yer imaginings are over active and 'tis the cause of uneasy dreams?"

Connor choked on a cough. She looked up and frowned.

Damron's hard stare quieted his cousin.

"I feel fit, sir," Brianna murmured. Drat the man! Of course she was tired. A nightmare would be easier on her nerves than the erotic dreams she'd been having. *Could* it be her imagination? No. It was much more than that.

Several times, she caught Damron eying her, a smug look on his face. He glanced away without speaking. She was glad when they mounted and started the day's journey.

After that first day, Damron allowed her to ride Sweatpea close behind him. Today, as they neared the foot of the Grampian Mountains, she felt that prickly knowledge that someone watched her closely. Others, too, must have sensed the hidden presence of men in the woods.

"Bleddyn. Do ye feel them?" Damron asked.

"Aye. About thirty surround us. Their leader's hair is the color of the sun. A man in his prime wearing a green tunic. A likeness of a boar's head is on his herald."

"Ah, 'tis Eric, the MacLarens heir. His brother is chief of the MacLarens." Damron's sword was in his hand in a flash. His men followed suit.

"Eric. Enough of this cat and mouse." Damron's voice vibrated through the air. "Appear afore me and give me greetin', or draw yer sword and hasten yer death."

"Mayhap 'twill be your death, Morgan. Are you no' wary of the Campbells, and you with a lovely lass in your midst? Hm, she is a wee, scrawny lass, no match for your heavy weapon. I will think on relieving you of her." As he spoke, the man came from the forest and rode confidently up to Damron.

Eric's confidence was mistaken. Before he drew his next breath, Damron's sword rested at the base of his throat.

"Ye will keep yer thoughts of swiving off her." The tip of his sword pricked the skin there, causing blood to dribble down Eric's neck, before Damron drew back and buffeted Eric's shoulder in friendship.

"You were never so stingy when I fostered with your family," Eric grumbled.

"Aye. But this *scrawny* lass is my wife." Damron squinted his eyes at Eric. "E'en though the Campbell chief is yer granda and ye'll give us much needed protection, behave yerself or I will skewer ye and not think twice on it."

Over the next several hours, Brianna learned much about the years Eric had fostered with the Morgans. As daylight waned and they made camp, Eric stood before her and smiled. Charm radiated from every pore.

"Eric MacLaren, lovely lady, Damron's foster brother." He promptly kissed her on both cheeks.

Brianna chuckled at the man's audacity.

"Unpucker yer lips. My wife is no kissin' kin to ye. Find

yer own lass to maul." Damron frowned and shoved himself
between them.

Eric provided an amusing addition to their nightly camp-
fire, for he told many stories about their youthful exploits at
Blackthorn. In each of his tales, he came off as the bravest.
No doubt he exaggerated, for Damron laughed. Damron also
frowned when Eric's gaze studied Brianna from head to toe.

"Eric!" The cold anger in Damron's warning didn't seem
to faze Eric. He grinned and goaded Damron at every
opportunity.

"Lucifer's arse!"

Damron jolted awake with a raging, rock-hard rod. Every
nerve in his body screamed for release. Brianna, shivering from
cold, slept all but atop him. Damron had never known anyone
to fall asleep so quickly. So soundly. A tree could fall and she
would not hear it. Her cheek nuzzled over his heart, her left leg
rested between his thighs. Though her hot center pressed against
his flesh, it wasn't what caused his distress.

Her hand, nestled in the curls of his sex and holding his
shaft in a firm grip, was. Each time his member pulsed, she
sighed, and her warm fingers tightened. Sweat beaded his
forehead. He held his breath and fought to restrain his urges.
A groan of pleasure burst past his clamped lips. She stirred.

He thanked the saints for all the lessons in self-control he
had learned. If he did not contain himself, she would be
rudely awakened. He choked on a chuckle. She startled
awake. He watched her through barely slitted eyelids.
Mayhap, she would return to sleep.

He hoped in vain.

Brianna's eyes opened wide, then blinked. She frowned
and tried to draw her hand closer to see.

She gasped. Loud.

His head clamored with his pounding heartbeats; his ears noted the rush of blood through his veins.

Finger by finger, she released him.

Fortunately, Connor called from outside the tent. She stilled, pretending she yet slept. When Damron slipped his shoulder from beneath her head, he kissed her closed eyelids. Her lashes fluttered like butterflies. With great care, he freed himself from her limbs. Upon leaving the tent, he heard her sigh of relief.

They rode hard for several hours that morning. Brianna had ample time to think. To worry. Before this crazy switch in time happened at Blackthorn's ruins, Brianna had resigned herself to being in love with the likeness of a man long dead.

Her dreams and flashing visions of him had made her doubt her sanity. She even considered seeking psychiatric help. Surely her obsession, as she considered it, had become so intense because of her disappointment in Gordon. She had trusted her husband completely, and completely he destroyed her trust. Her soul had yearned for the man in the drawing. The man whose face fascinated her with its strong character.

Damron.

Merciful God. Now she was with that same flesh-and-blood man—the very challenging flesh-and-blood man—not the likeness. He was so much more complex in life than she had sensed in the drawing.

The force of his personality would not let her ignore him or allow her to keep her distance. His dominating ways challenged her. The physical attraction that crackled in the air between them was unbelievably forceful. More than she had ever felt in her life.

Ha. In both lives.

To fall in love with Damron, and not know if or when she

would suddenly be whisked away, was more than her soul could bear, for she would leave her heart behind.

Damron called a halt beside a stream where the forest had thinned. At the noise of their arrival, birds scattered from the trees, and forest creatures hurried to find safer spots. He lifted Brianna from Sweetpea, and led her farther downstream.

Did he plan to complain? To blame her for his friend's interest? Eric had often ridden beside her that day and entertained her with his wit. When Damron had noted it, he scowled and demanded Eric return to his side.

Damron stopped suddenly. Brianna crashed against his back and muttered a garbled oath.

He turned to scowl down at her.

She folded her hands and smiled up at him.

When he placed his powerful fists on his hips, she studied the laces of his shirt and tried to look attentive. When he didn't speak, she shifted her feet and looked at him. His eyes looked hot. Sultry. Glancing down, she was sorry she had. Whatever his thoughts, they affected other parts of him.

Oh, my. The vision that had greeted her eyes at dawn flashed into her mind. Is that what he wanted to discuss? Her cheeks burned. His member tented the tartan enough for even an innocent to understand.

As if proclaiming himself the winner of their contest of wills, he growled and stalked around her. After he completed his circle, she noted he had adjusted his clothing. He stood, feet balanced wide apart. Even his dusty boots appeared menacing.

"Look at me when I speak." Damron's voice was firm and authoritative. Her gaze flashed to his face. "I have many responsibilities and little surcease from them. Is it too much to ask that ye give me time to renew my strength? Far from peaceful nights, my sleep is oft broken."

Merciful heavens. Had she grabbed him before?

Consternation flashed through her.

"A dutiful wife must think only of her lord. She should be a helpmate and cause him no problems. She should see to his food if he hungers. If his mood is on bed sport, she should comply. She should be as obligin' as his faithful wolfhound, to greet and give comfort."

"A dog? You want me to act like your dog? Ha! If you expect me to beg, to pant and drool, you've a long wait coming." She folded her arms across her chest. Her fingers twitched as she glared at him.

He held up his hand. "That isna necessary." He again launched into what he expected of his wife.

She stopped listening. She cringed. In her sleep while she was having her erotic dreams, had she drooled on his bare chest? Begged and panted for him? His next words caught her attention again.

"Ye must seek me out when ye have a question about a man's body." He scowled at her.

Oh, damn. Did he refer to her grasping him in her sleep? How would the early Brianna have reacted to what he said?

"I have lived in an abbey, husband, but I know men have different, ah, you know. Body parts? I cannot help but notice your men when they go into the trees." Maybe that's how she would have responded.

"By Christ's cross. A lady shouldna look when men are, uh, busy in the trees."

"They didn't look busy. More like they took their time and enjoyed themselves." She batted her eyelashes at him.

"Jesu! Ne'er look into the trees."

"Since you are being so helpful, could you explain why men call, uh," she hesitated, "*it* a wick?"

Seeing his surprised look, she hardly suppressed a giggle.

"Whom did ye hear speakin' of such at Saint Anne's?"

Oh, goodness, he seemed awfully upset.

"Merciful saints. Not in the abbey. It was you, of course."

"Ne'er have I said such in yer hearin'."

"Have you forgotten laughing earlier with Eric? He told a story about his wick being aflame. You said he didn't know how to dip it properly in the right honey pot." She frowned and looked up at him before continuing. "Surely he didn't get too close to the hearth? And why did he not dip it in a tankard of water?" She bit her tongue, stilling a laugh.

"Ye needna understand such things." His face turned redder with each word.

It was the first time she'd bested him. It felt good.

Damron could not take his mind from thoughts of Brianna. Each day had followed a pattern of traveling and resting. Each night had its own pattern. A sensual one. He knew her growing need. Her eyes watched him, studied him like hot, ardent fingers rustling over his body.

After stripping in front of her, he kissed and caressed her, becoming bolder and more persuasive each night. Her skin had become so sensitive to him, she quivered if he brushed against her. He whispered what he would do to her when she became one with him, crooned his pleasure at the *almost lovin'*, as he called it, that he did to her now.

Brianna drew slow, deep breaths when he was close by. His scent pulled her. Feeling her resistance, he would stroke her face. She lowered her lids to shield her eyes from him, then with a sigh, turned her cheek to nestle against his palm. Her response pleased him. If he kept to his sensual teasing, she would soon be the passionate lass he wanted for his bed sport.

He had yet to quell her troublesome personality that challenged him at every turn. Her father had neglected to teach her that a man owns his wife, that she was his property and should submit to his will. When he had instructed her on how to be a dutiful wife, she had refused to understand him. Were Saxon men so different? Did they not believe a wife's duty was to see to the husband's comfort, his pleasure? She took umbrage at his likening a wife to a faithful hound. He frowned, remembering her angry expression. Why, the woman acted as if she thought she was his equal.

What a strange thought.

At meals, Brianna ate less and sank deeper into her own thoughts. She tried to resist Damron. She began sleeping lightly. Her growing need for him unsettled her. Her increasing worry of loving him and suddenly being wrenched from him filled her thoughts. She could not speak of her fears. No one would understand, and if she let drop even a hint of how she came here, they would think her a witch.

Noon one day found them at the side of a steep hill covered with beautiful yellow and white wildflowers. Spencer stood guard as Brianna refreshed herself at a stream.

His lady cried out strange words. He gasped. When she came from behind the trees, he was frightened by her pale face. "Be you ill, Lady? Please, dinna worry. I will get help."

He broke into a run toward their camp.

"My lord, come quickly. Your lady wife cried out she had been pinched from a 'frigging crap.' From the looks of her, she may have a fit!"

Damron's mouth flew open. With a stern command for Spencer to say no more, he went to find his undisciplined wife. Several steps from the woods, Brianna appeared, her face white and strained, her clothing rumpled. His jaw snapped together. His face twitched.

"I suppose you wish to lecture now, my lord?" Brianna rolled her eyes and squared her shoulders.

Damron frowned at the men giving her sympathetic looks. "Ye will sit and eat. For now." When Brianna had choked down most of her meal, he poured her cup half full of ale.

"Drink it."

"I don't need ale for courage, lord husband."

Without a word, he held the cup to her lips. She would drink it or he would hold it there until she did. After she gulped down the ale, he guided her away from the camp. Neither spoke as they studied each other.

"'Tis yer woman's time, wife?" His gaze swept over her.

"It's personal, and nothing to do with you."

"Everythin' about ye has to do with me. Even the words springing from yer mouth that are fit only for a slattern's speech. Time and again I have ordered ye to cease speaking such."

Damron frowned at her. The longer he knew her, the more he realized no one had schooled her to be an obedient wife. From this day on, he would be more diligent in correcting her. He must needs curb her unseemly behavior, or he would soon lose the respect of his men if they thought his wife could defy him.

"Which words did you think unfit?"

"Ye well know there were two. I need not know the words to ken they be crude Saxon curses. I warned ye when we first met not to curse, and ye have defied me."

"Why would you think they were curses? Surely you have seen friggin' crappers before?"

Astonished at her nerve, his mouth gaped.

"Why, they are large spiders. They have very hairy legs and a shell-like body." She avoided his eyes and shifted from one foot to the other. "Their ugly green eyes protrude. Surely you know of them?" She peeked up at him and opened her mouth to speak again.

"Nay. Not another word."

His shout made her hesitate. But not for long.

"Wait! I suppose you also don't know Frigg was the name

of the Norse goddess of love? She was Odin's wife, the goddess of heaven who presides over marriage and the home."

"Dinna ye ken when to surrender?" He tugged her arm and hurried her toward the camp.

"The goddess is doomed to sorrow if she thinks to preside over this marriage," Brianna muttered.

He pretended not to hear her.

He heard her grind her teeth.

"Medieval ass," she whispered so low had he not a hawk's hearing, he would have missed it.

He near stopped again, but decided to ignore it. From the corner of his eye, he saw her stare at a rock ahead. He grabbed her waist and lifted her as she swung a leg back to kick it. Her foot met thin air. She was astride Sweetpea afore she knew what had happened.

He set a fast pace.

From the moment he first laid eyes on Brianna, the man had watched her. He was welcome amongst them, for he rode with his laird's brother, Eric. At the edge of night, he crouched behind bushes to spy on her as she tended to her bathing.

Fools. They know not the one they seek is amongst them. The Welshman willna sense me. I ha'e my own tricks. You willna long have her, Damron. Soon it will be within my arms she sleeps, my body warming her, my rod making her moan. Her belly will swell, and e'en to the day she whelps, she will be mine.

Chapter 12

Thunder rumbled and lightning flashed, startling Brianna awake. Careful not to rouse Damron, Brianna eased off the pallet and slipped from the tent. She drew in a shuddering breath as she lifted her face to the flashing night sky. How could she survive in this primitive world? She had thought hard about trying to find a way back. Since the elements helped send her here to the past, couldn't they also take her back?

Closer now, bolts of lightning streaked the velvet-black sky, beautiful to the sight but fearful in their intensity.

Heavenly Father, what am I to do? Damron believed a horse is more important than a wife. He didn't want a partner, a helpmate. He wanted a brainless woman to see to his creature comforts. She couldn't be that woman. Well, hell, she didn't have a submissive bone in her body. How could they ever find happiness together, when they were always butting heads like two angry rams locking horns and pawing at the ground?

Lightning struck ever closer. Tears slipped from her closed eyes as her body arched, arms raised, inviting the storm's power.

Damron jolted awake. Lightning silhouetted Brianna's form against the tent wall as she raised her arms as though entreating the heavens. His heart lurched as a man raced toward her, a cape billowing as he threw it over her head and snatched her up in his arms.

Damron burst from the tent, his sword ready to strike. Her captor turned. Waited. Bleddyn's gentle eyes gazed back at him.

"Bloody accursed Lucifer. What has happened?" Damron shouted above the crashing thunder.

"I awoke to see Brianna facing the advancing storm. She was walking in her sleep," Bleddyn said as he sprinted into the tent with Brianna. He set her on her feet, then wrapped a blanket around her shoulders.

"Wife, what say ye? I would have the truth." Though his voice softened, his stern gaze did not allow hers to shift away.

"As Nathaniel said, I was sleepwalking." She glanced at the Welshman. His lips were pressed together, his brow furrowed. He knew she had dared the elements, and was angry.

"Pray excuse us, Bleddyn." Damron's gaze pinned her to the spot as the Welshman left.

She swallowed, and her gaze shifted.

He grunted and nodded his head, as if acknowledging she had every right to be uneasy. "Lady, tell me the true reason ye stood facin' a storm." He held up his hand. "Nay. Not the handy excuse Bleddyn fed ye. Look at me, not my chest, when ye speak."

"How can I? You're too blasted tall." She glared up at him. The stubborn man was near to a giant. She could sure use some spike heels now. She spied a small chest about a foot high, and stamped over to climb up on it. Unsteady, she wobbled and threw her arms out to the side for balance.

He rolled his eyes. "Ye dinna see past yer nose. Ye canna find yer way around a circle, and ye are as graceful as a sotted chicken."

"Not a day passes that you don't lecture me and complain."

Her breath hitched, and she clamped her lips together.

His lips tightened, causing the nearby scar to turn white. "I but list your faults so ye may mend them. Ye try to distract me, wife. I am waiting."

"You're naked. I can't talk when you're naked." She looked up at the top of the tent, avoiding him and trying to think of a way to divert his attention from her attempt to test the storm.

Damron huffed. After hearing the rustle of clothing, she looked back at him. A shirt covered him down past his manhood.

He'd think she was a witch if she told him she thought the storm's fury could send her soul flying. She cleared her throat and blurted, "I don't know why I went outside."

He glared all the harder.

She started to get down from the chest.

"Stay!"

Crud. She wasn't a blasted dog. "Don't yell commands at me like I'm some hound sniffing at your footsteps."

His face darkened. She had gone too far. As she thought about her options, it took only seconds to know she had none. His rule was law. He was a medieval man. She could not change that fact, though she didn't have to like his boorishness.

"Well? I await yer reasons." His tone lashed her.

"I had a frightening nightmare and couldn't go back to sleep. I love rainstorms, and figured the worst of the storm was leagues away. I went outside to watch it approach, but it came faster than I expected. I got scared and couldn't move. I'm thankful Nathaniel saw me."

His scowl started to fade, and she could see he mulled over her answer. She'd better not linger too long, else he'd start picking holes in her story. She hopped off the chest, tripped on the corner of the blanket and landed on her hands and knees.

With a loud, huffed sigh, he hooked one arm around her

waist and stood her on her feet. "Mayhap I insulted chickens. Chickens have more dignity."

The storm passed, leaving a soggy dawn. Throughout the day, Damron watched Brianna's brooding face. The sooner she learned to be a proper wife, the easier it would be for her.

Eric sidled his steed close to Angel, who snapped at the other horse's ears.

"I take my leave of you here. Ah, Damron. I envy you your pleasure in your wife. You had best be discreet, else sparks will fly should she learn of your leman."

"Ye tempt me to rid ye of yer manhood, Eric."

"Dinna think it. I would add to mine own family." He raised his hand in farewell and waited until Brianna pulled alongside them. Quick as a fox snaring a chicken, he leaned over to grasp Brianna's face in his big hands and, with a roguish grin at Damron, kissed her on the lips.

Before Damron could react, Eric wheeled his mount and led his men at a hard gallop back down the path. His laughter floated above the pounding of the horse's hooves.

"My lord, I seek a boon."

Rollo, Eric's cousin, pulled his warhorse close. His blond hair and blue eyes accented his Danish ancestry, the single trait they had in common.

"I ha'e planned to wed for some time, but the lass isna of my village. I must steal her away."

Eric quirked his left brow. "Does the lady favor your suit?"

"She acts coy, but she will be content with her lot. After I have bedded her, she willna hesitate to wed."

Eric frowned at this hint that mayhap the lass was not willing. E'en so, 'twas the way of their world. Women's feelings were of no import, for they did not last. Once you showed them the way of it, they soon resigned themselves and were grateful.

"Begone, then, but dinna harm the lass." As Rollo and his men rode off in a westerly direction, Eric rubbed his jaw and watched them till they rounded a bend out of sight.

Just as the sun started its descent, Damron's scouts found an ideal spot to bide the night. The area was beautiful. The grass was so thick even a horse could walk quietly. Pines scented the air as sweet as a balsam forest in Maine.

Spencer led Brianna to a waterfall surrounded on all sides with dense pines, green oak and birch trees. The earth had formed the falls in four levels. Water cascaded from one plateau to the next, and the last was a flat shelf about twenty feet wide. From there the water filled a large natural basin.

After Spencer left, Brianna took her time to enjoy the beautiful setting as she undressed. The last of her clothing fell. Throwing her head back, she inhaled and savored the pines' scent, then stretched and studied the water. It was clear. She didn't see any rocks or submerged debris. She dove into the pool and swam along the bottom.

What bliss to swim in such a lovely setting. She broke the surface to take a breath. Had something moved behind the falls? She dog paddled while squinting her nearsighted eyes, but decided it was her imagination.

Her body arched, and she again dove deep. Though the water was cold, it was refreshing. On the next stroke, she drew her arms back and headed for the surface. The water's current changed, rippled up her back as she darted upward. Something other than she had disturbed it.

Fear struck when hands circled her waist and pulled her deeper beneath the water. A man's hard, muscular legs brushed against hers. She kicked and thrashed, and tried to break away. His hands gripped all the harder. Desperate for air, she pried at calloused fingers, tried to break his grip. Sunlight filtered through the water and revealed fawn-colored hair that swirled and merged with her own brown. He gave several strong kicks, and they sliced through the water toward the surface.

Brianna's face broke free. She gasped and tried to scream. He clasped a hand over her mouth and, holding tight to her, swam to the opposite bank. She fought as he pulled her from the water. Another man came to throw a blanket over her. Before she could get her balance, they had secured it tightly around her.

She screamed as loud as she could. Someone lifted and threw her face down across hard thighs. An arm snaked around her waist.

"Blessed Lucifer, ye have smiled on me today," a man exulted.

High above the camp, Cloud Dancer screeched. Damron, Bleddyn and the men ran hard. They burst from the forest in time to see horsemen disappear into the trees on the opposite side of the falls. When squires brought their mounts, they raced in hot pursuit.

As the distance closed between them, Damron shouted a battle cry. Bleddyn and Connor attacked the first two men while Damron streaked past. The third man swung his mount, trying to block his path. Damron's sword whipped up and out. Their weapons clashed. They were well matched. In one desperate swing, Damron found an opening beneath his opponent's chin. Blood spurted, splattering Damron and speckling Angel's white coat. Before the body toppled from the horse, Damron urged Angel to a gallop.

Cloud Dancer dove toward his target. Only the man's swift reflexes kept the eagle's talons from tearing the hood from his head and ripping into his scalp. He drew his double-edged dagger and grasped it upright.

Slung across his lap, Brianna twisted her head back and

forth until she found an opening and uncovered her mouth. She stretched her jaws wide and bit down hard on the man's thigh.

"I will make ye sorry for that," he snarled. His hand closed around her neck and cut off her air.

She released him, and thrashed around trying to dislodge his hand. His fingers eased their pressure, but pressed enough in silent warning.

When Cloud Dancer swooped low, his blade was ready. The eagle veered and threw off the knife's aim. He turned to search out the eagle's intended flight, but another sight surely chilled his soul. Damron gained on him, the maniacal look on his face leaving no doubt of his intent. The man could not escape with her, but he could save his own neck. He lifted her in his arms and drew the blanket back, baring her face.

"I will yet have ye! Wait for me, and remember me by this." He lowered his head. His open mouth came close.

Brianna could see only his nose and lips lifted in a snarl over crooked, rotted teeth. His breath near gagged her. Thinking he meant to kiss her, she clamped her lips closed. His hot, wet tongue glided along her jaw. Fiery pain of teeth piercing her skin shocked her. She screamed. When he released her, his tongue rasped over the wounds to lap the blood welling there.

Brianna gasped. Before the next scream tore from her throat, he tossed her from his lap. She landed on a bush, then rolled to the center of the trampled path.

The thunder of approaching horses did not mute Damron's bellow of rage as Brianna hurtled to the ground. Great clods of dirt flew as Angel reared and pawed the air. Damron forced the great horse to move to the side. When his hooves struck the dirt, their thud jarred the ground. Damron vaulted from the destrier and braced his body over his wife, protecting her as his men galloped near.

Bleddyn and Connor were already hauling back on the reins as they turned the corner, for Cloud Dancer had trilled a warning. Beside Brianna on the grass, Damron rose to his knees. Connor yelled orders for Malcolm, commander of Brianna's original guards, to stay as Connor and the warriors raced through the dense forest. Connor followed Cloud Dancer's lead to capture the last man.

Brianna lay sprawled on her stomach. When Bleddyn's knife ripped through the blanket to expose her back, they saw her fair skin already bruising. He reached to run his hands over her flesh, but Damron grasped his wrist to hold him from touching her.

"I am a healer." Bleddyn's voice was calm.

Damron released him and watched as Bleddyn felt her backbone, her neck, shoulders and each of her limbs. When assured nothing was broken, he rolled her into Damron's arms.

Blood covered Bleddyn's fingers. Damron's heart lurched. Upon spying Brianna's savaged jaw, his stomach churned. Bleddyn wiped the blood away, revealing the teeth marks.

"Afore I have the pleasure of gutting him, I will find this bastard and set my wolf, Guardian, to him. He will feel the fangs of a demon as bestial as he. I vow this afore God."

As Damron talked, Bleddyn took a small vial of white fluid from a pouch hanging from his saddle. He soaked the puncture wounds, for such wounds festered quickly. After making certain she had sustained no major injuries, they wrapped her in Damron's cloak and carried her back to camp.

Each time Brianna moaned, Damron flinched. His hands shook. Upon reaching the camp, he carried her into the tent and placed her on the pallet.

Bleddyn retrieved his herbal pouch from the saddle and followed Damron into the tent. "Malcolm, fetch as much of your Scottish whiskey as the men might have. Set it inside the tent flap."

As they tended her, the ugly imprint of a man's fingers darkened her neck. Her jaw swelled, red with heat. The Welshman blended crushed leaves in hot water and stirred the potion until it cooled. Damron lifted her head while Bleddyn dribbled tea laced with feverfew into her mouth. Gently, he stroked her throat until she swallowed.

Bleddyn murmured to her in Gaelic. When she blinked and opened her eyes, they flashed with fear. He moved so she could see his face. The fear vanished.

"Hold her firmly," he whispered, and reached for the jug of whiskey at the tent opening. Damron anchored her head to his knees. Bleddyn poured whiskey over her jaw and the ugly gouges on her neck from the lout's fingernails. She cried out, her voice hoarse, then went limp. Taking advantage of her faint, Bleddyn cleaned each wound with more whiskey and packed a poultice made from calendula petals over it. If the wound healed well, it would reduce the scars that would forever be with her, for he had no needles fine enough to stitch a lady's face.

Damron remained by her side. When the warriors returned, he ordered Malcolm to search the dead abductors for any clues as to whom they had pledged their loyalty.

Malcolm found they had recently shaved off their beards to hide their identity. They had no jewelry, or items with any markings. Even their weapons were unmarked. Damron ordered the warriors to toss the bodies into a ravine.

Never before had Damron denied a Christian burial to an enemy. But these men had not been worthy opponents.

They had dared harm his wife.

Bleddyn watched the sky for Cloud Dancer. When the eagle called, the mystic whistled, and his arm lifted. With a great flapping of wings, the eagle landed on his forearm. High whistles trilled between the two, and when Bleddyn pointed to the tree that loomed over the tent, the eagle flew off to perch on the branches. His eyes searched all that moved.

"The hunted one hid himself. He escaped into the densest part of the forest where he could not be seen from the air," Bleddyn told Damron.

"God's wrath," Damron shouted. "Ye said ye knew when danger threatened Brianna. What happened to your all-knowing gift of warning?" Damron's voice was near a snarl. He was furious that he had placed any belief in Bleddyn's powers.

"The raiding party was here afore we arrived. I could not sense their leader, for the roar of the waterfall covered his thoughts."

Damron regretted not giving Brianna time to recover, but they would best be served by leaving the next morn. The whoreson who harmed her was likely from this area and might return with more men. Damron would not give him the chance.

Bleddyn coaxed a potion of strong whiskey and sweet herbs down Brianna's throat. Soon her body stilled its tremors, and she slept quietly.

In the darkest hours of the night, Brianna started to talk. "You're never here for my birthdays, Gordon. Please, love. You promised. I planned a special day with you," Brianna cried out. She began to sob.

Lucifer's tarse! Who was this bastard Gordon? How many men had she loved? Damron wanted to pummel someone. He clamped his teeth together and wiped her face with a wet cloth. Her eyes were open. Her gaze followed this unseen Gordon. She seemed to listen, too.

"You break your promises. Yet you swear you love me." Tears streaked her face.

Damron clenched his teeth. His hand holding the cool cloth stopped its motion.

"I laced the brew with poppy. Brianna is unaware of what

she says." Bleddyn handed Damron another wet cloth. "The person to whom she speaks is but a dream in her mind."

The Welshman's matter-of-fact air soothed Damron's ire. Until she began to whimper and thrash about.

"You made me come. I know it's my fault, but please, send me back." She cried out as she stared up at him, seeming to know him.

"Ne'er will I return ye. Ye will always be mine," Damron vowed. He did not understand his violent reaction to her plea to return to the abbey. His arms went under her to lift her onto his lap. "Ne'er again beg me to release ye," he added, his tone harsh.

Great, ragged sobs tore from her throat past her swollen jaw. Watching the agony her sobbing caused, low growls of protest burst from Damron's lips.

"Jesu, mystic. Give her somethin' afore she harms herself further."

Bleddyn prepared a potion and coaxed her to drink. When Damron heard what the mystic crooned to her, his hand flew up ready to grab Bleddyn's neck and throttle him.

"Gordon is faithful and awaits you, *mo maise*." At the growl curling from Damron's throat, Bleddyn shook his head. Brianna's lips tilted in a smile, and her eyelids eased shut.

"Ye call Brianna 'my beauty' and 'my pretty,' but she is not yers. She is *mine*. Ye tell her she will return to another love, but I will cut his heart out should she try."

"Brianna has been my beauty, my pretty, from the day she was born. She needs the security of total love now, for she has no Alana, no father, no Galan, aunts or uncles to make her secure. Only I am here to give her love. The poppy makes her see and hear things which are not there. Her mind gives her a love to hold to."

The depth of his own feelings stunned Damron. From the moment he knew of Brianna's danger, he wanted to kill. When the whoreson injured her, a powerful need to not only kill but to do so slowly, agonizingly, gripped him. Now, the pain she suffered tore his heart; her grief and longing for this Gordon tore his mind. Was it truly imaginings from the poppy? The thought that she could so deeply love another that it brought her such terrible distress rent his soul, his being.

Brianna awoke the next morn with a driving headache, and a body that felt run over by a train. She heard Damron's movements as he prepared for the day's travel.

"How fare ye this day, wife?" His voice was gruff, but the hand smoothing her hair was gentle. "After we have tended yer wounds, we will hasten from this accursed place."

"Please. Don't shout. My head pounds something awful." Her words slurred, for she could barely move her jaw without sending hot shards of pain through her face and bruised neck.

Bleddyn tucked the blanket around her before he helped her to sit. He brought the hot tea laced with feverfew to her lips, for the herb was also a remedy for headaches. Waiting until she drank the tea, he examined and redressed her wounds. None showed angry streaks of infection.

"Brianna, tell me what ye know of yer assailant." Damron's voice was impatient, cold even.

"My lord, I saw no one. I was swimming toward the surface when he grabbed my waist, taking me deeper. Once, I thought long hair mixed with mine. It could have been something in the water. It was light. Blond? When he took me from the water, they wrapped me in a blanket."

"Be there aught else, wife?" Damron probed.

"He was naked beneath his cloak. When he fought Cloud Dancer, I bit his thigh. He squeezed my neck until I opened my mouth." She shuddered, remembering his nasty taste.

"What else, my lady?"

"He said, 'I will yet have ye,' and to wait and remember

him by this. His teeth were jagged, rotted. His breath stank when he bit my jaw."

Damron bolted to his feet and went to stare out the tent opening. After long moments, he turned back to her and helped her dress. When done, he carried her to Malcolm, who waited atop his horse with a blanket across his lap. Without a word, Damron handed her up to the waiting warrior.

"See ye cushion her, and that yer mount's gait is smooth," Damron cautioned and started to turn away.

"My lord, can't I . . .?" she began, but he held up his hand.

"Ye will do as I say. Ye canna ride alone. I must be free to battle should the whoreson plan an ambush." He whirled and left.

They had not gone a league before Brianna grew drowsy and slept. She didn't fully awaken until they stopped to water the horses. After a short time, Damron handed her to another man. She looked at the Scotsman and held her breath. His name was Hector. According to Eric, the warrior thought water would make him sicken, lose his sanity and, most important, render his rod forever flaccid.

Noting his wet hair and clean-shaven face, she took a deep breath. His shirt smelled of drying in the sun, and he had changed his tartan for breeches. She tried to smile. Hector grinned and began to tell her amusing tales of growing up with the men at Blackthorn Castle. He was a great teller of tales. She steadied her jaw when she giggled. They rode for some time, and soon her eyes drifted closed.

For several days they followed the Cromarty Firth north to Ardgay. The mountains were easy to climb, not being of a great height. They kept to the valleys when possible. Brianna enjoyed the full Scots pines, junipers and less abundant yew trees.

Early one morn, she awoke to find Damron's feet mere

inches from her face. Her gaze traveled up over him. He was elegantly attired with a blue-black shirt. He had pulled the last yards of his plaid up over his shoulder and pinned it with the Morgan badge. The scent of sandalwood and spices made her take a deep breath. Spencer had again braided Damron's midnight-black hair at his temples.

Her gaze searched his face. Raw desire flashed in his eyes. Wondering what caused his interest, she glanced down to see why he studied her pillow.

She had dropped it. The neckline of her sleeping garment gaped and bared her breasts, their rosy nipples upright, begging attention.

With a strangled gasp, she covered herself.

"'Twould please me, wife, if ye would dress in all possible speed." He left the tent.

When she joined him outside, he held the plaid she had worn when first they left Ridley. He draped it around her waist and across her shoulder and secured it with the silver brooch he had given her as her morning gift.

She did not have long to wonder what was special about this day. An ear-shattering series of cries that sounded like evil spirits escaping purgatory split the air as men crashed through the trees.

"Blessed Saint Edgar," she whispered.

Never had she seen such a display of dirty bodies, bare limbs, unkept hair and beards full of tangles. Here and there, a man with a smidgen of pride wore a tartan that covered his masculine attributes. Others had donned skimpy loincloths. Her face heated. She averted her gaze from men so careless their nether parts peeked from too short a covering. Damron's hard scowl sent many a hand down to hide what they had assumed was already hidden.

"'Tis men from my outlying lands, wife. Dinna let them think ye affrighted," Damron murmured, then introduced her.

They studied her bruised face, no doubt wondering what manner of woman required discipline when so newly wed.

The men banged their swords against their shields and bellowed, "A Morgan." It was a frightful din. As she drew close to Angel, he bumped her shoulder with his head. Without thinking, she cuffed the brute lightly on his thick skull.

"Don't make me have to hurt you," she warned. She was sure Angel knew it was a game they played.

Spencer grinned and interpreted her comment to the clansmen on their small Highland horses, and they stared wide-eyed at her. No doubt they wouldn't get close to the huge warhorse, much less threaten their lord's steed. Damron's lips twitched, but he kept his stern expression.

They rode northward, fording a stream at the end of Loch Loyal. They entered the pass between Ben Loyal and Ben Stumanadh, where Damron called a halt for Brianna to refresh herself. They would soon reach the Kyle of Tongue, the narrow strait of Tongue Bay where Blackthorn Castle stood. It loomed on a hill overlooking the inlet on the eastern shore, halfway in the strait.

Damron motioned his piper to the forefront. They passed over the crest of a hill and out of the deep woods, where the land gently rose for miles. The green forests ended at a village, all neatly spread out with fields and lush pastures behind the huts.

On a span of land that ran north and south, parallel to the bay's inlet, the castle rose. Tongue Bay cut into the western ridge and formed river cliffs protecting the castle from attack. The rectangular keep sat in the middle of the cleared area, with a walled bailey on either side. Curtain walls surrounded the castle and grounds. To the north, they followed the cliff outline, and to the east was a steep valley.

Brianna's heart raced. This castle was imprinted on her heart and soul, both with love and fear. In the twenty-first century, she had spent many months over the years exploring its ruins. Nothing she had imagined had prepared her for the vastness of the castle she saw before her.

Damron signaled the piper to ride ahead before he urged Angel forward. Brianna kept pace at his side. When the castle lookouts spotted the standard bearer and heard the first skirls of the bagpipe, Blackthorn's pipers atop the battlement joined in with welcome.

While they climbed the steep trail to the castle's entrance, the massive portcullis rose, creaking and clanging. The castle entrance was a pointed arch through the curtain, with an outer gatehouse. A rounded tower stood to the right of it, another at the end corner of the curtain wall.

The walkways of the battlements swarmed with men on either side of the pipers. One piper appeared to be a slender youth. Lusty signal cries rose from Damron and Connor's throats. The sound was so forceful she could hear them above the scream of the pipes. The slender piper echoed the cry.

Thrills of excitement went through Brianna on hearing the horses' hooves clattering over the wooden bridge. Though in the future most of the castle had been in ruins, the drawbridge and gatehouse had been much the same. Riding through the confining entrance, she studied the slits in the sides made for archers, and the murder holes on the ceiling above. When they came out into the bailey, she saw people awaited them at the foot of the steps to the keep.

The massive door burst open. A tall, beautiful woman picked up her skirts and dashed down the steps, evading hands reaching to halt her progress.

Brianna studied the woman hurtling toward them. Not one iota of doubt entered her mind about the woman's identity. She was Damron's leman.

Her hair was blond, long and straight, pulled back and se-cured to better show her features. Her face was the color of pale porcelain, with ice-blue eyes and lips thin and small. She wore a sheer white smock with long, trailing sleeves under a dark red tunic trimmed in gold. The tunic was cut so daringly low over full breasts, that her pink nipples threatened to burst free.

Never before had Brianna felt inadequate. Even after marrying Gordon, she'd had more admirers than she had cared for, and felt they were a nuisance. Now, with her face bruised and hurting, and after traveling by horseback over God knows how many miles, she knew her appearance was not at its best. She wished she was close enough to trip the damned woman into the nearest mud hole.

Damron slid from Angel's back. The woman flung her arms around his neck, and pressed herself so tight against him she'd have to crawl inside his shirt to be more intimate. He steadied himself, but made no move to embrace her.

Her lips locked tight on Damron's.

Chapter 13

The courtyard was as quiet as snow falling on a deserted mountaintop. Before anyone could aid her, Brianna gritted her teeth and dismounted with as much grace as she could muster. In seconds, she reached Damron, and the woman clinging to him like a leech.

"Am I to assume this is a member of your extended family, my lord husband, or are you about to introduce me to a *longtime* friend?" Brianna kept her voice calm and smooth, but her gaze flashed over the two with icy regard.

Freeing himself from the woman's arms, Damron cleared his throat. "My lady wife, I present to ye Lady Asceline de Monceaux of King William's court. As ye surmised, a special friend from Normandy. Lady Asceline, my wife, Lady Brianna."

"I see." Anger buzzed in Brianna's veins. She had her answer now. He was like Gordon. Short on honor. Along with anger was disappointment. Grief, even. Much as if she had learned of a loved one's tragedy.

Before she could say more, the young piper launched himself at Damron. A glimpse of shapely buttocks showed Brianna the longhaired piper was no man.

"Ye great gowk! Ye did not make a smart beginnin' by greetin' yer doxy afore ye introduce yer wife." Light green eyes and a broad forehead were above a wide, generous mouth. Had her eyes been brown, she would have appeared Connor's twin.

Brianna stepped forward. "Since Damron is otherwise occupied, I'm Brianna Sinclair. I take it you are Connor's sister?"

"Brianna Morgan, wife," Damron's voice was strained. "And, aye, this is my cousin Meghan."

Brianna ignored him.

Meghan squinted her eyes and studied Brianna. An explosion of Gaelic burst from her lips, before she whirled on Damron. "Ye eejit. Have ye no decency in yer great, lumbering body?" Her fist whipped up to cuff Damron on the shoulder, hard. He didn't budge.

"'Tis not as ye think, henny." Connor clamped Meghan's arms to her side. "A lout abducted Lady Brianna. 'Tis he who harmed her. Damron isna responsible."

"Aye. He is. He should have taken better care of her."

Without words, Damron shouldered Meghan aside and turned to a stately older woman. She stood white-faced, her eyes shooting sparks at Damron.

"I am Damron's mother, Phillipa." Her arms enveloped Brianna in a gentle hug. "I am most pleased to greet you, daughter."

"And I you, milady," Brianna responded. Sensing Nathaniel's presence behind her, she introduced him as a prince of Wales.

Thankfully, Lady Phillipa's graceful greetings eased tensions, and they turned to enter the keep.

Brianna eyed the formidable number of steps leading to the second-floor entrance. Wooden stairs led to a landing, and the next series of steps ended at great wooden doors. The last time she had stood before the castle entrance, the steps had led up to a shell of what the castle had once been. Now, her heart pounded in anticipation.

As they entered the great hall, Brianna's gaze darted from one end of the massive room to the other. Brightly colored banners hung from the ceiling. One wall was near covered with semicircles of broadswords and short swords, a row of maces of all kinds, shields and spears. A large tapestry depicting the castle and grounds brightened the wall behind the dais holding the lord's table. Fresh rushes covered the floor, and as they walked, the scents of rose, thyme and rosemary drifted on the air.

"Meghan, who will think you a lady if one cannot tell you from a warrior?" Lady Phillipa scolded. She smiled at Brianna. "Meghan is oft called the Warrior Woman of Blackthorn. She is as skilled as many of our soldiers, if not more so."

Damron, his brows drawn near together and his jaw firmed in a hard line, eyed Meghan. "Lass, are ye hidin' yer curves to steal outside the walls to meet someone ye should not?"

"Nay, 'tis not so. I have been long in the castle, tryin' to do as Aunt Phillipa asked. But what I worked on has not come out like what I planned in my mind."

"If it looked like what was in your mind, you are a bairn," Asceline snickered.

"What are ye talkin' about?" Damron's eyes narrowed.

"When we received word that you were to wed, Meghan designed and stitched a tapestry to celebrate the event," Lady Phillipa began.

"Look at this disgrace," the Frenchwoman interrupted with a triumphant look. She threw her arms wide, the offending tapestry gripped in her hands.

Brianna's lips spread in a delighted smile, and Damron's lips twitched at the corners, ruining his stern expression. The tapestry was done in brilliant colors. Trees in various shades of green made up the background with a trail leading from them. A brilliant blue sky with fluffy clouds was at the top, and along the right side was a sparkling brook. Everything was beautifully done except the people and horses. They were stick figures. By the colors of the hair, she saw what Meghan meant to be Damron and his new bride, along with Connor, riding on the path.

"It's wonderful. It's colorful and lovely. I'd be happy to have it where I can see it each morning." Brianna pried the tapestry from Asceline's long fingers and turned to hug Meghan.

"Come, Brianna, I will show ye to yer room so ye may wash the grime away." Meghan grinned and hurried Brianna from the room and up the stairs into a bright chamber. "This is Damron's room. The men have brought up yer trunks and Mari here is to be yer lady's maid."

Mari smiled warmly after her first shocked expression upon noting Brianna's injuries.

"I'm sorry for your trouble, Mari, but I won't be sharing Lord Damron's room. A small one close by will suffice." Before she could turn, Damron's voice spoke behind them. The man was near kin to a giant, yet how did he walk so quietly?

"That willna be necessary, Mari. Ye may leave." Damron jerked his head at Meghan, and the two women left, closing the door quietly. He crossed his arms and stared at Brianna.

"You lecherous, caterwauling tomcat," Brianna hurled the words at him. "I'm not sleeping in this room while *she* is in this keep." Never would she put up with a man who was unfaithful. The anguish of Gordon's betrayal had taught her not to let her heart, her dignity be torn to shreds again.

"Ye will share the room, and ye will share that bed with me." Damron eyed her sternly. "Dinna blather about it!"

"Blather? You haven't heard blather before. You can sleep elsewhere. You sure as the devil aren't going to crawl into bed with me after being in one with her."

"I will be in this bed with ye every night. Dinna think to demand I live as a monk when ye deny me yer body." His glare shot sparks at her. "Be on yer best behavior if ye dinna wish to feel the flat of my hand on yer skinny arse. As for my leman, she is no concern of yers." The door slammed behind him on his last words.

Fortunately, the walls were too thick for him to hear the futuristic curses she yelled.

* * *

Damron near knocked Asceline over, for she lurked outside the doorway, awaiting him.

"How came ye here from Normandy afore I sent for ye?" Damron shoved her ahead of him up the circular stairway to her room above. He kicked the door shut with his heel.

Asceline whirled, and her mouth clamped onto his. Her tongue plunged boldly while her hips ground against his groin, for she was a tall woman. When he responded, her hand moved between them. It was only seconds afore she had what she sought: Damron's tarse free from beneath his tartan and hard as a lance. She tugged, greedy. Blood roared in his ears as she cupped his throbbing ballocks and squeezed.

"Bitch!" He shoved her from him and straightened his tartan. "Ye have not answered why ye came here on yer own."

"You know you can never go overlong without sharing my bed." Asceline toyed with the bodice of her gown, deliberately baring the tip of one breast. "This marriage to the scrawny Saxon was not of your liking," she said as she thumbed her pink nipple. "Only I can satisfy your needs."

Remembering how she satisfied his needs, Damron's tarse heated and bucked. His tongue darted out and moistened his lips. He could not take his gaze off the swollen nipple that jutted out at him. Inviting him. His knees brushed hers, and his hand reached to grasp her full breast. He realized what he was about to do and cursed, low and furious. Filled with self-loathing, he turned and slammed out of the room.

Asceline brought out the worst in him. He had not meant for her to come to him. He well knew he should not have his leman housed with his wife. Truth to tell, he did not want her here. When he had seen to all that needed his tending at Blackthorn, and he could spare the men to escort her, he would decide where she should bide. Until then, they would have to make the best of it.

As Damron heard his granda's irritated bellows, his stride lengthened. He entered the room at the end of the landing to find Laird Douglas propped up on pillows, dark shadows beneath his eyes.

"Dinna think I will forget what I ha'e heard of ye," the laird said as Damron hugged him. "I would not blame the lass if she kicks ye from her bed, with ye greetin yer doxy afore her eyes."

"Dinna yammer about my leman. Brianna will learn it has naught to do with her. I will have my pleasures, and I will have my heirs. They need not be from the same field."

Being in this room was like stepping back in time, for it never changed. Animal hides covered the window openings, rushes were strewn on the floor and furs on the bed. Damron settled in to talk over the problems awaiting his return to Blackthorn. Though he had been gone two months, nothing more serious than raiding cattle had occurred. His men had retaliated, and what had been taken from Blackthorn was replaced from the raiders' own stock. He shook his head on hearing Meghan had led several of the forays.

Not many seconds after Damron had slammed out of the room, Meghan came back to be with Brianna. They talked while Brianna brushed the dust from her hair and freshened her clothing. She was delighted with the high-spirited and assertive Meghan. In the past hour, Brianna answered and asked so many questions her head was spinning. She was anxious to meet the "Old One," as Meghan called her grandfather with much affection. Brianna sat in the middle of the bed with her legs crossed, her hair tumbling in unruly curls, which hid most of her bruised face.

"Laird Douglas awaits, if ye can manage to act the lady and not a troublesome imp." Damron's voice was heavy with sarcasm as he thrust open the door.

"Bring the bonnie lassies and be quick aboot it," Laird Douglas bellowed from his room.

"Dinna fash him by delayin' us." Meghan made a face at Damron as she grabbed Brianna's hand to sprint with her down the dark corridor.

Brianna looked about her when she entered the room, taking in the burning peat, the covered windows, the furs and stale rushes. Her gaze met the deep blue eyes of the man who studied her with the same curiosity. His white hair and beard, sprinkled with black, were long and shaggy.

"How do you do, Lord Douglas? I am Brianna Sinclair."

"Brianna *Morgan,* wife," Damron interrupted to remind her for the second time.

"Come. Let me greet ye properly." Lord Douglas motioned her to sit beside him. He stared into her eyes and examined her face, his rough hands gently brushing aside her hair.

"Yer bruises will soon disappear, but these crescent marks on yer jaw will always remain." He patted her on the shoulder. "Why did he bite ye, granddaughter? A man usually sinks his teeth in a softer spot beneath yer clothes where only a bench can see."

"I couldn't free my hands, sir, so I had to use my teeth. I bit his thigh." She scowled, then muttered. "I hope his leg festers and spreads to rot off his male parts."

Damron's jaw dropped. Meghan hooted and pointed at his stunned face. The laird started laughing and coughing, then fell back, exhausted. Brianna jumped up and smoothed back his hair.

"We have overtired you, sir. May Lord Bleddyn and I attend you after the evening meal? He is a highly skilled healer. You'll like him very much. Come, we'll let you rest now." She motioned for Meghan and Damron to follow her.

Damron's brow quirked, no doubt questioning her nerve to

give orders. She shrugged and called over her shoulder as she went through the doorway, "I'll see you later, Papa Dougie."

"Ye dinna call the head of the family by such a name." Damron eased the door closed behind them "He is milord or Grandfather, not this 'Papa Dougie.'"

"I'll call him what I want, with his permission." She quickened her steps when she saw Connor and Bleddyn lingered at the head of the stairwell to accompany them to the evening meal.

Damron led Brianna to sit on his left at the table, with his mother on her other side. As each person reached their position, he introduced them to Brianna.

He frowned when Asceline smirked and wedged herself onto the bench on his right. She wore a low-cut tunic revealing the tips of her full breasts whenever she leaned toward him. His tarse stirred in remembrance.

Never had Damron been so tense at a meal while sitting between two beautiful women. He strove to ignore his leman's attempts to draw his attentions as they dined. By meal's end, when servants set bowls of apples and grapes alongside platters of cheese, the tight muscles in his neck had led to a pounding headache. He kept his face impassive as Asceline's hand slid over his thigh, then searched farther to clutch his tarse through his clothing and squeeze. His sex surged and bucked. He grasped her wrist in a steely grip and forced her hand away.

Asceline's hair flowed free, and her clothing looked rumpled. He could smell his own scent of sandalwood on her as she flounced about, angry. Brianna stiffened beside him. He heard the hiss of her indrawn breath.

When Brianna rose to excuse herself and Bleddyn, Damron rose when his wife did. Though he tried to cover his obvious state of arousal, she noted it.

Brianna ignored him and took Bleddyn's arm, then beckoned

Damron's squire to her. "Spencer, would you please grant me a favor?" she asked sweetly. "The Lady Asceline does not seem to have access to a bath. It would be a favor to everyone if you would provide her with hot water and strong soap. Surely a randy goat visited her, for she reeks with his scent."

Asceline shrieked. Meghan burst out laughing. Damron glared at his cousin, warning her to silence.

"A wolf is within about whom I have heard," Nathaniel warned Brianna as they approached Laird Douglas's room. "His name is Guardian. He will seek to frighten you with his bluster."

When they entered, Guardian sprang to his feet, bared his teeth and snarled ferociously. When he spied Brianna, he came slowly off the bed, his body low to the floor as he stalked her.

"Guardian? He's named as a guardian angel, isn't he?" She looked at Laird Douglas, who nodded with a smile. "Stay," she commanded the wolf and pointed to the ground. The animal advanced another step. "I said stay, you miserable heap of fleas." Before the beast knew what was happening, she tugged hard on the fur at the ruff of his neck. "When I speak, you obey," she ordered and pressed down on his haunches. His eyes looked startled. "Don't you growl at me again. I've enough trouble without a flea-bitten beast adding more." Guardian whimpered, his tongue lolled and adoration spread on his face. She nodded and turned from him.

"Hello, Papa Dougie. Do you mind the name?" She was pleased when he grinned and shook his head. "This is Lord Bleddyn, a great healer. He has prepared a potion to ease your cough."

"I wud like the name ye give me, but I dinna want potions of bat dung, snail slime or goat's piss if that be yer remedy. I will no' swallow anythin' comin' from critters' nether ends."

"Laird, I have used the juices of onions, carrots and parsley. 'Tis most agreeable and will give you much needed rest."

"I will try it. If 'tis better than the potions Phillipa makes, I will not be mad." He sniffed the potion. "Pleasant." He took a sip and nodded with satisfaction. "Tastes right good. Now get ye to yer room, Brianna, afore my grandson comes lookin' fer ye. I would talk with this healer of yers." He winked at her as he made a shooing motion with his hand.

Brianna kissed his cheek and turned to pet Guardian. She took his chin in her hand and rubbed his head as she whispered, "We will be friends and have a good time together." The gray and white wolf licked her fingers, before she left the room.

Meghan awaited Brianna in her chamber when she returned. A weapons chest, banded with steel studs and straps, stood against the wall to the left of the door. A large bed was on the outside wall, with two large shuttered windows, with window seats, opening above the inner courtyard. A washstand with the essentials was on the wall to the right. Above the fireplace hung a tapestry depicting hunting dogs killing a stag. It was done in such realistic detail, Brianna could feel the pain of the hunted, smell the blood and hear the gnashing of the hounds' teeth.

"No way am I going to see that scene every morning," she said. "Come, Meghan, help me take it down." She and Meghan pulled the table to the fireplace and put a chair on top. While Meghan held the chair steady, Brianna removed the tapestry.

"There, and good riddance," she said as she tossed the offensive tapestry backwards. She heard it land against something solid and turned to see it flapping over Damron's head, its rod bouncing against his back. As he fought to be rid of it, dust puffed in the air. His head finally emerged, and he glared menacingly at them. Brianna wobbled, the chair gyrated, and she threw her arms up to steady herself.

Damron gave a gigantic sneeze and raced to catch her.

Brianna toppled backwards yelling, "Ohhh, shit!" She landed in his arms.

"I have no doot ye are the gawkiest henny in all of Scotland, England and Wales for ye have no more grace than a Heeland coo. Does either of ye have a brain in yer heids?"

"Brains aren't in hides. When I got in trouble, my papa always said, 'If you had a brain you'd take it out and play with it.' Hm. We both have very good brains, though. I'm sure of it."

"Will ye tell me what ye were doin', and why ye did not call for help from someone with more sense?"

"You talk about missing brains? A child can see we're changing the tapestries. I didn't know the danged thing would be so hard to get off. It's been there for a century. Huh! Why anyone wanted to look at something so unsettling is beyond me."

"By Christ's cross! That *danged, unsettlin' thing* as ye call it was made by my great-grannie Elspeth. She loved the hunt." His cheeks twitched. "Now I think on it, I spied her more than once wringing a chicken's neck. She seemed to enjoy it. She was quite old. We did eat a lot of chicken for meals. Enough of this yammerin'. Give me Meg's tapestry and I will hang it."

Brianna and Meghan hid behind her tapestry, biting their lips, while they fixed it on the rod, then handed it to him. When he finished, he ordered his cousin to bed and put the furniture back in place. Brianna watched as he placed a fist-sized rock on the mantelpiece. She raised her brow at him.

"I deem 'tis best I display the rock that split yer head to bring to mind yer forever fallin' and totterin' about. The sweet Lord only knows how ye survived past a nursling." Damron paused. "This Saxon word shit. 'Tis the same as shite?"

"Why would you think so? They are nothing alike."

"Did it not come from yer lips? Though ye quibble, I have added one to yer total. When ye reach the limit I will allow, the rock will be on yer pillow. Ye will then prepare yerself."

"Allow? Limit? Prepare for what? Not that I'm worried, mind you." He couldn't be serious, could he?

"Ten. On yer arse. Ye will be well served to think afore ye speak. I rule with a firm hand on the reins."

"Reins! Now I'm a horse?" Brianna smiled sweetly up into his eyes. "You, husband, are a humongous knucklehead."

"Are ye cursin' me in strange words, wife?" he demanded. "I wud have an explanation now, or yer total will overflow!"

"Lord husband, humongous but points out your well-muscled body. As for knucklehead, your men say you have a splendidly hard head immune to the rap of knuckles. It's a wonderful feature. My own is soft and forever getting dented." Brianna watched frowns flitting across his face as he mulled over her words. "My lord, don't worry. I'm not pulling your leg," she added and smiled.

"Of course ye are not pullin' my leg. Ye are not touchin' me." He squinted, studying her. "Did ye e'er suffer blows to yer head afore ye fell from yer horse?"

"There's nothing the matter with my head. The place I come from has different expressions which you haven't heard. Now, let's get back to the subject. Well?"

"Well, what? What subject? Ye talk in circles like a daft creature. What are ye talkin' about?"

"Allow and total. Does that ring your bell?"

"Ring a bell? Why wud I ring a bell?" he yelled. "The total is five, not worth the effort till it reaches ten. One for each finger. That will leave a lasting impression on yer scrawny arse. At the rate ye are goin', the total may be a breath away."

"Five? It can't be five." She put her hands on her hips and glowered at him. "You cheated, adding extra points over nothing."

"I added two each for yer attempts to lie about friggin' and crap, and another for arguin' about the lie. Five," he yelled.

"Must I remind ye of yer word tonight? 'Tis now six. Get ye to bed afore I deem 'tis now worth the effort."

"You'd better call Spencer for a pallet." Brianna glared at him. "You're not sharing a bed with me tonight."

"Oh, I am sharin' one, wife, and dinna suggest *ye* sleep on a pallet," he retorted as he spun her around to face him. He lowered his face until their noses touched. "Ye will forever sleep beside me unless I go raidin' or sleep elsewhere."

She backed up several steps as he advanced on her. With a loud "humph," she turned her back and stripped to her smock. She stepped onto the dais and up the two-step footstool to climb in. On the last step, he grabbed the hem of her smock and whipped it up over her head. Her arms flapped like a bird learning to fly. She dove into bed.

"Ye will sleep bare. See ye remember it."

"I told you I'll not share a man. See *you* remember *it*."

She hissed the words through her teeth so he would know she meant each one. She stared into his eyes as he slowly pulled the bottom of his shirt free, then ignored her as he stripped.

Once abed, Damron propped himself on his elbow. "I will offer a compromise, and I ne'er compromise. When we are wed afore the priest as ye insist, and ye become a true wife to me, I will not come to ye from another. 'Tis more than any man need allow."

"I, too, will make you a vow, husband. I will not come to you from another." Her words were like arrows striking true.

Bounding to his knees, he grabbed her shoulders and lifted her till his face was so close her nose near touched his. "Dinna dare think such if ye value yer life. No man will ever ha'e ye but me." His sensuous lips thinned with anger.

Brianna tried to squirm away. Her nipples raked the mat of hair on his chest. It caught his attention, and he bent his head to stare at her breast. Startled, she lifted her head. It cracked against his nose.

"Lucifer's bowels, wife. Ye broke me nose." He turned her loose. The rope bed creaked and swayed.

Brianna tottered and grasped for balance. She fell backward. He grabbed for her—and missed. She disappeared over the side of the bed. He bounded after her.

The door crashed open, and Connor and Bleddyn charged into the room, their swords drawn. Connor's mouth gaped at the sight of Damron, naked, blood dripping off his chin. Brianna lay on the floor tangled in the sheet, her eyes squeezed shut.

Damron dropped to his knees, blood staining the sheet.

"Where is the intruder?" Connor's eyes searched the room.

"Nay, Connor. 'Twas Damron alone," Bleddyn said with disgust. "I vowed to protect Brianna from someone unknown, but the louts won't have to bother if he keeps this up."

Brianna opened her eyes. "Oh, hell. I'm still here," she muttered, and blinked at them. "Damron, if you're dripping blood on me for sympathy, you'll not get any. My head is pounding."

Bleddyn grinned and lifted her onto the bed. "I will bring something for it. Connor, hold a wet cloth to the back of her head." He sighed and added, "Damron, 'tis a wonder your brains do not also drip, for I believe they have turned to broth." He left and was back shortly with a potion for Brianna. Damron, his head tilted back, watched from the corner of his eye.

During the night, the healer came in to ask Brianna her name. She replied, "Lydia." When he again repeated the question she answered, "Brianna."

Damron feared he had caused his wife to again scramble her memory.

Chapter 14

"Damron, tell me all since William forced ye to acknowledge Brianna," Laird Douglas said from a chair beside his bed two mornings later. "She is a wee bonnie lass. Her character is strong, and I dinna ken what stands between ye."

Damron had always unburdened his heart to his grandfather, and did not hesitate to tell him of his and Brianna's confrontations. When he began to speak of their unusual wedding night, his voice stumbled. His grandfather burst out laughing.

"It wudna be so funny, sire, had *ye* been left with a ragin' tarse fair to burstin'." Damron scowled at his grandsire.

"So, this marriage can only be consummated when ye both speak vows afore the priest? Send this day for her family and all pledged to the Morgans. Ye will wed afore the moon again fills. Woo her gently. The lass may be afeared of the marriage bed."

"Brianna is not afraid of anythin'." Damron wished she was.

A clamor in the hallway interrupted them as his wife and Meghan swept into the room, leading a motley crew of servitors. At the old man's first shout, Damron grinned. His grandfather would learn firsthand of Brianna's independent character.

Brianna and Bleddyn had consulted with Damron, and he saw the wisdom of their request. They believed the dusty tapestries, animal skins and rugs were harmful to his grandfather's breathing. Not to mention the smoke from the peat and the strong smell of the many candles the old man required.

For many years, his grandfather had fought his mother whenever she attempted to change anything in his room. Mayhap Brianna could persuade him. For certs, she was stubborn enough to get her way.

As he eased the door closed behind him, he heard a stern command from Brianna. He waited, his head cocked and expectant. When he heard his granda's roar, he chuckled and walked away.

"Ye're goin' to do what? No' as long as I am in this bed!"

"Anger is bad for your heart, Papa Dougie." Brianna shuddered and handed him a decanter and a small goblet. "Here's a wee dram of the Scotch brew you all favor."

Laird Douglas's eyes lit as he sipped the whisky. He watched while she issued quiet commands and organized chaos broke loose. The musty animal hides were soon stripped from the windows, the fur covers and the pallet containing feathers from the bed. All went sailing out the window opening to the bailey below. The fireplace was emptied, cleaned and scrubbed, as were the floors and walls. Several hours later, the room smelled of soap and waxed wood.

Husky servants brought fresh bedding, linens and blankets made of heavy cotton. They placed pillows, prepared by Bleddyn's orders, on the bed. Large braziers were set about the room.

When Bleddyn entered, Guardian burst into the room, sat and scratched so vigorously wolf hair flitted through the air.

"Stop," Brianna yelled. He did. "Come with us, you flea-bitten monster. You're not going to ruin all our hard work."

She tugged Guardian from the room, fussing under her breath. Meghan raced after her, and when they reached the castle gates, Malcolm followed to guard them. They hurried to a small lake sheltered with trees about four hundred yards from the castle walls that Brianna had seen when they arrived.

"Thank you for your protection, Sir Malcolm. Please turn your back until we are through."

After seeing he did as she asked, she undressed to her smock. Meghan took a pot of strong soap and helped Brianna get Guardian into the lake. Brianna gasped and shivered in the cold water. Maybe she wasn't too smart doing this, for she felt like she might be coming down with a cough. Too late now, she decided, and slapped soap on the beast. She and Meghan began to lather and scrub Guardian. When all was clean except his head, she pulled the wolf's soapy hair into silly spikes atop his head and down his neck. She grinned, then winced from the effort, for her wound was still tender.

"What foolishness are ye about, Brianna?"

Brianna jumped, and loosened her hold on Guardian. The beast bounded out of the water, tail wagging and tongue lolling like he had not a wildlife gene in him. She ducked, hiding her shivering body in the water.

"Where'd Malcolm go?" she asked.

"I sent him to warn the healer."

"Whatever for?" She was truly puzzled.

"Ye are a wee, scrawny lass unused to our cold winds and water. Do ye think to do yerself harm? I heard ye coughin' afore I cleared the trees. Come from the water. Now!" It was not a request. It was a stern command.

"Turn your back first. I need to get the unruly beast and rinse him."

"Meghan, what were ye thinkin' to aid her in this? She is not a hale-and-hearty Scots lass. Wife, Meghan will tend Guardian. Ye hie yerself from that water. I will wait but a moment. If I need to fetch ye, ye will not like it."

"Aye, Brianna. I wasna thinkin'. Ye had best get dry clothin' afore ye catch yer death." Meghan sprinted to shore, water pouring from her wet shirt and breeches. She grabbed the wolf and started to rinse him, eyeing Brianna with a worried expression.

Brianna was conscious her wet clothing did little to hide her body from Damron. She turned her back on him and stepped backward toward the shore.

"My lord husband, please hand me a dry smock."

"Closer, wife. I dinna wish to wet my boots."

"Now, my lord?" Brianna huffed and was sorry she had, for it started a new round of coughing. She stepped back.

"But two steps more, my lady."

She stepped back again and bumped against his hot body. Before she could pull away, he turned their backs to Meghan and removed Brianna's smock, blotted her dry with a cloth and dropped a warm linen tunic over her head. When her arms reached for the armholes, his palms covered her breasts. He kneaded them gently while his rough thumbs slowly stroked her nipples. She gasped and jerked, but he held her close as he wrapped her in a heavy wool cloak. Lifting her, he placed her on Angel and mounted.

When they reached the keep, Damron carried her to their chamber where Bleddyn awaited them with the same potion he had given the laird. Damron sat with her on his lap beside a large brazier of hot coals.

"Drink all of it, wife. I will not have ye coughin' all night and disturbin' my rest."

Brianna would have given him a tart reply, but she couldn't catch her breath. She had to admit he was right. The honey in the potion soothed her throat. It tasted much like a hot toddy and was quite good. By the time she finished drinking two ample portions, she felt warm as toast, and her coughing eased.

She looked up at Damron and blinked.

"Why are you s-so pale, hmmm? I had a lovely t-time swaming, uh," she frowned and searched for the right words,

"sweeming with Greeper, uh, oh, heck, I know. Gardeener."
She beamed at him.

"Lucifer's ballocks!" Damron glared at Bleddyn. "Ye crazy
sorcerer. Ye have scrambled her brains. She is a wee daftie.
What did ye give my Brianna? Look at her. She canna look
straight out of either eye. By God's love, she ne'er smiled
crooked afore."

His roars brought people running. Asceline shoved her way
past Connor, before Meghan blocked her. Brianna turned
toward the tumult at the door and beamed. She felt marvelous!

"Hi. Wha's all the commotion? Demanor, uh, Damrorer, uh,
oh, crud, husband, stop squishin' my ribs." Her eyes lit, and
she held up a finger. "You know what? They'll break. Jus'
like"—she frowned and tried to snap her fingers together to
show them.

"Dolt," Meghan laughed. "'twas no poison, nor has her
wits been taken. At least not for long. Whiskey was in his
potion. Yer wife is a little fankled." She laughed all the harder
at Damron's expression.

He flushed and held Brianna off a little to get a better look.
She breathed slowly and evenly, then she grinned at him
before flinging her arms around his neck to pull his head
down.

She nuzzled his neck like a hungry kitten searching for a
teat. "You feel greath, and smell wunnerfull. I love your smell
when you are clothes, uh, near." She drew back from caressing his neck with her lips. "Did I ever tale you how saxy you
are? Ohh, whut you do to my head." She gave a gusty yawn,
snuggled even closer and slept. His arms tightened around her.

Damron turned a baleful eye on the occupants of the room.
Bleddyn grinned at him as he herded everyone out the door
and secured it behind him.

Why did Damron feel he must protect his wife from critical eyes? All who had gathered there had smiled when they heard her slurred speech. Ah, except Asceline. His eyes narrowed remembering her scornful look.

Soon Damron had Brianna tucked in bed beneath warm blankets. He discarded his clothing and climbed in beside her. After he pulled off her smock, he gathered her close to his naked heat. What would it be like to have a wife who snuggled so sweetly as Brianna had done just a short time earlier? Would she ever do so again? His neck burned where her lips had nuzzled him.

Brianna felt his warmth, flung her arm around his chest and snuggled her head beneath his chin, sighing. Such a little sound, yet it tore at his heart.

"Aye, ye ken where ye belong, ye fankled wee beauty," he whispered. "Whatever were ye thinkin', goin' into the cold water? Hm, defyin' me, no doubt. Ye knew I would forbid it had I been there." He clamped his teeth together, for her soft breasts pressed enticingly against his ribs. He rolled his eyes and stared at the canopy over the bed, trying to quell his raging sex with thoughts on the cruelties of battle.

He lost. His sex won.

His hands stroked down her spine and over the soft curves of her hips. He massaged her bottom, and she snuggled even closer, throwing her leg over his hip.

Since arriving at Blackthorn, he had not caressed her. Her soft whimpers of pleasure in her sleep made his heart speed crazily. He tilted her face up and brought his lips down to flutter over hers. Reluctantly, he moved his hand to stroke her back and make soft shushing sounds.

Damron shuddered. He wished she was awake and willing. His rod bucked and throbbed against her warm flesh as he thought of gazing into her eyes while entering her. She would have to acknowledge him as her master then, and he planned to pleasure her many times afore he took his own. Groaning, he clenched his teeth and composed himself for sleep. He smiled, remembering Brianna and Meghan laughing together in the water. He was still smiling when he nodded off.

Deep in the night, he dreamt of Genevieve wielding his sword with venom. He broke out in a sweat and moaned, as his hand twitched over the ragged scar on his thigh.

Several days later, Brianna was not in the great hall when Damron returned from training the men in the practice field. It was time for the afternoon meal and, worried that mayhap her cough had returned, he took the steps two at a time and was through their bedchamber door afore she could move. His gaze narrowed, for she stood fidgeting in front of his clothing chest.

"What do ye seek, wife? Were ye lookin' fer coins?" His left eyebrow rose high. "No? Weapons, then? Ye will not find either here."

"Don't be a sheep's patoot. I'm looking for my necklace."

"And what part of a sheep is that, pray tell? Should I add another two to yer tally?" He advanced like a panther stalking his kill.

"It isn't what you think. A sheep's patoot is a domineering ram. Ask any shepherd. He'll tell you." His slow advance did not stop. She began to blather. "They call babies sweet patooties when they cry all night. Ask anyone."

"Ye can be sure I will ask. What ye seek has always been safe." He withdrew a large velvet bag from the chest behind her. "Ye may wear it when I say ye may." He turned her back to him and fastened the chain about her neck. The pendant took on a warm glow.

When they entered the hall, Brianna knew everyone felt the air crackle between them. Asceline's eyes lit with glee when she looked at Damron. Brianna glanced at him and wished she had not, for his face was set in grim lines.

Damron addressed the room. "I have learned a new expression today: a sheep's patoot. I know not the meaning. We all ken sheep, but what of patoot? We will discuss what it means to ye at the noon meal on the morrow." He motioned for everyone to sit and start their meal.

Damron's chuckle was wicked as Brianna studied the trencher between them.

"I can read yer face, but can ye read mine?" Damron gazed down at her. "I think not. Do ye ken my thoughts, madam? It has to do with totals. I would have ye keep up yer strength, for ye may need it afore many suns rise if ye dinna curb yer tongue."

He held a bite of wild duck with wine sauce to her lips, but she didn't take it. When the sauce dribbled onto her chin, he leaned over to lick it off. She quivered and jerked, but he was too quick for her to stop him.

"Ye will open for me when my fingers are close." His voice was soft, suggestive. His words must have struck him, for he shifted uncomfortably.

She took the meat, and a hot flush covered her face and neck. She dipped her head and kept it down until the end of the meal.

"If my lord husband will allow, I would wish to retire?" Brianna asked courteously.

"Dinna forget, people." He stood and addressed the room. "I will await yer understandin' of patoot on the morrow." He looked down at her expressive face, and a sound rumbled up from his chest. He did not laugh often, but a laugh it was, though it held a hint of danger.

Brianna could not shake the clouds of doom when they entered their room. The air felt heavy with a storm closing in on the castle high on the cliffs. Thunder began to roll.

"Why dinna ye disrobe?" Damron asked. When she started to go behind the screen, he acted. "Nay. Afore ye say a word, listen to me," he commanded. "When I say nay, it is what I mean. Nay, ye willna hide yer body from me, and nay, ye willna hold yerself from my attentions." Their eyes locked in a battle of wills as he settled in the chair beside the window opening.

Well, hell. She turned her back and began to whip her clothes over her head and let them drop to the floor.

"Mari is no slave to ye. Ye will pick up yer clothes and fold them," he said, close behind her.

How had he crossed the room without making a sound?

She broke out in goose bumps and bent her knees with her body straight, careful not to touch him. After she gathered and folded her clothes, she stood on one foot to remove her shoes. She wobbled and swayed until he grasped her waist and lifted her onto the bed.

"Ye are as ungainly as a wee pup. Or is it yer way of askin' for my help?"

He bent to hold one foot in his hand and slid off her soft shoe. When his hand moved up to untie the ribbon holding her stocking in place, her heart pounded. His hands lingered, and she looked up to see he was staring, fascinated, at the vee of her body.

Oh, God. Was she supposed to have plucked her pubic hair? She knew highborn women did this in early times. Almost as if he had heard her thoughts, his gaze moved to meet hers. The blazing intensity in his look made her mouth go dry as the Mojave Desert.

"Ye are beautiful there, Brianna."

A bolt of lightening flashed and lit the room, making the passion in his face look diabolical. He turned his back to bring the branch of candles close to the bed. After placing it to his satisfaction, he began to remove his own clothing. His gaze challenged her to look away. She scooted beneath the covers and clutched them beneath her chin.

The candlelight cast a warm glow over his bronzed body. Was

he often naked at practice to be such a golden bronze? She gasped, realizing how she knew, for he had released the string of his breeches. They slithered past the heavy nest of black hair surrounding his sex. When that frighteningly large part of him burst free, she blinked but couldn't turn her gaze away.

She watched, spellbound, as the falling breeches unveiled hard thighs and bulging calves. Gordon had been slender and lithe, his body toned from playing tennis. When Damron bent to retrieve his clothing, his heavy ballocks swung free. While he neatly folded his garments, she had ample time to study his beautiful, muscular back, his firm buttocks and magnificent legs. When would she learn about the horrific scar there on his thigh?

Swallowing, she slid deeper in the bed and pretended she'd had the blanket over her eyes all along. Cold air chilled her when he tossed aside the covers. His body's weight pulled the mattress on the rope bed, and she slid toward him.

"I would gaze on ye, wife," he murmured. Kneeling, he cupped each foot and explored its softness. His fingers closed around her ankles, enfolding the small bones there. Callused hands smoothed slowly over her calves, across her knees and came to rest at the top of her thighs.

Brianna's heart jitterbugged against her ribs. When had she learned to respond so rapidly to his hands? Her body quivered and quaked like she suffered a raging fever. She held her breath.

Sounds hummed deep in Damron's chest as his gaze followed his hands' path. They swept over her flesh to tangle his fingers in the curls hiding her sex. After a slight tug and another low growl, he brought a hand to lay it flat against her stomach from the top of the curls on her mons to her rib cage. His fingers touched her ribs. He frowned, deep in thought.

His assessing gaze pricked Brianna's temper.

"I am no brood mare, if that's what you're checking."

"When I plant my seed, ye will hold it. Surely ye have more growin' to do."

"Grow? I'm no longer a child."

"Ye will," he ordered.

His scowl was so fierce she clamped her mouth shut, not wanting him to start proving the point. As stubborn as he was, he would likely put her on a rack to see if he could stretch her another inch. That was her last coherent thought as his hands moved up to cup her breasts and gently heft them.

Damron's nether parts ached, watching her nipples grow to pink hardness while his thumbs played over them. He forced his hands to leave there and travel over her chest, shoulders and down her arms.

He flipped her over without warning, and she gasped. He tugged the pillow from beneath her face to give her ample breathing room.

Beginning with her feet, he again studied her body, moving his hands over her heating flesh until they cupped her sweet arse. His big fingers kneaded her cheeks, then moved on up and over her waist to her hair. He murmured, a content sound, as he played with it, fanning it over her silky back so her buttocks peeked through the curls. He placed nibbling kisses on each sweet nether cheek and felt her tense as though to spring from the bed.

"I willna hurt ye, Brianna," he crooned. His hot, wet tongue wandered from the dark mystery nestled there to follow the crack in her bum and lick its way up to the nape of her neck. "Ye are honey and whiskey goin' straight to my head." He chuckled, acknowledging it was not that part of him with a brain that troubled him at the moment.

"May I turn over, Damron?"

"I wud be pleased, love," he crooned, his voice husky.

He turned her until she lay with her neck on his left arm that folded around her to fondle her breast. His head low-

ered and, as he nibbled and drew on her lower lip, his other
hand traveled over her body. He caressed her until his mouth
coaxed her lips open to sweep her resistance away. His hand
became more urgent.

He stopped to comb his fingers through the hair there between
her thighs. He slid his lips from hers to rain kisses across her face,
down her jaw and past her neck. Slowly, he reached his target.
Closing his mouth over one straining pink bud, he released his
breath in a sigh that sent shivers over the dampened flesh.

He sensed Brianna nearly came unglued when he suckled
lightly and then more urgently. Her breasts swelled; her stomach quivered. Her eager body was ready for him, but she
clamped her legs together to deny him.

Damron's hand cupped her mons, his fingers delving between her nether lips to find unmistakable hot, wet heat there.
He sighed with pleasure, then damned himself for his fool's
promise their first night. He grasped her bottom to grind his
manhood against her. When that hard and scorching part of
him tangled in her curls, she stiffened.

He knew Brianna fought for control. Why did she deny him?
Deny herself, when he knew she wanted him? He would not let
her hide from her need for him. Seductively, he pressed his slick
tarse against her mons and rubbed her there. When she gasped,
his middle finger sought the tight entrance he longed for. Her
heat and slickness were almost his undoing. He probed deeper
and felt the tight membrane proving she was his alone.

He wanted to roar with triumph when her body finished
betraying her. His mouth left her breast and covered her lips
to catch her moans of release. Her muscles clenched, pulsated
against his finger as she arched against him with the ferocity
of the release she could no longer deny.

When her tremors ebbed, he kissed her cheek and murmured soft words he knew she did not understand. Each time
she tried to speak, he touched her lips, stopping her. He

soothed and comforted her until her eyelids drooped and her body softened in sleep.

Thunder rolled and lightning lit the room. Brianna startled awake. Without looking, she knew Damron was not beside her. Where had he gone? She put on a cloak and shoes. When she opened the door and left the room, Guardian awoke and followed, but the sleeping squire did not stir as she headed for the winding staircase.

She wanted to watch the beauty of the approaching storm from the parapets and went up to the next landing. She heard moans coming from within the first chamber. She paused, and Guardian growled and stared at the door. A woman cried out in ecstasy, and Brianna fancied it was Asceline's voice. A deep male shout told of a man's own release.

Cold dread swept through her. Surely that wasn't Damron? She wanted to fling the door wide to see if it was, but Guardian shoved between her and the door. He pushed her with his great head and tried to herd her back to the stairway. She shoved the wolf aside and flew up the last flight, her tears near blinding her.

Reaching the battlements, she thrust open the door. A gust of wind wrenched it from her and crashed it tight to the outer wall. Guardian struggled to pull her back, but she leaned against the wind and made her way to an opening between merlons to stare out across the storm-tossed Kyle of Tongue. Driving rain lashed her. Wind whipped her robe high.

Lightning flashed closer and closer. Guardian scrabbled back to the opening, and raced down the steps howling with all his strength.

Chapter 15

Damron jolted to a stop, his hand gripping the massive door to the keep, his foot raised to step outside on the wooden stairway landing. Fear for Brianna kicked the breath from his lungs on hearing what sounded like a demented animal wailing, the eerie sound rebounding off the keep's walls. He spun around to the great hall and leaped up the stairwell, his feet barely touching the steps long enough to spring to the next one.

Guardian near bowled Damron over as the wolf raced to find him, then stopped to scramble around, its paws slipping and sliding, to head back in the opposite direction.

Damron followed and burst out onto the battlements, Bleddyn but a few paces behind. Brianna stood close to the edge of the battlement, defying God and the elements. The dark beauty of the scene struck Damron's heart. Thunder crashed, rain pounded and lightning streaks crackled so close together there was no silence in between. Her hair and cloak flew about her like dark angel wings.

"Lydia. Nay!" Bleddyn's voice roared above the storm's din and Guardian's howls. The mystic leapt and wrapped his arms about her waist. The screaming wind lifted his peacock-colored cape around them. His ancient talisman glowed with the light of a hundred stars. Bleddyn clutched the amulet just as lightning struck.

Time suspended. The air smelled strange, sharp. The small hairs on Damron's neck and arms stirred. He stood dumbfounded, gaping at the scene afore him. Bleddyn and Brianna hovered in the air. Blinding light surrounded them. Their bodies doubled—like a shadow above them. A blue aura circled Brianna. Purple lights spread around Bleddyn, encompassing her blue.

'Twas then Bleddyn again commanded, "Lydia. Nay!"

He had called her Lydia. The auras locked together, each seeming to battle the other's will. Their images, surrounded by the lights, rose higher above their bodies. Damron's heart near stopped. In desperation he fought an unseen barrier to reach them, her name tearing from his throat.

"Brianna!"

His demand swelled with the wind to tame the thunder. With arms stretched wide and grasping, he reached them and fell to the stone floor with Brianna and the mystic locked in his arms.

Dr. Christian MacKay gazed into his patient's expressionless eyes, hoping this would be the hour she would show some sign of recovery. He didn't understand his need to be with her, but every minute he could wrench from his hectic life, he spent by her bedside. He stopped only to grab for fast foods, whenever he remembered to eat. At night, he showered and slept a scant three hours before returning to stay with her until time for morning rounds.

The backs of his long fingers gently stroked the soft face on the pillow. Suddenly, strange lights flashed into the room to settle at the head of the bed. He was rooted to the spot.

Oh, my God. The fresh scent of spring rain filled the air,

chasing off the cold, antiseptic smell of the hospital. Heaven help him; he was hallucinating. Why else would he see strangely dressed people hovering over his patient? They were arguing. He could see their wills clashing, but he couldn't hear their words. With his barbaric face and cape, the man looked like a ruler from some ancient time. She looked to have come from bed. Beautiful. Her disheveled hair fell to her waist. She was blending with the woman on the bed! The man was commanding her to stay with him.

Shrill alarms beeped. Christian's gaze jerked back to his patient. Shock pierced him. Startled, lucent eyes stared back at him.

Recognition flashed. Rocked him. Near stunned him. He knew her. An overwhelming urge to grasp her in his arms pulled at him. His soul screamed in his mind. Willed him to remember.

He gripped the bed rails and took a deep breath. Of course he knew her. He'd tended her unceasingly since the wind during the freak storm had thrown her down, and she'd hit her head. But now, more than that, he knew her heart and soul as well as he knew his own. But how could he? He shook his head and rubbed his face hard. Surely his imagination ran rampant from lack of sleep?

The strange, cloaked vision reached out to her. At his touch, she tore her gaze from Christian. The strange man was reassuring her. She turned back to study Christian, smiled sweetly and squeezed his hand.

"Don't," he choked out. The harsh plea for her not to leave tore from his tight throat. She squeezed his hand harder, comforting him. In a split second, she detached from his patient on the bed and joined with the man. Both looked back, smiled and disappeared. The medical instruments returned to their quiet rhythm. His heart sinking, Christian's gaze searched the woman's still face. The antiseptic smell again filled the air.

The essence of his patient had again left, though now her face was peaceful. A sweet smile curved her lips.

"For God's love, Connor," Damron's shout rose above the din of the storm. He rose, clutching Brianna in his arms. "See to Bleddyn. Someone hold this crazed wolf."

Meghan raced to grasp Guardian's ruff. Damron shoved past the people on the stairway, shouting for them to get the hell out of his way. Connor and Malcolm lifted Bleddyn in their arms. His head dangled, and his hand still clutched the talisman. Their knees near buckled under his weight.

In their chambers, Damron stripped Brianna of her wet clothing and snuggled her under warm covers in but a few moments. Connor and Malcolm pulled off the mystic's cloak and leather shoes, but when they started to remove the strange, floor-length tunic, Bleddyn's steely fingers grasped their wrists. His eyes opened, he took a deep, rasping breath and rose. His fingertips rested on Brianna's forehead.

"Awaken now, *mo fear cridhe,* my little heart. All is as it should be." Bleddyn's scarred face softened with tenderness.

Brianna opened her eyes. She looked up at Damron. Her feelings flashed across her face as swiftly as the lightning had struck. Puzzlement. Recognition. Understanding. She stared at Bleddyn, then buried her face in the pillow. As Bleddyn's gentle hand smoothed over her head, her shoulders quaked with silent sobs.

"Ye great ox." Meghan cuffed Damron on the head. "Canna ye see yer wife needs comforting?"

Damron shot Meghan a quelling look and stripped off his wet clothing. She grinned, undaunted by his nakedness. He shrugged on his robe, then wrapped Brianna's shuddering body in the sheet and gathered her tight against him. Bleddyn nodded and ushered everyone from the room.

Tears seeped from the corners of Brianna's eyes, soaking

her cheeks. She stiffened when Damron settled down in the chair with her and started kissing them away.

"Don't dare kiss me after you have been with your leman." She shuddered and tried to pull from him. "I told you. You can't have us both."

"I have not been to Asceline. I vowed I would not come to yer bed after I had been with my leman, and I have not."

"Fool! I heard you." Brianna slapped his cheek. Hard.

He stilled, his face rigid with fury. "Never do that again, or yer back will feel the stings from my belt. And dinna ever name me fool nor doubt my word. What were ye doin' atop the keep in such weather?"

"I went to watch the storm come in over Tongue Bay."

"Nay, wife. Ye lie. Guardian howled with fright and raced to find me. Bleddyn knew somethin' was amiss."

"Nothing was amiss. I felt closed in when I awoke. Not much air came through our window opening, and I wanted to feel the wind on my face."

"Ye stood with yer arms entreatin' the clouds to lift ye, as ye did on our journey." His jaw set, and he fixed her with a level stare and waited.

She shrugged, uneasy. "The wind felt so good, so fresh. I wanted to feel it over all of me."

He frowned and his eyes narrowed as he studied her, then he blurted, "Ye dinna dabble in the black arts, do ye?"

"Of course not." Her eyes closed, but not before he spied the fear lurking there.

Hearing Laird Douglas's agitated shouts, Bleddyn went to reassure him. Connor and Meghan followed.

"Why was wee Brianna about in the storm, Bleddyn?" Laird Douglas asked. "And why did Damron not keep her in their bed?"

"Because he canna keep his shaft from leadin' him to that French bitch in heat," Meghan hissed through her teeth. "He would lie with both. Ye great eejits that call yerselves men. Ye follow yer prick wherever it points, and no' yer minds. His vulgar grunts must have caused her to wake afrighted. Dinna gaup, Connor. Ye will catch flies."

"'Tis nothing from what you will catch if you dinna seek your room. How know you of such things?"

"How? Do ye not remember the grateful looks ye and Damron got from the maids of a morn? Their gazes went not to yer eyes but to those bulges betwixt yer legs."

"Meghan, lass, you are wrong," Bleddyn said. "Damron was not with Asceline. He was coming from the stairwell off the great hall when I came upon him."

Meghan's brows arched in surprise. Her grandfather beckoned, and she went to him. His expression was stern, but his eyes were alight with amusement.

"I am sorry, Granda," she said, kissing his furry cheek. "I dinna mean to shock ye, do ye ken?"

"I ken, lassie. Morn approaches, and ye need yer sleep." He patted her cheek, then waited until she left the room. He turned toward Bleddyn. "Having a leman is proper, but a man must not flaunt her afore his lady wife." Anger hardened his voice.

"Brianna will not take it lightly if Damron shares himself with another. He will lose her." Bleddyn responded.

"'Tis not his heart she would be sharin'," Douglas chuckled. "I ken, Bleddyn, I should not make light of it."

"Brianna insists on fidelity from him as much as he demands it from her. Should he be unfaithful, she will not stay."

"Where would the lass go? Nowhere from the top of Scotland to the toes of bloody England could he not find her."

"The heart that is Brianna would slip away, and only the shell of her would stay, never to be the same sweet woman you are learning to love." If Brianna did not win this battle for Damron's heart, he could not deny her pleas for help. She knew now that he, combined with his talisman and the storm's power, was her way back to her future life. Seeing the old man's tired face, Bleddyn took his leave and went to roam the battlements.

Bleddyn's gaze searched the darkness in the great field between the fortifications and the forests, and he took deep breaths of the fresh night air. Connor came to stand with him. Neither man spoke. Cloud Dancer screeched, then circled lower. In the softening of the night before matins at dawn, horsemen emerged from the wall of trees.

Their leader, a giant of a man, rode a brown destrier as huge and powerful as Angel, or Thunder, Bleddyn's own steed. The man's hair was light, neither brown nor golden, and it flowed around his face and shoulders. His bearing was that of a knight, but he bore none of the trappings to name him such. Furs were thrown around his shoulders, held with a huge brooch, and leather armbands circled his wrists. He wore a Morgan tartan belted about his waist as he straddled his horse's bare back.

"Come," Connor said, "let us welcome home Damron's half brother, Mereck. No doubt, ye have heard of him as the warrior Baresark."

While Connor introduced him, Mereck's face was impassive as he studied Bleddyn standing with Cloud Dancer clasped on his wrist. Mereck nodded, then turned his gaze to Connor. "Where is Damron? 'Tis unlike him not to know I am near."

Connor sketched the night's happenings as they entered the

keep. Mereck solemnly dipped his head to Bleddyn, clasped Connor's shoulder, then took the steps two at a time.

He halted afore Damron's door and scratched lightly. After Damron's soft "Come," he entered the room. Damron sat on a chair in the dark, his wife on his lap. After studying the lady to see if her eyes were closed, Mereck squatted and coaxed the peat fire to new life, then raised his plaid high and turned his cold buttocks to the hearth. His face took on a look of utter comfort. His head fell back. His eyes closed.

Brianna sensed someone else in the room and awoke. Her gaze fell on a man's naked loins that were as impressive as Damron's own. The stranger met her gaze and lowered his tartan.

"Good Lord Almighty, here's another one. Don't bother to tell me." Then she lowered her voice to a whisper and contradicted herself. "Why didn't you tell me you had a brother? Everything about him is the same." She flushed when she realized the part of him from which she compared the two men.

"You have shrewd eyes, my lady. Many people dinna note our likeness," the man said wryly. "I am Mereck, Damron's half brother, born just hours after him."

"Hours? You're not twins? Oh, my God. Lady Phillipa must have wanted to castrate your father," Brianna whispered. The men's brows rose on hearing the strange word castrate.

"Nay, wife. Mother knew it had naught to do with her. Mereck's Welsh mother died birthin' him. Mother took him to suckle at her breast while she fed me. She pleased Father with her acceptance of his second son. Mother loves Mereck dearly."

"Nothing to do with her? You think his leman had nothing to do with his wife?" Brianna's voice rose. "It had everything to do with her. It showed he didn't love her enough for fidelity. I bet he'd have felt it had something to do with *him* if *she* had taken a lover."

"Had she done so, he had the right to kill her." Damron's

eyes squinted coldly at her. "At best, he would have locked her in a tower for the rest of her life. The day Father learned of him, the man would not have lived to see nightfall."

Brianna grabbed the sheet and jumped off his lap. Mereck watched her, seeming fascinated.

"I'll say it again. *I will not share a husband.* I will go. My body may remain, but I'll not be within it. If you doubt my word, ask my Nathaniel. If not for him, I wouldn't be here now."

Damron shot to his feet. "Ye will go nowhere without my leave," he shouted.

"Ask my Nathaniel." She turned to walk away.

"Dinna turn yer back to me, Lady." He grabbed her so swiftly she lost her grip on the sheet.

Mereck's appreciative gaze swept over her slender body. "I envy you the taming of such a lass, brother. You have no need to seek comfort elsewhere when you have a bride with such fire." He was gone afore Damron could respond.

Damron feasted on Brianna's supple lips as he lifted her high against his chest. 'Twas easier. For him. Not her.

"Dammit, you're hurting me, Damron. Put me down."

He ignored her command and put a hand under her bottom to hold her more comfortably against his hard length. Too late, she marked the curse. Had he noted it? She peeked up at him.

"Six," he murmured, then his lips tried to recapture hers.

"You can't count it because you were pulling off my skin."

"Nay, Lady." He set her on her feet. "I did not grant excuses. Stop trying to entice me and don yer clothin'. I canna keep Mereck waitin' while ye satisfy yer greedy eyes."

She spluttered and hoisted her nose high. "I have no desire to entice you, my lord. Don't keep your brother waiting."

He watched while she wriggled her smock about her hips. She noted his appraising regard and turned her back. When she looked again, he was tending his teeth with great care, naked as a babe.

"Clothe yourself, you strutting rooster. Find Connor and Mereck so you can crow and wrestle each other in the mud." She grabbed his wet cloth and lathered her face with heather-scented soap. When she ignored him, he dressed and was soon gone.

"Blasted viper," she whispered. The door reopened just wide enough for his head, and she near dropped her cloth.

"Good. Ye are learnin' to yield to the reins, wife," he said and ducked back out again.

When it was time for the noon meal, Brianna led the men who aided Laird Douglas down to the hall. Bleddyn's potion had done wonders for the laird's cough, and he wished to dine with the family. For the occasion, she had dressed in shades of gold, and her hair fell free down her back. She held her head high and trilled a tune in homage to the man being escorted. A deep baritone voice joined her with words to the melody. Her gaze flew to the singer. 'Twas Mereck. He smiled when the song was completed.

"Your voice is as beautiful as they told me, Lady. Why do you not sing the words?"

She shrugged but couldn't tell him of her vow never to sing where his brother was present. "Where did you learn them, Mereck?"

"Galen of Ridley went each night to a watchtower north of the keep and sang into the sky. I formed the habit of meeting him there."

"Enough!" Damron broke in. "Ye meddle where ye have not the right." His jaw thrust forward.

Mereck's chin rose in challenge, then his gaze swept to Bleddyn. He looked to have found his answer in the mystic's gaze.

An increased number of men awaiting their meal sported bruises and split lips. They laughed and jostled each other, and bragged about their fighting prowess. All but Bleddyn looked to have been in a melee. The men at the high table had taken pains to wash their faces and hands and rinse the dirt from their hair, but even so, their odor was so pungent she wrinkled her nose.

The grunts and belches as they shoveled food into their mouths disgusted her. After the men left, Brianna whispered a plan to Meghan. They went to each woman they could trust to ask for help. Soon, the women were giggling and nodding agreement.

Late that afternoon, Damron called to his men training in the open field to join him at the river to wash away the day's filth. The usual number followed him, but the rest jostled each other to see who would be first to enter the keep.

After they bathed, Damron and his men mounted and rode at a leisurely pace for the drawbridge. At the sight that greeted them, their mouths gaped open. Men stood bellowing and cursing with rage and refusing to pass beneath the barbican.

He soon saw the reason why.

All who passed through into the bailey were doused with soapy water poured through the murder holes and over the top of the barbican. The scent of lavender and roses wafted on the air.

Damron spied the culprits.

"If you want to dine with women," Brianna yelled in a commanding voice, "then don't come to us reeking of sweat, urine or anything else. You men outside the gate go to the river and bathe or we'll help clean you." She stood in an open embrasure. A stout older woman gripped her waist. Brianna glared down at the warriors, her hands fisted on her hips, her legs wide apart in a belligerent stance. "What sissies you are," she taunted. "Afraid your sex will shrivel from soap and water? It won't hurt, and it might improve your love life."

She had not noticed Damron, so intent was she on the smelly horde below. Meghan peeked around her and saw him. She threw him a cheeky wave, and her loud, boyish whistle filled the air. Brianna teetered. Meghan grabbed her arm to steady her.

"Brianna, get ye down. Now!" She looked down and shook her head. He narrowed his eyes and glared. She raised her hand in a strange gesture, her middle finger pointing upward. He need not know its meaning to ken it was not an affectionate gesture.

"Go, Guardian," she shouted. The wolf streaked through the portcullis. With growls and nips at their heels and buttocks, he herded the cursing men toward the flow of soapy water. The water was less menacing to their manhood than was her four-legged champion.

"Well, ladies, we willna ha'e to hold our noses this night." Meghan laughed, and stuck her tongue out at Damron.

He watched his men jumping and pulling off their clothes as they loped to the horse troughs to rinse themselves of the sweet-smelling soap. As they ran, they shouted curses to the heavens. Others went to the well where giggling women poured buckets of water over their soapy, naked bodies.

Damron's long legs made short work up the stairway to the barbican. He stalked up to Brianna, grabbed her waist and turned her in the direction he wanted to go. Grasping a handful of hair at her nape, he propelled her before him. She swatted at his hand, to no avail. Mereck lifted Meghan and carried her like a bag of grain. She fought like a wildcat. He didn't flinch.

Inside the great hall, Damron released Brianna.

"Don't ever pull my hair again, you freaking monster." She rounded on him, her fist aimed at his chin.

He caught it in midair. "Have we now reached seven,

Lady?" His anger built, thinking of her precarious stance on the battlement.

"Nay, Damron," Bleddyn said quietly. "Freaking is not what you think."

Damron nodded, accepting his word. "Do ye realize, lass, ye could have fallen and broken every bone in yer body?" His voice made her flinch. "And what will ye do if my men decide to take matters in their own hands?"

Brianna huffed. "You'll stop them, of course." She looked at him as if he lacked the wits of a child. "I won't have a stubborn herd of unwashed louts stinking up the place."

"Ye have not the right in this."

"Ha! Ye have not the right," she mimicked, "to expose women to their filthy bodies. They *scratch!*"

"Scratch? Why canna they scratch?"

"Can't they keep their hands off their private parts until they at least finish their meal? Every time I look up, some man has his hands where he shouldn't, looking at us like we've given him a rash."

"Ye are tellin' me they are lookin' at ye and doin' things they should not?"

"I didn't say that. I said they scratched when they shouldn't." Brianna muttered. "You can't talk to men who have no horse sense."

"Horse sense? What horse sense?" He took a deep breath and tried mightily to control his temper. "If ye have a special task, ye should come to me. Ne'er do anythin' like this again."

"A lot of good that would do us. Ye all are near as guilty," Meghan said. "Ye shift and wiggle in yer seats like ye were sittin' with tight breeches. And stink? Ye think because ye wash yer face and paws ye dinna smell? Bleddyn and Granda are the only ones who dinna reek of sweat and piss by day."

Connor grabbed her shoulders and shoved her toward Damron. "For love of God, cousin, pull Meghan's hair, too."

Damron snorted and turned on his heels. He motioned for the men to follow him to the stables, where they saddled their mounts and rode into the woods. When he called a halt, Bleddyn's face broke into a smile. Connor and Mereck howled with laughter.

"Did you see the men's faces when they smelled the suds?" Connor asked when he caught his breath. "'Twill make for a sweet-smelling garrison. By God's love, I've near pissed myself," he added as he vaulted off his horse and ran behind a tree.

"Did you see Angus cup his ballocks? He believes water will shrink his treasures." Mereck shook his head and chuckled.

"The dairy maid calls his weapon her 'battering ram,'" Damron replied. "'Tis likely he fears she might change the name to rosebush."

"This count of yours, Damron. You dinna plan physical punishment, do you, brother?" Mereck's eyes narrowed as he asked.

"How I handle Brianna is my right. Ye willna interfere. She is the most unruly woman in all of Scotland." He hesitated, shook his head, and then added, "Except for Meghan. I must have an obedient wife. I canna allow a woman to thwart my orders, or argue over every issue. I would lose all respect from the men."

In Meghan's room, Brianna and Meghan laughed and compared notes on the different shapes of the men's buttocks, shanks and other interesting areas. Suddenly, Damron's threat flashed to Brianna's mind. She told Meghan about his disgusting total, and about being but a few points away from a thrashing.

"Do you think he will really beat my bottom? Would he shame me like that? I'll not stand for it."

Meghan's hands fisted on her hips. "He willna think twice about shamin' ye." Her eyebrows near met in a scowl. "He took my own punishment into his hands when Connor was unwillin' to attempt the task. The first time was terrible. After that, I stitched a drying cloth to my smock. He smacked away. I pretended to cry. Afterward, he patted my head and said he was sorry I had pushed him to be a brute. Mayhap ye should try the same trick."

That evening, Brianna wore a loose-fitting tunic and spread her clothing as she sat. For the first time, the food's aroma didn't have to compete with the odor of sweat. Angry looks were cast her way. Here and there, loud arguments broke out. She gripped her trembling hands in her lap.

"Ye dirty scum! If ye think to bed me agin with yer dirty shaft ye can go back to yer sheep," an angry woman shouted, then poured a tankard of ale over the head of her latest bed partner. Other women picked up the clamor. The men were hard-pressed to lull their shouting women so they could plead with them.

Meghan jumped to her feet. "Ye blarsted auld sheep lovers. Ye smell like rams with yer piss and dirty arses, and then ye expect yer women to swive with ye. Afore we ducked ye with a wee bit of water this day, I doubt ye have had a drop of it on yer bodies since last summer."

"Hold your tongue. You talk like a slattern, not a lady," Connor scolded as he grasped her shoulders and forced her to sit.

"Dinna tell me to shut up! They try to cause our Brianna shame."

Damron drew his short sword and slammed the flat of the blade on the table.

"Haud yer clack." His voice near rattled the rafters. He turned to hold Brianna's arm. "Well now, wife. I have talked to all this day and heard a score of meanings for the word patoot. Many think it the sound a ram makes when mating, a sheep breakin' wind, the name for an old ram or a ram's sex rod."

Brianna relaxed somewhat. But not for long.

"But, as I suspected, most deemed it somethin' else," he added silkily. "Callin' yer husband a sheep's arse brought the total to eight. Lyin' about it, nine. This day's events brings ye to ten." He took his hand away.

She swallowed and watched him from the corner of her eye.

Brianna stood. "Laird Douglas, if you will excuse me? I'd like to visit Cloud Dancer tonight."

Damron reached to haul her back to her seat.

"The lass did not ask your leave, Damron, but mine. Sit. Lord Bleddyn, if you would escort Brianna, I would be grateful."

"Thank you, Papa Dougie. I'll visit you in the morning." Mustering her dignity about her, she left the room.

Her fingers trembled on Bleddyn's arm and, when they were out of sight of the great room, her hand tightened for firmer support. The falcon trainer was settling the raptors for the night and smiled as they came into the glow of the rushlight.

Cloud Dancer and Damron's falcon, Gawky, stretched their necks and twisted their heads side to side to get a better view. True to Damron's strange naming of creatures, Gawky was the complete opposite of what he was called, for Brianna had seen him soar to the skies as gracefully as Cloud Dancer did. Both birds made soft sounds in their throats, and she smiled.

"I wonder what they talk about?" She tilted her head as she listened, unconsciously mimicking the raptors. The men looked at each other and smiled.

She sighed and thanked Bleddyn for escorting her when they left the mews. She kissed his cheek good night. Not once had she asked him what her husband had in store for her.

Chapter 16

Brianna stood outside her bedchamber door, one hand outstretched to open it. She drew it back, then leaned her forehead against the heavy wood and closed her eyes.

Bleddyn was the catalyst to her way back to the future, though by his actions, he had made it amply clear he wanted her here. In this century. He knew everything about her. How she had no love who awaited her return to the twenty-first century. No parents. No siblings. *No one*.

Had he known about the other time? When she had thought life wasn't worth living? And for just a brief moment had wished to give it up? Anyone would have despaired if in her shoes.

Gordon had followed her home that dreadful day. He had argued against divorce, saying she would never leave him, for she needed him. They'd always had a passionate sex life, and he had thought to rule her by it. He threw her down on the bed, and when she fought him, he used his fists while spewing his venom at her. He called her a fool, and said he had never loved her. Her global reputation in genetic research had opened doors for him, had made her *palatable* to him.

Her assistant, Harvey, had turned to boxing to pay his way through college. Upon learning Gordon had followed her, he had become uneasy and driven to her house. Harvey used his feet to nearly kick in her front door. He used his fists when he found Gordon beating her.

She didn't leave the sanctuary of her home until sunglasses hid her fading bruises.

Gordon didn't leave his hotel room for well over a week. He didn't contest the divorce. If he had, Harvey swore he'd testify Gordon had tried to murder his wife.

Brianna shuddered at the memories. Bleddyn would not have kept her here if he believed Damron would treat her violently. Would he? She wiped her sweat-soaked hands and threw open the bedchamber door.

Her heart slammed against her ribs. Every candle burned, chasing the creeping twilight from the room. She spied the bed. That damned rock rested on her pillow. She bolted from the room and sped to find Meghan.

"The rock. It's on my pillow. Do you know where Damron is?"

"With Granda." Meghan grabbed Brianna's shoulders and peered into the corridor. "Quickly. Hide in one of the rooms below till his temper cools."

Brianna nodded and sprinted out the door. She made her way to the bottom of the keep, where there was a weapons room, the men's bathing room and at the end, a storage room. In it were barrels of goods, heavy bags of wheat and flour, bolts of cloth on shelves on the wall and every possible item needed to supply the keep. Spying an opening between the bags of flour, she scrambled toward it.

She shivered and rubbed her arms, muttering, "When did I become such a coward?"

Two floors above, Damron did not stop at his own door but went instead to Asceline's. He would ensure she stayed well away from the corridor outside his chamber. He would not have his leman gloat over his disciplining his wife.

Asceline was naked. She sprawled on the cushions of her window bench, her blond hair spread over her shoulders and breasts to allow her nipples to peek through. Her legs were bent and open, inviting him. She smiled with triumph as his gaze went to the center of her that she so brazenly exposed.

"Do you not have the courage to punish her?" She licked her lips as her gaze traveled down his body, looking for the effects her exposed womanhood would have on his shaft. "Church law allows you a stout rod as thick as your thumbs. I will hold her if you think she will fight you." Her nipples hardened. One hand moved to play over her breasts while the other caressed her mons.

He shuddered in distaste, for Asceline took pleasure in other people's misfortune. He silently watched his leman prepare herself for him. It was a game she often used when he was in a temper.

He did not speak, and he did not remove his clothing. Instead, he tossed her over his shoulder, turned and landed her face first on her bed. He raised his hand high and gave her a hard, stinging slap on her buttocks. She yelped and scrambled to the head of the bed.

"That is for enjoyin' the humiliation my wife must endure this night. Ye will stay here, in this room, or be on yer way back to Normandy with a goat herder for escort come the morn." He stalked from the room and slammed the door.

He found his room empty, and it suited him. He gathered clean clothing and went to the bathing room, mindful that he might smell of Asceline. She had doused herself with her favorite essence of jacinth, made in Normandy especially for her. Where before he had found it enticing, now it brought naught but distaste. He much preferred the teasing fragrance of heather when Brianna walked past.

Two large wooden tubs and several buckets of heated water stood warming by the fireplace. He filled a tub and scrubbed as he would after a battle.

Dressed in fresh clothing, he checked his chamber and knew Brianna had seen the rock and defied him, for her scent lingered. When he barged into Meghan's room, she thrust her chin forward and narrowed her eyes at him. He crossed his arms and stared at her. And waited.

"Well, man, dinna stand there like some great beastie."

"Where is she?"

Meghan shrugged. His gaze swept the room and came to rest on the large chest against the wall. He threw open the top, expecting to find his wee wife within. When she was not, his steps carried him to the bed. He tossed back the covers. Finding only pillows, he scooped aside a tapestry to check the window seat. With a disgusted grunt, he left the room.

Damron crossed to his mother's solar where she and three of the castle widows were stitching a tapestry.

"Brianna is not within, Damron." His mother's voice was cold. He knew she was angry at what she called his "unbending attitude" toward his wife.

His hands fisted. The longer it took him to find Brianna, the more his temper simmered. "I am sorry, Mother, but I must check."

Lady Phillipa rose to her full height and delivered a stinging slap to his cheek. "Question my word again, and I will take that great sword from the wall below stairs and beat you with the flat of it."

For a moment, Damron felt like a foolish lad who had raised his mother's ire. He fought to keep from shuffling his feet like an embarrassed youth, bowed stiffly and apologized. He had deserved her temper. His cheek still smarting, he left there and went to his grandfather's room. The Old One sat high in his bed, where he and Dudley, his friend and manservant, were playing chess.

"Granda, have ye seen Brianna since we supped?"

"The wee one is missing? God's bones! You checked the battlements above?"

"Brianna thinks to defy me yet again and has hidden herself from me. The lass *will* learn to heed my directions. I willna have an unruly Saxon to wife."

Guardian bounded up at the mention of his mistress' name. His tongue lolled, and his tail wagged in circles so fast it created a draft.

"Find Brianna, Guardian," Damron ordered, and the hound's eyes lit. Damron's jaw clenched. His search would soon be over.

They left the room and headed for the battlements, where Guardian raced out the door and searched over the rooftop. He came back thumping his tail, delighted with the new game they played. The wolf streaked down the hallway to stop at Damron's door, then ran across to Meghan's before he turned to the corner stairwell. Damron followed to the bottom of the keep.

"Lucifer's arse, Guardian, not my track but Brianna's," he grumbled. Guardian raced past the door to the bathing room and stopped at the storage room door. When Damron patted his head and thumped him on the side, he looked up and wagged his tail happily.

Damron stalked into the dim room and hooded his eyes. His gaze swept over everything stored there, and he grunted on spotting an opening between the bales of flour.

"Brianna, I know where ye are hidin'. Dinna make me come after ye. Believe me, wife, ye dinna want to anger me further." His voice was as soft and caressing as velvet.

"I wasn't hiding," Brianna said as her head popped up above the sacks. She squared her shoulders and frowned at him. "I was checking the flour for weevils and didn't hear you come in."

When he quirked a brow at her, she tilted her nose in the air and boldly met his gaze. Her nostrils started to twitch and she sneezed, took a deep breath and sneezed again, then near rubbed her nose from her face.

She stood and lifted her skirts just enough to free her knees so she could scramble across the tops of the bales. She looked much like a reluctant ant crawling toward the waiting tongue of a lizard. When she came to the last bale, Guardian stood on his hind legs and placed wet, sloppy kisses on her face.

"Huh. Go back to your master, Guardian." She scowled at the wolf.

The beast whimpered, flattened his ears to his head and looked at her with sad eyes. He put his tail between his legs and lowered his head, dislodging flour from his heavy ruff. He made several loud, snuffling noises, then sneezed and rubbed his muzzle against Damron's leg.

Brianna pulled her clothing about her and took the short jump to the floor. Her tunic caught on the wire tie binding a bale of wheat and exposed her bare legs up to her creamy thighs. Blushing, she jerked the material loose. She did not meet Damron's gaze, but stared at his arms crossed over his chest.

"Come." He held out his hand.

She drew back and shook her head. "I'm not through checking the flour and wheat. Did you notice the flour floating around? The sacks must have loose seams. If I don't mark them, we'll likely do without bread this winter."

He rolled his eyes at her, reached out a hand and grasped her chin to force her to look at him.

"Have it yer way, Brianna, but ye will come when I command. Come easily or with force. 'Tis yer choice." His calloused hand slid through her flour-coated hair to rest on her nape. From the tension in her neck and shoulders, he knew she wanted to yell at him as he guided her up the stairway and past the great hall.

When they chanced meeting anyone, she nodded and greeted them with a cheery voice. He smiled with the air of a man enjoying the feel of his wife's slender neck.

At their bedchamber door, Damron slammed it shut with his foot.

"Eleven!"

Brianna's eyes widened. "Like he . . ." she started, before he clamped his hand over her lips.

"Dinna think to quibble. I have no doubt ye saw the rock on the pillow. I told ye to prepare when that occurred. Not only did ye not do so, ye dared defy me by hidin'."

"Prepare? How do I prepare myself to be punished like some hound that stole meat from your plate?" She shouted, "Don't dare. Try it and I'll not forgive you."

"I willna ask forgiveness. I demand honor and obedience from my wife, and *I will have it!*" Before she could move, he grasped her tunic's hem and whipped it up over her head, then yanked it off her flailing arms. The smock was a bit more trouble, for she grabbed hold of it and tried to tug it back from him.

His heart pounded at the sight of her. Her hair was in wild disarray, and her beautiful body was bare to her creamy thighs. Pink ribbons held white stockings above her knees, adding to the erotic picture. He tore his gaze away to study the bundle of clothing puddled at her feet. He spied the drying cloth sewn to the back of her smock.

"Did ye think me a fool? That I did not know Meghan padded herself? I wouldna shame my cousin by barin' her body to my hand. Nay!" He held up his hand, letting Brianna know his wife was another matter. "Dinna say it. I warned ye from the first day not to defy me."

Damron sat on the edge of the bed and eyed her. And waited. Brianna's chin lifted. She stared defiantly at him and crossed her arms over her breasts, shielding them from his gaze. His eyebrows arched. His mouth set in even grimmer lines.

When he grabbed her waist, she shrieked. He bent her across his spread legs. She became a spitting tigress, clawing and trying to bite him.

He anchored her firmly, pulling her tight against his body. His left hand held her waist. His groin stirred to the erotic sight. He groaned and fought himself not to nuzzle his face against the creamy skin of her bottom and place nibbling kisses there.

A bitter taste filled his mouth. He did not want to strike her. Why had she challenged him after he had warned her? Every warrior at Blackthorn waited to see if he could control his wee wife. Not a one of them would respect him if he did not. He had been unable to curb Genevieve, and he had vowed never again to let a woman make a fool of him. He clamped his teeth together.

"One!" His right hand came up. And wavered. "Yield to me, Brianna. Vow obedience and I will pardon ye." He stilled, waiting to see if she would agree. His hopes sank. He could not let her win this constant battle of wills. Life in the High- lands was harsh and dangerous. If a woman was to be kept safe, she had to obey the men in her family without question.

"Let go of me, you obnoxious, overbearing Neanderthal!" she yelled. Struggling wildly, she freed an arm and raked her nails down his hard thigh.

He tightened his hold, looked down at her lovely arse and shook his head. His raised hand clenched, then stretched flat again as he steeled himself to smack her tempting flesh.

"Oaf! Blasted lummox. Hit me, and I'll slam a brick on

your fat skull the first chance I get." She tried to thrust herself up from his lap.

His hand was halfway down to her creamy cheeks, but it bounced back up. Again. He began to wonder if his elbow was a tightly coiled spring.

"You wouldna dare." He flipped her over on his lap and scowled down at her angry face. Never had he had trouble disciplining Meghan. But then, even as a young lass, his cousin had been much bigger than Brianna. And he had known she was well-padded, and he couldna hurt her.

Brianna glared daggers at him. "Ha! Try it and you'll be damned sorry. I'll not be treated like an unruly child." She grabbed the braids at his temples and used them for leverage to hoist herself up.

"Ow! Lucifer's hairy back! Are ye tryin' to snatch me bald?" Damron grabbed the sides of his head and rubbed.

"I will if you keep acting like you're my father and I'm three years old," she shouted.

Brianna hurtled out of his arms and grabbed her tunic off the floor. Her face burned with embarrassment. She had never been so humiliated in her whole life. No. In both lives. For God's sake! She was naked, her private parts exposed to his eyes and hands. The more she had struggled the harder his sex had become. Had it gotten any more rigid, it would have bruised her side.

"Then agree to heed me and dinna ever again cause me to treat ye as such." Damron bounded up to come nose to nose with her.

"Ha! Who died and made you king?" The idea that he demanded unquestioning obedience to his dictates stoked her anger into maddened foolhardiness.

She fisted her right hand and whacked him on the nose. On seeing the astonished look on his face, and the bright red drops starting to dribble toward his lips, she brushed her hands together like she had finished an accomplishment.

He grabbed his nose and stared at her, undecided. She glared daggers at him. A soft rap at the door and Mereck's voice sent him swiftly to unlatch it.

Mereck raised an eyebrow, seeing the blood coming from Damron's nose. "Come," he said and jerked his head toward the stairwell. Neither spoke until they came out into the bailey.

"Well, brother," Damron began, "why did ye come for me?"

The words were barely out of his mouth before Mereck's fist smashed into Damron's chin. He hit the ground with a thud. Mereck followed to kneel on his shoulders.

"You have insulted a proud woman." Mereck, normally a man of few words, took a deep breath. "Have you not learned the strength of her will? Her dignity?"

Mereck was right in his judgment. Damron did not fight against his half brother, nor did he tell him he had not punished Brianna as he had promised. Were his men to learn of it, they would look on it as a flaw in Damron's ability to command respect from all at Blackthorn.

When he did not answer, Mereck continued, "Brianna expects honor from others. Once she calmed down, she would have come out on her own. But you hunted her like a forest creature. She is angered at Guardian, for he broke faith by leading you to her hiding place."

"He is right, Damron. She isna a woman to bend easily to your will." Connor stood over the two sprawled on the ground. "Did I not tell you she had the temper of a Mereck? She is as proud as any man."

"Surely Damron realizes by now that he made the wrong decision on how to deal with Brianna." Bleddyn appeared where before no one had stood. "She will not forgive you for allowing anyone to know you meant to correct her like a child. It offended her dignity. Come. I have taken leave to order Angel and Thunder saddled. We must talk."

Their horses' hooves pounded like crashing thunder as they crossed the drawbridge. Once they stopped to talk, Bleddyn did not tell Damron all of it, only that Brianna was not as other women, and should she become unhappy enough, she would become but a mere shadow of herself.

"What?" Damron's shout caused creatures settling for the evening to scramble from their lairs, and birds ruffled leaves on the trees above them as they made haste in flight. "Have ye fallen victim to the old fables of strange happenings, of people appearin' and disappearin' from other places? 'Tis naught but foolish imaginings."

"Nay, Damron, 'tis no tale I recount." Bleddyn's voice rang with truth. "Is she not different from other women? Do you not question the strange words and expressions she uses, though now she has adapted more to our own way of speaking?" Bleddyn waited patiently for him to think about it.

Trying to make sense of it, Damron rubbed his face hard, then ran his fingers through his hair. Brianna was different. No other lass was as pretty, as clever, as defiant or as headstrong as Brianna. Not even Meghan.

"Aye." Damron shook his head hoping to clear it. "But how would she change? Would she not still be the same Brianna?" His heart thudded in his chest, and bile rose to his throat as fear washed through him.

"In looks, aye. But the Brianna we know today as a strong woman will become the bride Malcolm and William told you about. Docile. Shy. Willing to follow your dictates without question."

Damron shuddered. They were no longer the attributes he wished for in a wife. She would not be exciting. Her voice would not fill his soul with longing. Nor could she stir his lust with but a defiant gaze. Far worse, this weak version would not be the helpmate he knew this strong Brianna would be.

His gut twisted. But how was he to ensure Brianna would be faithful and obey him in all things? Sweat trickled down his back.

Genevieve had also been strong-willed. He had the scars to prove it.

Above, in their chamber, Brianna snatched the offending rock from the bed.

"You damned, stinking, miserable, stupid-looking rock," she hissed at it between her teeth. She flipped it back and forth from one hand to the other, glared at it, spit on it, then rolled it in her hand like her favorite pitcher on the New York Yankees would do. She wound up for the pitch, stepped forward with her left foot and hurled it as hard as she could at the stone wall. It bounced back and landed at her feet.

"Crap! You were supposed to break, dammit." She grabbed it back up, marched to the window opening and heaved it out.

"Now, there's an end of your *Strong Hand* rock, by God."

She huffed, put on a night garment and crawled into bed. "I'd better not see that damned thing again." She pulled the covers up to her chin.

Closing her eyes, she tried to come to a decision on how to manage her life here. Though Gordon had physically hurt her, Damron had wounded her in a worse way. Her pride. She would not give him the satisfaction of knowing how badly.

Below, in the great hall, Damron stood by the window opening, a goblet of strong ale in his hand. He hoped Brianna would soon understand she could not be a proper wife if she believed herself equal to her husband. How could any woman be so sadly mistaken about her place in life?

Something thudded onto the ground below the window, interrupting his thoughts. Already suspecting what he would find, he went out to investigate. Moonlight illuminated the rock, and he knew it was not yet time to seek his bed.

He returned to brace himself against the door frame, away from the many sleeping bodies on the floor. He occupied himself picturing faces to match the snores. He did not attempt the task when it came to the varying tunes of breaking wind. In the darkest hours of the night, he took off his boots, went above and slipped into his chambers.

Until the sky started to lighten, he sat beside the bed and studied Brianna's face, thinking. How could a person change as completely as Bleddyn suggested? His heart lurched, and his hands fisted. What if the Welshman had not told him all?

It was not possible that Brianna's soul was from another time? Was it?

Chapter 17

For several days, relentless storms raged, driving everyone inside. Grumpy men sat about, tired of idleness, restless and weary of each other. The castle began to feel cramped and too small for them all.

Damron leaned back, arms crossed and shoulders braced against the wall, and scowled at a group of near-drunk men arguing over a game of chance in the hall's far corner. When the armorer lunged to his feet and stalked over to the blacksmith, Damron's eyes narrowed. 'Twas likely a brawl in the making. He huffed in disgust and lurched to his feet. In a voice that boomed over the din, he called out, "Meghan, lass, do ye think a lively tune or two can chase the sour moods away?"

"Aye." She bounded to her feet, snatched her pipes from beside the door and shouted above the din. "Listen well, ye blustering louts. I can play louder than ye can carp, so save yer breath." She squeezed out a screeching note to get the arguing men's attention and began to play. Blaringly.

The quarrelsome voices softened, then faded away. Bleddyn left the room for a time, then returned with his ancient bodhran. His fingers rubbed over the round drum and caressed the white leather skin, then slowly traced the Celtic knots and horses he had painted there in vivid blues and reds. Catching Meghan's attention, he nodded.

"Little one, sing for me," Bleddyn called to Brianna.

He grinned and waggled his brows at her, drawing her to stand beside him. Picking up the beaters, he struck a wild, savage rhythm on the bodhran, and his deep voice rang out in the language of his ancestors. Meghan joined the tune with her pipes, and Merrick's rich baritone rose to blend with Bleddyn's.

Bleddyn stared intently at Brianna. Memories flashed in her mind of being in woods surrounded by his people, singing and dancing. She knew he had taught her this tune when she was a youngling. She turned her back to the high table. To Damron.

Damron's heart lurched on hearing Brianna's beautiful voice soar up and around the men's words, twisting and turning, a striking contrast to their deep tones. Her arms lifted as graceful as swaying willow limbs. Her hair swirled about her face while she danced around Bleddyn. Her body flowed to the music like a breeze stirring the calm waters of a loch.

Brianna's voice caressed every part of Damron. 'Twas more erotic than anything any woman could do to entice him. He cursed himself for causing her vow not to sing for him.

The music softened and faded into the wall's stones. The sounds floated like a whisper as she disappeared into the hallway shadows.

His chest ached, like she had struck him a mighty blow by her denial.

Not once had she looked at him.

Damron waited. When he finally followed her to their chambers, he found the bathing tub was still full, the water warm and clear. She had bathed elsewhere.

"Mari, where did yer mistress cleanse herself?"

The woman's startled gaze met Brianna's.

"Speak, lass. Dinna look to yer lady for permission," he ordered.

"I went with my lady to the baths below, milord."

"Ye well know men oft go there to cleanse themselves. What if someone came while yer mistress was unclothed?"

"Nay, milord, I would not let that happen. A man I be seeing stood guard with his sword ready. Protecting us."

"Never do so again. 'Tis my wish the lady bathes within the safety of our chamber." Damron frowned and motioned for the maidservant to leave.

With abrupt movements, he grasped his tunic and bent to pull it over his head. Brianna ambled over to the window opening and pretended to watch the waning daylight, while he got into the tub and settled back in the warm water.

"Come, wife. I would have ye wash my back." His quiet tones rumbled oddly in his chest, imprisoned there, sounds that had yearned to soar with hers in the hall below. He watched and waited for her to do her duty by him. Slowly, she came over, took the cloth he handed her and lathered it with ginger-scented soap. He leaned forward and sighed with pleasure.

Brianna decided it wasn't such a chore after all feeling his muscles ripple beneath her hands. Her movements slowed and sometimes nearly stopped while she stroked over his bronze skin and the scars there. Most were white, while others were still pink. She finished washing his back and stepped back, only to have him hold up one dripping arm.

"I thought you needed help only with your back, my lord. Are you not able to tend your own bathing?"

"'Tis what a wife and squires are for, Brianna. In this room I prefer yer hand. A Scottish lass attends not only her husband's bath, but anyone else he wishes her to aid." He kept his arm up. Waiting.

"Huh, tough luck on what Scottish women do. I'll never bathe a sweaty stranger," she muttered.

Seeing his narrowed eyes glinting at her, she decided to be quiet. She gritted her teeth as she rubbed the soapy cloth over his arm and down to his hand. He spread his fingers for her attention. While she scrubbed, she inspected his calluses.

"Huh. You can wield a sword but you can't wash your own hands?"

Once satisfied even his nails were clean and white, she glanced up to find him studying her.

"My chest, wife," he murmured. When she hesitated, he studied her face.

"Whoever heard of a grown man needing a nursemaid?"

He ignored her, closed his eyes and rested his head back against the tub's rim. Her hands lingered as she washed his bared neck, fascinated by the feel of the blood pounding there below his jaw. No matter how calm he looked, his heartbeat claimed something else. She soaped across his collarbones and soon became engrossed in the thick mat of curly black hair covering his broad, muscled chest.

Well, hell, why not be honest with herself? She enjoyed touching him. He was beautiful. All over. When her cloth moved down to wash the hard slab of his belly past his navel, she again tried to give him the soapy cloth.

He shook his head. "My legs, lady."

A flush warmed her face while she tended the hard smoothness of his muscled thigh and calf. He lowered his left leg and lifted his right. When she finished with his foot and moved up over his calf to his knee, the soapy water flowed off, revealing a horrendous, jagged scar that began on the inside of his knee all the way up to meet his groin.

"Oh, my God, Damron. How did you ever survive such a wound?" She reached out, wanting to comfort his flesh, but he jerked his leg back and stood. Water sloshed onto the floor.

He shook his head and turned his back to her.

"Pull the stool close and bring the rinse water."

Her gaze flashed down his body; her arms began to shake. When she came close, he took the bucket from her and held her elbow as she climbed onto the stool and poured the water over him.

He seized a large drying cloth from a short stool nearby, wrapped it tightly around his hips and turned to her.

"I thank ye, Brianna." His gaze probed her face. "Ye broke yer promise tonight, my lady. Why?"

"Promise, my lord?"

"Yer promise ne'er to sing afore me again. Tonight ye did so." He paused, his gaze searching her face. "Why?"

"I neither sang for you, nor before you. I gave you my back."

"If ye will not sing at my request, for whom will ye sing?"

"For my Nathaniel. He favors music as wild and mystical as he is. And it's a favorite of mine. We went into the woods at special times of the year. His people would join us there to dance and sing the ancient tunes."

When they sought their bed soon after, Damron attempted to gather her close. She stiffened.

"Let go, Damron. Until our wedding, please keep your hands to yourself."

Damron drew back and anchored his arms behind his head. He stared, unseeing, at the bed's canopy. Was she still angry because of his stupid attempt to curb her? Or, worse, now she had seen what Genevieve had done to him, did she find his body repulsive? Knowing Brianna would not sleep until sure that he did, he forced his breathing to slow and deepen until he snored lightly. Weariness finally claimed her, and she sighed and slept.

Damron fanned her hair out over the pillow and burrowed his face in its silky sweetness. When her legs jerked and her arms twitched, he murmured and ran his hand over her head, much as he would do when Angel was upset, until she stilled.

He knew Bleddyn hid some secret from him. He struggled with believing what the mystic did tell him, and he determined to keep a close watch on Brianna. He brought the covers snugly to her neck, then left the bed, dressed and slipped from the room.

Guardian lay outside their door and whimpered and tried to barge into the room, but stopped obediently when Damron ordered him to stay and guard her door.

Not long after, Brianna awoke with a fright, sure that she heard a voice cry out. Damron was not beside her. She threw her robe about her as she ran to the door, afraid Papa Dougie was in pain. The blasted door wouldn't open.

She pounded on the heavy wood with her fists. "Help! Someone help me. The door's stuck."

When Bleddyn wrenched it open, she started to run from the room, but he restrained her.

"Please hurry. I heard a man cry out as if in pain."

"Nay, little one, you but dreamt it. Though now you are awake, I do have a matter we must discuss." He looked down at the floor.

She followed his gaze to see Guardian wedged between them, quivering. Had he shrunk? Why were his eyes and coat dull? "Has Guardian been ill?"

"He does not eat, and he drinks only small sips of water since you became angry with him. He thought it a game his master played at finding you, and now he suffers for it."

Brianna's heart went out to the great, sad beast looking up at her. She sat on the floor and crooned silly words to him as though he was a small puppy. He whimpered and shoved his head against her chest, so she would pat and kiss him.

Reaching for a plate of bread and cheese on the table beside her, she broke the cheese into small portions and dunked the bread in water to feed him. He opened his mouth when she bade him, and she patiently fed and talked to him. After he had eaten enough, she folded a blanket and coaxed him onto it. The wolf closed his weary eyes and surrendered to her comforting presence.

Damron strode into the room and halted when he saw Brianna sitting on the floor beside Guardian. He pushed his windblown hair out of his eyes and watched her face.

"Damron, I heard someone cry out. I ran to help, but the door stuck." She frowned, went over to it and found an extra latch. Through narrowed eyes, she stared at it, then at him. "Is there a reason you locked me in this room?"

"I had the latch added to keep ye safe if ye sleepwalk, and I am not here. It will ensure ye dinna go out into the storms that come so oft this time of year."

"Oh? And what of a fire? Who will release it then?"

"I will post a guard for yer safety. Now enough yammerin'. We have but a short time afore the sun's rise. I wish to sleep."

Brianna glared at him and pressed her lips together. He nodded to Bleddyn and shut the door after the Welshman left.

After Brianna slept, Damron rose and pulled the bed curtains tight. He slipped on his robe, and lit a candle to examine the ceiling above their bed.

Satan's fetid breath! He may as well have told Brianna he had gone to Asceline for her ministrations. He had not. What had awakened his wife? Directly overhead was a gap wide enough to allow sounds to travel from the room above. Where Asceline slept.

He quit his chamber and made his way to the corner stairwell, and up to the floor above. He thrust open the Frenchwoman's door. She jumped up with a shriek, but seeing Damron, sprawled back against the pillows.

"Clothe yerself, and be quick about it." He seized her arm and pulled her to her feet while evading her groping fingers. He had no doubt she was swiving another, nor did he care. Seeing a braided rug beside the bed, he shoved it away with his foot. He spied what he looked for. Kneeling, he peered through an opening that had been recently enlarged, for fresh knife cuts were visible between the boards. Below was the canopy of his own bed.

Disgust roiled through him knowing Asceline had likely tried to spy on Brianna and him in bed. Thanks be to the saints, the canopy had foiled that attempt.

He did not care who Asceline took to her bed, but what did stoke his anger was her vocal attempts with her lover to convince Brianna he was still swiving her. His leman's voluptuous beauty no longer drew him, for he was a helpless slave to his building desire for Brianna. Each day, it became harder for him to keep his vow not to take her and make her fully his. The thought of her sweet body beneath him was in his thoughts when he awoke each morn, and even plagued his dreams by night.

Dawn's soft rays peeped through the hall's window openings the next morn, casting a gentle streak of light over the room. Brianna and Meghan hurried with eating their porridge and scones, for Damron had told her when she woke that he had arranged an outing for her and Meghan's pleasure.

Simon, the head falconer, waited in the bailey with Meghan's sparrowhawk, Simple. The sleek raptor transferred to her wrist with eager little hops, while Meghan calmed her with soft cooing sounds and light caresses down her wee head and back.

Damron smiled at them and motioned toward the drawbridge. "Get along with ye now, for 'tis likely to rain this day. Malcolm, dinna let them stray from yer sight." Before they were through the barbican, he was bounding up the steps to the keep.

Brianna closed her eyes and took a deep breath of the pine-scented air, savoring it. The sun filtering through the canopy of leaves looked like streaks of golden air. She turned to Meghan, curious. "What possessed you to call your hawk by such a lowly name as Simple?"

"Because she be right glaikit, of course," Meghan chuckled and brushed falling leaves from her dark hair. "I am not like Damron, naming my beasties the opposite of how they act. As bonny as she is, she is not so canny in catchin' her prey. She forgets to watch where she goes and slams into trees or anythin' else in her way." Her eyes danced with humor.

"Mayhap I should have called her Stupid. One day whilst chasing a white sea bird twice her size, she dunked onto Angel's rump. She dropped to the sand, out like a wet candle. My cousin was not well-pleased. He had the devil's time of it tryin' to calm the fright she gave the great steed."

They spent most of the morning laughing and watching Simple's antics. The wind picked up, and mindful of Damron's warning, they headed back to the keep.

Brianna hurried to her chamber to change her damp clothes. She tugged a clean smock over her head, and though it muffled the sounds, she heard Damron's footsteps enter the chamber. Her head cleared the smock's neckline, and she glimpsed him leaning against the wall, watching her. She was still puzzled over why the sparrowhawk was so agile while pursuing its prey at high speeds, but after the catch, collided with anything in its way.

Damron's deep voice rumbled something about "the time has come," while she continued to dress.

"Yes, my lord," she said when she finally settled a heavy blue tunic over her shoulders.

"I am pleased ye agree, lady wife." His soft voice became a purr. "I thought to hear a long list of new reasons against it, but ye have settled my mind."

Brianna looked up at him, confused. Maybe she should ask him to repeat what she had missed hearing while her head was smothered with clothing? Before she could, the daft man winked at her without cracking so much as a smile. Damn. What had he meant by "ye have settled my mind"?

Meghan burst into the room, distracting her.

"Our outing wasna a treat but a ruse to be rid of us whilst servants moved Asceline's belongings to another room," Meghan said in such a hurry the words near blended together.

Brianna lost the warm glow of pleasure she'd felt during her outing from the castle. Determined to find out what was happening with Damron's leman, she and Meghan bribed Johanna, the blacksmith's burly wife, now Asceline's maid, to talk Asceline into going to the village to look for ribbons. Asceline no sooner was over the drawbridge than Brianna and Meghan ran up to the Frenchwoman's room. The room had been freshly scrubbed, and bright, colorful tapestries hung on the walls to keep out the chill.

"Hm. Do you have your knife with you?" Brianna asked.

Meghan unstrapped a blade from around her thigh, and they grabbed the pallet and pulled it onto the floor. Brianna studied the exposed rope structure to see where it had to be the strongest to support the greatest weight and strain. After she finished, they hastily put the bed back to rights.

The hours passed swiftly to afternoon. A lathered horseman arrived to advise Damron that raiders had attacked a nearby village. Damron and Mereck examined each warrior's equipment to see that every knife and sword would slice though a blade of grass. They hefted maces and battle hammers to assure their shafts were sturdy, and ordered the men to cover their shields and helmets with a dark paste, which would keep them from reflecting light.

Damron found Brianna in the great hall and led her to stand with the family members close to the hearth. He motioned to Father Matthew.

The priest stepped forward and held up his hands. "By

your leave, may we have quiet in the hall? Lord Damron wishes to make an announcement." Conversation stilled, and he stepped back.

Damron put his arm around Brianna's shoulder. "As ye know, my lady and I married by proxy. She has felt the lack of a proper weddin', so I have sent notice to the clans. Within a sennight, visitors will arrive. When all are gathered here, we will wed the way she wishes."

Brianna startled and looked up at him in surprise. No wonder he had winked at her. The blasted man knew she hadn't heard him in their bedchamber. Damron folded his arms around her to bring her tight against his hot, muscular flesh to kiss her senseless. His loins stirred against her belly, and she pictured him as he had stood in his bath, naked with water droplets winding their fascinating way down his glistening skin. Her body melted against his, while heat pooled at the joining of her legs. She gasped and pushed back from him.

After the shouting and thumping faded away, the hall quickly emptied as everyone made their way out to the bailey. Spencer carried Damron's broadsword and shield. Brianna felt an uneasy flutter of fear.

"Will you be back soon, Damron?"

"Dinna worry, Brianna. Ye willna be without protection. Someone will always be close by should ye need aid."

"Huh, I don't need protection or aid. 'Tis your own men's protection I question. Do you take enough warriors in case there're more raiders than you expected?"

"Think ye I need instructions from a Saxon lass?" He arched a brow at her, and the corners of his lips twitched.

Father Matthew pointedly cleared his throat, raised his arms in supplication, and called blessings on all their heads, bidding God to bring them safely home. Brianna handed Damron a stirrup cup, and in a quivering voice, spoke the same wish being offered to Connor and Mereck.

"Godspeed and bring you home in good health."

Her heart lurched in fear. Damron could be badly injured. She tried to swallow the lump in her throat.

He drained his cup, handed it to a squire and grasped her to him. "Have no fear I willna return, wife. I leave much unfinished between us." Holding her steady, he kissed her, his tongue gently exploring her mouth, then withdrawing so he could nibble at her lips. His arms hesitated, then tightened in a fierce hug before he released her and gracefully swung up onto Angel's saddle.

Bleddyn, his clothing as midnight black as his great destrier, Thunder, came over to them. "Hold, Lord Damron. I go with you." He had again divided his face with blue dye. The right side, where the great scar stretched from scalp to chin, was even more evident painted a vivid red. He had drawn purple symbols over that half of his forehead and cheek. His strong jaw and neck were outlined with black to match his hair. Some of the younger men sidled nervous glances at him.

But Brianna did not fear him. His was a face glorious in all its starkness, outlined by the shaggy black hair hanging wild and straight about it. She kissed his painted cheek.

"Godspeed, Nathaniel. Come safely home." Before she could blink, he vaulted astride Thunder's back and shouted the chilling, high-pitched, warbling cry Brianna had told him the American Indians had used.

When Brianna echoed the sound, Damron's startled gaze jerked down to study her. She knew his people had their own battle cries, but when he and Bleddyn galloped down the line of men to take the lead, Bleddyn warbled the cry again. Damron's warriors mimicked it, and the sheer volume of their voices made up for their lack of practice.

Brianna and Meghan watched until the last man disappeared, then hurried back inside the quiet castle.

"Aunt Phillipa will ready the hall to care for the wounded. Ye must have a proper blade to help strip them of clothin'," Meghan said, her head deep inside her large wooden chest. She brought out a narrow dagger etched with holy symbols, and its sheath, and held them up for Brianna's inspection. "This fine blade is a misericord. All knights and squires carry them. If a fellow warrior's wounds be mortal and they canna stay till his passin', they deliver him from misery and degradation. 'Tis like the one I carry."

"I'm glad for the weapon, Meghan," Brianna said. "Ever since that lout grabbed me at the waterfall, I've wanted some means to protect myself, should the need ever arise again." Though the early Brianna had died by falling or being pushed from the parapets, she knew her being brought to this time could change the past. That early Brianna would have been too timid, too used to being chattel, to have fought overmuch when things went wrong.

Her confidence grew as Meghan helped her tie the sheath to Brianna's inner right thigh.

Sun crept through the windows of Bleddyn's medicinal hut the next morning, giving enough light for Brianna to study all the labeled earthenware jars, the vials of powders and the herbs hanging in small clusters from the ceiling. In the years she had studied to become a geneticist, she had also taken courses in pharmacology. She selected a goodly amount of every herb and powder she knew would be needed when the men returned.

Picking and choosing amongst them, she and Meghan prepared powders for potions and ingredients in healing wounds.

Brianna ordered large barrels of water be brought to the hall, and for the kitchen staff to keep a steady supply of hot water. She no sooner finished her preparations than trumpets blared, and rasping chains signaled the raising of the portcullis.

Returning warriors who were not able to ride their mounts were supported by others. All were splattered with so much mud and

bright blotches of blood that Brianna had to study their faces to
recognize them. Her heart pounded in her ears until she finally
spotted Damron at the end of the long line of men.

Many of the warriors made their way or were carried to the
hall, which now reminded Brianna of an emergency ward.
Calling them by name, Laird Douglas spoke words of praise
and comfort to each man.

"Place the badly wounded on the trestle tables close to the
fireplace," Brianna instructed the men as they entered.

The supplies she and Meghan had prepared stood ready for
use. Bleddyn insisted everyone scrub their hands before
touching the wounded men, and several young boys scrambled to bring fresh buckets of water from the barrels.

Servants passed from man to man, helping them to drink as
much wine as they could, before it was their turn to be treated.

Brianna tied up her tunic's long sleeves and scoured her hands,
preparing to clean around a gaping wound in a man's shoulder.
Her movements were quick and efficient, handing Bleddyn whatever he needed before he asked. With precisely placed stitches,
she closed the wound, then spread a healing ointment over it and
nodded to Meghan to bind the man's shoulder.

Bleddyn motioned Brianna to come with him to the next
table, where the man had an ugly gash from the side of his
knee down to his heel. His blood-soaked breeches were in the
way, and they had no time to strip them from him.

On seeing Brianna draw her misericord and reach toward
him, the poor man fainted. She sighed, relieved, and slit his
breeches from groin to ankle. She and Bleddyn worked rapidly to repair his wound and spare the man pain. As she
worked, she wondered in what battle Damron had fought to
receive his terrible leg wound.

The boys kept up a steady rhythm of replacing the water,
for everyone followed Bleddyn's directions to make ample
use of it and soap. Each time the Welshman or Brianna used

an instrument from his amazing stock, they washed and poured whisky over it. Her misericord flashed often, but now the men no longer flinched.

Sunlight was fading when they finally cared for the last man. Bleddyn beckoned Damron, Connor and Mereck to come over for treatment, but they held back, much like small boys called for a scolding.

Mereck approached Bleddyn like he trudged through thick mud. Meghan grabbed Connor by the arm and drew him over to the table, where she searched him for any injury, no matter how minor.

"I have naught but mere scratches," Damron claimed and moved back from Brianna. His clothing was blood soaked, his face pale.

"Sit!" She scowled at him and pointed to a bench. He sat.

Though he claimed he had mere scratches, she found deep gashes on his chest and arms.

"Why didn't you come to me right away, Damron? For God's sake, man. What were you thinking?"

He looked surprised, like she had asked a foolish question. "As long as I have my wits about me, I ne'er seek aid until my men are tended."

When Bleddyn finished with Mereck, he hurried over to help her.

Damron watched Brianna through lowered lashes while she tended him. She was as fastidious with what he considered his simple wounds as she had been with the life-threatening ones of the badly injured warriors. He gritted his teeth to keep from wincing, while she closed his flesh with neat stitches. Vomit surged to his throat. He swallowed it back, then bent his head, hoping no one had noticed.

"The louts' leaders kept their precious hides well behind the fightin'," Damron said to Laird Douglas. "Ne'er have I seen such reluctance to show their faces."

"Always, the Gunns flaunt their plaid, but today, we did not see their colors," Mereck added.

"Mayhap they are men not wishin' to be known?" Laird Douglas suggested.

"Aye. I felt 'twas so." Damron shoved a lock of hair out of his eyes. He grimaced as Bleddyn probed a wound on his back.

"Lean against me, husband." Brianna moved close and put her arms around his shoulders to steady him. "The blade must have been ill kept. There're rust flecks deep inside the wound that must come out, else it will fester."

"Umpf," he breathed when Bleddyn dug deep. "Their leader had blond hair. It made me curious. Something wasna right about them." To Damron's shame, his voice wavered. To divert himself from Bleddyn's torture, he thrust out his left arm and admired Brianna's needlework.

"Ye stitch a fine seam, lass. Mayhap ye can teach Meghan the 'ins and outs' of a needle?" When Meghan snorted nearby, he grinned.

"The next openin' ye have on yer thick skull, cousin, I'll gladly close for ye," Meghan said with a huff.

"Nay. I dinna think so. From what I have seen of yer stitchin' on the tapestry, my ears might rest atop my head when ye finished."

"Huh. Better that than the knot I'll place there if ye linger," she said and advanced with an empty basin raised high.

He chuckled, and after Bleddyn motioned they were finished tormenting him, he followed Mereck and Connor down to the bathing chamber.

Though the two men's wounds were above their waists, and they could soak their aching bones in hot water, Damron could not chance getting his dressings wet. He stripped off his bloodied clothing and filled a large basin.

"Only a bairn should use a basin to bathe," he grumbled.

"Ruin Brianna's fine artwork on your feeble body and she will box your ears," Connor teased.

Swift as a badger, Damron grabbed Connor's head and shoved it under the water, then grunted with the pain it cost him. "Puny did ye say? Not so feeble I couldna tromp ye into the mud, cousin." He let go and stepped back as Connor started to lunge out of the tub. "Nay," Damron said and shook his head. "Wet my bindings, and I will tell Brianna ye took advantage of a poor, wounded man."

Connor and Mereck barked with laughter. He grinned and turned to scrub from his hair down to between his toes, not quitting until all traces of grime and blood were gone.

As dusk fell, the great hall filled with boisterous men making light of their wounds. They bragged and preened before the women. Once their bellies were sated, they would plow their way through the willing females of the keep in a night of debauchery.

Brianna was beautiful tonight. Her hair flowed free, and Mari had drawn a little from each temple and secured the sections with yellow ribbons. The ends hung down the middle of her back and mingled with her curls. Seeing her lean close to speak in Mereck's ear, Damron frowned. His brother looked down at her as she talked, shook his head, then turned to stare at Damron.

By God's blood! What had she told him?

Asceline boldly flounced up to Damron, ran her hand across his shoulders and tugged the braid of hair at his temple. She bent and boldly nibbled his ear. He jerked away, his gaze fixed on his wife. Brianna's lips set, and her eyes flashed fire. But she held her tongue.

Mereck came close to clamp a hand on Damron's shoulder and hiss in his ear, "If you took the time to sample your wife, you might find her far tastier than the Frenchwoman. Brianna would give you less trouble, if you taught her the ways of pleasure."

His words flowed over Damron like scalding pitch. He surged to his feet and pulled Brianna up with him. His gaze burned into hers. His voice was a violent whisper forced between clenched teeth.

"Why did ye break yer vow, wife? Did ye not believe me?" His thumbs rubbed up and down her soft neck, and his fingers tightened. "Are ye not going to plead?" One hand stroked down over her shoulder. "Ye knew full well what I promised, if ye told anyone I had not taken yer maidenhead. Though that man be my brother, ye will pay the penalty."

"Do you think I'd be stupid enough to tell anyone?" Brianna struggled to break his grasp without disturbing any of his injuries.

"Your wife told me nothing, Damron, but your actions have. You wear the look of a man bursting with need," Mereck said bluntly.

Damron snatched Brianna up and over his shoulder, and stifled a gasp of pain. He turned toward the now deathly quiet room.

"Dinna fash yerselves. I am impatient to claim my wife this night." His arm clamped around her knees and he tilted her farther over his shoulder to quell her struggles. He ran his hand over her rounded bottom and winked. "Ye will seek yer own pleasures soon enough."

Chapter 18

Brianna beat on Damron's hips as he lunged up the stairway. "For God's sake, Damron. Put me down. You'll hurt yourself. I didn't tell Mereck anything."

Damron fought to regain control over himself, knowing battle fever had him in its grip. Over and over in his mind he kept telling himself, "Wait till yer temper cools. Ye canna treat an untried woman as ye would yer leman."

"Out, Mari!" He hurtled into his bedchamber and jerked his head toward the door. She flew out of the room like a chicken running from a fox.

He slammed the door with his booted heel, then bent over until Brianna's feet were firmly on the floor. He watched her without speaking. She stared at him as if she saw some strange creature.

"Remove yer clothes, wife." Damron's voice sounded husky, and he coughed to clear it. Brianna's heart ticked a frantic pace in that special hollow low on her neck. She crossed her arms over her breasts.

He stalked across the room, his eyes hard slits, and threw his sword atop his weapons chest. He whipped his shirt over his head. It landed behind him. Sitting on the edge of the bed, he shoved off his boots and stockings, then unbuckled his belt. He stood, letting his tartan slither to the floor.

"Ye dinna plan to be an obedient wife, do ye, Saxon? I should not have listened to yer pleas those months past and denied myself the pleasures of yer body. I will have ye and wait no longer."

His hands reached for her. She did not move. Her eyes were large, and her face so white even her lips were pale. Quick flashes of anger and regret passed over her features. He ignored them.

Brianna watched the blue vein in Damron's forehead throb and bulge. His lips were nearly a straight line. She swallowed, wanting to calm him with words, but her thoughts tumbled, remembering her futile efforts to fight off Gordon. The more she had tried to elude him, the more vicious his touch had become.

She did not resist as Damron pulled her tunic from her body and dropped it onto the floor. Her chin high and firm, she stood clothed in her gold smock.

His gaze roved over her and halted on the dagger strapped to her thigh, then traveled back up to linger on the dark triangle between her legs, up over her flat stomach and on up to her breasts. She didn't recoil when he lifted the smock from her. Only her weapon, her stockings and shoes remained. His gaze mocked her.

"Ah, wife. Will ye, too, try to unman me?" His voice faded to near a whisper. "Like Genevieve?"

Brianna gasped, horrified. One arm snaked around her waist and lifted her high. He had the weapon off in seconds and tossed it across the room. He stalked over to stand her beside the bed.

His words streaked like adrenalin through her veins. Her fear vanished. She grabbed a sheet off the bed and quickly wrapped it around herself. Knowing who had given him that dreadful scar explained why he did not trust her. Or perhaps any woman, for that matter. What could have happened between him and Genevieve? Now was not the time to ask. Not when he was so agitated, believing she, too, had proved deceitful. She took a deep breath and squared her shoulders.

"I didn't break my vow to you, Damron." She raised her chin and met his angry gaze. "I would never discuss our mating with anyone. It is no one else's affair."

Indecision flashed through his green eyes. His lips lost some of their tension.

"You have already sent notice to your people to gather here for our wedding, like you promised. Why would I endanger that? Especially since it's what I asked for in the first place?"

Raising his hands, he scrubbed them over his face. His shoulder muscles eased and the vein in his forehead stopped looking like it would burst at any moment. He dropped down on the side of the bed, his elbows on his knees and his head in his hands.

"Damron," she murmured. "You may still doubt me, but do you really believe Mereck would lie to you?"

Damron heaved a sigh and looked up at her. His eyes looked so haunted, so vulnerable, she caught her breath.

"Nay. Mereck has never told a lie in his life. Not even to save himself a thorough thrashing when we were lads." His face paled and his body seemed to soften as his rigid back relaxed. He cleared his throat and eyed her ruefully.

"I think ye need to repair yer needlework, wife. Mayhap carryin' ye up the stairs wasna a good . . ."

Before she could move to help him, his eyes closed. He toppled over sideways onto the bed.

Knowing Damron's pride, Brianna did not call for help. He would be humiliated if anyone learned he had collapsed, and they believed swiving his wife had laid him low.

She climbed onto the bed, pulled and tugged at Damron until his head lay on her pillow. She scrambled off the foot of the bed and grunted as she hefted his right leg onto the sheets. Stepping back, she grabbed his left calf to do the same, but hesitated. On seeing his male parts so openly displayed between his widespread legs, heat spread over her face. She blinked, gulped and forced her eyes to behave as she took a deep breath, let it out in a whoosh, and finally maneuvered his leg onto the bed.

It did not surprise her that his body had shut down and forced him to rest. Exertion after the battle and the hard ride back to Blackthorn had taken a heavy toll on him. Of course, his wounds and too much wine didn't help. Not to mention bounding like a jackrabbit up the stairs carrying her on his shoulder.

She dressed quickly and opened the door only wide enough to beckon a passing servant. "Bring a pitcher of hot water and clean linen, please. Lord Damron's bindings need changing."

She paced beside the bed, waiting. On her tenth trip from the foot of the bed to the head, she realized her gaze kept straying to one particular area. One that had no need of her ministrations, as far as she knew. But she really hadn't checked.

Her heart skipped a beat on spying a streak of blood on his penis. She bent over, her brows near drawn together as she squinted nearsightedly at his flesh. She lowered her head until she could see more clearly. She was so close her agitated breath fanned the hair nestled there. One hand reached out and touched his flaccid flesh. He groaned and tossed his left arm across his chest, hit her on the back of the head and almost knocked her face onto his male parts. She jumped back, feeling like a lecherous peeping Tom, uh, Tomasina.

When the supplies she requested were brought to the door, she heaved a sigh of relief. Once she had them spread on the table, she inspected each wound, repaired his stitches and applied clean dressings. Her hands roved over his smooth, warm chest muscles, down across the hard slab of his belly and even further to prowl over his long, powerful legs. As she washed away the smeared blood on his sex, she told herself she searched for any missed injury. When she realized she was touching and admiring his sexy body far more than was necessary, she pulled the covers up to his chin and slid into bed beside him. She didn't trust her hands not to start straying again, so she pressed her cheek to his forehead to be sure he had no more than the normal amount of fever after such an ordeal.

She inhaled his scent, that scent that forever made her heart trip, for her soul had remembered it throughout centuries. Earlier, bitterness had gleamed in Damron's eyes and showed in the grim set of his lips. If he had no feelings for her, why had she been sent here?

With her hands behind her head, she stared up at the bed canopy. What had happened between Damron and Genevieve that caused the woman to give him such a vicious wound? Was it something he had done, and she had defended herself? Or did she attack him in a jealous rage? Had this distrust, this unwillingness to let another woman close to him, caused the marriage between him and the early Brianna to end in tragedy?

Well past sunrise the next morning, Brianna woke to find Damron had drawn the bed draperies. It was dark and deliciously warm, but not from his body next to her. She stretched and knew he was not in the room, or she would have felt his presence.

"Good day, milady," Mari said as she opened the drapes, a cheerful look on her face. "The master said to have a warm bath waitin' when ye stirred."

"Um, that sounds heavenly." Brianna swung her legs over the side of the bed and groaned when she stood on the cold floor. Though she was in good shape, every muscle in her body squawked. Lugging Damron around on the bed had taxed her strength to the limit. She sighed, relaxing in the hot water.

Mari bustled about picking up discarded clothing and putting it away. Her eyes near bugged out of her head when she saw the blood-stained sheets.

She clucked and shook her head in sympathy. "Me mither told me to lay all quietlike, with me arms at me sides and me eyes closed. She claimed 'twould make me marital duties easier. Mither said a man doesna like ye to see his rod all shriveled like. Ye must wait till it be full grown with heat, for it do look right hapless afore it gets excited."

Brianna covered her face with the soapy cloth, hiding her grin.

Mari pursed her lips and added, "Whimper and beg that such a massive weapon will surely kill ye, but dinna scorn that part of him that holds a large share of his brain."

"A large share? Huh. I think it's *all* housed there." Brianna huffed and rolled her eyes at Mari.

"Aye. To be sure some do." Mari stooped and gathered the soiled linens in her arms. "After the master be done, sigh that he is a most powerful man. It wudna hurt to say he has a wondrous pintle." She giggled and made a face over her shoulder as she left the room.

Brianna finished dressing, and secured her hair with two braids at her temples tied in back with a bright yellow ribbon. Hearing a distant crash, she startled. Thunder? Did a storm approach? But the room was bright with sunlight.

Fear flew through her that someone attacked the castle. She stumbled over her feet as she ran and peered out into the courtyard. Men looked up at the floor above her and scratched their heads. She rushed from the room and up the corner stairwell. Shrill shrieks and curses led her to Asceline's room. The door was thrown wide as if someone had left hastily. Brianna stopped and stared at the room.

The leman's bed had collapsed in the middle, folding the pallet into a giant sandwich, trapping Asceline inside. Her hands scrabbled like frantic crabs trying to reach the frame at the head, and her feet were high and thrashing against the raised foot of the bedding.

Whoever had lain with her there had slithered out like a worm, for half the sheet trailed across the floor. Brianna shrugged and studied the leman's predicament. Damron burst into the room, with Connor and Mereck arriving seconds later. Half a dozen people gathered behind them. Meghan peered over a man's shoulder and, seeing Asceline's dilemma, her eyes sparkled. On hearing her throaty laughter, Asceline shrieked even louder.

"Hush yer blarsted screechin', woman," Damron bellowed. He shoved a lock of windblown hair out of his eyes and stared at the bed like it had become a monster that had decided to gobble up the hysterical woman.

Brianna's heart sank. Had he been on the stairway behind her, or had he been much closer but timed his arrival after hers? She jerked around and left the room. She would not ask him.

Damron and Mereck freed Asceline, and when Damron spied the cut ropes, he raised a questioning brow at his brother. Mereck's lips twitched, but neither man spoke. Damron knew his thoughts on keeping a leman while one had a wife. He decided his brother was wiser than he.

When they finally returned to the dusty bailey, Damron grinned at Mereck. "What do ye think happened?"

"Hm. No doubt Brianna had help from Meghan to weaken the bed," Mereck said and chuckled, then his face became serious.

"Aye. Though this is one mischief I dinna intend to lecture about." Damron frowned and rubbed his jaw. "Asceline has taken a new lover. She tries to convince Brianna that I still visit her."

"'Tis a shame the man freed himself afore we got there. How long do you think Asceline has lured another to her bed?" Mereck met Damron's gaze and quirked a brow.

"I kept her well sated until I brought Brianna here. Only these past weeks has she been actin' like a bitch in heat." Damron huffed in disgust, then turned when guards atop the barbican called out that Eric MacLaren approached. He was the first to answer the summons to gather for Damron's wedding.

In the next days, Brianna busied herself helping Lady Phillipa prepare for their expected guests. When she joined Damron in bed, she was so tired it didn't take as much of her will to close her mind to her body's response to his drugging kisses, and his warm flesh pressed to hers when they slept. If she didn't allow herself to want him, maybe she could protect her heart.

As the sun started to lower two days later, Damron entered while Brianna lounged in her bath. He sent Mari for more water, then lifted Brianna from the tub, wrapped a warmed cloth around her and stood her before him. He took his time drying her with exquisite tenderness. When the housemaids arrived with his own water, he put Brianna's robe around her and belted it.

"Come, wife, I would have ye tend my bath. I wish to please someone special this night."

Brianna's temper flashed. So he wanted to please Asceline, did he? "One moment, husband. I'll wash your hair with one of Bleddyn's special soaps." She went to her chest, drew forth two small vats and held them close to her body as she went to his back. When she reached for his head, his hand shot up to inspect what she proposed to use. It had a heady scent of sandalwood, herbs and juniper. He released her and she spread it over his back and chest. She took her time lathering his black hair and scrubbing his scalp before massaging his neck and shoulders. His wounds were healing nicely, and her fingers were especially gentle around them.

She grasped his head and nudged it forward so she could rinse it, then rubbed it with a towel before again running her fingers through the hair at his nape. After she finished bathing him, he dried himself while she dressed with all speed. She peered at him from the corner of her eyes, and began to regret what she had done.

Damron donned a soft white shirt, wrapped his plaid and buckled it around his waist with his heavy ceremonial belt and sword. He wore white stockings and black leather shoes and, when he was done, he looked so handsome her heart jumped a beat.

"Sit, my lord, so I may comb and braid your hair." He looked surprised at her solicitude, but he smiled and thanked her.

When he brought his wedding gift from his chest and buckled it around her hips, unease quivered down her spine.

No sooner had they descended the stairs than Brianna wished she could haul him back to their room and fix what she had done, even if it made him so angry he punished her. She grabbed his arm, opened her mouth to urge him to return upstairs with her, but the bagpipes called a merry greeting from the barbican.

It was too late.

"'Tis a Sassenach greetin' they play," Damron said, smiling down at her.

On hearing the word for someone across the borders, she would have dashed forward, but he kept a tight grip on her elbow.

"Walk beside me, lady wife." His green eyes flashed, and his smile disappeared. "Ye need not display such eagerness. All will think ye unhappy in our union."

As her gaze scanned the approaching riders, she could hardly control her excitement. Seeing men dressed in the Morgan tartans, she craned her neck and tried to see the people behind them. Finally, she spied whom they escorted. Aunt Maud and Uncle Simon rode at their center, and between them rode a woman clothed in white garments and a wimple.

"Alana!" Breaking from Damron's grasp, Brianna hurtled down the steps, her arms outstretched. The abbess was beautiful. The white cloth wound around her head, framing her face, was drawn in folds beneath her chin, flowing down across her back. Her eyes were the same deep brown as Brianna's and, by the color of her eyebrows, so would be her hair. Her eyes held inner peace and love.

Bleddyn put his arm across Brianna's shoulders, keeping her from harm's way as the laughing party dismounted. She waited anxiously until Alana, Aunt Maud and Uncle Simon reached them. She flung herself into her sister's arms, crying and laughing, until her aunt and uncle demanded attention. She turned to them with the same exuberance. When she finally caught her breath, her gaze scanned the people around them, looking for Elise and Galan.

"'Tis sorry I am Elise and Lady Cecelia could not join us." Baron Ridley patted her shoulder. "They have traveled with Sir Galan to Normandy. I sent him to purchase an Arabian stallion and mares for breeding. Elise is happily buying cloths and spices. They will be sorely disappointed when they return to find they have missed this visit."

"Now, my lovely, we will join the others," Damron said and smiled down at her. "We wished you to have this private time with your family, and they waited within." He put Brianna's hand on his wrist and led them all into the hall where his family stood by the fireplace.

After all the introductions had been made, she again hugged her sister. "Alana, I have longed to see you."

"You have changed much, my little one." She held Brianna at

arm's length to study her face and form. Bleddyn stood close. "No longer are you the unruly lass who must be watched like a hawk." When Damron snorted, she glanced up. "I have come to see you take your wedding vows afore God and man."

"She will need support to stand when my lord is finished with her. Unruly? He should whip her more often." Asceline's triumphant laugh poured from her throat as she pointed to Damron's head. "Have you joined the savage Welsh with their wild paints, my dear lord?"

Damron stiffened. He stood as still as a standing stone.

Bleddyn broke the silence. "Lord Damron has allowed his wife to stripe his hair in our fashion. It is a great honor he does me. I thank him for it." He bowed deeply toward Damron.

"Indeed, I would always honor you and your people thus, my lord. I have much respect for your customs." Damron's eyes flashed fire at Brianna. She recognized the anger in his soft voice and knew he would retaliate.

He did, when he whirled from her and took Asceline's elbow to escort her to the table. Brianna felt as if he had slapped her in front of everyone. When he had said he wished to please someone, why hadn't she kept her temper under control? What she had feared—that he would favor Asceline—she had brought about.

The evening meal progressed with Alana and the Ridleys answering Brianna's many questions. As trays of sweets were placed on the table, Alana turned to Brianna.

"Please, love, sing for me? It seems forever since I have heard your and Bleddyn's voices together." She clasped her hands in delight.

"Yes, my loving wife. Do sing for us." Damron crossed his arms over his chest and sprawled his legs out in front of him.

Hearing his sarcasm, Brianna hesitated. Bleddyn helped her rise and whispered, "You will sing for Alana, my little one. She does not have the joy of being with us and will soon return to her abbey. Let not your vow stop you from giving her comfort."

He sat on a stool, his bodhran on his lap. When the sounds and rhythm of the beat filled Brianna, husky warbles started low in her throat. The volume of her voice increased until it lifted high in an ancient Celtic song.

Damron listened to a song of such passion and wildness that his heart beat in rhythm to the bodhran. Delight shone in Alana's eyes and wide, happy smile. She held her hands tightly clasped at her chest as if in prayer. The tune ended and they began another. Damron's head jerked when Mereck joined them. His eyes widened in surprise, and he leaned forward when his brother took Brianna's hand and they danced gracefully, uninhibitedly, as they continued to sing. The dance ended and their voices picked up with the next beat.

Too soon, night fell. Brianna turned to Bleddyn with questions in her thoughts. She wished she could be content with her life like Alana, but then her sister knew she was much loved by Bleddyn. Would her father have vowed to found an abbey with Alana as the abbess had he known one day Bleddyn, the Welsh boy he loved like a son, would so dearly cherish her? And, had he known the healthy heir he prayed for was but another daughter, would her father have made that vow?

It was her fault Alana did not have the happiness she so deserved.

Bleddyn's arm tightened around her while they made their way back to the table. "It is no fault of your own, *mo maise,* my beauty. Your father could not know Alana's and my love was so intense when we were not full grown. He loved you both dearly and did not regret you were not a boy. If he could have foretold the heartbreak, I do not think he would have vowed as he did."

Brianna's chin quivered, her steps lagged. Damron rose,

and the abbess stood and touched his arm, looking up at him with a sweet smile.

"May I see my sister to her bed? She is pale. It looks to have cost her much to please me."

Damron nodded, bent and kissed Brianna lightly on the cheek and whispered in her ear, "We will deal later, wife." His gaze bored holes in her back as she left the room.

Bleddyn moved to sit beside him. "What do you intend, Damron?"

"To lecture my wife that she may not humiliate me in any way. If not for yer words, my men would have viewed me as a gutless fool who couldna control his wee wife."

Mereck dropped down on the other side of him. "She may have tried to take revenge, for she thought you prepared for your leman. Have you not thought of that?"

"Aye. 'Tis likely. But remember this. She is my wife and belongs to neither of ye."

He strode from the room to find Alana leaving his chambers. She smiled serenely up at him and patted Guardian before she wished him a pleasant night.

Damron stood beside the bed and studied Brianna's sleeping face. Tear tracks marred her creamy cheeks. She lay unusually still in her sleep. He picked up a cup from the bedside table, sniffed it and tasted the remaining drop of milk. Alana must have added a mild sleeping potion.

He gathered his robe and descended to the bathing room to wash the coloring from his hair. And to be alone to think. He recalled the haunted look in Brianna's eyes when she spied Asceline folded in the collapsed bed. And he remembered his wee wife had suddenly stilled on hearing he wanted to please someone.

Never had he known a woman to be so strong-willed as Brianna, who thought more like a man than a weak lass. He grimaced and shook his head. Huh! Meghan also was such a one.

He wrung the water from his hair and shoved the dripping mass over his shoulders, then turned on his heels and returned to his room. He stripped off his clothing, slid between the sheets and gathered Brianna close.

Would she be pleased when guests began to gather on the morrow? He grinned, thinking of the beautiful dress his mother and the widows had sewn when Brianna was occupied. Preparations for the wedding feast were well under way. The flaming crosses that gathered his people had all been delivered. Surprisingly, Meghan had not blurted out his secret. In two days' time, they would hold the ceremonies.

He would move Asceline to the village, until he could spare an escort to return her to Normandy.

Chapter 19

The skirl of bagpipes playing the Morgan ceremonial greeting startled Brianna as dawn broke. She stumbled to the window to watch Meghan and the family piper, Angus, who stood atop the gatehouse, welcome a line of visitors so long they nearly reached the woods beyond the castle wall. A standard-bearer, waving aloft the family's colors, preceded each group cantering across the drawbridge.

Mari bustled about the room, her lively face split with a happy grin. "My pretty one, ye must prepare for yer guests. We have not had so grand a gatherin' since . . ."—she shrugged and threw up her arms—"since I dinna know when."

Damron stood inside the doorway and shook his head. "Last eve ye slept, wife, afore I could tell ye the time has come for the gatherin'."

He sauntered over to her, his vibrant body moving with sexual grace. Brianna swallowed and tried to ignore the twinges in her nipples that shot sparks of desire to the pit of her stomach. Damron's lips lifted in a broad smile, and his eyes lost their usual wariness.

"They come to witness the weddin' ye wished for with our families. After the feast, we will join in our old Scottish ways." He bent his head and placed a warm kiss on the soft spot below her ear.

Shivers raced down her back. She could no longer deny the excitement coursing through her, though she tried to convince herself it was because she would witness firsthand the gathering of a clan. It was a lie. One look at the bed proved it, for her body clamored to be joined there with his.

"I would have ye bound to me in all ways, Brianna," he whispered.

"Surely not today?" Oh, God, why did she have to go and lick her lips?

"Nay, Sunday. Two days hence. Mother and the widows have sewn yer weddin' attire. All that needs to be done is the fittin'." His face lit with a smile before he turned and left.

Her mind and heart were at war. The early Brianna's love for him had lasted through the centuries, else why had she, as a child, felt he was *hers* from the moment she saw his likeness? She was still trying to calm her mind when she went below.

Alana came to stand beside her in the crowded hall, their shoulders brushing together. Damron stood at the foot of the dais, Jeremy beside him. The squire held a thick ceremonial staff carved with images of the sun, mountains, oak trees, deer and wolves.

Eric MacLaren led off the long line of guests to greet and pay their respects. He stomped up to Damron, grinned, then took the heavy staff and banged it on the floor. The blow resounded throughout the hall, making Brianna jump.

"Eric MacLaren, tanist for the MacLarens, brings the laird's greetings and wishes for a fruitful union," he shouted.

"The Morgans thank ye and yer clan," Damron responded.

They cuffed each other's shoulder, and then the next man in line moved up to take the staff. Some greetings were brief, like Eric's, others long-winded and elaborate.

Names buzzed through Brianna's head. When Meghan finally

joined them, she helped Brianna and Alana sort out faces with families, as the hall filled with boisterous travelers.

"Most are Highlanders, with a sprinklin' from the Central Lowlands. If the clan chief canna leave his stronghold, he sends his elected heir, his tanist. Those who travel the furthest dinna bring their wives because of the danger of kidnapin'."

Now and again throughout the day, minor skirmishes erupted between men not on the best of terms.

Mereck stalked up to them, drew up to his full height and fixed the offenders with a gimlet stare. His fingers twitched as he caressed his sword hilt. They quieted. All were wary of provoking Baresark.

The next morn, Damron rose and pressed Brianna back onto the sheets. "Stay abed, wife. Ye should store yer energy for bed sport." He gave her a noisy, smacking kiss on the forehead and, with a broad smile and a wink, pulled the bed drapes closed.

She awoke later and had a light meal of apple pasties and milk. The widows bustled into the room and began fitting her wedding outfit to her breasts and waist, and measuring the hem.

When they were done with the fitting, Brianna thanked them for working so diligently to surprise her. The sweet ladies were soon laughing and racing back to the solar to place the last stitches.

Mari helped her dress in both bright and light shades of yellow and wound yellow silk ribbons through her brown hair. They no sooner finished than Damron arrived to escort her below.

"Ye are most lovely, wife," he murmured. "Come, we must seat ourselves. The guests have been at the kegs most of the day and need food or they will soon be wrestlin' on the floor. I have no wish to sport a bloody nose on the morrow. It seems to bleed much of late." He rolled his eyes at her.

Brianna's breath caught, seeing Damron so relaxed, so at ease. And he had teased her about his nose! So many preparations had gone on without her knowledge. He'd put himself out a great deal to see their wedding planned to the last detail.

Happily, Asceline did not sit nearby, but at a table below the dais beside a blond-haired MacLaren clansman. When Brianna looked up, the man eyed her, undressing her with his hot gaze. The skin on her nape prickled. He pursed his lips, narrowed his eyes and stared at her cheek. Uncomfortable, she put her hand over the small scars, for she could almost feel his hands on her. When all had eaten, mummers, acrobats and musicians took their turns entertaining.

Brianna tugged at Damron's arm. "Is that Eric's brother who sits next to Asceline?" she whispered.

Damron glanced up and frowned. "Nay, 'tis Rollo, Eric's cousin."

The room became unruly as the mummers started rows between the most drunk of the men, who were more than happy to oblige. Damron signaled it was time for the ladies to seek their beds. He surprised her when he accompanied her to their bedchamber.

After they undressed, Damron blew out the candles and drew the bed curtains. He gathered her to him and cuddled her head against his chest. "Sleep, little wife. The morrow will be a long day." He kissed her gently and soon snored.

Finally Brianna relaxed and slept. How long could he continue to fool his wee wife with snoring? As Connor had told her, he never snored. He had trained himself to be a very light sleeper, aware of the faintest sound.

Would wedding her afore a priest finally make Brianna a willing wife in his bed? These past weeks seemed like a lifetime of need to him, for whenever Brianna was near, his body reacted like a randy goat. He was forever adjusting his clothing to hide his rampaging sex. Each day he had spent longer and longer hours on the practice field. He never lacked for a partner, for the men did not try to keep their tongues behind their teeth, but needled him about his bulging sex.

Damron stroked Brianna's hair as she slept. He wanted her to be well-rested come dawn, for he could not have her rebellious during the ceremonies.

He would be asking much from her.

Brianna awoke, hearing people bustling about. Who could be in her room in the middle of the night? She peeked through her eyelashes, just as her sister bent over her.

"Come, lazy bones, or you will be late for your wedding." Alana laughed. "You must bathe, and we are to help you dress."

Brianna's heart pounded. Her mouth went dry. Damron had done all she had requested that night at Ridley. She could no longer deny him. Her stomach churned. If she gave her heart to him, would she stay? Or would she be whisked forward to the future, leaving her heart—and Damron—behind?

"Here ye go, lovie," Meghan said and placed the bathing screen for Brianna's comfort. "Mari will feed ye and give ye a little watered wine to soothe yer spirits."

Once Brianna had bathed and Mari wrapped a drying towel around her, Alana drew a wooden comb through Brianna's hair, then used silk cloths to dry and rub the strands. She leaned back and inspected her work, then took a curl and stretched it out. When she released it, it coiled back again.

"Your chestnut curls are shiny and lively enough to delight the most fiery of lovers." When Meghan burst out laughing, Alana shrugged her shoulders and looked sheepish. "I may be a nun, but I was a woman first."

Alana and Meghan tied ivory ribbons around Brianna's

knees to hold her stockings. They slipped soft shoes on her feet and slid a lovely smock, a deep ivory color, over her head. Its long, trailing sleeves and hem were trimmed with roses made with ruby-colored thread.

Ladies Phillipa and Maud helped her don a light ivory tunic with wide, flowing sleeves, designed so the smock peeked from her wrists and through slits in the tunic's sides. On either side of the slitted openings, the widows had used sapphire-colored thread to embroider the trunk of an ancient tree. They had sewn curving patterns of the tree's roots on the hem. The gold wedding girdle with rubies and sapphires that Damron had given her rode low on her hips. Brianna was sure the widows had designed the dress to enhance his gift.

"You will be a most beautiful bride." Lady Phillipa wrapped her in a gentle hug and kissed her forehead.

"Dear Brianna, 'tis such a pity your mother and father could not see you today." Tears slid from Lady Maud's eyes.

Instead of a circlet, Meghan placed a garland of flowers on Brianna's head. Ivory, blue and red silk ribbons trailed from it down the middle of her back.

Brianna felt her Nathaniel approach, and she bade everyone except Alana to meet them below. He had dressed all in black, his face again painted, looking savage and handsome at the same time. He smiled at Brianna, his dark eyes filled with moisture. When his gaze sought Alana's, her eyes also pooled with tears. Brianna's heart ached for all that the two of them had missed of life. Much as a father's would, his strong arms embraced her.

"Come, your impatient husband waits." He smiled and opened the door.

There stood Guardian, fresh from an early bath and looking quite handsome. Someone had fastened a garland of purple heather around his neck. The beast did not seem to mind. He nodded his great head and trotted to the stairwell.

Alana walked beside him, with Brianna and Bleddyn following. Brianna came through the great doors into the sunlight, and cheers rang out from the people assembled to follow her progress to the church.

Connor, holding Angel's reins, grinned at her. Grooms had braided the horse's mane with silver ribbons, and bells hung from each. His freshly brushed white tail flowed, its tip touching the ground. Jewels studded his halter and a Morgan tartan lay across his back.

Bleddyn lifted her to sit as if she were on a sidesaddle. He walked beside her as Connor led the great destrier. Guardian started the procession, his steps haughty and proud. His great head swept from side to side, assuring his mistress's safety. Angel stepped with such gentle grace, Brianna could not believe it was the same horse she thought of as Lucifer.

Simon Ridley escorted the women following Brianna, and crowds of villagers lined the way, shouting approval and showering Brianna with flowers. The crowd of wedding guests made way for Guardian and Connor to lead her to Damron. Seeing Brianna approach, Damron started to descend the church stairs, but Mereck put a hand on his arm, halting him.

"Nay, Damron. Let Bleddyn do these things her father would have done."

Connor halted Angel, and Bleddyn stepped forward to offer Damron a black slipper—part of the pair she had worn in defiance with her black gown. He smiled at the symbolic gesture, for the Welshman was giving Brianna over to him and promising that she would forgo her former resistance.

Never had Brianna been more beautiful than she was at this moment as Bleddyn led her up the steps to him. In Damron's eyes, she was the loveliest of all women.

He, Connor and Mereck stood to Father Matthew's left, Laird Douglas and Baron Ridley on the priest's right. Damron tensed. Brianna would truly be his wife now. The ceremony with King

Malcolm, King William and Queen Matilda had been no more than a contract. It did not hold the power of today's ceremony.

Bleddyn placed Brianna's cold fingers in Damron's. She clutched his hand, her eyes wide and haunted. He sensed her fear. Pray God it was not of him and their wedding night to come.

Father Matthew began. He spoke each word clearly, so everyone could witness and attest the legitimacy of the wedding, and any offspring that would come of the union. Damron responded with his vows in a strong, carrying voice.

Brianna's stomach fluttered like butterflies filled it, and she licked her dry lips. Marriage vows had not changed much over the centuries. Dear God, after speaking vows with him, how would she ever survive if she was sent back to her own time? What if she became pregnant? It would rip her heart out to be taken away from a child. And what of the early Brianna, so woefully unable to handle the dangers here?

Her voice quavered, repeating her vows. When time to promise to obey him, her hands twitched. Beneath her breath so only he could hear, she added, "If it's not something I believe is foolish." His grasp tightened.

Mereck handed over a gold band studded with red stones that Damron had chosen for her.

"With this ring I wed ye. With my heart I honor ye." He placed the ring in turn on her first two fingers. As he spoke the next vow, he fitted the ring snugly on her third finger, where it belonged. "With my body I will cherish ye." He stared intently into her eyes.

Sparks flew between them at his words. She blushed and dropped her gaze. He chuckled, the sound wicked.

Laird Douglas stepped forward. "'Tis time for the bride's fealty oath to her lord. Once done, we will celebrate the mass."

Surprised, Brianna turned to him and asked, "What oath, Papa Dougie? We just said our vows."

"Aye, that ye did, granddaughter, but there is another important oath in this case."

"Why 'in this case'?" She frowned suspiciously at Damron.

Damron stared hard at her before answering. "Because, I am tanist of our clan and marryin' a Saxon. 'Tis not meant as insult, but to assure everyone ye will be a loyal Morgan." He studied her face a moment, then added, "Kneel and place your hands within mine."

"Kneel? I don't think so." She shook her head.

His big hands clamped on her shoulders. He stared into her eyes as bit by bit, he urged her to her knees. Alana gasped. For her sister's sake, Brianna stopped resisting and knelt. Her teeth ground together when he clamped her hands tightly between his. There she was, on her knees and her arms uplifted with her hands between his, as if in supplication.

"Mereck will read the words for ye to repeat."

Mereck took the paper Damron gave him and quickly scanned it. He cast Brianna an uncertain glance, cleared his throat and quietly read the oath.

"I, Brianna Morgan, vow fealty to my lord husband, Damron of Blackthorn." She repeated it easily.

"I vow to honor him in all ways, and to be loyal to his clan." She also had no conflict with this and spoke the words.

"I will forsake all other loves by thought or deed." She hesitated, wondering why Damron would request such an oath. After his grip tightened on her fingers, she spoke the words.

On hearing the next vow, "I will obey, keep myself only unto him, and will never leave him as long as breath is in my body," she startled, tugged her hands and tried to stand.

Damron refused to let her rise, and waited. His hands gripped hers with a new urgency, willing her to respond. Her gaze traveled slowly from the tips of his shining black shoes to finally rest on his face. He seemed to hold his breath. His body looked chiseled from solid stone.

"Promise me ye will never leave me, or ye will stay on yer knees till morn and beyond." His eyes blazed with determination.

She believed him. "I vow to obey him within reason. To follow his lead in keeping myself only onto him." She ignored his low curse. How could she repeat the rest? To promise to never leave him? What if he grew to love her? Her throat tightened and ached, thinking of his anguish if she suddenly disappeared. She shuddered, fearful for him. Finally, she cleared her throat. "And never willingly leave while breath is in my body."

Bleddyn moved close behind Damron. "Do not force more from her than she can honestly give. You cannot break her to your will, but in time, you may bend her to it. The way of it you will have to discover for yourself, or it will be your undoing."

Damron lifted Brianna to her feet and wrapped his arms around her. He kissed her, and with his lips and his tongue, he vented his frustration against her strong will. When he released her, he straightened her garland, then gently cupped her cheeks and kissed that small spot between her eyes.

He did not regret forcing her vows. Though he could not quite believe Brianna could be from another time, she had threatened to leave him before. The thought that she could elude him filled him with fear. He would force her to stay.

He wanted her. He loved her. He would keep her.

Damron held Brianna tight against his side, while they followed Father Matthew into the church.

The doors were propped open so everyone outside could participate in the mass. When they emerged, a path led to the doors of the keep. Damron walked slowly, for Brianna's legs seemed unsteady.

Food already rested on trestle tables in the inner bailey for the village people and the retainers who had come with the clans. Servants began filling tables in the hall for the feast.

Brianna stood dutifully by Damron. She did not protest when men grasped her in the air and kissed her. When

Mereck came close, Damron stamped hard on his brother's toes, pretending to stumble.

Mereck kissed Brianna's cheek. "'Tis sorry I am to be the one to read ye the vows."

She smiled and hugged him. "I know, Mereck. I am grateful that it was you who read them. How can a wife keep a vow to never leave under any circumstances? There are some things a person can't control, no matter how much they wish to."

The feast could not begin until Damron and Brianna sat at the board, so he escorted her to sit beside him at the head of the table. He chose the best morsels of goose with a sauce of grapes and garlic, roasted pork, quail and poultry for their trencher. He placed a small bowl of carrots glazed with honey near her, knowing they were her favorites. Whatever he thought would please her, he set before them, tempting her to eat.

Everything seemed to stick in Brianna's throat, for cold fear coursed through her. She kept remembering standing in the castle's antique shop when his hands had reached through the mist to pin the brooch to her clothing.

His deep voice, laden with tension, had entreated, "Promise me, promise me ye will never leave me," just before her soul was brought here. His words drummed through her head. Her heart skipped a beat knowing she had, centuries later, finally answered his plea.

Damron's gaze entreated Bleddyn, for Brianna had eaten but a morsel of food. The Welshman stood and motioned for Meghan.

"Come, my heart," he murmured to Brianna, "eat while I sing for you."

Meghan stood with her pipes, while Bleddyn sat on a tall stool in front of the table.

He started a rhythmic beat on the bodhran and began to sing in his beautiful Welsh tenor. Meghan's pipes chimed in. How could she coax such sounds from the strange instrument?

Brianna saw his gaze go to the food on her trencher, and she obediently started to eat. They did not stop their music until she had eaten enough to last through the grueling hours.

'Twas a tedious day. Damron never left her side. The weather was cool, so they gathered out of doors. Often throughout the day, Brianna felt the hair rise at the nape of her neck. She turned to find who stared at her, but noted only Asceline with the same blond man she had seen before. The Frenchwoman glared at her. She pulled him by the hand, and they disappeared in the crowd.

Night began to fall, and stars lit the sky. It was time for all of the gathered crosses to be lit for the Scottish ceremony. Damron helped her up the steps to a platform, where Lord Douglas raised his hand for quiet.

"The time has come where I no longer am able to run hither and yon to keep peace, to quell raids or lead armies into battle. For many years, I have trained my grandson Damron. Ye have elected him tanist, to take o'er as chief when I pass. I dinna want to watch from heaven above. Nor do I intend to. Greet and give homage to the new Laird of the Morgans, Damron Alasdair, a Morgan of Blackthorn. Tomorrow, he will stand on this very platform, and ye will give him yer vows."

"Grandfather, ye canna do this. Ye have many years left to lead our people," Damron protested above the approving shouts.

"Nay, Damron, dinna deny me the pleasure. I will be with ye as ye say, and I will have the joy to play with yer children, to write and sketch like I have always wished. I do not envy ye the burdens that now fall on yer shoulders. Know I will be here to help whene'er ye need me."

When Damron still hesitated, Connor handed Lord Douglas the great sword that belonged to the Chiefs of Clan Morgan. Damron's hands shook as he accepted it from his grandfather. Lord Douglas handed a symbolic eagle feather to Mereck.

With pride beaming from his eyes, Mereck fastened it

behind Damron's brooch that held his plaid at his shoulder. Mereck's face lit in a beatific smile as he turned to hug his grandfather, then swung back to Damron.

"May I have the honor to be first to vow fealty, brother?"

Damron clutched Mereck close. "It will be so at first light of morn." He turned to his grandfather, went down on one knee to kiss his hand, then stood and held up his arms to quiet the men making a din as they thumped their swords against shields or anything else handy. It would be as his grandfather wished, but they would wait until the morrow for the vows of fealty.

"We have yet a small ceremony to finish afore I can take my bride to my bed," he said, then laughed at their bawdy shouts.

He took Brianna's hand. Meghan and Angus stepped onto the platform with them and started the wedding music. Lord Douglas faced them and asked that they repeat parts of their vows, with the pipers playing softly in the background. For Brianna, he wisely left off the word obey, and asked only if she would love, honor and cherish Damron until death they did part. She said her vows as strongly and earnestly as Damron did. Connor then handed Lord Douglas a finely honed misericord.

"My wee kelpie, dinna be afeared I will do ye harm. I will place a small cut on yer wrist, one on Damron's, and then join the two with our colors. Bleddyn has seen to cleansing the blade, so it willna corrupt the wound. Will ye trust me in this?"

"I trust you with my life, Papa Dougie."

"Give me your left wrist, Damron, as 'tis closest to yer heart." Damron obediently bared his wrist to the blade. Lord Douglas made a cut just large enough for blood to flow freely. "Now, little one, let me have yer right wrist so that his lifeblood can mingle with yers, and yers with his." Brianna lifted her wrist to him. She held very still. Only a quick intake of breath showed the sting of the cut. Mereck joined their wrists together, blood against blood, with a thin strip of Morgan plaid. He draped a Morgan tartan about Brianna and pinned it at her left shoulder with the brooch Damron had given her.

Meghan and Angus piped a joyful melody as they preceded them down the steps. Damron and Brianna's palms were clasped together, his fingers entwined with hers. He anxiously watched her face. She did not look unduly upset. The pipers, with Guardian ahead of them, led the wedded couple. Lord Douglas, Mereck and Connor solemnly followed to circle the platform, around the burning crosses and back to where they had started.

The crowd parted, and the pipers then led them to the keep's doors. When they returned to the great hall, it had been cleared of all food and the extra tables. Benches had been set along the walls in several rows, ready for the evening's entertainment.

While their guests were occupied watching the entertainers, Bleddyn came to unbind their wrists, cleanse the wounds and apply a healing salve.

Damron tenderly gathered Brianna in his arms and started up the stairs. Guardian padded close behind, his long tongue lolling out, making his great wolf face look foolish.

Chapter 20

Damron's riveting stare froze Mari in her tracks. Her gaze darted from him to Brianna, and then to the door.

"Mari, yer mistress needs yer help." He cleared the huskiness from his voice. "I am afeared I would ruin her wedding finery were I to assist her."

His gaze searched Brianna's blushing face as he leaned slightly backward and lowered her down his body. His rampant tarse nudged the juncture of her legs and bucked, revealing its impatience to be buried deep within her heated flesh. A raspy chuckle slipped from his throat on seeing her face flame as though she had never been in his arms afore. When her feet reached the floor, he waited until she had her balance, then brought over the modesty screen to give her privacy undressing.

For the first time in his life, he fidgeted. He glanced around the room and saw the mead he had brought from Ridley, and a pitcher and chalices sitting on the table beside the bed. Hearing Brianna's surprised gasp, he grinned and listened to her soft words.

"Why, it's so light, so fine I can hold it on the palm of my hand and still not feel its weight."

Anticipating the sight of Brianna's beautiful, lush body in the exquisite garment his mother had painstakingly made for her, his blood ran hot. While his wife prepared herself for him, he prepared himself for her.

In his haste to strip, he grabbed for the large brooch holding the tartan at his shoulder and stuck the pin into his thumb. "Lucifer's prickly arse," he muttered. Blood stained his tartan. He jammed his thumb in his mouth and sucked the blood away, then whipped off his belt and sword. By the time he placed them across a chair, his tartan had slithered from his hips. He glanced over at the screen, then nearly tore off the rest of his clothing. He rolled his eyes, sheepish now, when he had to step over the garments strewn over the floor. Never before had he been so careless of such costly attire.

Gathering his finery, he laid it atop his chest. He loosely belted a black silk robe around his waist and, just as he swiped his hands through his tousled hair, trying to do something with his hands other than yank away the screen, Brianna came from behind it. She hesitated and started to fold her arms across her chest, then changed her mind and dropped them to her sides, her hands shaking.

Damron forced his face to show only pleasure at her beauty, though his heart near sprang from his chest, his loins from his skin.

"Ye are most lovely, wife, e'en more today than e'er before." He was grateful he could turn his back to her with the excuse to see Mari out, for he did not want to further unnerve Brianna. His shaft was like to burst with longing. He could not hide his impatience, no matter how he adjusted his robe.

"Dinna slabber on yer bride, milord, and take care not to tear the wee un's pretty gown," Mari warned, looking pointedly down at the bulging black robe as she went out.

"Sassy woman," he grumbled and latched the door behind

her. Brianna shifted from one foot to the other, her eyes looking everywhere but at him. He tried not to smile.

"Is my face so changed these last moments, wife?"

She did not answer, but shook her head and lowered her
gaze to stare at her pink toes peeking beneath her gown.

He poured the wedding mead into a chalice they would share
and placed it on the table near his chair. Brianna looked so unsure
of herself, so vulnerable standing there. Tenderness filled him as
he picked her up and sat, settling her comfortably on his lap. He
held the mead for her to sip before he drank.

"Have I done everythin' ye wished for our weddin', love?
Alana is here, and yer family is below wishin' us well. Grandfather, Mother and all my family were present. Yer Bleddyn
is here, and we have thrice been joined. Will ye now stop
fightin' me and be a dutiful wife?" He almost groaned aloud
as his foolish question left his lips.

"I can't ever be the dutiful wife you expect, Damron. It's
not my nature to sew and gossip with the women. As for
blindly obeying, you well know what I think of that."

"I dinna expect ye to bow and scrape on yer knees to me,
love. I demand loyalty from ye, and I will ne'er allow ye a
lover like in the royal courts. Ye will obey me in this."

"Humpf. I don't want a lover. But you insult me by having
everyone think me inadequate for one primitive man."

"Primitive. Did ye say primitive?" His eyes widened in disbelief. "I am one of the most learned men in all of Scotland.
I read, write and speak six languages, have been knighted earlier than most, have helped plan battles, fought and won many
contests, razed many castles, and have the power over life and
death of hundreds. I doubt another can rival me in this." He
thrust out his chin and stared down at her.

"Bleddyn can." Her words were near a whisper.

His rampant tarse deflated like a popped soap bubble.
Damron sighed. His foolish wife never knew when to keep

her tongue behind her teeth. His brows drew together as he mulled over his reply. He nodded.

"Bleddyn does not count. He is Welsh."

He rested his chin on her head and waited before he again spoke. "I have said that I would be faithful when ye became a true wife. We have stood afore the priest and made our vows. I will make another to ye now, love. I will ne'er go to another as long as ye dinna deny me yer comfort." He felt her body relax against him.

His fingers threaded through her hair's clinging warmth to grasp her nape. Her breath caught as he lowered his lips to kiss the corners of her mouth. The tip of his tongue ran along its seam, and he drew her lower lip between his teeth and nibbled. His lips moved up to her eyelids to close them, to make her more conscious of his touch. Each time her lids flickered and tried to open, he kissed them shut again. He trailed kisses along her hairline while he murmured all he wished to do to her. He found her ear and lightly tugged the lobe, then the damp tip of his tongue traced the outline as his breath tickled its depths. Her moan of pleasure delighted him.

He caressed the silky skin of her arms up to her shoulder, then traced her collarbone. His calloused fingers found a warm, pliant breast, and she shivered. He pressed it in his cupped hand, his thumb circling the nipple until it peaked and hardened. When he rubbed his rough palm over it, she quivered. He kissed her eyes closed again, then gazed hungrily at her body displayed through the sheer gown.

Though he wanted to rip the garment off and bury himself deep within her, he cautioned himself to go gently. She would never seek to leave him if all went as he hoped, for she would still remember this night when she was a grandmother many times over. Nuzzling his face against the soft hollow of her neck, he arranged her across his lap so she was more open to his greedy mouth and hands. Did she hear his heart hammering against his ribs?

To relieve the painful tightness returning to his groin, he slipped his arm beneath her knees and lifted her enough that he could spread his legs.

Brianna peeked through her lashes at Damron. His robe gaped to reveal his broad, sculpted chest with its dusting of curly black hair. His iron-hard shaft pulsed against her side. If she lowered her gaze, she knew she would see his sex fighting to be free of his robe. She had an almost irresistible urge to peek. Her mouth filled with water.

Heaven help her! Did she drool for him? She did.

Her hands flew up to grip his shoulders, and her cheeks burned when she brushed against his hard member. His mouth lowered to lick and nibble at her nipples through the fabric. When he began to suckle firmly, fire streaked from her breasts down to the center of her being.

Damron's fingers crept under the hem of the gown to skim lightly over the sensitive flesh of her legs and, when they reached her thighs, she tensed. He smiled wolfishly down at her. He did not linger where she expected him to, but continued up over her hip. He lifted her with his left arm and, before she could draw her next breath, the gown lay puddled on the rug.

Damron made little shushing sounds, soothing her. Gazing at her body stretched between his arms, murmurs of pleasure rumbled in his chest. His teeth clamped together when he eyed the brown triangle between her legs. He didn't touch her there while he teased her body, and his fingers stroked where she didn't expect them. Her mewling sounds, so light to be almost unheard, brought a gleam to his eyes.

Damron's lips, tongue and teeth explored her. His humming, guttural murmurs reminded her of a giant panther who licked and savored his kill before devouring it. She quivered and throbbed from head to toes.

His palm grazed the curls at her mons. She gasped, knowing he was going to explore her further. He didn't. His hand moved around her hip to caress her plump nether cheeks and squeeze each, then traced the crease between them. When he tightened his arms and stood to carry her to the bed, she clutched the hair at the back of his neck.

His hard shaft bumped against her bottom with each step, tantalizing her. Her heart moved its way up into her throat. His gaze held hers as he placed her on the bed. Slowly, he untied the silk rope at his waist. First his right shoulder, then his left, shrugged slightly. The robe slithered slowly down his arms. Inch by inch, Damron bared his body to her. She watched in fascination as the sliding cloth exposed the hair on his powerful chest, his hardened nipples. It was a fascinating sight.

His bent elbows stopped the silk's slow descent. His gaze examined her face. She studied his. What did he want? He smiled, eyes heavy with passion, lips wet and glistening. She yearned to tease his lower lip as he had done hers. Those lips were more sensuous now, fuller when he was aroused. Her eyes widened when her gaze came to rest on the taut, ridged muscles of his stomach. Finally, his arms lowered to let the robe fall. It caught on his rigid, upright shaft. His smile was wicked as his engorged rod bucked. The silk fell. Brianna blinked, and giggled. He went to the foot of the great bed and crawled to her on hands and knees. His black hair fell to frame his face as he moved with all the grace and beauty of a great jungle animal. A little frightened, she grasped the sheet in her fists, until he stretched his massive, hot body over her.

Damron began his seduction again and, this time when he came to her velvety mons, his hand cupped her. He growled his pleasure at the slick wetness there. Her hands began to explore him. Her fingers glanced over his hardness. He couldn't suppress a groan as he waited, hoping she would grasp him firmly. She didn't. She looked satisfied, smiled and began to tease his body as he had teased hers. Each time she came close to his sex, her hands fluttered away.

He straddled her and buried his face between her breasts. Each time he suckled, her grip tightened. Her hands roved over his back, down to his muscled buttocks. His heart skipped a beat when her hand slipped between their bodies, searching for his hardness. Her fingertips flirted over the silky head and around the fold, and then down the engorged shaft. His groans deepened. He gasped as her hands over-flowed with his ballocks. She squeezed, gentle but firm. He buried his head against her neck and held his breath. Hearing her slow, husky whisper in his ear, he near spilled his seed.

"Mmm. Nice balls, Damron."

His lips clamped on hers, his tongue plundered her mouth. He settled himself between her legs as his lips traveled down and over her stomach. His fingers raked through the curls protecting her sex and searched out her hidden nub to stroke and play havoc with her swollen nether lips. His tongue thrust between her teeth when he circled her tight entrance. He teased her slick flesh until she writhed beneath him. When she stiffened, close to release, he moved to plunder elsewhere. Once she was back from the brink, he redoubled his assault.

Finally, she panted for him.

"What is it ye want, love? This?" His tongue plunged, claiming her mouth. She whimpered and writhed, but refused to answer.

"What is it ye want, love? This?" Relentless now, he teased her breasts, laving and drawing each in turn into his hot mouth while rolling and plucking the opposite nipple be-tween two fingers. She gasped and bit her lip, but kept silent.

"Hmmm. What is it ye want, love? This?" He spread her wider with his hand. His fingertips caressed the petals around her open-ing. He moistened his middle finger with drops seeping from his tarse and slowly pressed it into her hot, tight innocence.

Sophia Johnson

Then, he asked for the last time.

"Ah, is it this, love?" He rubbed his thumb against her swollen bud until she could deny him no longer.

"You, Damron. I want you!"

He rumbled his satisfaction and nudged his tarse to enter her. Her body tightened, resisted his invasion. He stilled, and returned to lave and tease her breasts until her muscles softened and surrendered around him. Encountering her maiden's barrier, his breath rasped between clenched teeth as he held himself in check.

"Open yer eyes, love. I would have ye look at me and know to whom ye belong when I claim ye," he whispered. He tipped her chin until her face tilted to him.

Brianna gazed into blazing green eyes near black with wild passion. She caught fire feeling his fingers circle her flesh around his thrusting tarse. His hands and lips refused to relent in their exploring. Each touch became more gentle, each kiss more coaxing until she responded to his lightest demand.

Whimpers of arousal escaped her lips. She clutched his shoulders. His touch softened even further. Holding her gaze with his, he thrust deeper.

Brianna winced and tried to draw away. Surely Damron was too large for her? When she had gone to Gordon a virgin, she had no trouble adjusting to him.

"Easy, wife. Look at me," Damron crooned.

She blinked and met his gaze. He thrust again, but the barrier refused to give way. He stopped. Waited.

She read indecision in his eyes.

"Yield to me," he ordered, then sighed.

She tried to relax, hoping her body would adapt.

He pulled back. She took a deep breath, thinking he had changed his mind. He hovered, the tip of his shaft still entered, for what seemed a goodly time. She began to relax around him. He lunged forward.

Sharp pain ripped through her. She cried out and beat at his chest. He stilled and gripped her shoulders when she tried to squirm from beneath him.

"Ah, Brianna, I did not mean to hurt ye, but ye were so tight. I thought it would be better done quickly. I hoped to shorten yer pain."

He didn't move, but waited, patient. She shuddered and nodded. He began to move slowly, testing her pain. When she no longer seemed in distress, his movements became more urgent. Her legs wrapped around him, and her hips rose to seat him firmly. Finally, she writhed, moaned and thrust against him, demanding all of him. He drove her relentlessly until she stiffened. She arched her back, panting.

A cry burst from her with such an explosion of passion he clamped his mouth to hers to catch it. Wave after wave, her hot core rippled and clenched him. He lunged deeper, faster, surging against her womb until he reached his own release. His head reared back. A great roar burst from his lips as he filled her with his seed.

Damron rested his face against her neck, his gasps tickling her ear. He stayed within her until their breathing calmed, then lifted himself to her side. He cuddled her in his arms and crooned endearments in French, German and Spanish. Brianna knew they were endearments, for she recognized his whispered Spanish.

"Mi alma, mi tormento." My soul, my torment.

Damron stroked her hair and soothed her until she slept. He worried he had not been tender at the end, though she had not cried out in pain. Finally the candles guttered out, and he closed his eyes and slept.

Brianna heard Damron ease the door shut behind him shortly after dawn. She stretched and grimaced. Remembering her heated response to his lovemaking, she blushed. Though sex with Gordon had been satisfying, never had she felt the consuming passion that Damron called forth in her.

When she went down to the hall, she tried to disguise her sore body with slow movements. The men grinned and teased Damron, saying if he did not go more gently, she would ne'er be able to sit for her meals.

Below the lord's dais, servants cleared away the spilled pitchers of ale and wine, and stored the trestle tables in their wall niches so they would have room to present the men to Damron for their fealty oath. Damron stood, his grandfather by his side.

Mereck kneeled on the cold stones, placed his hands between Damron's, and gazed up at him.

"I vow, on my honor, to be faithful to ye as our Laird of Blackthorn. I will perform all acts and services due ye, and ne'er do ye harm." Mereck's voice rang out loud and clear.

After Damron bid his half brother rise, he clasped him around the shoulders. Connor came next. Then Lord Douglas called up one man at a time. Each knelt before Damron and vowed fealty. Damron in turn promised to protect them and their lands with his army should they ever be in need. The ceremony was finally completed, and the men ate and drank themselves into a stupor.

Damron and Brianna tended guests by day, and made love throughout the night. Their visitors slowly left, reluctant to leave Blackthorn's generous hospitality. The Ridleys and Alana lingered, for their journey had been long. Brianna gloried in being with the women, who smiled at her and showered her with hugs and kisses. She blossomed, but as the weeks passed, she began to tire easily.

He continued to make sensuous, gentle love each night and

coaxed her to rest after the noon meals. Sometimes she spied a sweet smile curling his stern lips. She guarded her heart and soul as best she could, fearful she would be taken away as swiftly as she had been brought here.

Damron wanted to savor each night, even though they had a lifetime ahead. He knew she did not give him her all, but he was too proud to ask her reasons.

He did not believe himself unreasonable in wanting her soul to belong only to him, but he did not think he should give as completely to her. It was a wife's duty to love her lord, to give him heirs and to cleave only unto him.

Brianna had finally accepted her role as his wife. He wanted nothing to upset her. One day late in the morning, Damron searched out Brianna.

"Simon complains that Gawky spoils for an outing and needs exercise. Mayhap we can gather yer family and ride out to hunt this night's meal?"

Brianna's eyes lit with pleasure. "That would be fun. Meghan can bring Simple. Alana doesn't believe the stories we've told her about the little hunter."

When they all went below, stable boys had their horses waiting at the foot of the stairway, but Sweetpea wasn't there.

"I've missed ye all morn, love. Come, I would have ye sit across my lap, so I can have ye in my arms." When she blushed, he chuckled and lifted her to sit across his thighs. She smiled up at him, a fragile trust budding in her eyes. His heart lurched. Thankfully, Guardian barked at the horses to follow him. Brianna laughed at the wolf's antics.

As they rode through the forest path, Damron spoke.

"Brianna, I wanted us to be gone from Blackthorn for a while. I have moved Asceline to another holding." She stiffened against him and started to speak. "Nay, wife. She will bide there only until we can spare the men to see her safely to Normandy. We will speak no more of her," he said, his voice stern.

She was tense for a time, until Simple's attempts to copy Gawky's graceful landings with his prey brought forth her laughter. From then on, the day was peaceful.

Brianna, Alana and Meghan spent many hours together. Though Meghan would rather be whipped at a stake than sew, she would wait patiently while the sisters mended Damron's clothing. Brianna's favorite days were when the three women and Bleddyn went into the woods to gather herbs not grown in the castle gardens. Damron didn't object to their forays, for Bleddyn's formidable presence and Meghan's, who had earned her reputation as the Warrior Woman of Blackthorn, were more than adequate to protect the two women.

On the day Alana and the Ridleys were to return home, Brianna forced a cheerful smile. They broke their fast with hot fruit scones, clotted cream, fresh churned butter, cheese, cold meats and sweet ale. All in the household went down to the bailey. After Meghan said her farewells, she raced to the top of the gatehouse to play a *Ceol mor,* to salute the departing guests.

Her family rode through the gatehouse and out over the drawbridge with their escorts. Brianna insisted on going to stand beside Meghan to watch as they crossed the open field to the forest road beyond. She didn't move until they disappeared into the dew-washed trees.

Damron watched Brianna learning her duties as The Morgan's wife under his mother's guidance. Brianna rose with the bells of matins as deep night lightened to beckoning dawn.

No duty seemed too menial for her. She worked from the sun's rise to its setting, studying how their clothing was made, from shearing the sheep, to weaving the wool, to watching the seamstresses stitch clothing for the villagers. She inspected the dairy, the bakers' ovens, the cow byre where they milked the cows, the kitchens, the brewery and the chandler's.

The sleeping chambers smelled fresh as a spring garden, for when she visited the chandler's, she took them small vials of lavender, rose and heather essences to add to the candles. She even saw to having heavier bags made to hold the flour, and supervised cleaning the storage room from ceiling to floor.

Damron welcomed each sunset, for Brianna was ever more receptive to his nightly advances. Still, he was not fully satisfied. From the lingering glimpse of fear in her eyes, he knew she withheld something from him.

Brianna woke one morning when the sun was high, for Damron had been particularly insatiable through the night. Noting the late hour, she jerked upright. Her head spun. Her hands flew to cover her mouth. Mari rushed to hold a basin beneath her chin.

"Ye should eat the bread first." She washed Brianna's face, then gave her a hunk of warm bread. "Just ye lie there, lovie, and nibble away. Ye will see yer stomach settle."

Brianna took a mouthful and started to chew. Suddenly, she went still. She gasped, and nearly choked. When she looked at her hand and stared at her fingers, mentally counting, Mari smothered a giggle.

"Good God Almighty," Brianna whispered. She took a deep breath and yelled, "Nathaniel!" He did not surprise her when he immediately entered her room. She looked at him and then at Mari. "All right, dammit, how long has everyone known I'm pregnant? That's why you've been treating me with kid gloves, telling me to eat bread before I rise, drink milk and take a daily nap."

"Pregnant?" Mari gasped, her eyes bright with worry. "What malady be this? I thought ye were breedin'?"

"It's the same as breeding, Mari," Brianna said quietly. She dropped her head into her hands and groaned pitiably. "Nathaniel, what am I going to do?" Tears welled in her eyes.

Bleddyn wrapped her in a sheet, took her into his arms and sat on the bed's edge. He rocked her as his hands glided over her hair, soothing her.

"Fetch your laird, Mari." He nodded, satisfied, when she hurried away. He studied Brianna's face. "Did you not suspect, when your time of the moon has not appeared since the night you lost your innocence?"

She shook her head. "I've been so caught up in all that's happened these past two months, I forgot to count the days. And don't forget, there's no such thing as a calendar here." She stared up at him as icy fear twisted her insides. She gulped. "Nathaniel, what will I do? In my time as Lydia, I lost two babies before their term. I've tried to keep my soul intact, or I'd never survive if I left Damron. What if I went while I'm pregnant, or after the child is born? I couldn't bear it." Brianna sobbed and clutched her arms around Bleddyn's neck. She had fallen deeply in love with Damron.

Damron stormed into the chamber, his face grim.

"Leave me, wife? Do ye make plans to leave?"

Chapter 21

"Do ye so hate the thought of my bairn in yer belly? I have been waitin' for ye to tell me ye were breedin' and thought ye would be happy. Ye are always holdin' and kissin' the wee bairns whenever they are about." Damron's tone was harsh, his body stiff. Brianna sobbed all the harder. He took her from Bleddyn's arms, and the Welshman left.

"Ye did not weep so even after I shamed ye afore all of Blackthorn when I threatened to thrash ye." Her tears unmanned him. After all the hardships he had dealt her, she wept over carrying his bairn. Fear squeezed icy hands around his heart. "Did ye not tell me for ye planned to leave, carryin' my bairn and heir?"

"I v-vowed to be with you unto d-death, and I wouldn't break it by any will of my own. I d-didn't tell you because it n-never dawned on me I was carrying!"

His pent-up breath whooshed from his chest, ruffling her hair. An idea struck. He loosened her fingers from his neck and studied her, shaking his head.

"Little wife, did ye not know how bairns are made?" He yanked up the hem of his shirt and wiped her face and nose, being as tender as if she was a youngling. "Ye argued about ploughing yer belly and planting my seed, and I thought ye knew why yer time of the moon had not come."

He cuddled her against him, kissed her forehead and coaxed her to relax. "Did ye not notice yer body's soft signs?" Moving his hand up beneath the sheet, he cupped her left breast. "See how much fuller yer beautiful breasts have become?" He felt down her waist and over her slightly rounded belly. "Have ye not felt this tiny burden when ye bathe? I thought ye waited for a special time to tell me. I had forgotten yer innocence from livin' with the Sisters at Saint Anne's."

"I've been so caught up in learning my duties as the laird's wife, I thought I was late from being busy and worrying over missing Alana. Even when I couldn't keep my meals down, I owed it to eating food different from what I am used to."

Truly, she did not lie to him. She had known her time was late, but she thought her system had been shocked by all that happened since she awoke in the field with Damron and Connor looming over her.

The sickness, she had thought, was caused by food that hadn't been refrigerated, and the tiredness from worry, and even her body changes had all seemed normal. She thought she was filling out from eating the extra bread, scones, cheese and milk they had coaxed on her.

Heaven help her. All the signs of pregnancy were there.

"Now that ye know, why are ye so heartsick? Is it knowin' 'tis my bairn and not Sir Galan's ye carry? Do ye still pine for him?" His heart squeezed near dry while he awaited her answer.

"Oh, Damron. I don't love Sir Galan. Never would I wish him in your place." She buried her face against his neck and whispered, "I'll love your bairn with all my heart."

Tears flowed freely down her face, soaking his shirt. He was truly puzzled until another thought struck him.

"Ye are afeared of the birthin'?" His eyes flew wide, for the thought also haunted his mind. "Bleddyn has told me he will be with ye, and he is well prepared."

Her head popped up from his neck. She stared at him, her mouth agape.

"He has gathered special herbs and met with midwives. He is sure ye and the babe will thrive. Did ye not note Alana promised to return in five months' time? 'Twas so she can be with ye for yer last month." He struggled to hide a smile when she tugged the sheet up tight to her chin and gaped at him.

"Well, for God's sake. Did everyone in this whole blasted country know I'm pregnant except me?" Her tears stopped, and her face was red with indignation.

He shook his head, as solemn as a priest. "Nay. Not everyone. Most of the women, the couples with bairns of their own, and mayhap the older pages and fostered children," he teased. When a look of horror crossed her face, he laughed.

Brianna scrambled from his lap, grabbed the trailing sheet in her fists and stormed over to her bedside table, muttering the whole way. She tore off a large chunk of bread and jammed it in her mouth. He knew she smothered her curses so he could not hear them. She swallowed several times before she got the mouthful down, then huffed and disappeared behind the privacy screen.

She grumbled and cursed again when she stubbed her toe on the stool, where Mari kept a basin of clean water and cloths for Brianna to wipe her face. Damron grinned and decided today was not the day to take issue with his wife's unseemly language.

Brianna struggled to come to terms with her greatest fear: being torn from Damron's arms and thrown forward to her future time. She ate all the choice morsels he piled high on their trencher and even planned meals with the cook that included more vegetables. She drank milk fortified with honey and eggs, and ate more fruits and cheeses, and a variety of meats, fowl and fish. She didn't resist her body's needs when she grew sleepy.

Each day, for additional exercise she climbed the stairs, from the ground on up to the rooftop. She took deep breaths of crisp air as she circled the curtain wall several times and drank in the beauty of the changing leaves in the forest. She walked from one bailey to another going about her duties and, instead of asking a servant to fetch someone or something for her, she went herself. Her muscles were as firm and sleek as if she attended a gym every day. Her breasts and belly rounded softly.

Damron's new duties kept him occupied all through the day, and he sometimes missed coming to the hall for meals. Each night when they were abed, he was especially tender with her.

He delighted in pointing out the changes in her body. He would grin and say, "In case ye did not notice . . ." One such evening, he rested his face against her rounding stomach, just as the babe decided to make its first sturdy move.

Damron gasped and clutched her hips. "Did ye feel him, wife? My son greeted me!"

"What you felt, husband, is your daughter," she teased.

Brianna had felt flutters before, but this was the first time her child had moved so forcefully. She smiled and ran her fingers through Damron's hair and pulled his face up to hers. He came to her willingly and braced his weight on his arms as he covered her with his body. For several long breaths they stared into each other eyes. Finally, she gripped the braids at his temples and tugged.

Fire swept through the pit of her stomach at the hot passion of his hungry kiss. Parting her lips, she offered the tip of her tongue between his teeth. He groaned and drew it into his

mouth where his own tongue swirled and danced lightly
around it, allowing her to explore him.

Her restless hands roamed over his head and down to explore the broad, smooth muscles of his shoulders and back.
When she could not reach his hips, she returned to the corded
muscles of his arms holding his weight from her, and pushed.
He raised himself as she sought to explore his chest's hardness, then straightened his arms when she kept urging him
upward.

She slithered beneath him and teased his nipples the way
he had done her own. Her teeth grazed the hard nub, and she
suckled it until he gave a sharp intake of air. Still not content,
her hands searched over his taut buttocks. Damron panted
like a dog left too long in the heat.

Feeling Damron quiver in anticipation thrilled Brianna.
Her fingers trailed over his massive thighs and searched
inward to trace the scar leading up to his manhood.

He stiffened, starting to pull away. Willing him to be still,
she grasped his hips. Her hands roamed to explore the silky
skin of his engorged rod and the sensitive, velvety tip. She
held him still, wrapping her fingers around his shaft with one
hand, while she hefted and caressed the huge sacs hanging so
heavy behind it.

"Ah, little wife. Ye torture me," Damron said in a hoarse
whisper as he fought for control. He could stand no more or
he would spill against her and waste their pleasure. He pulled
from her grasp and inched toward the foot of the bed. He
kissed and stroked and suckled his way until his knees
reached open air. He slid to the floor, kneeling at her feet. He
drew his tongue up the soles of each foot, then kissed each
toe before drawing it lightly between his hot lips to caress it
with his tongue.

Little by little, he pulled her toward him as he worked his
way back up her legs. She moaned and writhed and, for the

first time in his life, he was grateful for the skills that had made women seek him out at the royal courts.

He eased Brianna's legs over his shoulders, then gripped her hips to pull her to the edge of the bed. He nuzzled the silky cleft between her legs, keeping a firm grip on her so she could not scoot away. When his tongue flicked out to find what he sought, she startled and tried to pull his head away.

He pressed a finger inside her heated body and began a rapid but gentle thrusting, while his lips, tongue and teeth continued their persistent assault. He did not stop until her body became taut as a strongly pulled bow, and her grasping muscles rippled and tried to draw his finger deeper. Rising to his feet, he teased her by slowly lifting her to let his shaft nudge and enter her as she exploded around him.

Desire for Brianna near swept away the control he fought so hard to maintain. He took a deep, shaky breath and kept up an ever-increasing rhythm. He leaned forward to kiss her, and tweaked and fondled her breast until he felt her passions build again.

His tongue plundered her mouth. She arched against him, straining closer, until he could go no deeper. They reached their release together. Her moans and sharp cries startled him. His hand cupped her head to his neck, and her arms wrapped around him as he held her against him.

"I am sorry, love. Did I hurt ye? Are ye sure we will not harm the wee bairn?"

The wee bairn took that moment to give her father a sound kick. Brianna laughed. "I think we might have spoiled her nap, and she's annoyed with us, but what we did won't harm her. We'll have to be less, uh, energetic, the last two months of my time."

The following day, before the sun reached its highest point, Damron and Mereck came from the armory and halted when they heard loud arguing. Damron's gaze darted toward the barbican entrance, where he saw Spencer restraining a woman from entering.

"Satan's puckered arse! What goes there?" Damron yelled.

"If you did not send for Asceline, it appears your discarded leman is bent on creating more trouble." Mereck squinted in distaste.

Damron snorted and shook his head. "Do I look dafty, brother?"

Mereck clapped him on the shoulder and grimaced. "'Twould be best if you handle her quickly. I will see that Brianna is not disturbed." He loped off toward the hall's entrance.

Damron's long strides took him over to Asceline. He grasped her arm and forced her to cease her struggle to evade Spencer.

"Keep yer voice down, else I will shut yer mouth for ye," he said with a threatening growl. He hurried her along the length of the outer wall to the carpenter's shed. On seeing a shadow in the entrance, the carpenter and his apprentice looked up in surprise and stilled their hammers.

Damron jerked his head toward the doorway. Though annoyed Asceline had come, he sighed with relief. Mayhap she wished to return to Normandy and meant to take issue with him for not having provided an escort. Averting their gazes, the men scurried out into the dusty bailey.

Asceline lifted her chin high, thrust her breasts forward and threw open her cloak. "I am breeding, Damron." She smirked, looking triumphant. "I used the precaution you ordered, but the sponge must have been too heavy with your seed. You are well and truly caught, my lusty lover. A bastard you have spawned, and I will not have you deny it."

He looked down in horror at her distended belly. "Why did you not come to me when ye knew yer moon's time did not come? Ye have been absent from my bed for months, and I know ye have taken a lover here at Blackthorn. How do ye know the bairn is mine?" If Spencer had not been posted outside keeping the curious away, anyone walking nearby would have heard his furious voice coming from the hut.

Asceline shouted back, "My moon's time had not come when you arrived here with your Saxon bride. I hid it well. I would not let you force me to take a potion and rid you of your duty. Besides, if your sickly wife dies in birthing, this may be the only heir you will have," she finished with an ugly sneer.

"Dinna e'er speak such about Brianna! Get ye back to the village. I will prepare for yer departure." Fighting the urge to throttle her, Damron fisted his hands and kept his arms clamped against his sides. She flounced toward the doorway, a victorious smile on her face. He hauled her back into the shadows, beckoned Spencer over and ordered him to return her to the village.

Mereck had reported having more than once seen Asceline steal into the woods with a light-haired man, but they were too distant for him to recognize the man. He wondered if it was Eric who shared her favors. Damron had not cared who she took to her bed. He would no longer be in it.

After Spencer left with Asceline, Damron strode over to the well and yanked up a bucket of cold water, took a deep breath and plunged his head in it. Could the bairn be his? By the looks of her belly, had he planted his seed that last night in Normandy? Or was the babe the fruit of this blond man?

Damron exhaled in a flurry of bubbles, raised his head and shook it like a hound coming from a swim. How would he know until the babe was born? He sighed, squeezed his eyes shut and pinched the bridge of his nose, thinking.

'Twas unfortunate his plans to return Asceline to Normandy had to be set aside, for wet, stormy weather prevented him from sending a breeding woman traveling over mountain roads. Though instinct told him she had lied, guilt ate at him. He had always been careful not to sire a child he couldna rightly claim as his heir, but what if the bairn *was* his? He could not abandon it.

Brianna sensed his unease, for she no longer slept soundly but awoke with a start and reached for him. Once her hands touched him, she would sigh and relax into sleep again.

One night, after servants cleared the tables in the hall, Bleddyn brought out his bodhran and Malcolm, looking shy, produced a psalterion. He brought the zitherlike instrument close to his chest and stroked his fingers over the strings. They played bright melodies while Brianna nibbled on apple slices. Meghan picked up her pipes and joined them. Damron glanced from them to Brianna and back again, then made up his mind to do what his heart had longed to do since he first heard Brianna's voice.

Damron strode over to Meghan and asked her to play a certain melody. She looked up in surprise and grinned.

"'Tis about time, cousin. Why have ye waited so long?"

Meghan lured sweetness from the strange instrument, and the sounds floated through the room. Malcolm's fingertips flew over the psalterion's strings, and Bleddyn feathered the beaters over the bodhran.

At the first sound of Damron's rich baritone, Brianna's gaze flew to him. His was the voice her heart remembered. From the way his body moved and his eyes stroked her, though the words were German, she knew it was a love song.

His was a tone like chocolate velvet, reminding her of a great Argentine singer, José Cura, in Lydia's time. Her heartbeat quickened, and her body responded to him, filled with the emotion he drew from her. His marvelous voice flowed over her like silk-clad fingers that searched her mind and found her soul.

Damron did not miss the signs of passion building on her

flushed face. It was not the same look he had seen when she sang with Galan.

This was different. Intense. Yearning. Straining.

His gaze strayed to her breasts. Her nipples thrust against her tunic's bodice. He longed to grasp her in his arms and take her breasts in his mouth to suckle.

It took but two long strides for Damron to reach her. She gasped in surprise when he went down on his knees and held out his hands in supplication.

"Please, my love. Sing for me," he whispered.

Talking ceased. Men playing games of chance stilled, and women stopped their soft chatter to lean forward, waiting. All knew of her vow not to sing for him.

Brianna's gaze flew to Bleddyn's, and he nodded and smiled. When they spoke of it later, those nearest to her swore they heard the mystic say, "'Tis time to set aside a vow made in anger. Do not deny yourselves the healing pleasure of your greatest gifts."

Mereck's face bore the satisfied look of a barn cat certain of a juicy mouse for his next meal.

Brianna took Damron's hand, and they stood pressed close together. He listened intently as she sang of love and longing, and when she came to the final verse and would have stopped, the players resumed at the beginning, prompting her to sing again. Damron's full tones echoed her words. The effect was startling.

His shaft, which had stirred at the first sight of her, was near bursting with need. His gaze never left hers. His hands and arms moved in gestures fitted to the song of wanting to know how to love her, to show her his heart was hers for the taking.

Heartache sounded in her words. Damron wanted to cry out that he did not mean to bring her such pain. He held her arm so she could not leave him, and started singing the happy, lilting tune that Meghan urged from her pipes.

Damron launched into his next song. 'Twas a tale of love a

woman had for a man but refused to show him in any way. The man pined for his wife to love him. One day, they carried her husband home from battle. He had no will to live without her love. She lamented that she had kept her love from him, and vowed to return his love for the rest of her days.

> *We started wrong, my fault, not thine,*
> *My soul, my heart I kept as mine.*
> *Begin again with me, my love,*
> *And meet anon by heaven's gate.*
> *In sorrow now I know 'tis true,*
> *My life, my love, belongs to you.*

At the song's end, Mereck grinned and rose to come stand with them, he on her right and Damron on her left. When Mereck began the haunting tune Galan had composed, she started to protest, but hearing Damron join him, she relaxed. Her words floated to meld with theirs.

By his actions, Damron strove to make amends for his jealous deeds at Ridley. This night, they had given each other a precious gift: their joined voices.

Damron asked Angus to pipe them a tune so they could dance. Mereck nodded, made a beeline for Meghan and ignored her protests. Eric MacLaren hauled Elizabeth Neilson, a redhead with a fiery temper who aided Brianna and Meghan to dunk the men with soapy water, to the center of the room. He stated they would start the dance so Brianna could see how it was done. After Brianna watched for a while, Damron led her to teach her the steps. It was her first attempt at Highland dancing.

Her softness and heady scent made his body ache with love. When she finally begged fatigue, he worried over the dark shadows under her eyes. He breathed a kiss on the forehead. She surprised him by rising on her toes and kissing his chin.

Damron's heart surged with that unexpected, public kiss. He cuddled her in his arms and carried her to their bedchamber.

One cold, blustery night, a messenger with torn clothing and bruises on his face galloped over the drawbridge to bring news that brigands had raided a Blackthorn village ten leagues away. Damron and Mereck summoned knights and warriors to aid the hamlet. Before first light, they rode out.

When the sun was at its prime, they had yet to see signs of strife along the much-traveled path. Damron halted and ordered the villager brought to him. Spencer went in search of the man, but returned with word that the villager had dropped to the end of the line, after he claimed his horse had picked up a stone. No one had seen him since. Spencer found signs that a horse had left the trail and headed off into the woods.

As his suspicions raged, Damron's heart thundered with worry for Brianna. He ordered the men to make haste watering their horses and return to Blackthorn. He and Mereck far outstripped the column as they galloped back the way they had come.

Bleddyn walked deep into the forest, searching for herbs which could be picked only as dawn rose. He carefully lifted a small plant into a sack. Tree leaves began to rustle and murmur, and then Cloud Dancer circled above and screeched. Bleddyn stiffened, then broke into a run back to the castle.

Within the keep, David fought sleep after downing his last cup of ale. At last, he slumped against the wall outside Brianna's door. Guardian also could not keep his eyes open. Neither man nor wolf heard footsteps approach.

Brianna heard her name. She opened her eyes to see some-one stood beside her bed.

"Little love, awake for me," he whispered, as Damron was wont to do.

"Dear God, is something wrong, Damron?"

He turned to her bedside table to pick up a cup of milk mixed with honey, and emptied a small vessel into it. "Awake and drink, Brianna, for I will make slow and passionate love to ye."

Too late, she knew it wasn't her love's voice. She tried to scramble to the other side of the bed to escape and screamed, "Get out!"

The man gripped the back of her head, jerked her back and held the cup to her lips. She clawed at his wrists, choked and tried to spit out the liquid. Until the last drop passed her lips, he kept flooding her mouth with the potion. Tossing the cup aside, he clamped his hand over her lips and dug into her soft cheeks to stifle her screams. He crawled onto the bed to strad-dle her.

Brianna fought, knowing this was the man she had feared would find her again. God help her! Why had she not put her misericord beneath her pillow? She tried to scream.

"If ye wish no harm to the bairn, do not fight me. When I took ye from the waterfall, did I not say that ye would yet be mine?"

Brianna aimed a knee at his groin. He cursed and back-handed her face, subduing her until the drugged milk began to take effect. Her struggles weakened. Her body relaxed. The man ripped off his black mask and clothing and began to kiss her face. With greedy eagerness, he made his way to her swollen breasts, leaving bruises wherever he suckled. With his knees, he forced her legs wide as he freed his turgid shaft. He pressed his rod to her, his breath loud and labored with excitement.

Asceline burst into the room and grabbed his shoulder. "Get

dressed, Rollo. That lovesick fool is returning." Her voice vibrated with hate. Two men entered, carrying a naked man.

"Satan take ye." Rollo shook off her hand and snarled. "Ye said I'd have her. I'll not leave her behind. She comes with us."

"Simpleton! She would slow our escape. Do you want Damron's blade at your throat?"

Asceline and the men posed the naked body beside Brianna. Rollo's rod was rigid, more huge and swollen than at any time in his life. His gaze never leaving Brianna's ripening body, he muttered obscene words as he gave a few fast jerks of his hand. His seed spurted onto her thighs. Before the spasms ended, he shot his last over the flaccid member of the unconscious man.

"Explain this to the mighty Laird of Blackthorn. He will discard ye now," Asceline sneered.

They crept past the unconscious David and Guardian, dashed across the open areas and stole past the guards slumped at the postern gate at the castle's side wall. They heard the chains grating as the drawbridge was lowered.

Damron and Mereck thundered across the meadow, shouting for the guards to lower the drawbridge and open the portcullis. They galloped into the bailey and flung themselves from their steeds at the foot of the stairs. Both ran until they reached the sleeping guards. Seeing Guardian and David, Damron's heart lurched. He burst through the doorway, his sword gripped tight in his fist.

Damron stalked to the bed and jerked open the bed hangings.

Chapter 22

Damron spied two pale, naked figures sleeping side by side on his bed. White-hot fury sped blood through his heart till it near burst with it. Nay! It could not be. Not again!

"Bar the door, brother. Light the candles. I would see the man clearly afore I spill his blood." Damron snarled the words through taut lips.

As Mereck lit each of the four candles in the holder beside the bed, the scene unfolded through the brightening light. Eric lay sprawled close against Brianna's side, his right arm thrown across her and his hand cupped over her breast. Bile surged to Damron's throat, for he recognized the unmistakable sight of a man's milky seed on their bodies. Gripping his sword hilt with both hands, he raised it high, its sharp point ready to plunge into the sleeping man's heart.

"Hold!" Mereck's shout stopped Damron. "By God's blood, something is amiss. Look at them." His steely hands on Damron's wrist forced the blade away.

"I am lookin', brother, and 'tis not a sight for any man to bear— his wife, swollen with his bairn, and his good friend beside her. I see Eric's seed on his tarse; I see his seed on Brianna." His voice, forced out of his throat with effort, near choked him. "'Tis worse than Genevieve's betrayal. How will I know if my wife carries my child or Eric's?" He tossed the sheet over Brianna and hauled Eric off the bed onto the cold floor. He yanked off one of the braided bed curtain ropes, and tossed it to Mereck.

"Tie the bastard. Then find out why Connor and the men we left to guard the keep failed in their duty." His nails cut into his palms as Mereck did as he asked, then left.

Bleddyn pounded up the stairs, his cape sailing behind him, and near knocked Mereck over. Marcus opened the door only wide enough for the Welshman to enter. Bleddyn glanced at Eric on the floor, then went immediately to the bed. Without speaking, he grasped Damron's shoulders and moved him aside, for Damron stared at Brianna like he had turned to stone.

"Brianna's neck is limp, as are her limbs," Bleddyn pointed out as his gentle fingers checked them. "Someone's hands have bruised her face, neck. Her breasts, too." He picked up her hands and studied them. "Blood is on her fingers, flesh beneath her nails." He frowned and went over to kneel beside Eric.

He turned the unconscious man to find a huge lump covered with blood on the back of Eric's head. "Damron, did either you or Mereck do this? Have you known a man to make love after a blow savage enough to kill?"

Damron clutched the sheet with white-knuckled fingers. Brianna had said fawn-colored hair mingled with hers at the waterfall. He glanced at Eric's light hair, then his gaze roved down to the tracks of semen. "Explain how he spent himself, and why 'tis on my wife's thighs."

Bleddyn bent and picked up the cup to sniff and taste the drops of milk there. "Someone drugged her, Damron, and I see no gouges on Eric's body to account for the flesh under her nails."

Damron stared, not moving. Finally, Bleddyn prodded him to action. "Examine your wife. You will find proof she did not swive with Eric." He turned his back when Damron bent over Brianna.

Damron found cuts and scratches between her legs, but

no sign of a man's seed. His breath whooshed from his lungs, but right after, wrath turned his body rigid. He stormed to the door and jerked it open.

"Mari, have a bath brought for yer mistress," he bellowed, his face a rigid mask of anger. Mari, already pale and shivering, near jumped out of her skin. Lady Phillipa started to enter the room, but Damron shook his head and closed the door. When the water arrived, he barred the door with his body and passed the buckets to Bleddyn.

Damron carried his unconscious wife to the tub. He bathed her, his hands gentle, as he cleansed her flesh of the man's filthy touch. His heart ached that he could not wash away her hurts.

After Bleddyn bandaged Eric's head, he turned to Damron and shook his head. "Come. Her skin will be sore if you do not stop."

Damron swallowed and nodded, then wrapped Brianna in a warm cloth and sat beside a glowing brazier with her. Bleddyn knelt and placed a tube against her chest and listened to her slow and labored pulse. At last, he turned his attention to her swollen belly. As his splayed hands stilled on the sheet, waiting for the child's movements, his face paled.

Eyes closed, Bleddyn clasped his talisman and cupped a warm hand over her babe's shape. For long moments, energy seemed to flow from his hands into her. Each time Damron started to speak, Bleddyn shook his head. After some time, he looked up.

"I feel slight movements. As if the babe wakes and tried to stretch. A tiny foot kicked." He frowned. "Whoever drugged our little one and her babe also rendered the guards unconscious and struck Eric a mighty blow. Your return foiled them. They planned to ruin Brianna and Eric in your eyes." Bleddyn added softly, "Someone hoped you would kill Brianna, or at the least, cast her aside."

"I dinna doubt I am well-hated by more than one man." Damron's voice was bitter. "By Lucifer's wicked heart! Had we not suspected something awry, he would have had all of her. Surely 'tis the same man who stole Brianna on our journey here."

Bleddyn prepared a potion, one which would not harm the bairn, to offset the sleeping brew. Damron spooned it past her lips, while Bleddyn and Marcus carried Eric to a pallet in Connor's room.

Damron sat with Brianna in his arms, holding her nestled to his chest, her head beneath his chin. She soon became restless in her cramped position. Damron, reluctant to release her, put her on the bed and snuggled the covers over her shoulders. He sat beside her, guarding her while he waited for her to awake and tell him who had attacked her.

Mereck returned carrying Guardian in his arms, and lowered him to the rug beside the bed. "This great beastie will be upset when he awakes. 'Tis best he be by your side. He will be calmer." He straightened and nodded to Bleddyn. "Within the keep, the intruders drugged only those closest to this chamber. Connor struggles to fight off the sleeping potion, but Meghan sleeps as soundly as David."

Bleddyn nodded, then left to tend those who were drugged.

Mereck poured wine into two cups and motioned for Damron to come sit with him beside the table. He watched as Damron swirled the wine in his mouth, his brows creased in a frown as he stared at the rumpled bed.

"Brother, how can you mistrust Brianna? From what I can see, she has been naught but honest and caring. I dinna ken how you can think she has betrayed you."

Not speaking, Damron studied him through narrowed eyes.

"What happened with Genevieve? I expect Connor knows, but I have never questioned him on it. I have sensed your thoughts, but I would not pry into your mind seeking to learn what you did not want me to know." Seeing Damron had drained his cup, Mereck refilled it. "Mayhap it will ease your mind to speak of it."

Damron leaned back in the chair, a grimace distorting his face. "Aye. Mayhap it will." He kneaded his forehead and wished he could rid himself of his painful thoughts. He sighed, then leaned forward with his arms braced on his knees.

"Genevieve and I were married less than a year. King William sent me to Rouen on a matter, and I stopped to visit Mother's kin. I returned to the court a sennight earlier than expected . . ."

His shameful tale unfolded. "I rode hard to surprise Genevieve. A locket studded with blue stones—her favorite—rested in my pocket. 'Twas her name day.

"I was cautious not to startle her when I opened our chamber door. The first rays of dawn crept through the window. It streaked her hair with golden highlights. Her back was to me. She was naked. Her alabaster skin glistened with sweat." His words choked off, and he took a deep breath.

"She straddled a man. She combed her fingers through her lover's ebony hair and fanned it over the pillow. I didn't even know I drew my sword until I heard the rasp as it left the scabbard. Genevieve stiffened. Her head whipped around and she stared at me.

"I yelled at her to move aside. My voice quavered like someone ancient." He looked down, shamed. "She screamed at me to get out. Called me a Scot's whoreson and asked why I was not in Rouen mewling with my mother's family. Hate filled each word she spat at me. She hovered over her lover, protected him with her own flesh." Damron squeezed his eyes shut for a moment, then cleared his throat.

"I tossed her aside, then raised my sword high. When I spied her lover's face, I froze. At the same time, another head popped up from beneath the covers beside them. My sword crashed to the floor."

"By all the saints, Damron. Who were the men?" Mereck sprawled back, his legs stretched wide in front of him.

"Nay. 'Twas but one man. Clasped between Genevieve's legs was Danielle, the most beautiful, the most licentious woman in William's court. Beside her, his eyes near bursting from his head, was Robert." Seeing Mereck's brows rise in alarm, he nodded. "Aye. King William's eldest son. Neither was an opponent I could meet on the field." Damron drained his cup and held it out for Mereck to refill.

"I felt stunned. Heartsick. Serene as if she rose from a night's sleep, Danielle rose and draped a sheet around her naked body, lifted her dainty hand and blew me a kiss, then sauntered out the door. A crowd had gathered there on hearing Genevieve's screams. Smiling, she passed through everyone there. She was unaffected by what had happened."

"For God's love, brother. Did you kill Genevieve?" Mereck swallowed, his stiff face mirroring Damron's horror.

"Nay. By rights, I could have. Still, my humiliation did not end there. Not even with the shame of having half the court gaping into my chambers and chortling at my expense. That came when Genevieve spewed her hate at me. She screamed that I was a misbegotten, wretched nithing of a man. Said I repulsed her with my gentle hands and soft embraces.

"Afore I knew what she was about, she swooped down and grabbed my sword. She slashed me from my groin down to my knee. She meant to geld me. 'Twas Robert who wrenched the sword from her."

"Brother, ne'er did I suspect a woman gave you such a wound. How did you not die of it?" Mereck's face paled.

"Aye, Mereck. Robert clamped hold of my leg and screamed for his father. The king was already sweeping into the room. William's physician saved my life; William's influence secured a speedy annulment."

Mereck's lips twisted in a bleak, tight-lipped smile. "Ah, Damron, 'tis a blessing I, and not you, am the one called Baresark. I fear I would have struck first and been drawn and quartered for killing the king's son." He leaned forward and shook his head. "From what you told me afore about Genevieve, Brianna is nothing like her. Your little wife is gentle. Loyal. By far, too much in love to betray you."

Damron's gaze studied Mereck's face, hoping he had seen into Brianna's mind and judged her right.

Mereck swept his long hair back from his face with an impatient hand and stood. "Rest now, brother. I will gather the men and inspect each for scratches. All are loyal to you. I dinna think I will find any marks not caused by practice. We will get to the bottom of who plotted this." He clapped Damron on the shoulder and left the room.

Damron leaned over Brianna to cover her bare shoulders. At his touch, she cried out and tried to scramble from the bed. "Brianna, calm yerself, 'tis me." Her eyes cleared, and she grabbed his shirt in a frenzy of fear. She flung her arms about his neck, panting and shaking.

"Tell me what happened, wife. Did ye think ye welcomed another to yer bed?" Damron couldn't shake the memory of Genevieve in bed with her lovers from his mind.

"You can't believe that. Someone came in. He forced milk down my throat. When I tried to scream, he put his hand over my mouth."

"Did he say anythin'? Do ye know who came to ye?" Damron stared at her, waiting for her to admit she knew who had crept into her bed.

Brianna swallowed. "Someone whispered my name. I woke and saw a man in black clothing beside the bed."

"And? Did he wear aught else?"

"A mask over his head. A cloak. He called me 'little love.' It didn't sound like you. When I struggled, he cursed and said he had warned me at the waterfall that I would be his." She shuddered when Damron's gaze bored into hers.

"For a moment, I thought it might be Eric. I told him to get out. He grabbed me and poured milk down my throat. That's when I saw his eyes and knew it wasn't Eric. This man's eyes were close-set. Nearly without lashes. His hands were scarred and calloused, his fingers short."

"Had it been Eric, would ye have fought so hard?" Damron stiffened with jealousy.

Brianna shoved him away, clutched the sheet and wrapped it tightly around her swollen stomach. "You don't deserve an answer, Damron. I vowed to be faithful to you."

Guardian wobbled around the room, and when he sniffed the rug beside the bed, he bared his teeth and growled ferociously. The hackles on his neck stood up while he searched the room and over to the door.

Damron's eyes narrowed, watching the wolf. He went over to hold him by the ruff, and opened the door. Mari waited there, her eyes fearful.

"Mari, stay with yer mistress. Dinna leave her alone, should ye need to fetch anythin'."

Mari bobbed her head and scurried around the growling wolf. He glanced back to see her go to Brianna and grasp her hand, crooning as she smoothed Brianna's hair back from her face.

He released Guardian and followed him down the back stairwell, through the rear courtyard, across the bailey and to the postern gate. The wolf sniffed the ground, savage growls rumbling from his chest. At each place the beast stopped, Damron searched the ground, hoping the culprits left a clue in their hurry. In a wooded area twenty paces outside the gate, Guardian whined and ran around in circles, sniffing. From the churned-up grass, Damron knew 'twas where the louts had mounted horses and fled.

He ordered a patrol to enter the woods, though he knew whoever had been there was long gone.

After the sun set, Damron went to Eric's room and found him awake. He squinted painfully from the candle Damron held close, and he groaned and grasped his head.

Damron leaned so close his nose near touched Eric's. "How came ye to be in my bed, with my wife, naked as the day ye were born?"

"What! In your bed?" Eric struggled to sit up. "Naked? How?"

"'Tis what I am askin'." Damron's lips thinned to a hard line.

"Damron, the last I remember is climbing to the battlements to meet Cook's daughter in the shadows of the barbican. Someone struck me from behind when I reached there." He looked around, puzzled. "I was fully clothed. Where are my clothes?"

Damron snorted. "Where ye took them off."

His face ashen, Eric tried to rise from the bed.

"I dinna ken how ye believe I would play ye false." Hurt echoed in his voice as he rubbed his pounding forehead. "Marcus said if Mereck hadna stopped ye, ye would have dealt the fatal blow afore learning the truth." He struggled to reach a bucket as his stomach emptied its contents.

"My blade would not have struck ye, Eric. I would have come to my senses afore it reached yer flesh." Damron held him about his shoulders until the last spasms quieted, wiped his face and coaxed him to drink more of the liquid Bleddyn had prepared for him.

He stayed with Eric until he rested. When Damron sought his own room, David and Guardian were outside his door. Meghan sat beside Brianna, and he nodded and motioned for her to leave. The bed shifted with his weight when he slid between the sheets. Brianna cried out in her sleep. He put his arms around her, and she thrashed around until his murmurs soothed her. When he felt his bairn kicking and refusing to rest, he put his face against her stomach and sang, his voice soft. Soon, both Brianna and the babe quieted.

Brianna no longer sought Damron out by day, and during mealtimes, she was quiet and withdrawn.

At night, it was like a switch had turned off her passion. His touch didn't thrill her as it had before. He caressed and kissed her body, even whispered erotic thoughts, as he patiently tried to arouse her. She became slick and ready for him, but her passion did not mount enough to gain her own release. Finally, he could wait no longer.

Damron felt her mental withdrawal from him. She no longer caught fire at his lightest touch as she had before. Did she pine for another? Distrust ate at him and struck him where it hurt the most: his heart.

He still had not found who had attacked Brianna. He ordered Mereck to question the men, for Mereck had inherited his mother's ability to hear another's thoughts when he put his mind to it. But Mereck could find no one who had seen or heard anything that could give them a clue who had attacked Brianna and Eric. It preyed on Damron's mind until it consumed him.

He watched the men around him, and he became angry over the slightest things. If the stable boy did not have Angel ready and waiting when Damron stepped out into the bailey, he yelled until the poor lad quivered. During weapons practice, if a warrior took mere moments to gain his breath, Damron took him on as an opponent. He battled with him until the man dropped from exhaustion. Damron knew he was being the Demon that Brianna had called him on first coming into his life, but he could not stop himself.

One night, his anger spilled over into the very worst place, his bedchamber. Brianna's stomach had increased, and he had been entering her sweet center from behind to spare any pressure on the bairn. He wooed and aroused her, until she was ready to accept him. He guided his engorged shaft to her entrance and rubbed it around her nether lips, keeping up the gentle pressure of his fingers on her slick nub.

"Yield to me, love," he whispered, his cheek pressed to hers. She stiffened. He lifted his head and saw her eyes squeezed tight and her teeth clamped together. Though her body had yielded, her heart had not. He wanted all of her, not just her flesh—he wanted her very soul. Anger streaked through him.

"Ye give me only yer body, Brianna. Ye dinna want my love. I must thank ye for stirrin' my blood enough to pleasure another, who will not hesitate to give me her all."

He had not thought before he spoke. Pride had put the words in his mouth; pride kept him from taking them back.

Damron heard her shocked cry. His hands clenched at the sound, but he steeled himself not to relent. Pictures of Genevieve and her lovers pummeled his mind, followed by the images of Brianna and Eric sprawled on his bed. Within a couple of heartbeats, he was up and out of their room, his robe belted tight around his body.

He made his way to Angel's stall, wrapped himself in a wool blanket, and sat propped against the hard wall. He would never go to another for solace, nor would he break his vows to her.

Why had Brianna not fought with him as she had before she began increasing with his child? The way he had baited her, she should have spat and clawed at him. It would show she had some feelings for him, some tenderness.

He needed proof Brianna loved him, that she needed him with her heart and soul. But she had ignored him as if he did not exist.

Miserable and hating himself for what he had done, Damron slumped there in a corner of the stall until the first bells of matins.

Chapter 23

Brianna's soul was breaking. Dark shadows smudged beneath eyes that saw little, for they looked inward to her thoughts. How could Damron have thought for even a moment that she could be as treacherous as Genevieve?

Suddenly, a glimmer of understanding struck Brianna. He did have good reason to doubt her. From the start, she had not been wholly honest with him. He had sensed her secrecy and thought she was withholding her love for him. How could she have told him she came from far into the future? Surely a medieval man would think her insane or possessed, like Elise's great-grandmother Elyn. Or worse yet, believe she was a witch.

She grew listless and talked little. For the babe's sake, she walked daily and willed all the nourishment and energy she had into the little growing body inside her. To comfort herself as much as the babe, she wrapped her arms around her swollen belly and smoothed and patted the babe nestled there.

One day, Bleddyn strode up to Damron, grasped his shoulder in a demanding grip and urged him toward a deserted corner of the outer bailey. He turned to face Damron, his face stern.

"Brianna cannot keep on in this way, Damron, or she will

not live through the birthing." Bleddyn's lips thinned and his voice was deathly quiet. "If you had thrust a knife into her body, it would have been less painful than what you did that night."

"How did ye know? Did yer mind intrude in our bed?" Damron's nostrils flared, his chin stuck out in defiance.

"Her soul was in such torment, how could I not know?" Bleddyn lips curled in disgust.

"If Brianna was yer wife, would ye not do the same, if ye knew she did not love ye?" His voice rose and broke. Spasms crossed his face.

"Brianna would never break her vow. She would not allow another in her bed, and well you know it."

"'Tis not her bed but her heart and soul that are not mine. When I touch her, I feel her yearning. She has ne'er given me all of her." His tone dropped near a whisper. "Though she denied it afore, I think 'tis Sir Galan she still loves." He whirled and hurried away.

Damron made every effort to please Brianna. He neither left her bed, nor tormented her with his jealousy. She slept more soundly, and the shadows beneath her eyes began to fade. On clear days, she spent most of her time outdoors. Always, Guardian kept so close he brushed against her skirts. She was well into her seventh month.

'Twas the end of fall, and the lovely painting of leaves that had made the surrounding forest a feast for Brianna's eyes had now fallen, leaving naught but skeleton trees. One day, after her noonday rest, she and Meghan strolled along the curtain wall. David trailed behind. Cloud Dancer patrolled the skies, soaring high above, flirting with the clouds for which he had been named. The wind was colder than expected, and Meghan went below to fetch heavier cloaks.

Brianna sighed, enjoying the beautiful day. She watched Mereck ride across the drawbridge, entering the front bailey. Not far from him, a movement startled her. She shaded her eyes to see what it was. A woman with a large falcon on her gauntlet moved stealthily from behind a cart, where she must have hid, waiting. The raptor looked like a gyrfalcon, the largest and fastest of the falcons. But how could that be? All thoughts fled as Brianna saw the woman's stomach was very heavy with child. Brianna's gaze flew to her face. She gasped, feeling like a fist squeezed her chest. 'Twas Asceline.

While Asceline removed the raptor's hood, untied the jesses and raised her arm in triumph, her peals of laughter reached the parapet. The great wings took the wind. The falcon spotted its prey. Within a span of seconds, the predator plunged. David shouted and sprang forward. Meghan burst out onto the parapet, dropped the cloaks and sprinted to Brianna.

Guardian howled and jumped into the air, his teeth gnashing as he strained to reach the falcon. Standing in front of the opening between two merlons, Brianna bent over to protect her stomach and flung her arms around her head. The falcon sped to her, and its talons grasped her wrist. The momentum and weight behind the large raptor jolted her forward against the edge of a hard stone merlon. She screamed. Cloud Dancer plunged through the air, shrieking.

The falcon released Brianna's wrist. She stumbled, her hands clawing and grasping for some hold to keep her from falling to the ground far below. Meghan lunged to wrap her arms around Brianna's hips. Leaning far out, David grasped Brianna's shoulders and lifted her back to safety.

Bleddyn and Damron burst through the doorway, the same doorway through which Guardian now streaked downward. The wolf was soon out into the bailey, with bloodcurdling growls and snarls coming from his throat. Just seconds away from the wolf's jaws, Mereck galloped over, and with one arm, jerked Asceline up onto his horse.

But 'twas not only the leman the wolf sought. The wind carried the remembered scent of the man who had attacked Brianna in her room. The culprit, seeing the wolf loping toward him, mounted and tried to escape. A cart filled with hay was in his path. The horse reared, and tossed the man to the ground. In a trice, Guardian was astride him, his slavering jaws wide. Just as his teeth clamped on the man's neck, Cloud Dancer dropped the dead gyrfalcon on the ground beside them.

Damron raced with Brianna in his arms. In their chamber, he placed her still form on the bed. Meghan, who never showed fear, stood ashen and trembling.

"David, run quickly," Bleddyn ordered. "Fetch my black pouch from the medicinal hut. 'Tis on the table at the far wall."

David nodded and dashed out the door.

Phillipa patted Meghan's shoulder, then urged her from the room. "Please, love, tell everyone to wait within your grandfather's room. I will come to you when we learn more from Bleddyn."

After the room emptied, she hurried over to help Damron as he straightened Brianna on the bed. He smoothed her hair back from her face, his jaw clamped hard to keep from crying out.

Bleddyn's fingers felt alongside Brianna's neck and collarbone. "Her heartbeat is too slow and faint." His face did not change expression at any time while he listened to Brianna's body and probed with his hands. He checked the sheets beneath her, and seeing no telltale red stains, sighed with relief.

David, out of breath and gasping, hurried into the room and handed Bleddyn's pouch to him. "David, now I must ask you to bring sturdy logs to prop up the foot of the bed. 'Tis important we raise her lower body higher than her head."

Bleddyn tended the cuts and scrapes on Brianna's arms and

face, then looked for further damage. Finding none, he mixed herbs and dribbled small amounts past her lips.

"We must wait until she wakes. She needs more than I can give her in this way." He moved back from the bed so Lady Phillipa could cover Brianna with a warm blanket.

Damron stood, mute. This terrible happening was his fault. It would have been better to have sent Asceline over a cliff than to have given her this chance to harm Brianna. He looked up, expectant, when Mereck entered.

"I assigned ample guards over Asceline. They will watch her door and all windows to see she never again shows her face at Blackthorn."

"What of Guardian's kill?" Damron straightened, his jaw thrust forward.

"Neither Connor nor I could identify him. The wolf savaged his face so thoroughly we were unsure of who he was. Seeing his long, pale hair, we asked Eric if he knew him."

"And?" Damron waited, expectant.

"Eric also had trouble making out the mangled face. The hair and forehead looked like Rollo. He couldna be certain. After he spied the man's belt buckle, he said aye, 'twas his cousin. Rollo won it as a trophy while wrestling last All Hallow's Even."

"Was there aught else to identify him?"

"Aye. A scar high on the man's thigh." Mereck's face tightened, his lips thinned. "Small crescent marks. We have found who abducted Brianna on her journey here."

Just before the first perfect glow of sunlight made its way above the horizon in the wee hours the next morn, Brianna's eyelids fluttered. She took refuge in the darkness within her mind, and resisted the voices calling her name. She heard Damron's pleas while he smoothed her hair.

"I am so sorry, Brianna, 'tis not what ye think," he murmured.

She jerked her head away and opened her eyes.

"No? What isn't what I think, Damron?" Her voice was faint. "Though my eyesight is poor, didn't I see the woman you supposedly sent away? Wasn't she heavier with child than I?" She shook her head, warning him to silence. "What she did isn't a surprise to anyone but you. Your cruelty is beyond hers, for you took vows to honor and cherish me, yet you kept her here." She stared deep into his eyes.

Foreboding swept over Damron, feeling the torment that filled her soul.

"Drink this, little one," Bleddyn spoke softly beside Damron. "'Twill strengthen the blood flowing through the bairn." He lifted her head, and she swallowed the bitter brew.

She was so very tired. Her eyes closed and she slept.

"I will see she sleeps often until she regains her strength." Bleddyn spoke with deliberate calm.

Damron read the worry behind his words. "It will not harm the bairn?"

"Whatever harm comes to the bairn will not be by my hand, Damron. We must keep the babe safe, until she grows big enough to stand the rigors of birthing."

"She? How do ye know 'tis a daughter?"

"Brianna senses it. She has talked and sung to her all these months. Do you not realize by now your wife is not as ordinary women? You, who are closest to her, know her the least."

Damron shivered as he watched her. Thankfully, she was no longer sickly pale and, when he laid his hand over her heart, he felt its stronger beat.

Bleddyn sat and prepared a missive seeking Alana's support. At the window opening, his whistled summons brought Cloud Dancer silently over to perch on the ledge. The mystic secured the note around the eagle's sturdy leg. His long fingers stroked the regal head and back, while he murmured in

strange, high-pitched tones to the great bird. Cloud Dancer
answered with strident bursts of sound, then soared off into
the darkening sky.

For days, Brianna slept soundly, waking only to drink
Cook's nourishing broths. When she finished and took whatever potion Bleddyn held to her lips, she sighed and returned
to sleep. Either Damron or Bleddyn was always by her side.

Damron chafed when his duties took him from Brianna's
side. Where once he had thrown his whole being into settling
disputes and making decisions for the whole of Blackthorn,
he was now impatient until he could return to find how she
fared. One day, his suspicions roused on seeing her eyelids
flicker. Realizing she feigned sleep when she heard his tread,
he removed his boots before again ascending the stairwell.

When he spoke to her, she was polite, but no expression
was in her eyes or her voice. The only time she showed feeling was when Guardian whimpered and nuzzled her arm for
her to pat his head. After she did so and crooned a soft
melody to him, his big mouth spread with a grin, and he slept.

The day Cloud Dancer returned, Bleddyn untied Baron
Ridley's answer and read that they would begin their journey
the next morn after fetching Alana from Saint Anne's.

He and Damron removed the lifts from beneath the foot
of Brianna's bed. She was up and about more each day. Her
stomach continued to grow, while her face became paler,
more strained. Her gaze reflected lost dreams and heartache.
She resumed walking along the curtain walls, and stared into
the distance that was England, or down at the waters of the
Kyle of Tongue.

Damron watched, his fists clenched. Did she long for her old life? He would never let her go. He had to have her with him always. He vowed one day she would learn not to hate him.

Cloud Dancer patrolled the forests, and one early morn, he circled above the parapets, letting them know their guests would soon be within the keep. Damron insisted Brianna stay abed until the Ridleys were close. He came to the room to be sure she slept. Her head moved restlessly, and tears seeped from her eyes. He knelt beside the bed, his eyes stinging, and leaned close to her ear and stroked her head.

"I would have yer vow, Brianna. Promise me! Promise me ye will ne'er leave me! I canna live without ye, for I love ye with all my heart," he pleaded. He pressed his cheek to hers and sang to comfort her. His chest tightened and ached with the emotions he could not release. The warrior in him wished for the distraction of battle, to hack and butcher, and ease the fear and pain in his mind.

Brianna awoke the next morn to find Mari had prepared a warm bath. The faithful woman never ceased trying to make her more comfortable, and was cheerful and bright while in the chamber. Brianna relaxed in her bath, and after she was done, Mari helped her dress in a forest green tunic with an ivory smock beneath.

Damron strode into the room and placed his hands on Brianna's shoulders. "Wife, ye are the most bonny lass in all of Scotland. Ye look like a fairy queen that dwells in the forests or deep within the lochs. Ye could tear the heart from a man." Damron's voice whispered soft and bittersweet.

"I never sought to tear any man's heart. All I've ever wanted was to love and be loved."

"Ye canna say ye are not loved, wife. Not a man or lass in our clan has failed to take ye to their heart. Grandfather loves ye as his own. Mother thinks of ye as her bairn, and ye are sister to everyone. Come, let us greet yer Alana. She is crossing through the barbican and will be impatient to see yer lovely face." He carried her, carefully maneuvering the many stairs down to the bailey. When Alana stood before them, he lowered Brianna to her feet.

Alana's arms opened wide. With a low cry, Brianna snuggled into them. Her sister held her close and smoothed her hand over Brianna's dull, lifeless hair, down and over her back. Alana's gaze searched out Bleddyn's. A low cry escaped her lips.

At the sound, Damron's body tightened with fear.

"Come, my heart, you will be happy to see who else brings you love and lightness," Alana said, a strained smile on her face.

Brianna sensed Damron behind her, for no matter where he was, she felt his presence linked to her. Tense waves flowed from him. Puzzled at what caused them, she searched up and over Alana's shoulder. Uncle Simon and Aunt Maud stood there. Then someone moved from behind them. She met Galan's beautiful blue eyes.

"Come, Alana, you take overlong hugging my Brianna," Galan said, his arms outstretched as he came to her.

Damron hissed air through his teeth, but Galan paid no heed. As his arms closed about Brianna, he laid his face atop her head. He squeezed his eyelids, trapping his hurt there. Before he took her chin to peer down at her, he spread a comical look on his face.

"Never did I expect to see my Brianna so fat. Why, I have my doubts I could lift you without lurching like a man in his cups. That must have been a great apple seed you swallowed to fill you so."

Brianna laughed up at him, and for seconds her eyes lightened. "For shame, Galan. Elise and I were such silly twits to believe you. How you and your friends must have laughed when we refused to eat an apple."

"Come, greet yer aunt and uncle, Brianna, so we may go into the hall. Ye grow weary," Damron prompted beside her.

After Maud and Simon kissed her cheek, Damron gathered her in his arms. He did not put her down until they reached the fireplace in the hall.

The weather was cold and clear, and Damron placed a warmed plaid over Brianna's lap. She sighed with pleasure, feeling its warmth. Galan sat on the floor in front of her chair, his knees drawn up and his arms crossed over them. Damron looked at Brianna, and for the first time, he realized she wore the gift Galan had given her before they left Ridley. The gold chain and pendant with the dancing horses nestled between her breasts. His jaw twitched, but he quelled his jealousy and relaxed. He would do nothing that would take the smile from her face.

"How is everyone? I knew Alana had planned to come, but I hoped Elise would also make the trip."

"I fear Elise could not stand the pace. You know she can barely keep her seat on Buttercup," Aunt Maud answered with a grin. "Lynette of Wycliffe has come to Ridley for a visit. Cecelia was delighted having the two of them to herself."

The evening passed pleasantly, but Damron could not stop watching the expressions in Bleddyn and Alana's eyes. The sweet face of the abbess stilled as she looked at Damron and searched his eyes. He flushed. Somehow, she sensed all that had taken place at the keep since her last visit.

After a while, the room became too tense, too quiet. Meghan rose and suggested the room needed a little music. She grabbed her bagpipe from beside the fireplace, and Bleddyn smiled and picked up his bodhran.

"Come, Brianna, sing with me and welcome me to your home," Galan murmured. "We will choose only happy tunes, and the wild Welsh music that you favor." Galan's gentle eyes gazed down on her.

Damron could not believe that with just a soft word from Galan, Brianna joined them. His hands clenched until his knuckles turned white. He forced a pleasant smile, determined not to let his jealousy ruin the moment, and placed a stool amongst the musicians for her.

Galan started with a merry, romping tune that made Brianna chuckle, then she sang alone her favorite melody. Mereck rose to join Galan, and rested his arm over the younger man's shoulder.

"Galan, let us sing the ballad that has become famous even here in the Highlands."

Bleddyn started the beat, and the others joined as they recognized the tune Mereck sang when he first returned from Brianna's holdings at Stonecrest. It was Galan's song. Their voices merged, and they stood before Brianna, paying her homage.

She joined them in the last verse. Sorrow and pain came through in her voice. Damron swallowed hard, realizing the loneliness and fear she kept so well hidden. The minute their voices stilled, he gathered her in his arms and held her tight to his chest, while he sang the German love song she seemed to favor.

When he finished, Brianna waved to the extended family around her. "I'm so sleepy, I'm afraid I'll start to snore like Damron. I'll see you in the morning."

"Huh! Snore, wife? I ne'er snore. 'Tis yer imagination." Damron grinned down at her, then turned and started up the stairs.

By the time Bleddyn reached Brianna's bedchamber with her nighttime drink, Damron and Mari had propped her up on pillows, ready for her hot potion. They talked of the enjoyment of the evening as she drank, and when she was finished, Bleddyn kissed her forehead.

"Nathaniel," she whispered, "ask Alana to meet with us in your herbarium after we break our fast. I have much to say, and I will need you both with me when I say it."

"My heart, we will be there for you. Now you must sleep and rest." He patted her cheek and left the room.

Damron got in bed and held Brianna in his arms. He snuggled the covers over her shoulders and back, then sang softly to her until she slept.

Soon after the sun's rise, Brianna felt Alana's presence and awakened. She gazed into her sister's serene brown eyes. Alana always seemed at peace with the world, and now Brianna needed her presence and her guidance. Meghan burst into the room, vibrant with energy.

"Connor and I are going to show Galan the grounds and then go huntin'. I agreed to take Simple, for Galan canna believe the sparrowhawk is as ungainly as Alana has told him."

After Brianna dressed, Meghan and Alana held firm to her elbows to see she did not falter as they made their way below.

Damron and Galan stood talking together before the fireplace, and Brianna heard Galan laugh at something Damron said.

Bleddyn turned toward Brianna, and when he came close, she murmured, "I'm happy to see Damron and Galan together, Nathaniel. Damron has been pleasant to him. It surprises me. I thought it would be a 'cold day in hell' before he stopped hating him."

"They will be friends, my heart. Have no fear for Galan. You look much better this morn. When the others have gone on their hunt, we will meet as you asked."

Brianna rewarded Bleddyn with a warm smile just as Damron looked up and saw her coming toward them. He hurried to hold her arm and suggested they all should take their places.

Cook's helpers carried in large bowls of steaming porridge, cheeses, cold meats, sweet apples and grapes from France. The aroma of freshly baked bread made Brianna's mouth water. A servant filled Brianna's chalice with milk, then poured ale into Damron's. Mari's daughter placed a warm bowl of egg custard close to Brianna. Custard was one of many things Bleddyn insisted she eat each day.

Brianna's mouth gaped on seeing the next item. Cook arrived with a long platter, not filled with fish and meats, but oranges. Galan laughed at her surprised face.

"I thought you would like this special fruit. Bleddyn told me before you left Ridley that you had heard of this thing called an orange. At the end of my travels, I spied a ship being unloaded. Amongst the cargo were large crates of a yellow fruit. When I found what they were, I convinced the merchant to sell me as many as I could keep from spoiling. I set sail the same day."

"Thank you, Galan. It's truly a wonderful gift you have brought. I will keep one tucked in my pocket to enjoy as often as possible." His eyes lit with pleasure.

Damron spooned porridge into a bowl, added butter and heavy cream before he put it by her hands. She thanked him and, for the first time in days, smiled up at him.

He watched to see she ate every drop. When she had, he replaced the empty bowl with a large cup of custard.

"Goodness sakes alive. I don't have room for all of this."

"We will linger o'er our food until ye have room, wife. Bleddyn said ye must have it for strength."

Damron forced his face to softer lines as he reached up and stroked her hair. The babe drained much from her, for her curls had lost their warmth, their luster. They no longer grasped his fingers. He would be glad when the bairn was born.

After everyone finished eating, Brianna selected two oranges, and put one in each of her tunic pockets. Damron carried her down the stairs to the bailey, and watched as she waved to everyone leaving for their jaunt. He saw the bittersweet expression on her face and tried to reassure her.

"Afore long, wife, ye will be ridin' and doin' all ye wish to do."

Brianna lowered her gaze, then looked up to pat his cheek.

"Don't worry, Damron. I'm not unhappy to stay at home today. Alana and I are going to visit Bleddyn in the herbarium."

Alana moved to her side, and Damron nodded. He studied the men milling about, awaiting his attention. After kissing her forehead, he strode off, bellowing for the men to assemble in the great hall and be quick about it.

Brianna felt Alana's comforting arm around her waist as they entered Bleddyn's bright and fragrant hut. The herbal was sweetly aromatic from the lavender, mint, rosemary and sandalwood that hung from the rafters. Vats, tubs, vials and dishes held all sorts of ingredients. The quantity of herbs her Nathaniel had gathered, dried and stored to last through the season amazed Brianna. He rolled a pallet and placed it against the wall so she could sit and lean back in comfort. Sunlight streamed through the window, making the room warm and cozy.

"Now, little one, we must talk."

He tried to spare Brianna pain as he told Alana about the night someone drugged Brianna and attacked Eric. Fierce anger flashed over Alana's face. He spoke of the dreadful day Asceline had loosed her raptor, and of how they had fought to bring Brianna back to health. When he came to the present time, he stopped and looked to Brianna. She stared down at her tightly folded hands.

" 'Tis time to hear from you now, little sister. Tell all, for I suspect there is much we do not know."

Tears misted Alana's brown eyes as Brianna reached out to cling to her hand.

Chapter 24

Brianna's gaze was unseeing as she told Alana about her soul's journey back from the twenty-first century. "It began the day I fled Saint Anne's, and I fell and struck my head on the rock. The day Damron brought me to Ridley."

She told Alana her tale up to the past months. Her voice quivered and her eyes blurred as she looked from one to the other. "Something happened to the babe that night someone dishonored Eric and me. I realized it when I got my wits together. The bairn became quiet. Her movements weaker each day. I hugged and sang to her, and told her how much I loved her. I tried to support her in every way." Her face mirrored the agony of her mind when she described the day Asceline loosed the heavy gyrfalcon. "I felt the instant she lost the strength to continue. She didn't move again.

"I know you think I can't possibly tell what happens inside my body, but I can. You see, in my life as Lydia, I suffered the same horrible experience. I've waited, praying I was wrong. I'm not. My stomach is increasing because the baby's nest has pulled away from my womb." At their shocked looks, she shook her head, bidding them wait and listen to her. "I'm increasing because I'm bleeding inside. The baby, or the nest, has blocked the opening to my womb and kept my blood from spilling out." She squeezed her eyes tight to hold back her tears.

"I'm slowly being poisoned from what is happening. Soon, my stomach will heave as if the baby is strong and fighting to be born. I'll break out in a rash that will look like a dreaded disease, and finally my body will seek to empty its contents to try to save me. I'll tell you all you need to know so you may help me when the time comes.

"With all my heart, I thank Galan for the oranges. Inside the fruit's skin is a natural remedy that strengthens blood vessels. It will do much to help me survive." She took a shuddering breath. "In my future time, I studied the history of Blackthorn and learned I will birth two sons for Damron. It will be so." She gritted her teeth and fought to keep from crying out with the mind-numbing dread of having to go through the anguish of losing a child the second time.

Bleddyn nodded, pain filling his beautiful eyes. "What Brianna has said is true. I have seen in her mind all she speaks of, and what we must do when the time comes. Hopefully, we will do better by her than the doctor who near killed her as Lydia."

The door burst open, sending blustery, cold air racing through the room. Damron stood outlined against the bright day. He quickly entered and shut the door.

"I came to make sure my love isna drainin' her strength." His gaze searched the room, and his face relaxed when he spied Brianna sitting bathed in sunlight. The corner of his lips lifted in a soft smile, watching her nibble the white underside of the thick orange skins. "'Tis a strange thing ye crave, Brianna."

"To me it's the best part of the orange, Damron." She smiled up at him, a flicker of longing crossing her face.

Damron sat on the hard earthen floor, then reached for her and placed her on his lap. He took the orange from her hands and deftly finished peeling it. When she cleaned the rind with her small, white teeth, her face puckered, making him chuckle. His arm wrapped around her, eyes half-closed, concentrating. His big hand roved and stopped for minutes at a time over each section of her swollen body.

Damron's heart skipped a beat, then began to pound. He waited. With every breath he drew, his heart throbbed harder. Near frantic with worry, he stared into Bleddyn's eyes.

"Well noo, ma fey gawkie, I expect Alana wud agree 'tis time ye took a wee walk and rest. Ye must ha'e been sittin' for a long while, for I ha'e finished the petitions for the day."

Brianna wondered what stress had brought out such a thick brogue in his speech. Did he suspect the babe was no longer vital? Would he blame her for it? Her thoughts fled as he stood with her in his arms as easily as he had the first time he picked her up.

"What? No creaking and groaning under my weight? Surely with your advanced years, you should be complaining?" She poked him in the chest and grinned up at him.

He growled low in his throat. "Did ye really believe I did not hear ye mumblin' that 'the dratted man has a penchant for carryin' women'? I like feelin' my wife close to my chest. Have ye not noticed?" Before she could answer, he lowered his head and kissed her loudly. "Hmmm. I believe the taste of these oranges on yer lips makes them all the sweeter."

He walked out into the bailey, then turned to call to the others. "Come, let us take Brianna to visit her favorite spots." At the top of the stairs leading to the curtain walk, he carefully lowered her feet to the ground. "Look. Is it not a beautiful sight?" He waited for them to admire the water where Brianna herself stopped each day.

Sensing when she had seen enough, he put his arm around her waist to support her and moved to the next section overlooking the open field and paths that had brought them from England. With each area he selected, he surprised Brianna by knowing her favorite viewing points.

Halfway around the curtain wall, he insisted she have a brief nap before the rest of the family returned. He carried her down the wooden stairs, and asked Alana to take her noon meal in Brianna's room so his wife could lie abed. Her arms tightened around his neck, and she nuzzled a kiss on that tender spot below his jaw.

"As long as you are not struggling overmuch, my lord, you may as well take the whole burden of my increased size to our chamber."

"Bleddyn must make me a tonic, wife. Me puir muscles can barely take the strain."

Alana laughed up at him. "Poor muscles, like hell, my lord. You carry her as lightly as a dove."

He stopped a moment, then turned to stare at her, his brows raised. "Like hell?" he repeated.

Seeing his startled eyes, Brianna giggled.

"I believe I have shocked my new brother by law." Alana exaggerated a deep sigh. "My lord, your wife comes by her tongue naturally. One day, I visited Brianna at Ridley, and I stubbed my toes on a sharp rock. Not realizing Father Jacob was behind us, I grabbed my foot and cried out 'Lucifer's Hades.' In a trice, he had Brianna, Elise and me on our knees and lectured us.

"The poor dear had just left when Brianna whispered, 'Will blisters on my knees make up for it if I say cursed Lucifer's toes, but they hurt?' Uncle Simon came around the path and nearly called Father Jacob back, before we persuaded him we would be more careful in the future."

Brianna snuggled her ear close to Damron's chest to enjoy the rumble of his laughter coming from deep within. He had a beautiful, rich baritone of a laugh she had heard so seldom. Once in their chambers, he settled her comfortably on the bed. Alana and Brianna were soon engrossed in deciding which would be better on such a chilly day—hot porridge with cream or a steaming bowl of vegetables and meat soup.

He eased the door shut and left to seek out Bleddyn.

* * *

Damron led the Welshman deep into the forest, where he finally brought Angel to a halt. Wordless, he swung down to the ground and turned to study Bleddyn's face. He was tired of the Welshman's half truths. What did the man know about Brianna? What secret did they keep from him? Bleddyn's warnings that she was not as other women, that she could leave yet still be here, did not make sense. How could she become a meek, biddable woman, and yet still be Brianna?

Damron wanted answers. And he wanted them now.

"All of it. I want to know all of it." Damron circled Bleddyn like a prowling wolf. Every muscle in his body tensed until his skin felt like it was stretched over stone. "Ye have hinted Brianna is not as other women, yet always have ye and Brianna hidden the truth. That is not all of it. This morn, when I held her on my lap, I sensed something was terribly wrong. How can I help her if I dinna know what foe I am fightin'?"

"Brianna feared to tell you everything," Bleddyn said.

"Afraid? Nay. Brianna is not afeared of any man," Damron said with a disbelieving huff. He narrowed his eyes at Bleddyn.

"Not even if she felt the man would think her brainsick, or a witch? That he might lock her away in some distant tower?"

Cocking his head, Bleddyn waited for Damron's answer.

"What tale could she tell that she thinks so unbelievable?" He stopped, his boots near touching Bleddyn's own, then braced his hands on his hips and waited.

As Bleddyn spoke, Damron felt like his feet were rooted deep in the ground, as unable to move as a tall pine tree. Bleddyn's words rolled over him, at first like icy rain spilling over his skin. His arms prickled, his scalp crawled. Then, as Bleddyn said that Brianna, the woman Damron could not imagine living in a world without, could somehow be whisked away to a future time, he felt afire. He shook his head, swallowed and stepped back, as if distancing himself from the words would make them go away.

"Nay! Her soul? Her soul would be different? She would become that mindless girl that fled Saint Anne's Abbey?" Damron stalked back and forth as Bleddyn explained how Brianna's soul had matured over the centuries, had made her the feisty woman he knew today.

Damron didn't want the shell that would be the Brianna of the eleventh century. He wanted *his* Brianna. He had to keep her. Always.

Anguish ripped through him. His mind near exploded with it. He drew the broadsword strapped to his back. With a roar that sent creatures of the forest scurrying, he raised his blade high, twirled on his toes and brought it whirling and singing through the air to slash at every branch, tree and rock that he saw. His cape swirled about him, his hair flew out to whip his face, sting his eyes. And still, he roared like a wounded boar.

Finally, his breath caught on an endless sob. He fell to his knees, leaned forward, his forehead pressed to the damp forest leaves.

How long he stayed there, his face pressed to the earth, he did not know. He stayed on his knees, drenching the forest floor with his tears. Until he came to grips with what he had learned, he didn't move. Finally, Angel snuffled against his shoulder. Damron lifted his head and pushed up to his knees. He was alone. Though he had prayed till his mind was numb, he looked up at the darkening sky with one last prayer.

"Please." One word. No more than that.

Damron kept close within Brianna's call, helping her in every way and showing her loving concern. He held her close at night and, when she became restless, sang to her until she quieted. He whispered into her sleeping ear how much he loved her.

"Promise me! Promise me ye will ne'er leave me," he begged her again and again.

Her husband's close attention sometimes discomfited Brianna, for he insisted he tend her in her evening bath. He trusted no one else to aid her into the tub and sent Mari away. He bathed her, silently watching the changes in her body. Her face became more pallid, her veins clearly visible through her skin. Though her stomach and breasts grew larger, the rest of her body thinned and weakened.

One day, seeing a rash on her back, his hand stilled in shock. He swallowed his fear as he rinsed and dried her with a large cloth. He slipped a light shift over her head, laid her on the bed and told her not to move. He charged out the door, almost colliding with Bleddyn. Damron's eyes searched the healer's, and his blood ran cold. He stood aside as Bleddyn entered the chamber and went to her bedside. She held out an arm, and they saw the rash spreading there. Alana arrived in seconds. Damron knelt beside the bed, taking Brianna's hand in his. He held it tight to his chest and studied her eyes.

"Brianna, my love, dinna fear me. Bleddyn has told me of yer secret, but I knew ye did not wish to speak of it. I have known for days somethin' terrible is happenin' to yer body, and I want to help ye through it. Please dinna shut me out any longer." His throat worked in fear as he spread her hair around her thin face.

"Oh, my heart. I know you have not felt life in our bairn since"—she swallowed past the lump in her throat—"since at least a fortnight. My body has refused to give her up, and it's my fault. I wanted her, our daughter, so very much that I wouldn't allow myself to let her go. I can't fight it any longer. By morning it will be over."

"How long have ye known this fearsome thing, love?"

"From that day on the parapets." Brianna's low voice was full of sorrow. Tears streamed down her face as she looked up at him. "I'm so sorry, my love, but our little one left us then. Promise me you will bury her in hallowed ground. Father Matthew must say the prayers for her soul, and Nathaniel will have his ancient ceremony to see she is given her rightful place.

"Our daughter, Faith, must have a marker that each generation will promise to keep refinished, so it will last throughout the centuries. When it is time for each of you to pass, you will have taught your families to see that every name and year is kept distinct. Centuries later, those who come after you will read their histories set in solid stone. No one will be forgotten."

Brianna gasped as her stomach gave a giant heave. She had felt smaller surges for days now and knew her time was near.

Bleddyn went to the door where Connor and Malcolm stood guard. David waited with a short, narrow table covered with a pallet. Taking it from him, Bleddyn brought it into the room. Lady Phillipa covered the pallet with soft linen. Alana pulled over a table loaded with cloths they had prepared for this day.

Smiling, Brianna turned to Lady Phillipa. "Thank you for loving me as your daughter. Nathaniel and Alana will explain all to you later, but it would be best if no one else enters this room." She gasped as another spasm racked her body. "Kiss them for me and tell them I love them dearly. Please send in Mereck. I must speak with him." She kissed Phillipa's cheek and tasted the salty tears there. Mereck entered right away and went straight to her.

"Little sister, how can I help ye through this?"

"Damron needs your strength. Know I love you as a brother when I ask if you will stay with us. It's against custom for men to tend women in childbirth, but I'm not like other women."

"I will do whatever I can to help ye both," Mereck promised.

Brianna tried to smile through a wave of pain. Gritting her teeth, she held tight to Damron's hands.

"We must move you, my little one," Bleddyn told her.

Damron lifted Brianna, uncertain how to place her on the table so her head and feet would not dangle over the ends. Bleddyn had him lay just her body on the table, then placed a thick pillow beneath her head and shoulders to raise her. He took her feet and placed them in a strange extension attached at the end of the table, and covered her with one of the large, sterile sheets. Damron started to object, but Brianna insisted.

"Nathaniel had the table made from my drawings, love. It will help me."

Bleddyn worked swiftly to arrange everything around the room. Though he knew she would refuse it, he made a potion of poppy seeds to give her should the time come when she could take no more pain.

Bleddyn and Alana had everything ready. Damron shivered in horror when he saw the equipment Bleddyn unwrapped and laid out on pristine white cloths. They looked like instruments of torture.

"Alana," Brianna whispered, and her sister's face was immediately pressed to hers. "You know something wonderful?"

"What is it, sweetling?"

"You will be my mother in another time. I've recognized you since the first time I knew of you, and I've loved you. Promise me that if anything threatens your abbey you will give up the life you led for my sake. Father had no right to cloister you away, and I know he would want you to be happy with Nathaniel."

"I promise, little sister." Alana turned a worried face to Bleddyn. "She burns with fever, love."

"Mereck, please stand behind me, and don't watch my pitiful attempts," Brianna said. "Alana and Damron, place yourselves on either side of me and do as I tell you each time I ask."

They were no sooner in place when another wave of pain racked her. The right side of her stomach swelled near to bursting and was hard as stone, while the left softened, its muscles slack.

"Damron, massage my womb on the left while Alana holds the right firm." They did as she asked. She panted until the spasm had passed, and her stomach returned to its round shape.

Gorge rose in Damron's throat. He swallowed and gasped huge gulps of air, and felt Mereck's arm tighten around his shoulder in comfort. Damron looked mutely at him and, before anyone knew what he meant to do, he held Brianna up and slid her pillows to the floor. He climbed onto the table behind her, with his legs dangling on the side and her body rested back against his. He took her hands and held them tight in his own. Mereck took Damron's place beside Brianna. Every pain that struck through her, Damron felt in his own body. He willed his strength into her.

A scream of agony tore from her body, her soul. A scream Lydia had never allowed herself to release, but Brianna now let burst through bitten lips.

The anguished outcry reverberated throughout the room and into the forest depths.

It was a sound so primitive that Guardian and the dogs of the keep howled. The birds in the mews screeched. The wolves and beasts in the forest stopped, gave an echo of the pain of her soul and bolted.

Brianna's cry did not stop until she knew nothing was left for her body to do. She opened grieving eyes and looked at Bleddyn. She panted for breath, but had to speak.

"Please, Nathaniel. Let Alana clean her so I may hold her this one time."

Bleddyn nodded and tenderly handed the small body to Alana. Alana bit her lip, then did as Brianna asked, and when she was done, she placed a soft cloth round the tiny body.

Fighting back sobs, Brianna blinked at the bundle in her arms. She was a perfectly formed girl, her hair black like her father's. Brianna cuddled her to her face and kissed her, her murmurs breaking every heart in the room.

"Oh, my sweet babe. I wanted you so from the moment you were placed in my body. I'm so sorry I failed to keep you safe. You must wait for me. We'll be together again. I promise." She moaned, then whispered huskily to Damron. "I am sorry, love. She would have been a wonderful daughter. Her soul will now find another, and I pray she waits to be your child." Her voice stopped as his great hands came to cup the tiny head and body and bring it to his lips to kiss before he handed her back to Brianna. Alana took the bundle from her arms when Brianna slumped, unconscious.

Damron's shoulders shook with sobs he no longer stifled. Mereck supported Brianna so Damron could stand. Bleddyn wanted her flat on the table. Damron stroked her head and talked to her. Mereck kept a comforting arm around him. Bleddyn and Alana worked quickly. He carefully stitched the cut he had made on her body. When he was done, they did not pack her with mixtures of herbs, mud, spider webs or any other such common treatments of the time.

Brianna had an extensive knowledge of medicines in her own time and she had added her information to Bleddyn's. He had readied preparations of betony, St.-John's-wort, common rue, lady's mantle, wolfbane, columbine, white archangel and other herbs. All would aid Brianna in healing.

They knew little or nothing of many of them, but they did all she had told them to do, plus what Bleddyn himself had learned on that trip to Lydia's hospital. When done, they quickly replaced the bloody pallet with a clean one. Alana bathed her from her waist down, then packed sterile cloths against her body. She kept a steady pressure against them. As soon as blood seeped through, she placed another cloth over it and increased her pressure.

Damron and Mereck elevated the foot of the bed even higher than it had been weeks before. When it was ready, Damron lifted his wife onto the bed.

Brianna remained blessedly unconscious as they settled her in the freshly made bed. The room was cleaned and aired. Damron stood, the body of his daughter cuddled in his arms, and stared out across the night sky. He shook like a man too long on this earth, heartache and regrets tormenting his soul. Finally, Alana persuaded him to let her have the wee burden. She left the room and the women in the family met in Meghan's room. They would prepare the babe and dress her in the gown Brianna had made months earlier. When the sun rose, they would lay the bairn to rest alongside Damron's father and brothers. Father Matthew was a good man, and he would make no objections. He did not believe as others did that a stillborn child could not be buried in hallowed ground.

The first glimmer of dawn appeared, and Mereck persuaded Damron to leave Brianna's side. Phillipa stayed with her. A small rock wall, not more than two feet tall, enclosed the Morgan burial ground. In the center grew a huge rowan tree, magnificent with its massive trunk and spreading branches reaching to the sun.

Meghan and Angus's pipes wailed laments. Father Matthew said a prayer for the bairn's soul. He blessed the small spot before Bleddyn performed his own rites. The mystic beat his bodhran and sang his prayers for the small soul Brianna had asked Damron to name Faith.

Brianna believed the name carried the blessings of all the religions, for isn't that what religion is about?

Faith?

Chapter 25

Each time Brianna opened her eyes, Damron spooned elixirs between her lips, potions Bleddyn had cautiously prepared using black nightshade seeped with feverfew to ease the pains that came after birthing. On the third afternoon, Damron dared to breathe a sigh of hope, for the rash started to disappear.

Damron left her side only when it was necessary. He watched, lines of worry furrowing his forehead as Brianna began to heal. In the long hours by her bedside, he learned from the Welshman about her life in the future. Though she seldom opened her eyes, she spoke in her sleep to the people in her other time. He soon began to recognize their names. Her body was healing, but her mind seemed to drift away from them.

"Do not hide from us, Brianna," Bleddyn demanded in a stern voice. "Though Asceline is no longer Damron's leman, and you did not plunge to your death from the parapets, you have not completed all for which God sent you here."

Brianna's head shook and her arms moved, looking like she talked to him in her sleep.

"Would you turn coward and flee? In your century, you read Brianna would birth two stalwart sons for Damron and Blackthorn. Never was there mention of a daughter. Though it near breaks your heart, you knew the babe was not meant to be."

Brianna stirred. "I know you all love me, but it's not enough. Without a tie to my soul, I could never be happy here." She sighed and her voice wavered. "Damron, I'm sorry I was a disappointment to you. I thought a strong woman could bring you the happiness you so badly need."

Damron gathered her in his arms and rocked back and forth with her. "God's heart, Brianna. Ye were ne'er a disappointment to me. Ye are all the woman one man can e'er hope to have."

Brianna huffed, more like her old self. "So much a woman you held fast to your leman? No, I challenged the centuries. I lost. Do you know I've loved you all those years?" Brianna's face held a wistful expression. "Look at the sketch Papa Dougie created, when you didn't know he watched. You'll see the bitterness in your face. In my time, I'll see that drawing again. I'll never forget you, husband."

Bleddyn had explained what they must do should Brianna slip from them. His face was grim now, as he sat on the bed and held tight to Brianna's right hand. Damron clutched her left to his heart, while Mereck's fingers clamped on Damron's left hand.

Bleddyn would take Brianna to her future time. If he forced her to stay in the past, she would never be happy. She would have to decide whether she wanted to remain in the future, or return with him. When she started to leave, Damron should try with all his heart to convince her to stay. If he failed, and she pulled him with her, Mereck was not to break his hold on Damron's hand until they were all safely back. Alana and Mereck would watch over them and keep anyone from entering the room.

Brianna gazed deep into Damron's eyes, let out a deep breath and closed her eyes.

"Nay, Brianna. Dinna go. I canna live without ye," Damron cried out. "Promise me! Promise me ye will not leave me!"

Bleddyn commanded Damron, "By God's grace, keep her soul within the sound of your voice."

Damron's stomach contracted like a fist when a blue aura began to rise from Brianna's body, with Bleddyn's purple surrounding it. Damron's heart tore. Tears were in his voice as he started singing his soul out to her. Soon, the sound of Meghan's pipes drifted through the door, and his voice grew stronger. The blue light halted and wavered. Brianna's eyelids flickered.

Damron's voice, husky with love and heartbreak, rose in the love song Brianna favored. She wailed with anguish as her blue aura struggled to push past Bleddyn's essence. Bleddyn's body was as still and silent on the bed as hers. Damron was determined. He stretched out beside her and held tight to her hand. He willed his mind to fight for her the way Bleddyn did. Where she went, there he also would go. He felt his body relax against the sheets as he slipped away.

Beside the bed, Alana prayed while Mereck begged and pleaded for them to stay. The three auras joined, determined to remain together. The purple of Bleddyn's advanced soul and the light blue of Damron's enfolded the deep blue of Brianna's. The three bodies on the bed were still. Damron's voice floated through the walls of the keep as the beautiful lights disappeared.

The sounds of Lydia's monitors changed with her quickening heartbeat. Dr. Christian MacKay startled awake and jumped to his feet. Having been by her side for over forty-eight hours, he had dozed for a few short minutes. The two strange auras again surrounded his patient. His skin prickled, sensing the weak presence of a third hovered out of sight. Christian watched the struggle between the colored lights as they flashed around Lydia. Finally, the blue aura spread across Lydia's body until they merged. He saw that the other nimbus was determined she should come back with him. He knew it was the soul of a male, but how he knew he could not tell.

Lydia opened her eyes and stared at him. After several moments, she blinked and smiled. "Ah, Damron. You were here all along, weren't you?"

Christian didn't know who this Damron was, but it was obvious he was important to her. "Yes, love. I've always been here. You've been ill, but you're starting to heal."

"I'm so sorry, my heart, that I lost our bairn."

"I'm sorry, too, love. Keep talking to me and tell me what you feel." This woman's loving eyes and the sound of her sweet voice tore at his heart.

She noted his puzzled expression and realized it was not Damron, but someone in her time who looked very much like him. She closed her eyes to rest after her long struggle.

Bleddyn's aura whirled around the room in agitation. She argued with him in her mind, but he wouldn't leave her. Suddenly, Christian left the room, a blank expression on his face. She knew Bleddyn had caused him to leave.

Her heart thudded. Damron's rich baritone called to her, and begged her to return to him. She knew Damron could not appear while Christian was present, for a soul could not move through time and meet itself in another body unless it merged with that body. If he did so, they would forever change history. Damron would be as Lydia had been, in a coma. In medieval times, he could not survive. He would die.

Damron's essence entered to plead with her. "Love, I know yer soul is in torment. Mine own will ne'er know peace without ye. Ye vowed on our weddin' day ye would ne'er willingly leave while breath was in yer body. Ye canna break that promise, Brianna. Please, love. I canna live without ye."

Bleddyn took up the argument. "Brianna's lifetime can still be completed, little one. Return with us to Alana and all who love you. You can accomplish all you were destined to do there. In this future time, only a matter of days will pass for Lydia. When your time in Scotland has passed, you will awake again in this room."

Damron's energy color began to fade away. Lydia caught her breath. Scant seconds later, Christian reentered the room.

Christian noted the purple aura still hovered over his patient, but it no longer surprised him. He peered down at Lydia, intrigued by her eyes when they looked into his. She smiled the loveliest, sweetest smile he had ever seen. She stared up at him. Suddenly, scenes flashed through his mind.

A small woman in strange clothing smiled just like Lydia had at him. Her hair was brown, long and curly. She had large dark eyes and she lay beneath him! He was gazing deep into her eyes, while their arms were clasped around each other's heads. They were in the throes of passion, as pleasure exploded through them both. His body jerked with the emotions that coursed through him.

How could he possibly see and feel such a memory?

Shaking his head, he watched in amazement. A confident smile glowed on his patient's face as she spoke to him.

"Don't worry. I'll not be gone for long. Watch over this body that is Lydia and I'll return soon."

The bedside monitors started a frantic, high-pitched beeping, mimicking Christian's heartbeat. His hands shook as the blue shape rose again and the purple surrounded it. He knew it was not her love, but someone or something that would lead her to him. He heard the echo of her voice calling to the man.

"I am coming, my love. I am coming!"

Another echo sounded. MacKay's body shook as he heard it.

"I will always love ye, Brianna. I will ne'er let ye go, through life, through time, through eternity!"

The voice rose, and he knew this Damron called to the woman he loved, for he sang as if his heart would burst from longing.

My heart, my soul is in your hands,
Give me but a glimpse ye care.
Let me love ye as I long to do,
Forever in my soul, my torment.

Damron and Bleddyn lay slouched beside Brianna, breathing as if they had fought some great battle until no more was left in them to give to the fray.

"Damron, what is happening?" Mereck's voice quavered. He lifted Damron's head and held a goblet of wine to his lips.

Alana waited patiently beside Bleddyn. He slowly opened his eyes and turned his head to look at Brianna.

Her long brown hair lay spread about the pillows, with his and Damron's head resting on it. Blood seeped from between Bleddyn's fingers, cut by his tight grasp on his talisman. Silently, he took the cloth Alana handed him and wound it around his hand. Then, taking infinite care, he untangled Brianna's brown curl caught on the dragon clasp at his shoulder. Her cheeks were beginning to color and grow warm. He rose from the bed and stood beside Damron's still form.

Damron gasped and shook himself. He sat up in alarm, then wobbled to his feet. His eyes widened in panic. On seeing Brianna's still form, the blood drained from his face.

"By God's love, be she with us or not?"

"Jesu, Damron, the room was charged with such a feeling of lightning as to near set sparks to everything within." Mereck's voice was hoarse with fear, but Damron's concentration was on Brianna.

"Brianna, my love. Keep to me! Ye will always be mine," he cried, clutching her shoulders.

Brianna took a long, shuddering breath. She was desperately tired. Her mind wanted nothing more than to escape all memories and feelings. She willed herself back to that dark place to rest from the emotions that threatened to tear her apart. She would keep that "Brianna" locked in the back of her mind, until it was safe for her to come back.

"Lucifer's bloody toes! Open this door, ye great gowks. Ye ha'e no right to keep us from Brianna," Meghan shouted through the thick door. A heavy object banged against it.

"Meghan, put that down afore ye do yerself harm," Connor's voice boomed. "Quit yer battering. Ye canna break through solid oak. If the door were to open, ye might clabber Alana on the head with that Scot's hammer."

When Lord Douglas added his voice and bade them open to him, Bleddyn glanced around the room to see nothing told of the tumult caused by their souls' passages. He checked Brianna once more, then placed his hand on Damron's shoulder.

"If you do not want to injure her wee hand, do not clutch her so tightly," he said, then went to open the door.

Meghan burst into the room and hurried over to stand beside Damron. She brushed Brianna's dull hair back from her eyes, then her gaze searched the faces in the room. Her mouth set in a grim line. They would not easily put her off about what had happened here.

"Damron, ye look like ye have been through the gates of Hades and back." Connor's gentle voice was full of understanding as he looked at his grieving cousin. "If ye drop and yer great body falls across yer wee wife, ye would do her more harm than taking a few hours' rest in my room."

"Nay. I willna leave till I know she did not stay ahead." He started to weave on his feet. When he had willed his soul to follow and fight hers to convince her to return, the strain on his body had been great. Mereck took him by the arm before Damron all but collapsed beside Brianna. Before Mereck finished removing Damron's boots, his eyes shut.

* * *

For the next three days, Damron slept little and never left their chamber. More than once, Brianna cried out for someone to help her little one. He trailed the backs of his fingers down her cheeks and murmured to her.

"Her fever is gone. There is no reason for her not to awake." Bleddyn spoke just loud enough that Brianna could hear him if she wished. "I believe she hides from her pain. It does not help that I cannot make her milk dry up, no matter what brew I give her, nor how tightly we bind her."

He motioned Damron to follow him to a far corner of the room. "If you wish to bring her back more quickly, soothe her mind as you did before."

When Bleddyn left, Damron latched the door and went to her.

He whispered over and over again in her ear, "My little one, dinna hide from me. I pine for the sound of yer beautiful voice when ye sing for me. I will see that the rest ye need is free of all but gentle thoughts and of love."

His voice finally came through to her. She stirred, as if she listened. When he caressed her face, she whispered a sigh.

Damron held her. He sang the songs he knew comforted her, his face close to hers. It did not matter that the words were in German, and she did not understand their meaning. She listened. When he finished, he murmured how much he needed her.

Tears slipped through her closed lids. He tenderly kissed them away. They spent the night with Damron soothing her mind, and Bleddyn slipping his elixirs between her lips. Damron talked to her of his grief for their sweet Faith, and how much he longed for Brianna to come back to him.

Through her haze, Brianna remembered how he had tried so hard to help her through the birthing, and the tears of grief he shed when he held the bairn.

Maybe Damron really did need her?

* * *

By morning, she was aware of people in the room. Soon after, a great commotion and shouting occurred outside the chamber.

Damron threw open the door, cursing at the uproar that was sure to disturb his wife. Johanna, Asceline's maid, stood there surrounded by Alana, Meghan, Connor, Mereck and Lady Phillipa. Johanna looked like she had run a great distance. She clutched a small bundle to her chest.

Thin, mewling sounds of an infant came from the bundle.

"When it were no' a boy, Lady Asceline ordered me to drown it," Johanna said, spasms of horror crossing her face. "She up and left durin' the night. Said ye were welcome to the little . . . I willna call it the name she used, milord. She has vanished. She were an unnatural mother, Lucifer take her. 'Tis reason enough the little one cries and willna suckle."

"Hush, Johanna. Find a wet nurse in the village."

"Do ye think me so daft I did not try? Whene'er someone takes her to their breast, she kicks and screams and turns her face from their nipple. All say she be a changelin'. 'Twill cause their own bairns to die if they give it suckle." Johanna snorted. "She be no changelin'. I were there at the birthin' and have not left her side. When I threatened ye would send them from Blackthorn, they put her back to their teats. She refused to suck at any of them. I have tried until there be no one left."

Brianna's mind came farther into the light. She fought to keep from retreating back to the quiet black. Concentrating on the baby's wails, she opened her eyes to see Mari stood close. Brianna reached to tug Mari's tunic.

"Blessed saints. Brianna be awake. Help, someone! Milord Damron, dinna let her slip away again." Mari's tone rose to a frantic pitch.

Damron rushed to her side. Brianna held up her hand to keep him silent.

"Please, Damron," she whispered, struggling to sit up. "Let Johanna in. I will nurse the babe."

"Love, ye are ill. Ye dinna know what ye are saying."

"You would let a bairn die, because of its horrible mother?" Her weak voice was not much above a whisper, but indignation gave her strength. "Bring the babe. Please. A changeling! Who believes such stupid things as that?"

"Bleddyn, tell her she canna do this. She canna know what she is plannin' to do." Worry for his wife, and worry for the child, warred together on Damron's face.

"I think our Brianna knows what she wants to do. Bring the child to her. Let her decide."

Alana added a pillow behind Brianna's back and whispered, "Welcome back, little sister." Brianna's smile was fragile as she held out her arms to Johanna.

Joanna placed the little squalling bundle securely on Brianna's chest. With Alana's help, Brianna unwrapped the bairn until it lay naked on its soft blanket. It gave one more angry cry, its red face wrinkled, its eyes tightly shut. Little arms and legs beat at the air, as if to fight away anything that would try to take it from this world.

The babe had soft tufts of black hair on her head. She was so tiny she could not be more than five pounds. Brianna hardly felt her weight. The baby interrupted her crying to wet the blanket through to Brianna's stomach. Brianna dropped her head back on the pillows and chuckled. Hands reached to take the babe from her, but she clutched it tight.

"No. She'll just wet again after she has fed, and she is so desperately hungry. Please, cut these bindings from me. I'm bursting with milk." The binding cloths were soaked with the milk that would not be held back. She wondered at the ways of God.

Damron used his dagger to carefully free her breasts. He lifted the sopping cloth to the side. "I dinna ask this of ye. I know how ye suffer, love."

"I know, but do please hurry before she gets any weaker."

Alana washed her sister's bare breasts with warm water. The minute Brianna murmured to the babe, she stopped wailing, took a huge gasp of air and stared straight into Brianna's eyes.

Brianna's heart lurched. Joy filled her, for she knew her babe's soul had listened to her plea.

"Don't cry, little one. I will not let anyone take you from me. Come. See how hungry you are," she crooned as she lifted the small face to her left breast. The tiny mouth rooted around, but could not seem to fasten. While she tried to grasp hold, the babe's eyes looked frantic. Brianna held the sides of the tiny mouth closed at her nipple, and the bairn clamped tight around it. Her fragile chest heaved with quick breaths, and the first drawing of the milk came from the breast. Pain shot through Brianna down to her healing womb, and she winced.

Damron made to reach for the infant, but her arms tightened protectively around her. He sat on the edge of the bed, his shoulders slumped as he watched his wife nurse what might be his bastard daughter. He wanted to cry out that it should have been their daughter who was so greedy. Pain swept through his mind and heart.

Brianna concentrated on the babe's warm body against her chest. Cuddling her, she wrapped the soft covers close around them. It was not long before the suckling stopped, and the tiny rosebud of a mouth fell away from the still-flowing nipple. A sigh followed, and Brianna grinned as she lifted the babe to her shoulder. She patted gently until she heard the burp she sought. Brianna looked down to see the baby relaxed in sleep, well-satisfied and peaceful.

"Serena. Her name shall be Serena. See how calm she is now her needs have been filled? Alana, please tend to her for me. You'll find garments in my chest." Her head fell back on the pillow and, though she was exhausted, hope filled her heart. She watched as they cleaned and dressed the babe, then she reached out her arms for her.

"Damron, you have not yet greeted this wee love. She was too small to come into this world. She will need all the tenderness and care we can give her. Hold her to your heart. She will hear it beating and know she is not alone."

When he did not hold out his arms, she urged him. "Come. She is a special babe. Though she's not of my body, I feel love for her growing in me. Promise you'll never let anyone take our precious one from us."

"I promise, love. But how can ye love her knowin' from whence she came?"

"Your mother understands," she said as she put the babe in Damron's arms. At first, he looked like he would deny holding the babe, but then his eyes softened. He lifted the blanket away and gazed at the sleeping infant, pity and tenderness softening his face.

"I'm sure your mother loved Mereck from the moment she held him. He is a part of his father, as this little one may be part of you."

Damron's head shot up. His gaze met hers. "Aye. But my mother dearly loved my father," he whispered.

"Didn't I tell you how much I love you? That I have loved you over the centuries? If I had not loved you with my heart and soul, would I have come back to this time?"

A ragged sob tore from Damron. He laid the sleeping child next to his wife and put his arms around them. He rained kisses on Brianna's face.

"My love, my love. How I longed to hear ye say those words. Do ye have any doubt that I love ye as well?"

"My dearest Lord Demon. Your love was there in the timbre of your voice. When you tried to hold me to this time, I heard it in your pleading for me not to leave you. How could I ignore our hearts longing to be together? We've wasted so much time, but we will make up for it. With such a great love between us, how could we not?"

"I will always love ye, Brianna. When our time with this life is through, we will love again and again."

Peace and happiness warmed her. She laid her palm on his cheek and smiled up at him.

"As you promised me, my love. Our love will live forever in our souls. Through life. Through time. Through all eternity."

Dear Reader,

Please keep in mind that *Always Mine* is about a modern woman whose soul is sent back to the eleventh century to relive her tumultuous life as Damron of Blackthorn's wife.

The two kings mentioned in the story were King William I of England and King Malcolm III of Scotland.

In this tale of love through the ages, I have tried to keep *modern* words out of the manuscript dialog. This is Lydia/Brianna's story, so when Brianna is speaking, or in her point of view, she uses the language of today.

English Through the Ages, by William Brohaugh, provides words for the eleventh century. They fill a scant twenty pages, so I have borrowed from later centuries in order to paint word pictures for the reader's ease and enjoyment.

One instance is the bodhran Bleddyn plays. It was not called a bodhran until centuries later. It was first used as a Welsh war drum, for the steady noise brought fear to an enemy, much like the early use of bagpipes.

If an author used only words suitable to medieval centuries, they would be in Old English. I doubt that telling a story would be possible, for how could anyone but a scholar in old languages interpret it?

Relax and let my tales of love through the ages transport you to another time.

Visit me at www.sophiajohnson.net.

Sincerely,
Sophia